by

Frost Kay

Copyright

Enemy's Queen

First Edition

For information on reproducing sections of this book or sales of this book go to www.frostkay.net

Cover by Amy Queau
Formatting by Jaye Cox
Copy Editing by Madeline Dyer
Proofreading by Holmes Edits

DEDICATION

To the people in my life who have survived their own monsters and demons, and come out the other side scarred, but beautiful. Your strength and courage are not unnoticed. I see you. I accept you. I am awe inspired by you. Thank you for sharing your stories with me.

THE KINGDOMS

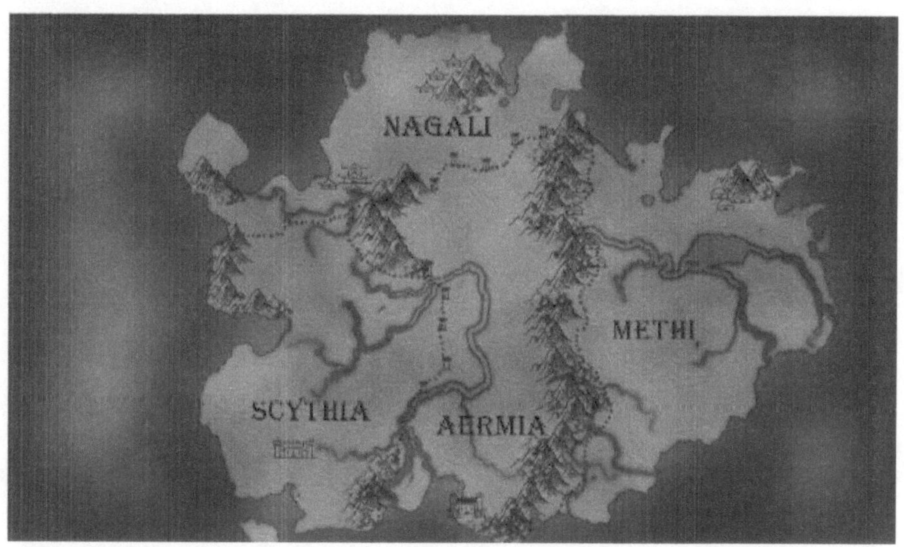

PROLOGUE

The storybooks had it wrong.

Prince charming wasn't always perfect, and monsters weren't always ugly.

The deceptive thing about monsters is they're never what you expect them to be. They're not always the shadows underneath the bed, but the hero expected to save you.

Those are the most dangerous.

Those devils are so beguiling that your breath catches when they look at you, and your heart flutters when they grace you with a smile. But therein lies the rub. They're the type of monster you want to hide from. The ones you pray never notice you.

Beware of the winks, and innocent touches. It's nothing but deception, an intricate trap. And remember, beauty and perfection have a price. Nothing is free.

Sage's monster was everything and nothing like she imagined, and this time there was no escape.

The devil had come to collect his dues, and Sage was short.

CHAPTER ONE

Jasmine

"Jade, we won't catch a thing if you don't tread more lightly. How can you make so much noise?" Stephen complained.

"Shhhhh...," Jade's tiny voice admonished, her fawn-colored eyes narrowed. "You'll scare the animals."

The young boy huffed. "Suuuurrree. *I'm* the reason we'll go without meat."

Jasmine smiled as she glanced over her shoulder at the young boy helping her niece through the underbrush. Each day, Jasmine checked the traps, and each day, she'd bring along either Jade or Ethan, the three-year-old twins. In the meantime, the other would stay with the widows of her village. Today was Jade's turn. Her niece was trying to walk quietly, but it seemed that the harder she tried, the louder she became. As Jade loudly snapped yet another twig under her feet, Stephen met Jasmine's gaze, exasperation clear on his face.

"At least the animals in our traps can't run away," she offered, grinning.

Stephen rolled his eyes and shifted an overly-large bow onto his shoulder, looking dejected. "I know."

Pain lanced her heart. The poor thing. He wanted so badly to have a chance trying out his new bow. She sighed. It had been months, yet, in many ways, the Scythian attack still affected them as if it had happened only yesterday. Stephen was but one of the many children to lose his father. She frowned, some of the pain in her heart giving way to anger. None of them would be in this situation if the Scythians hadn't been such monsters.

Jasmine tried to do what she could for the village, and Stephen was one whom she happened to be in a position to assist. He needed archery lessons and she needed help caring for the twins, so their arrangement was a win-win.

A small hand slipped into hers, jarring her from her thoughts. "Okay, Auntie?"

Jasmine blinked several times, focusing on her niece's round face as she forced a smile. She squeezed Jade's hand three times, reminding the little girl that she loved her—one squeeze for each word. It was something her family had always done. A toothy grin split the small child's face as she returned the three squeezes.

She pulled her gaze from her niece to scan the forest. At the edge of a meadow, a small plant sporting small, bright green leaves caught her attention. Dropping to her haunches, she brushed Jade's dark brown hair from her eyes and widened her own at the small girl. "Guess what I just spotted?"

"What?"

She leaned in conspiratorially and whispered, "I found strawberry plants!"

Her niece squealed and bounced on her toes. "I *love* strawberries!"

"Yes, I know." Jasmine pointed to the strawberry patch on the left. "They're right over there, so I need you to stay in the patch and do some picking while I help Stephen with his bow. Okay?"

"Okay!"

Jasmine released the child's hand and Jade rushed over to the patch where she immediately flopped down, her hands already searching for the sweet, plump fruit.

Jasmine shook her head and turned to her other charge. "You ready?"

Stephen smiled and nodded as he yanked his bow from his back. "Where can I shoot?" He skipped over to a flat spot.

She chuckled. "Slow down a second. You need to calm down, and be still."

"But I can't," he said, bouncing on his toes.

Jasmine smiled and wandered over to the boy. "Just close your eyes and breathe. In through your nose, and out from your mouth. Try to calm your mind, still your limbs."

He slammed his eyes shut and breathed in rapid succession. She hid a smile at how excited he was and repeated, "Slowly,

Stephen, slowly."

At her admonition his breathing slowed and, as she was hoping, his body relaxed.

"Perfect. Now, open your eyes and take up your stance."

Stephen planted his feet shoulder-width apart, rotated into a closed stance, and straightened. Jasmine eyed his stance. "Good, very good. Beautiful form. But don't forget your sequence. You need to perfect this form as well as the movement, so you can effortlessly repeat it each time." Adjusting his grip, she continued, "You must also remember to grip exactly here."

She stepped back, briefly glancing back to Jade. Her niece was happily munching on strawberries, oblivious to the rest of the world, with her face already stained crimson.

Jasmine turned her attention back to Stephen. "Draw."

He wobbled only a little as he pulled back on the bowstring, though his form mostly held.

"Excellent job."

The boy smiled at the praise and his cheeks pinked. She stepped forward to tap his hip where it stuck out a bit, and he quickly straightened into a smooth line, accepting the silent critique.

"Lower your bow."

He did as she said and looked at her expectantly. "Now what? Can I try it with an arrow now?"

"Yes."

He let out a joyful whoop and snatched an arrow from his quiver.

"But," she added, "you must first replicate that stance perfectly ten times."

His nose wrinkled, and he returned the arrow back to its

quiver. "Okay."

Leaving the boy to his practice, Jasmine found a comfortable tree, leaned her back against it, and slowly closed her eyes. She took the moment to enjoy the peace and quiet of the forest. She'd always been drawn to the almost magical stillness it offered, and now, like a plant in the desert, she soaked it up. It was something she needed.

After a while, she cracked an eyelid, checking on Jade. She was hardly surprised to note her niece hadn't moved, but she couldn't help checking on her all the same. Ever since the death of her brother, and the subsequent transfer of the twins to her care, she couldn't help but be overprotective of them. They were her only family now.

Her eyes had just closed again when a sound reached her ears, faint but familiar—thundering hooves. Her brows drew together as the sound grew closer. The hooves weren't slowing down.

Jasmine's eyes snapped open. The only reason for a rider to be charging in such a reckless fashion through the forest was if they, firstly, were guilty of a crime or secondly, were being chased by something terrible. Neither scenario boded well for herself and the children.

"Stephen," she barked, "we're leaving." Rushing to Jade's side, she urged, "Get up, sweet girl. We need to go."

"I'm still hungry."

"I know. You're always hungry. But I promise to make some lunch when we get home." Scooping up the little girl, she threw her on her back and instructed her, "Hold on."

As the sound of the rider drew even closer, Jasmine spun on her heel and swept toward the little boy, who was still struggling with his bow. "Let's go," she ordered, grabbing his hand as she passed him. It seemed like his feet were dragging behind her. "Hurry up!" Before they got anywhere her arm jerked, and he cried out.

Jasmine released his hand and turned to him, finding his clothes caught on a branch.

"I'm stuck," he said, pulling at his clothes.

Her heart picked up speed. The thundering hooves were much closer now. They were almost out of time. She frantically scanned the trees around them. She finally spotted a tree hollow behind a bush and sprinted toward it. She then pulled Jade from her back and pushed her through the bush and into the hollow. "Stay here. I'll get Stephen, and then we're going to play hide and seek."

"Okay."

She rushed back to Stephen and tugged on the bow. Somehow, he'd got it hooked in the limbs of a bush and it wouldn't budge. "We don't have time for this," she growled. Pulling a small dagger from her sheath she cut the bowstring.

"My papa made that," he cried, appalled.

"I know, and I'm sorry. I can fix it when we get home, but for now, we need to hide."

Desperation filled her voice. The rider was so close, she could hear the horse's ragged breaths. She yanked Stephen to her and shoved him in the hollow as well—it was just big enough for the two children. Carefully, she sank down behind the bush, sheltering the hollow entrance. "I need you both to be silent. Can you do that for me?"

Whispered yeses reached her ears as the horse and rider broke into their meadow. Sweat poured down the flanks of the horse, its chest heaving as the rider dug his heels into the poor creature's sides. The tall rider held a struggling woman in his arms and Jasmine hissed. If the woman wasn't careful, she'd fall. A fall like that could kill a person; she was surprised he could even ride like that. Almost as soon as the thought ran through her mind, the woman flung herself from the man's arms, and narrowly missed the horse's hooves as she crashed to the ground. Clutching one arm, she struggled to stand. Just as quickly, the man pulled the horse back and dismounted in one smooth motion, storming toward the woman. When he reached her, he yanked her up by the hair and Jasmine had to muffle her gasp of alarm.

"How stupid are you? Did you really think you could get away? And now all you've done is hurt yourself."

The young woman slammed her head into his nose and spat blood in his direction. He dropped her hair and clutched at his face, cursing. The woman collapsed to the forest floor, heaved, her face pale, and began to crawl away.

"Oh, no, you don't," he growled. "I think you need to be taught a few lessons."

Jasmine's stomach dropped when he pinned her to the ground. Oh God, she couldn't sit there and watch. She had to do something. She glanced back to Stephen and Jade, their small faces pale and frightened. "Don't watch, loves." She swallowed. "I need to help the woman, but you two do *not* leave this hollow unless I come and get you. Understand me?"

"Yes," Stephen whispered, voice shaking.

"I need you to keep Jade calm and quiet, Stephen. Can you do that for me?"

"Yes."

"Even if I get hurt or look like I'm not okay, do not come get me. You take Jade home and get help. You must not approach that man." Turning to Jade, she whispered, "Auntie loves you so much, but I need you to be a good girl and listen to Stephen, okay? Once

I'm done, we'll go home and make lunch. Okay?"

"Okay."

She kissed both the children's faces and pulled in a breath before slipping quietly from her hiding place. The man had flipped the woman onto her back and was now holding her down with his weight and pinching her chin between his fingers. The rumble of his voice filled the air, and Jasmine could only guess at what disgusting things he was saying. Anger burned beneath her chest. It was men like this who made the world an awful place for innocents. She glided through the forest on silent feet, drawing closer to the man and woman.

"You'll learn your place," the man threatened as he slapped the woman across the face, her eyes falling shut. She wanted so badly to charge across the meadow and teach him a swift lesson, but she knew better, so she did the opposite. Inhaling quietly, she continued her careful trek.

When she'd almost reached them, the woman's eyes popped open, revealing vibrant green eyes. The green eyes widened, and she opened her mouth to speak just as a hand clamped over Jasmine's lips. While keeping her gaze on the woman, she raked her nails down the arm detaining her. Her captor cursed, and the huge dirty hand pressing against her face pressed harder, now covering her nose. When she tried to breathe, no air would come. She thought frantically, trying to recall any of the things her mama had taught her to do in such a situation. She needed to offset her attacker. Jasmine threw herself down, becoming dead weight, hoping to upset his balance. Her move did little to aid her, however, for all he did was grunt and heft her against his body. Dizziness overwhelmed her, but she refused to give up. As a last resort, she bit down with all her might. She gagged as a metallic taste filled her mouth, but she didn't dare let go. When she felt a blow to her side, she was forced to release his hand as she gasped. Then, something knocked her in the head, and she found herself on the ground, staring at the raven-haired woman.

"This wench drew blood," a male growled.

"Well," a deep, smooth voice answered, "at least she has fight. That's exactly what we need. Are the men here?"

"They're waiting at the border with Blair. He was getting antsy, because you were late, my lord."

Border? She thought, *What border?* The treetops swirled together above Jasmine. *The only border close is ... No!* Jasmine tried to sit up, to escape, but the world lurched when she made the attempt and then she was right back on the ground.

"There were a few complications," the smooth-voiced male answered.

"Like abusing the master's woman, my lord?"

"She needed to be taught a lesson."

"He'll be displeased with what you've done, my lord."

"We'll see. Let's move. It won't be long before the Crown figures out she's missing."

Right before the world went black, the green-eyed woman mouthed something to her.

Fight.

She didn't need to be told. That was something she would always do.

CHAPTER TWO

Tehl

Tehl sighed as he snuggled deeper into the blankets, relishing the sunlight warming his back.

Wait...Sunlight?

Tehl squinted at the window. The sun was high. When was the last time he had slept in? He couldn't remember. His stomach growled. It was most definitely past breakfast. He stretched out a hand to touch the empty spot beside him, a smile on his face. Sage had slept beside him last night of her own volition and that was truly a victory. Her words from the night before came back to him, and his smile widened further as he rolled over to stare at the ceiling.

You have a loyal heart. That one statement changed everything. It meant she cared.

Finally, after everything they had been through, she was warming up to him. Admittedly, he had thought for quite a time that she never would. And after last night's misunderstanding, he'd expected her to cut him off completely, or possibly even stab him. But he was very surprised when, instead, she'd opened up to him and they'd been able to communicate freely and honestly for possibly the first time ever. At last, it seemed there was true hope for a friendship with his wife.

He clutched his stomach when it, once more, rumbled its displeasure. It was well past the time he usually ate. Tehl glanced again to the windows and Sage's empty spot. He had slept better last night than he had in a long time. Normally, Sage's nightmares woke up both of them frequently. It gutted him each time he had to reassure her that no one was hurting her, or when he had to hold her so she wouldn't hurt herself or him. What a cruel hand they'd been dealt.

Tehl shook off the glum thoughts and rolled out of bed, stretching his arms above his head. No matter what had happened in the past, today would be a good day.

He shuffled to the vanity and brushed his black hair, splashed water on his face, smoothed his rumpled shirt, and finally, pulled on his boots. It was well past time to get his day started, but first...breakfast.

Pulling the door open, Tehl paused, looking between the guards. Addressing the redhead, he asked, "James, do you have any idea where the princess is?"

"Garreth took her for a walk a while ago, but they've not returned."

"Probably training already," he mused. After nodding to the two men, he moved down the corridor and to the stairs where his brother lounged carelessly against the banister. Moving past him, he began to descend the steps, slapping his brother's shoulder good-naturedly as he passed.

"How are you this morning?"

Sam followed him. "Not as good as you, it seems. Why, you seem downright chipper this morning."

He raised a brow and smiled. "It's going to be a good day."

"I take it things went well with your wife last night?"

"She forgave me," he said simply.

A choking sound came from behind him. "She didn't make you grovel or anything? Or attack you?"

"She's not that type of woman."

Sam sniggered. "Uh, yeah... she is. She would definitely stab you."

"That's not what I meant. I meant she isn't a petty woman."

"Then you're a lucky man," his brother said.

Tehl stopped at the bottom of the stairs and turned to his brother with a smile. "I am. Last night resolved itself better than I ever expected. She can be so emotional at times, and yet, she can also be extremely rational. It's remarkable and confusing."

Sam grinned. "You act like you're surprised. Of course, Sage is remarkable."

Something in his brother's tone gave him pause. There was an intimacy there that he hadn't expected. His brows furrowed as he tried to work it out. When Sam caught his expression, he slapped the back of his head. Tehl rubbed it and glared. "What was that for?"

"Don't be stupid. You know I consider Sage my sister. I have no feelings for her, save the sort of love and admiration a brother usually has, so stop looking at me like I'm about to steal your wife."

"You've been known to steal women." His brother's lack of expression pulled a sheepish smile from him. "Sorry," he offered, continuing to rub the back of his head.

"Apology accepted. It happens to the best of us."

Now *that* made him snort. "Like you've ever been jealous. You don't keep company with the same woman long enough to become envious."

It was Sam's turn to furrow his brow as they began descending the arched, airy corridor. "Well… maybe one day, I'll find the right woman."

Tehl stumbled, gaping at his brother.

"What?" Sam shrugged. "I'm just saying one day it would probably be nice to have a family."

"Who are you and what have you done with my brother?"

"Very funny," his brother said, rolling his eyes. "I'm not saying right now, just… you know, in the future sometime."

"And what brought on this change of heart? You've always told me you're not a one-woman man."

"Things change."

"*Things?*" he asked incredulously. "What sort of things?"

Sam entered the private dining room and closed the door behind them before responding. "Sage," he said, with a shrug.

"Sage?" he repeated plopping into his chair.

His brother paced back and forth with his hands behind his back before placing himself in the chair across from him. "Well... She's interesting."

Tehl waited a beat before prompting, "And?"

Sam tilted his head back to stare at the ceiling. "She's strong, hardworking, loyal, funny, sweet, smart..." He paused. "She's a good person. She's even warm and empathetic, which is hard to find. Being her friend has brought me to the conclusion that, perhaps, marriage wouldn't be so bad after all."

"Because of Sage..."

"Yes, she's helped me realize that all women aren't the same."

Tehl plucked a grape from the table and tossed it into his mouth while studying his brother. He agreed that Sage certainly was unique. Like his mother. That thought stopped him mid-chew and a lump lodged in his throat. He forced himself to swallow. "Do you ever think about Mum?"

Sam smiled softly and dropped his head to meet Tehl's gaze. "From time to time. Sometimes, Sage snarks something at me and it reminds me of Mum. I think she would have liked Sage."

"Father said that, as well."

Both men fell silent, lost in their thoughts. His mum would have welcomed his wife with open arms, he was sure. She'd always wanted a girl in their family. Tehl pulled himself from his thoughts and asked, "Have you seen Sage this morning?"

Sam blinked and shook his head. "Not this morning. She's

probably skulking around somewhere. I heard her ladies-in-waiting wanted to go to the market this morning, so I bet my horse she'll hide out all day, just to escape the horrors of shopping."

The brothers exchanged a look and burst out laughing. "I've never known a woman to hate shopping more than Sage. I tried to have new dresses commissioned, but she about ripped my head off, spouting off about 'ridiculous and unnecessary things.'"

"Let me guess, she wanted you to use the money to fund some cause?"

"She's predictable in that way, isn't she?"

"Well, at least she isn't a power-hungry money spender."

Tehl swallowed a bit of honey cake and nodded. "She's special." He blinked, surprised at his own admission.

Sam grinned. "I'm glad you think so."

"What do you mean by that?"

"You're finally seeing her worth."

His brows wrinkled in confusion. "I've always seen her worth."

"No." Sam shook his head. "Not her worth as a consort, her worth as a *woman*."

Tehl's mind conjured up her sweet smile, the glint in her eye when she was about to do something crazy, and the curves she hid beneath linen and leather. "She's beautiful," he blurted. "My wife is beautiful."

"Inside and out," Sam said.

"Indeed," he muttered, staring at the table. He definitely appreciated her appearance, but he had to admit it was the person she was on the inside that had finally won him over. Sage had done many things for his family, but she'd received very little in return which benefited her personally. Maybe he could change that. But what could he do for her? Despite living with her, he didn't know her very well. All he knew was that she didn't care for extravagant gifts and she liked weapons, but, as she was a blacksmith, she liked to make her own, so that was not an option. What did women like?

"Sam..." He eyed his brother. "What do women like as gifts?"

"Jewelry, flowers, romantic dinners, things from the heart. Sage is a little different from the typical woman, but she still appreciates things from the heart."

What was in Sage's heart? Her friends and family. It was that thought which sparked an idea. He smiled. "I've a plan," he declared. "I'll set up a dinner with our families at her parents' home."

Sam slapped a hand on the table, excited by the prospect. "That'd be a perfect gift."

Echoing his brother's excitement, he expounded on the idea. "I want this to be a surprise. It can be Father, Gav, Isa, Lilja and Hayjen, her brothers, her parents, and the two of us. We can spend the evening together as one united family."

Sam leaned forward on steepled fingers. "Tehl, I must say, I think this is one of the best ideas you've had in a long time."

A moment of uncertainty plagued him. "You think she'll like it?"

"She'll love it."

He stood up and pushed back from the table. "I need to go see her parents and Lilja."

"Right now?"

Tehl felt like his smile couldn't get any wider. "Yes, right now. I want to get this underway as soon as possible, before the summer ends."

"Well, best of luck. Give Gwen and Colm my love."

"Give it to them yourself. You're coming with me."

Sam's face dropped. "I don't know. I haven't seen them since we discovered Sage at the forge, and I'm not sure they'd welcome my presence."

"Then it's about time to talk it out. Stop being a coward."

"Very mature."

"What can I say? Communication does wonders. Last night is proof of that."

Sam sidled up to him with a wolfish grin on his face. "What indeed did it accomplish, brother of mine?"

He punched his brother on the arm, ignoring the question, and headed toward the doors to the training yard. "None of your business. What happens with my wife is private."

"Your wife? Not Sage?"

He smiled. "Yes, my wife."

CHAPTER THREE

Sam

Sam tilted his face toward the fading sun and soaked in the last rays of warmth, reveling in the feeling of sand between his toes. Dropping his chin, he began scanning the beach as he walked, reminiscing. He'd spent innumerable hours here as a young boy, playing with his brother and his mum. A smile softened his features at the memory. His mum had cared nothing for propriety;

everything had been about their family. He knew she must have ruined countless gowns by wading into tide pools just to gather sea treasures or to show her sons some of the little sea animals.

Catching sight of something small and shiny, he moved toward a pool surrounded by porous rocks. He reached into the water and plucked the shell from the sand, holding it up to the light. The iridescent abalone was a mural of swirling blues, greens, and purples. It was just the right size to be made into a necklace, one his sister-in-law was sure to love. His sister-in-law had a love for sea baubles that almost rivaled his mum's. Grinning to himself, he pocketed the treasure and moved toward the entrance of a cave which lay hidden among the rocks. Just before entering, he paused. The large, arching cavern was still a source of wonder for him; it was a study in contrasts. Some spots had been so worn by the ocean's waves that it felt as smooth as glass, whereas others were sharp enough to cut your hand.

Just past the hidden entrance was a staircase carved into the stone walls. Sam stopped to pull on his socks and boots and grimaced. The sheer number of steps combined with the steep gradient made the hike a brutal one. Putting one foot in front of the other, he began the long trek up.

As he walked, his mind wandered to their recent reunion with the Blackwells—how his stomach had been in knots when Gwen had answered the door. How, much to his surprise, she'd looked him over, and before he understood what was happening, hugged him fiercely. She had then ushered them into her kitchen, where Colm stood. The four of them had awkwardly stood there until Gwen forced them to all sit down. As was his way, his brother had forgone any small talk and launched straight into his idea for their families to spend an evening together. That particular moment had amused him since, by the looks on Colm and Gwen's faces, they had yet to adjust to Tehl's straightforward manner of speaking.

But, what bothered him the most was when they'd discreetly catch his eye. The questions lurking in their eyes had him wanting to squirm in his chair. He knew he deserved it for lying to them for years. They were owed an explanation for his behavior.

After Tehl had talked everything through, he sat back and eyed all of them for a moment. Sam got a little nervous when he'd noticed a glint in his brother's eye. His brother had flashed them a smile before excusing himself to 'get some fresh air' while Sam had glared at Tehl's retreating back. The traitor. He hadn't even been subtle about it. Taking a deep breath, he'd then turned to face the only people that had given him one thing it was hard to find at the palace after the death of his mum. A sense of normalcy.

"I'm happy to see you, my lord. We appreciate your visit," Gwen had murmured.

The way she had spoken held a note of respect, but he detected wariness as well. He had felt his heart sink in his chest a little more, hating that he'd lied. His lies almost always hurt someone and he hated that, this time, it was someone he cherished. Carefully, he had reached out a hand and taken one of Gwen's. "There's no need for such formality. You still know me."

"Do we?" Colm asked.

That one question had felt like a punch to the gut. "Yes," he paused, then amended, "Well, part of me."

"And who is the other part?" Gwen asked.

"Brother, prince, commander. Take your pick."

"Those are merely descriptions of your roles, Samuel, not who you are. Your lot in life does not define you. Your actions do."

Gwen's words had struck him. The concept was both powerful and foreign to him. His roles did not define him?

"So, again, my lord, who are you?"

Sam had met her eyes, imploring her to believe him. "A boy looking for a family when his own fell apart, and please, call me Sam. That's who I am to you, just Sam."

At his response, Gwen's expression had shifted from that of wariness to understanding. "You'll always have a family here."

Sam had swallowed several times over the lump in his throat. He'd never expected them to be so understanding and forgiving so quickly. "Thank you."

"I've heard Sage's side. Now I want to hear yours," Colm interjected.

Sam had straightened and met the older man's serious gaze squarely. "First of all, we never meant for her to be harmed in the prison. That's not how we treat even the worst of our prisoners."

Colm nodded his head. "Sage said as much, but I would like to hear what you have to say on the matter."

He had then taken a deep breath and started the long story of how Sage had entered their lives.

***

Something crunched beneath his boot. Sam blinked, pulled from his thoughts. His brows lowered as he truly saw the stairway around him. Seashells, sea glass, and sand dollars were strewn everywhere, as if the sea had vomited trinkets all over the place. He squatted and fingered a particularly dark piece of sea glass. Odd. The only persons to travel these tunnels were members of his family. It was unlike Sage to leave her sea treasures, especially so strewn about like this. If she couldn't carry them all up, she would have piled them safely in a corner somewhere, so she could come back to get them.

He stood and ascended a few more steps to a platform with intersecting hallways. Had a servant found the passages and dropped their stuff when they got scared? He scanned the area for clues, freezing when he thought he heard something unusual. Trying to identify it, he turned to face a hallway to his left, holding his breath and listening, but he could identify nothing except the sound of wind.

Shaking his head, he returned to the staircase. He was being daft. Perhaps it was the creepy, old tunnels getting to him. He should know better. After all, it was here that, over the years, he'd frequently played tricks on both his cousin and brother.

"Sam." The word came from one of the tunnels. He spun toward it, his cloak flaring around him, as he pulled a dagger from his waist. That was *not* the wind. "What do you want from me?" he demanded.

Silence. He stared into the dark, trying to decipher any human shapes. It was dumb to go in blind, but he couldn't let a threat escape up into the palace. "If I have to come get you, you won't like it."

Something shuffled forward, and he kept his gaze focused ahead. Slowly, bloody fingers became visible, then an arm, and finally, a face. Sam blanched. The face was a familiar one. Rushing forward, he pulled Garreth into the dull light. As he did so, his friend cried out, his entire body seizing. "What the hell happened to you?"

Garreth tried to speak, but with his lips swollen and bloody, the best he could manage was a croak.

"Never mind, we'll get you some help." He tried to stand, but one of Garreth's bloody hands latched onto his forearm. Sam sank down to his haunches and ran his worried gaze over the member of his Elite. "What is it?"

"Sage," Garreth whispered.

Sam squinted at his friend, his heart picking up speed. "What about her?"

"Gone."

His blood turned to ice. "Gone?"

Garreth coughed, and it wracked his whole body. "Taken."

"By whom?" Garreth's eyes started to roll back in his head. Sam shook him hard, jarring his entire body. "No dying on me. Who took Sage?"

His friend's eyelids fluttered. "Rhys."

"No," he breathed out, horrified. How could that monster have gotten to her? He'd spent months hunting the man, but could find nothing, absolutely nothing. It was like he had vanished into thin air.

Sam grabbed Garreth's chin and looked him in his one good eye. "What's broken?"

"Ribs, but there are other wounds. I've lost blood," Garreth gasped.

He winced. That didn't sound good. "I'm sorry, old friend, but this will hurt." He grabbed the Elite's arm and slid it round his neck, maneuvering Garreth until he was draped over Sam's back and shoulders. Sam shifted until he had a good grasp on Garreth's arm and leg hanging over each shoulder. "I'm gonna try to lift you. Be ready," Sam warned, before he pushed up from the blood-smeared ground. Both men bellowed, one from pain, the other from strain. Garreth's body trembled hard against Sam's back.

"Just hold on. We'll get you some help. Maybe even from sweet

Mira. Don't think I haven't seen the way you look at her."

"She wouldn't have me," Garreth tried to shake his head and wheezed. "I'm too bitter for the likes of her."

"She said that?"

"No, but I've known women like her."

Sam just nodded and slowly trudged up the stairs, his muscles protesting. He stumbled near the top when Garreth's body suddenly went completely slack. "You better have passed out and not died on me, you bastard!"

At long last, he came to the secret door and crashed through it, catching his boot on the rug. The motion had him crashing to his knees in the royal wing hallway. An Elite standing outside his brother's door only gaped a moment before moving into action and pulling Garreth from his shoulders.

"Get him medical attention," Sam gasped. The door to Tehl's suite opened, his brother's dark head poking out. Spotting him, he immediately rushed over.

"That better not be your blood," Tehl growled.

"No," Sam said as he stood, willing his legs to keep him up. He closed his eyes, gathering the strength to tell his brother the bad news. When he opened them, he met eyes which perfectly mirrored his own and forced himself to just say it. "She's gone."

His brother's face scrunched up in confusion. "Why? I thought we worked everything out last night. Why would Sage leave? She makes me so insane. Why can she say what—?"

"No," Sam interrupted, "She was taken, Tehl."

Tehl's features hardened. "What do you mean *taken*? Where is she? Where is my wife?"

The menace in his voice gave even Sam a twinge of fear. He held his hands up. "I don't know, Tehl. I found Garreth in—"

Tehl moved around him and powered down the hallway, no doubt to find out for himself. Sam groaned and spun around, sprinting after his brother. He caught up as they ran down the stairs and toward the infirmary, startling the staff. He touched Tehl's shoulder, but he was shaken off as Tehl crashed through the infirmary door, where he skidded to a stop, causing Sam to plow right into him.

He watched over Tehl's shoulders as the healers buzzed around the bloody, unconscious Garreth. His gaze moved to his brother's profile, attempting to gauge his reaction. Only horror and rage were readily apparent.

"Will he live?" Tehl asked Mira.

The healer glanced up from her work, her face pinched. "He'll live, but only time will tell if his mind is still stable. He's taken a terrible blow to the head."

His brother nodded and pushed past him back into the hallway. Sam kept quiet, merely observing his brother as he paced the hall, tugging on his hair the way he did when he was thinking. Finally, Tehl paused to look at him. "What information do you have?"

Frustration bubbled up inside him. "Just what I told you. I took a walk along the beach to think..." Sam lowered his voice, "and entered through the cave to the stairs." He placed a hand over his mouth and focused on remembering each the detail. "There were sea trinkets scattered everywhere, and blood. That's when I found Garreth. If I hadn't taken that route, he would have died."

Tehl placed his head in his hands. "So, no sign of Sage?"

"I didn't examine the hallway, but most of the blood seemed to come from Garreth."

"Whoever came for them knew when to strike. She doesn't go for a walk every morning, she trains. Someone was watching her."

His stomach soured, and he had to force the words out. "I know who it was."

"Who?"

"Rhys."

Tehl stared at him blankly, then shouted a black oath. "How?" he demanded. "How did he get into my home? How did he take *my wife*? I promised Sage I would protect her! I looked her father in the eye and swore she would never have anything to fear." His fists clenched and his whole body shook. "Damn it!" He darted a look to the floor and back to Sam's face. "Why couldn't you find him? You swore to me you would do so!"

Although Sam knew in his head that Tehl was merely reacting to the situation and lashing out because he was worried, it still hurt to hear his brother hold him responsible. "I just couldn't," he replied, trying to keep calm. "I used every asset at my disposal ... and nothing. It is like the man's a ghost. I'm sorry."

His brother shook his head. "No, I'm sorry. I'm not blaming you. I just—when I think of her in his hands, it..." Tehl shook his head, as if to rid himself of the thought. "It makes me want to retch and strangle him at the same time. But blame and pity won't find her. Send the Elite into the city. Make sure they leave no stone unturned," he commanded. "Also, call the council together, and retrieve Lilja. We'll need her. Sage has been missing for far too long already. We need to find her. Now."

CHAPTER FOUR

Sage

Everything bloody hurt.

Munching on a stale cracker, Sage eyed the surrounding jungle, attempting to ignore the pain in her feet. Four days in the jungle of Scythia had taught her this: touch nothing.

That first day, Sage hadn't questioned why Rhys and the other Scythian warriors had left her and the other woman untied. She and Jasmine coordinated an escape, but they only made it thirty paces before stumbling upon a black feline creature that had been feeding. The creature had what looked to be human remains strewn across the ground. Golden eyes had clashed with green, and in that moment, she'd welcomed death. If the beast had attacked her, at least that way it would have been her choice and saved her from the horrors to come. But that was snatched out of her hands by an arrow. She had glared at the dying creature, feeling absurdly jealous.

A shudder moved through her body as she noted movement at the base of a nearby tree. She shuffled carefully forward, her eyes never leaving the enormous snake coiled around its trunk, the reptile's beady, black eyes observing her quietly. Sage hadn't been afraid of snakes until very recently, when one tried to make off with a horse two nights ago.

The rope which bound her wrists was suddenly yanked taut. It bit into her already tender skin and sent her cracker to the forest floor. She bent down, attempting to retrieve it, only to be pulled off her feet. She crashed into the foliage and cried out when the horse, to which the tether was attached, just kept moving forward, dragging her behind it.

"Sage, must you keep slowing us down? It's a wonder I even keep you around."

She scrambled to her feet and limped after the horse, ignoring the surrounding sniggers. Bastards. All of them. The warriors were as cruel as they were cold. She glared up at the monster on the other end of her leash.

Rhys.

Everything inside her rebelled at being near him. Her skin

hadn't stopped crawling since he'd first kidnapped her, nor had she been able to sleep. Each time her eyes finally closed, before she could drift off, a sensation of being watched would creep along her skin, jerking her into awareness. And she knew it was his dark eyes that roved over her. This was the only reason she was actually grateful for the other warriors. Without them around, he would no doubt have already tortured and raped her.

"Come now. Surely, you want to end your punishment?"

Sage clenched her teeth together to keep her scathing retort in her throat. Perhaps if she'd had only herself to think of, she would have spouted off, heedless of the consequences, but her actions wouldn't hurt just her. Each time she misbehaved, it was Jasmine who suffered the punishment. She craned her neck to check on the woman and grimaced. She looked as bad as Sage felt. The young woman's brown hair hung in limp strands, and every inch of Jasmine's skin was covered in bruises, even her face, a result of the fight left in her friend.

"Admiring your handy work? It's your little rebellions which created her pain, you know."

Sage pulled her eyes from Jasmine to stare straight ahead, forcing herself to look calm. Men like Rhys thrived off their victims' reactions and enjoyed blaming others for his cruelty. But no matter how hard it was, she would not allow him to gain any sick pleasure from seeing her react. It was one of the most difficult things she'd ever done.

She tensed when his horse slowed, and he moved right next to her. Her hands trembled slightly and sweat pooled between her shoulder blades as she forced herself not to move away.

"Look at me when I'm speaking to you."

Bile burned the back of her throat. She had no desire to look upon the face which still featured in her nightmares. But for Jasmine, she had to. Slowly, she pulled her eyes from the forest and up to his face. The satisfaction she saw in Rhys' eyes was enough to make her want to stab him, repeatedly. Her eyes dipped briefly to the dagger sheathed at his chest before quickly moving back to his chin.

Rhys' lips formed a smirk. "I can read you. You think you're hiding your thoughts, but they're written on your face for all to see. Take it, Sage. I know you want to."

Her gaze didn't waver from his chin. She wouldn't play his games. The last time she'd grabbed a weapon and attacked Rhys, he'd batted it away like it was a child's toy. He moved faster than anyone she'd ever seen, and her entire world had shifted in that moment. The Scythians were something unusual. Something unnatural. Something that, unfortunately, she couldn't outrun.

From that point on, she'd watched the warriors under the guise of examining the jungle. They all looked eerily similar, and they prowled in the same dangerous way she'd seen the large black felines move. One time, a warrior seemed to disappear, only to emerge a few feet from her. The Scythians also heard and smelled things she couldn't. She shivered. What sort of creatures were they?

"Given up already? I thought you had more fight in you."

She did, but fighting just excited him. So, she did the opposite; she didn't react at all. Not until a calloused fingertip caressed the shell of her ear did she flinch and jerk away, losing all composure. The rope jerked again, pulling her closer to the monster. Panic seized her body and tugged back, but she wasn't strong enough.

Soon, she found herself leaning against the horse with her arms held painfully above her head.

Rhys leaned down until the tip of his nose brushed hers, as if they were lovers. Fear paralyzed her as she stared into the mud-brown of his eyes.

"If you weren't property, I would've torn you apart already." His eyes ran over her face, an unholy glee plain on his face. "Maybe I already did."

It disgusted her that he was right, but she couldn't let him see that. Pushing through the fear, she whispered, "Filth like you won't ever break me." She regretted the words before the blow even came.

Pain radiated from her face, and she tasted blood in her mouth. She blinked several times. Stupid. That wasn't brave, it was just plain stupid. It was good, though, that he took it out on her and not Jasmine. Before she collected herself, Rhys grabbed her chin and forced her to meet his gaze. His eyes were lit with a demented kind of excitement, and beneath that, lust. The latter was more disturbing than the former. "You always thought yourself so much better than everyone else, so righteous, so honorable. But where's your honor gotten you?" He grabbed her hair and hauled her up higher. She sucked in a deep breath as the pain had tears pricking the corners of her eyes.

"When the warlord has had his fun—"

"Watch yourself, Rhys. She does not belong to you," a deep voice called from behind, moving closer.

Rhys' expression morphed into a sneer; he released her roughly and straightened in his saddle. Sage dropped to the ground in a heap, breathing hard through the pain, the damp dirt soaking through her pants.

"You don't command me, Blair. My uncle would hate to hear of your disobedience."

Uncle? Sage stared at the crushed plants beneath her knees, listening. Was Rhys' uncle someone important to the Scythians?

Cautiously, she picked herself up, standing on shaky legs. She peeked at the warrior from beneath her lashes. Blair. He was a huge man with broad shoulders and a wide, muscled chest. Sage had named him the leader in her mind, for all the warriors followed his lead. What he said went. He wasn't as cruel as others, but he wasn't a saint, either; both she and Jasmine had received a cuff or two from him. But overall, from what she'd observed with his men, he was fair. And Rhys hated him, which made Sage inclined to tolerate him slightly more than the others.

He spared her a glance through his long black braids before looking back to Rhys and bowing his head. "You're right," he rumbled. "Your uncle *does* hate to hear of disobedience."

Sage dropped her eyes to the forest floor. That was a threat if she'd ever heard one.

She snuck a glance at the two men as they stared each other down. Rhys with anger, the leader with tolerance. Rhys cracked first, shifting his eyes to the surrounding men, his feelings flitting across his face: embarrassment, no doubt that he'd been chastised, anger, from humiliation, and finally, hatred. She took a small step back, the wet earth and leaves squishing through her toes. She had been on the other side of his hatred. It wasn't a place anyone wanted to be, yet the leader didn't even blink.

"We camp here tonight," Rhys barked as he swung off his horse, clipping her in the ear with his boot in the process.

The blow disoriented her, and she stumbled into a warm, muscled chest. Horror dawned as two large hands curled around her biceps. Sage jerked from his grasp and put as much distance between herself and him as possible. She eyed the leader's blank face and rubbed her throbbing head. He was dangerous. His beauty couldn't hide what lurked beneath the surface. Beneath the skin of his perfectly symmetrical face was a killer. He was just humane enough for her to give him a little trust.

Rhys yanked on her bonds, knocking her off balance, and threw the rope at the leader. "It's your turn. I tire of her." He stormed off through the camp, yelling at a warrior about a tent.

Tension in her body eased as he moved farther away. She watched the exchange between Rhys and the other warriors, once again noting the differences between them. All of the men were extremely tall, but that was where the similarities ended. The warriors were flawless, like they were sculpted from stone. High cheekbones, cut jawlines, coal-black hair, smooth olive skin, and deep brown eyes. She'd always thought Rhys unremarkable, but here among the flawless warriors, he was downright ugly. A perverse sense of delight bubbled up in her. *He* was the damaged one here.

"Stop smiling or someone will notice your disrespect, woman."

Sage cleared all expression from her face and blankly stared at the bone and feathers woven into Blair's raven-colored braids.

"You'll have to do better than that if you want to survive us, woman. You need to have self-control."

Self-control? Anger pushed through the icy fear still gripping her. If she didn't have self-control, she and Jasmine would have been dead already. A grunt left his lips when she didn't answer, and he stepped closer to her, cupping her chin. Her body froze when he tipped his head forward, his braids falling around their faces like black silken curtains.

"Look at me, Sage."

She met his deep brown eyes at the soft tone. It unnerved her that, up close, he didn't appear so harsh.

"Stop baiting him," he breathed. "You're owned by the warlord. You're his possession."

"Possession?"

"All women are possessions of the warlord." The leader shook his head. "If you keep baiting Rhys, he will lose control of his berserker rage. He'll kill you before he knows what he did. You're putting all of us in danger."

Sage mulled over the information. Rhys was on the edge of losing it. She could see it and so could his warriors. "What do you want for that little bit of information?" she whispered back, just as softly. No one gave information away for free. It was every bit a currency as gold.

His eyes ran over her face, softening a little, almost friendly. If possible, her body stiffened even more. He was not her ally, and she was not a woman to be passed around. "No. My body is not payment." She'd die before she let them use her like that.

"It's not what you think."

A snort escaped her. "Then what? Are you my friend now?" she asked, trying to keep the sarcasm out of her voice. The last thing she needed was another beating. She was sure there had to be something wrong with her mind from all the blows to the head she'd recently received.

"I'm not your friend, and never will be. I'm just trying to save my men."

That was truthful. He may have been the enemy, but he did care for his men.

He leaned back and gestured to the men setting up camp. "They die if you die."

That disturbed her. "Why?"

To her surprise, he answered her: "Because we would have failed to complete our task. The warlord does not have time for things that are not useful."

Disgusted, she grimaced. No one should use a person like that, but in the back of her mind, an idea took root. If she died, they died. It was simple.

"I know what you're thinking." He shook his head. "You're not selfish enough to do it."

"You don't know me."

"I've known people like you. Despite what you know of us, you wouldn't sacrifice all these men. It wouldn't be something you could shoulder. It would destroy you."

"Perhaps, but none of you are *men*." His eyes narrowed, but she hurt too much to care. Maybe if he hit her, she would black out for a bit and find some relief.

He raised a brow. "Then what are we?"

"Monsters," she said, not losing eye contact. They were. They weren't human.

"Always remember that," he said as he tossed the end of the rope at her feet. "Tend to the other woman."

She let out a sigh of relief as the frighteningly intense warrior turned from her and prowled toward his men. She winced as she gathered up her leash and picked her way to Jasmine, who sat on the ground glaring at all of the surrounding men. Sage slid down the tree next to the feisty brunette and watched as a camp emerged among the trees.

"How are you?"

Jasmine scoffed. "Well, that's obvious. I am damn peachy."

The reply pulled a smile from Sage, despite her split lip. "What's the worst of it, Jas?"

Jas grimaced and pulled in a painful breath. "The cracked ribs. I think they may have broken one yesterday."

"Did you bind it?"

"Sort of."

Sage moved onto her knees. "Let me see it."

Jasmine shifted to the side. "Lift my shirt, please. My shoulder's not working."

Sage gently pulled up the woman's shirt. "Beasts," she hissed. Jasmine's skin was mottled purple, blue, and green. She glanced at her friend's pained face. "I'm sorry for this, Jas. This is going to hurt."

"Do what you must."

She sat back and stared at her shirt. There wasn't enough fabric. "Swamp apples," she cursed. "I will have to ask them for supplies."

Jasmine gripped her thigh as she moved to stand up. "Don't. They'll just taunt you."

She met her friend's remarkable blue-gray eyes. "I've no other choice. You can't go on without healing."

She squeezed Jasmine's hand once and forced herself to stand on her cut feet. Once again, she squished through the mud and leaves toward the men forming up camp. It discomfited her greatly, but it was better than being in Rhys' arms. She scanned the camp and caught sight of the leader. "Blair!"

The camp seemed to freeze at her shout. The large man turned, his mouth turned down. "What did you call me?"

Hell. She'd broken some sort of protocol. "Your name."

The black slashes of his brows rose as the whole camp seemed to hold their breath. "This is not Aermia. You may not speak to me as you wish."

Gritting her teeth, she calmed herself at his mocking tone. She needed supplies for Jasmine. Time to play nice. Sage dipped into a deep curtsey, humiliated. But it was worth it for her friend.

"My apologies. What shall I call you?"

"My lord."

She pulled herself from her deep curtsey and met his eyes. "My lord... I need supplies for Jasmine. Her injuries need care."

He eyed her. "Do you not have fabric?"

Sage blew out a breath. Obviously not, since she was asking him. "No, I do not."

Rhys sauntered back into camp, his gaze dipping to her shirt. "Seems to me you do."

Her lips thinned. "There's not enough material," she replied as calmly as she could. "And its filthy."

Lazily, Rhys smiled at her. "You do, but you're being selfish. Would you really let your friend suffer for the sake of modesty? Take it off and help her."

The blood in her veins froze; her heart seized painfully in her chest. He wanted her to strip in front of everyone. She looked over her shoulder at Jas, who was glaring daggers at all the men. Sage turned back to the leader and Rhys, meeting his gaze. They held a taunt and a dare. He might think to humiliate her, but she'd gone through worse things. If he wanted to punish her, so be it. She'd not cower.

Despite her resolve, her hands trembled and her cheeks burned as she began unbuttoning her shirt. Sage held her head high and locked her eyes on the leader. It was easier looking at him than the demon at his side.

The dirty linen slowly parted to reveal the half-corset she wore underneath. Her sleeves slipped down her arms, exposing her damp skin to the humid air. She peeled the soiled fabric from her wrists, one at a time, hung it over her bicep, and held her hands out, her body completely on display for the silent group of men gawking at her. "Anything else, my lord?"

Even though she tried to ignore the heavy stares of the surrounding men, she couldn't help the goosebumps that broke out across her arms. That one piece of linen was protection. It hid her curves from them; it was at least a barrier they would have to get through to get to her.

Or, at least, it had been.

The leader broke their stare-off and scanned her body, his brows pulling together. "So many scars."

Sage kept silent and swallowed the retort on the tip of her tongue. Her sarcasm was a way to protect herself. One more defense that the Scythians had stripped her of.

The leader crossed his arms and tipped his head, his raven braids sliding over his shoulder. "What happened to you?"

Surprise filled her. He didn't know?

"I did," Rhys boasted.

Stillness settled over the camp. The hair on her arms rose, and she shifted on her feet, wanting to hide from whatever was coming.

"You marred her?" the leader asked, his tone sharp as a blade.

"It was punishment."

"That's disgraceful," a lanky warrior said, venom clear in his voice.

"Silence!" Rhys snarled, a promise of vengeance on his face. The warrior immediately shut his mouth and stared at the ground, no doubt pondering his future punishment.

Sage shivered and brushed at her filthy corset, needing to do something with her hands. "Woman…" Something about the leader's voice scared her. He was not one to be trifled with.

She lifted her eyes and stared at his chest.

"You have your fabric. Go take care of the woman."

Her spine stiffened at the command, but, as it gave her the chance to escape being the center of attention, she simply nodded. Turning her back to the leader and Rhys, ignoring the gazes of the surrounding men, she started to leave. Her steps faltered as the leader issued a command:

"The prior rule stands. If you touch her or the other woman, your life is a forfeit."

Picking up speed, she reached Jas just as her legs gave out. As she fell to her knees beside her friend, every muscle in her body hurt. She studiously kept her eyes from Jasmine's face.

"I'm so sorry, Sage."

"Me, too," she whispered as she tore long strips from her shirt. Tears blurred her eyes, turning her task into a watercolor of greens, browns, and creams. She hated crying; it made her feel weak. A small hand halted her jerky movements, causing her to look up. She blinked repeatedly, trying to clear the tears from her eyes.

Jasmine's stormy gaze met hers. "Truly. If I could move right now, I'd go give them an earful."

Sage scanned her face, noting the sincerity, but right behind it lurked fear. "I won't let them do this to you. I'll protect you."

Her friend's lips curled. "We'll protect each other, sis."

The casual use of 'sis' about knocked the wind out of Sage. Jas had just claimed her as family. For the first time in four days, warmth bloomed in her chest. She held her hand out, and Jas clasped it. "We'll protect each other, sis." She'd found a friend and an ally in the most unexpected place.

Dropping Jasmine's hand, she plucked a strip of her shirt from the damp ground and said, "Hold still. This will hurt."

CHAPTER FIVE

Tehl

Four days.

Sage had been missing for four days.

The last four days had been hell. Pure, unadulterated hell.

After his wife's abduction, everything came crashing down: Garreth almost died; his father practically disowned him; the rebellion leader tried to kill him; and her mother slapped him across the face. The only ones who'd stood by him were Lilja and Hayjen. That surprised him.

Gwen's accusations still echoed in his mind. *You promised to protect her! You're a liar. A murderer. This is your fault!* He had taken it. The look on Colm's face gutted him. It bespoke deep pain and great loss. He hadn't spoken out and blamed Tehl in the way Gwen had, but the accusations were there in his green eyes, so similar to Sage's.

Tehl had failed them. He'd failed Sage.

He picked up his stride and weaved through the hallways toward the war room. So far, it seemed like she had disappeared along with Rhys but, hopefully, today they'd find something. His stomach clenched, thinking of her alone with that monster. He couldn't contemplate what was happening to her though for he needed to stay focused; he needed to find her.

But she had. Her cinnamon scent seemed to follow him everywhere. It was strongest in their room. He would sit by the fire, close his eyes and breathe. Something about it soothed him. She'd been as prickly as a sea urchin, but he'd grown accustomed to her sense of humour and brilliant smile. He kept expecting her to appear and chide him for his terrible people skills. From the beginning something had told Tehl that when the worst was over, they'd be allies, companions, friends. He was right, it had come and even quicker than he expected. Tehl was a solitary creature, but he'd found himself enjoying her company in spite of himself. He actually looked forward to teasing her. Previously, he'd never understood Sam's fascination with stirring the pot and causing mischief, but after living with Sage he discovered it to be one of his favorite pastimes. She was so easy to rile. And now, he needed to find her so they could continue building on that foundation.

Arguing voices reached his ears before he even opened the door to the war room. He leaned his forehead against the wood and took a deep breath to calm himself. Outside of the room, he worried over his wife, but inside that room he had had to see the bigger picture. He was their leader and future king.

He straightened, blew out the breath he was holding, and steeled himself. Pushing open the door, he strode to his seat at the far end of an oval table. The room quieted with his entrance. He lifted his eyes to scan the group of men and women around him. "Where is my wife?"

Everyone was eerily silent.

The small amount of hope he had harbored in his heart crashed and burned. They'd still found nothing.

"My lord, there has not been enough time to—"

Anger burned through his veins at William's statement. "Not enough time? My consort has been missing for four days! Where is she?"

Still silence.

He looked to Rafe. "Where is my wife?"

The rebellion leader seemed to vibrate in his chair. He'd almost turned feral at the news of Sage's disappearance. "I used everything, and everyone, to the best of my ability. There's no trail. Wherever Rhys took her, he did not want us to follow and he did a damn good job of making sure we couldn't."

The longer Tehl stared at Rafe, the more he felt the reins on his emotions slipping. Rafe had promised to take care of Rhys, yet obviously he was still alive. Not only alive, but hurting someone he cared about. Tehl blamed him as much as he blamed himself.

Silence still reigned.

Irritation pricked at him. "What is the purpose of this meeting if none of you have any information for me?" he asked. "You should be out searching instead sitting here idly."

"My lord, Sanee and the nearby villages have been searched," Lilja said softly. "There's no way in knowing which direction to go."

Some of his irritation abated at her mild statement. She was right. They needed a specific plan of action for their hunt to produce results. Each hour that passed was another Sage no doubt fought for her life so time was of the essence. "Suggestions?"

"Escape by sea would be smart," Zachael, the combat master, said. "The harbor is close, and it would be easy to conceal an unconscious woman."

"While you are right," Hayjen added, "Lilja and I have secured the logs of the ships and fishing boats in our bay. They've been searched and come up empty."

"She was missing for twelve hours before we discovered her disappearance," Zachael said. "Is it possible a boat left before you searched the others?"

"It's possible," Lilja admitted. "But unlikely. The merchant and fishing community are a tight-knit group. If there had been an unfamiliar ship among them, they would have alerted me."

"Are you so sure they would?" Jeren needled.

The captain's magenta eyes flashed as she speared the pompous duke with a look. "I'm not someone to be trifled with. I assure you, they know the consequences of lying."

The door opened, and Sam strode inside, his expression severe. "I have something you need to hear."

"What is it?"

His brother stared at the table of councilors. "I have a lead on Sage."

The air seemed to disappear from the room. He held his brother's blue gaze, hanging on his words. "Please," he whispered. "Please tell me she's alive."

"She's alive."

Something inside him loosened.

"But it would be better if she were dead."

Tehl's blood turned to ice. For his brother to say that, it had to be very bad.

Lilja glanced at him and then to Sam. "Where is she?"

"Scythia."

There was a collective gasp and then shouting erupted. Tehl's vision tunneled and a dull ringing filled his ears, canceling out the noise erupting around him. Scythia. Anyone who crossed the Scythian border never came back.

"Tehl..."

Sage was gone. As good as dead. How would he tell her parents? He'd failed her. Gwen was right. That monster had taken her from under *his* roof. He was guilty.

"Tehl!"

He blinked, and Zachael's face swam into view. "Yes?"

"Are you all right?" the combat master prodded, concern on his face.

Tehl glanced at the chaos and back to the combat master. "I killed her, Zachael," he rasped.

Zachael's shoulders drooped for a moment, but then he straightened, looking Tehl in the eye. "You did not. Sage is stronger than anyone I've met. No one is infallible, but if anyone could survive Scythia, it would be her, my lord."

Heat built behind his eyes, and, for the first time since his mum died, he shed a tear. He rubbed his eyes and stared blearily at the arm of his chair, giving himself a moment to recompose. "You're right," he said gruffly. "She has too much fire to die."

A chuckle rumbled out of the older man. "That she does. She's spunky, that one."

Tehl swiped at his eyes again and tucked away his emotions as the volume of his council rose. Being a leader came with responsibilities and obligations. His feelings would have to wait.

Turning to the table, he bellowed, "Silence!"

The group quieted and twisted to look at him as he addressed them. "Where did you come by this information?"

Sam rubbed his neck and began his story. "I received news of another Scythian kidnapping in a town along the Mort Wall. A young woman named Jasmine was apparently taken captive as well."

He frowned. That name sounded familiar. "The same young woman we met some months ago?"

Sam blew out a breath. "Yes, the same. It seems she was out with her niece and a young boy from the village. She was teaching him how to use a bow in the forest, but they never came home. The village created a search party and stumbled upon the boy and the little girl."

Tehl's stomach clenched, knowing what came next.

"The little boy explained that while they were out hunting, a stranger carrying a woman with brown hair interrupted their practice. The young woman, Jasmine, knew something wasn't right and hid the children and herself." His brother sucked in another fortifying breath. "Apparently...Sage tried to get away, but the man got on top of her, pulling at her clothes."

Lilja hissed and pushed away from the table to pace.

Sam eyed the captain. "It seems that Jasmine decided to take action so she had the children promise to stay hidden. She'd almost reached the man when the little boy noticed more men appearing in the surrounding forest. She never saw them coming." His brother's hands clenched. "They hurt the women and then carried them over the wall. The boy kept the little girl quiet, and they stayed hidden in the tree hollow for some hours before they were found."

"Rhys is Scythian?" Rafe rumbled.

The tone of his voice had everyone sitting up straight. Tehl's eyes slashed to the rebellion leader who was still trembling in his seat.

Sam watched Rafe before answering. "From what the little boy observed, the other men were Scythian and very friendly with Rhys."

"That son of a whore!" Hayjen shouted. Everyone glanced at the normally level headed man in shock. He looked to his wife. "Lilja?"

"I know," she growled. "We have to get her out of there."

Slowly, Rafe stood from his chair, his amber eyes locked on the captain. "What are you not telling us, Lilja?"

Hayjen held his hand out to his wife. "It's time, my love. This is what we've been waiting for."

The exotic woman stared at his hand, before striding to her husband's side. She cleared all emotion from her face. "I can only guess why they took Sage, but I can tell you of my own experience." She turned and met Tehl's gaze. "There was a time when I believed Scythia could be changed for the better. I wanted to make a difference. I was convinced that there was no way an entire people could be evil. It'd been hundreds of years since the war. Something had to have changed." She shook her head. "I was wrong on many accounts and right on just one. At first, I was welcomed with excitement and affection. I mistakenly thought it was because they'd left their twisted ideals behind." She chuckled bitterly. "They lulled me into a false sense of security, then sprang their trap. They wanted me, but not in the way I thought. Their excitement and affection were for what my body held. The key."

"What key would that be?" Gav asked gravely.

"My womb."

Silence.

Lilja's smile was brittle. "In all this time, the Scythians have never stopped their search for the perfect warrior nor their desire to be flawless. But something happened because of all their experiments, something they didn't plan for. Their women have become barren, or if they could have children, they're malformed. Given how much they've put into becoming untarnished I'm sure you can imagine their treatment of any child who doesn't fit that description. This has left them with a single option."

"I think I'm going to be sick," Gav muttered, his face going white.

"They need broodmares. They need wombs to grow more warriors. So...they've been taking women." She paused and let that settle in.

"The raids disguised the disappearances," Sam muttered with a hint of a growl. "How did I not guess?"

"You couldn't have known, Spymaster. The Scythians guard their secrets jealously."

"How do you know all of this?" Lelbiel asked, his whispery voice seeming loud.

"Because they used me as one of their broodmares."

More silence.

Lilja swallowed hard and continued. "I was strapped down and forced to take only God knows what draught. Then I was given to a warrior, and well...use your imaginations."

"Did they beat you?" Zachael asked bluntly.

A peal of bitter laugh rang out from Lilja, the sound eerie. "And harm the body that protected their young? No. But that's not the only way to hurt a woman. I would take a thousand beatings before I wished their kind of torture on anyone."

Tehl's stomach churned. "How long, Lilja? How long has this been going on?"

"At least twenty years."

He grabbed hold of the table to steady himself as the room tilted around him. "Twenty years? They've been raping our women for twenty years?" His voice rose. "How are we now just hearing about it?"

Lilja stared right through him. "Few have escaped, but those who have are turned away for speaking nonsense. Think about it, my lord. If you didn't have proof, would you have believed such a story?"

Tehl panted heavily and thought about it. No. Shame and guilt clenched his stomach. "I wouldn't. Without proof, such a tale would have seemed like a story spun for entertainment."

"Indeed."

"How many have...?" He stopped, he couldn't finish the thought.

"This is not on you, Tehl," Hayjen stated. "This problem rests at the feet of the Scythians, not yours."

"Will they do the same to Sage as you?" Rafe asked Lilja in a surprisingly gentle tone.

Her hands clenched at her side. "There's only one reason she would be taken to Scythia, especially when she was a difficult mark to obtain. She was targeted. Scythia wants her."

"And what will they do with her?" Tehl had the strength to ask.

Lilja's magenta eyes clashed with his. "Destroy her."

CHAPTER SIX

Tehl

Destroy her.

It didn't seem possible for anything to destroy Sage. She conquered everything that came her way. But Lilja would never say something like that unless she meant it.

"We can't know for sure that's what he plans for her," William offered.

Hayjen glanced at William, his expression grave. "We've seen this time and time again. Lilja's not the only one to have had such an experience. You should be afraid for the consort."

The gravity of the situation settled heavily over the group.

"Then what do we do? We can't leave her there," Gav barked.

"But what can we do?" Zachael asked. "If we cross the border, it will mean war. We have no idea what is on the other side of that wall. We cannot take them on."

"What about a small rescue team?" Lelbiel offered.

"I have sent some of my best spies over that wall. None have come back. None. We would send the men to their grave."

"So...what?" Rafe snarled. "We leave Sage to die? To be used as a broodmare of their young? I'll not do it! She's been hurt enough to last many lifetimes. I won't let her live in that hell where she'll be raped until she dies."

Tehl felt the same way. Their gazes met and understanding passed between them. For the first time since they'd met, they agreed on something. "I'll not leave my wife there."

"So, what do you propose? You can't go traipsing through the jungle to retrieve her. Aermia needs you here."

He glared at his brother. "You don't think I know that?" His swept the men with his glare. "You're all aware of how Sage came to become my wife. I did my duty, and so did she. I will honor my duty to Aermia, but I also have a duty to Sage, not only because she's my consort, but my friend."

"What about a treaty?" Jeren suggested.

"What?" William gasped. "You want to make a treaty with those monsters? They deserve to rot where they are."

"No, listen..." Jeren leaned forward in his chair. "Scythia has been preparing for something for a long time. Presumably to invade Aermia. But what if we threw them off balance by offering a peace treaty? Scythia has been excluded from other kingdoms for hundreds of years, and we have what they need. Women."

"Clever," Lilja mused. "But the warlord would see right through that. He's cunning, ruthless, and arrogant. He would see the treaty for what it was, a final attempt to keep them from invading our kingdom. He'd strike before you had a chance to rally your men, but his weakness is arrogance."

"So, we use that," Sam proposed. "We don't want them anywhere near Aermia, but if the warlord is as arrogant as Lilja claims, he'll want to meet. If only to flaunt his army and Sage in front of us."

"That's a huge risk to take," Tehl said, then glanced to Lilja. "Would that work? Would he fall for it?"

The captain pursed her lips before speaking, "He would suspect a trap, but it would be an enticing lure that he'd likely engage. The warlord would meet with you, but no doubt have his army at hand."

"We'd need to have ours ready," Zachael remarked.

"How much time would that take?" Tehl asked.

"We could be ready in four months."

"Make it two," Tehl commanded. "Every moment we linger here is another moment the princess suffers in Scythia." He turned back to Lilja. "Would the warlord bring her to the negotiations?"

A bitter smile graced Lilja's face. "He wouldn't miss the chance to bait you. He'll bring her, but you won't be able to rescue her."

Silence filled the room.

"Why?"

"You don't understand the enemy you'll be engaging. The warlord is not like you or me. He has plans, and then plans to cover those plans, and plans to cover *those* plans. He would never leave Sage open. She'll be so heavily guarded, you won't be able to breathe in her direction without a blade to your throat."

"Then, why the ruse?" William asked. "The whole point is to retrieve Sage."

Understanding dawned. "Because we'll coax him out into the open. For the first time in years, he'll be out of his fortress. He'll be vulnerable. Vulnerability means mistakes."

"We will never be able to get to her if she's locked away. We may not be able to get to Sage *at* the negotiations, but afterward..." Lilja eyes held a predatory gleam, "she'll be coming home."

Tehl fought a shiver at the bloodthirsty expression on the captain's face. Once again, he was happy she was on their side. She'd make a formidable enemy.

"So, we plan an assault for after the negotiations?" Sam asked, a faraway look in his eyes.

"Yes, but we also plan for one before and during," Rafe interjected. "If he's as brilliant as Lilja says, we need to have a backup plan and expect the unexpected."

"Indeed..." a deep voice said from behind Tehl.

The men around the table stilled, and then, in a flurry of movement, all stood and bowed. A heavy hand landed on Tehl's shoulder and gave a squeeze. "Always expect those who act treacherously to be treacherous."

Tehl peered up at his father, shocked at his presence. It had been years since his father visited the war room. "My king," he said respectfully, and began to stand. The hand on his shoulder tightened and pushed him back down into the chair.

"This seat is yours, Tehl," his father murmured. "I won't take it from you. You have earned it."

He blinked as he sank back into his chair, sifting through his emotions: pride, dread, and relief—mostly relief. It was reassuring to have his father by his side. Gav stood from his chair and pushed it over to the king. Tehl's father smiled and patted Gavriel on the back before sitting. His white-blond eyebrows lowered over his blue eyes as he took in the group.

"So, what is being done to get my daughter back?"

There was a beat of silence before Sam, Zachael, and Jeren began explaining their plan. Tehl sat back in his chair and watched his father as the plan was laid out before him. The king rubbed at his chin after the explanation finished. He let out a long sigh. "Two months? That's the best we can do?"

Zachael's face screwed up. "I wish we could get our men together sooner, but we'll have to collect the Guard from all over Aermia, gather weapons and supplies." The combat master shook his head. "That will take time."

"I understand. Thank you, Zachael, for your service." The king scanned the group once more. "Thank you. You've all been fine advisors to my son. Those of you who are new, welcome."

It still awed Tehl how his father could command people and bolster them. He smiled at the king, then addressed the group: "Start planning our assault. I would like to go over it tomorrow afternoon. Thank you, and good day."

At his dismissal, his advisors began to remove themselves from the room.

"Captain Femi, would you please stay?" the king called over the thumping of booted feet against stone.

Lilja glanced at the king in surprise, and then to Tehl. He offered a slight shrug and eyed his father with curiosity. What did he want with the captain?

The king stood as Lilja glided to his side, Hayjen following behind. To Tehl's shock, his father bowed low and kissed the captain's hand. "My lady, I'm honored to host you in my household. It's been a long time since the Sirenidae have graced these hallways.

Lilja's eyes pinched. She yanked her hand from the king's grasp and Hayjen pulled several daggers out. Tehl shot out of his seat and in front of his father. "What do you think you're doing, Hayjen?"

"Protecting my own," the big man growled.

Sam and Gav circled, letting their presence be known.

Tehl's eyes snapped to his father and back to Lilja and Hayjen, tension filling the room. "What in the blazes is going on?"

His father responded without looking from Lilja. "Her kind are very rare and are to be treasured. The fact that she's Sage's guardian is beyond special."

"Sirenidae?" Tehl repeated. "You're not making any sense."

"Your mum used to tell you tales of them."

"Some say they were real at one time," Sam said from his left.

"They are real, Samuel. Your mother has Sirenidae family."

Tehl's eyes rounded. Just when he thought his father was sane. Tehl shook his head in disappointment, then scrutinized the man and woman in front of him. He didn't miss how, throughout it all, Hayjen and Lilja kept backing away from them. "Everyone needs to calm down. Obviously, there's been a misunderstanding."

"There's been no misunderstanding, son." His father moved past him and held a hand out with a dagger resting on his palm. Tehl shot a look at Sam. Where did he keep getting blades?

His brother shrugged and crowded in closer.

His jaw dropped in shock when his father knelt and held the dagger out to Lilja. "My family and I mean you no harm. I did not unveil your secret to all the council, just to my family. My wife made sure I knew the original stories, not the propaganda that Scythia began spreading years ago. You're welcome in my home, not for what you can offer, but for the service you've done my family already. We are in your debt."

Lilja's unusual magenta eyes locked in on the king kneeling before her. She was quiet a moment before she plucked the dagger from his hand and handed it to Hayjen. "Friends should never bow to one another," she said softly, helping his father up.

"Are we at peace?" his father asked, equally soft.

"We are." Warmth filled her eyes when the king kissed her hand once again.

"Is no one going to explain the Sirenidae comment? Or the family part?" Sam demanded.

Tehl crossed his arms and raised an eyebrow. "Who are you, Lilja?"

A laugh bubbled out of the woman. "I'm many things: captain, pirate, survivor, guardian, wife, aunt, friend, lover, ally, Aermian, and...Sirenidae."

"What does it mean to be Sirenidae?" Gav asked, silent up until now.

"It means I'm different from you, yet your eyes mark you as my family."

Gav's jaw dropped.

Tehl ignored his cousin and took a step closer. "Different how?"

She pulled in a breath, releasing it once Hayjen placed his large hands on her shoulders. "I grew up in the fifth kingdom."

"Fifth kingdom? The underwater kingdom of legends?" Sam asked.

"Indeed."

"How...?" Tehl blinked, trying to wrap his mind around the idea. "You're telling me the myths are real?" He eyed the woman. The stories painted Sirenidae as bloodthirsty, dangerous people.

Lilja observed his expression before answering. "Some myths are real, even the bloodier ones, but as a whole, Sirenidae are not killers."

"You look so..." Tehl drew out, looking for the right word.

"Aermian?" she supplied.

"Normal."

Sam sniggered. "That wasn't rude..."

Heat crept into Tehl's cheeks. "I meant that she looks like a woman."

Lilja's eyes filled with mirth. "Am I not a woman?"

"That's not..." He heaved out a sigh and ran a hand through his inky locks. "I always imagined the Sirenidae as something akin to fish."

There was a beat of silence before Lilja threw her head back and let loose a husky chuckle. "You have a way with words, my lord."

He rubbed the back of his neck, embarrassed. "That's what my family is always telling me." He blinked, a thought occurring to him. "Does Sage know?"

"Yes," Hayjen answered.

Tehl scoffed. "Of course she bloody well knew. Nothing escapes that woman."

"She's a smart one," Sam muttered, plopping into a chair. "This is my question: how were they caught unaware?" Sam glanced at them. "Sorry for changing the subject, but I can't figure it out. Garreth is one of the best Elite I know, and Sage, well, her sneaking and self-defense skills are excellent. How did Rhys surprise them?" Frustration tinged his brother's voice.

Lilja propped a hip against the table. "I believe I can shed light on this as well. The Scythians are enemies like you've never faced before."

"You've said that," his father said. "What makes them so different? We vanquished them before."

"That was before they were flawless."

"They've always strived for perfection," Gav reasoned.

"True, so are you saying now they've accomplished it?" Sam asked skeptically.

"Not in the truest sense, but in the ways that mattered most to them. Unparalleled beauty and an exceptional thinking ability are two."

"Beauty is hardly dangerous," Tehl said.

"It is when used the right way," Sam said.

"Your brother's right, but there are more deadly qualities. Enhanced hearing, increased speed, and inhuman strength."

"That seems impossible," said Gav.

Tehl glanced at his cousin. "So did the annihilation of the Nagalians, and the existence of the Sirenidae."

Sam quirked a brow. "Are you so quick to believe in this

madness? You who never believes in anything but logic?"

Tehl tipped his chin at Lilja. "She's all the proof I need. Her story does not conflict with any of my knowledge. It makes sense the Scythians would be enhanced. They've had hundreds of years to do God-knows-what to their people."

"How did they accomplish such a thing?" his father asked.

"Science."

Tehl wrinkled his nose at Hayjen. "That's dangerous."

Lilja shrugged. "It's only dangerous in how it's used. They've discovered and manipulated different essences from their jungles, the ocean, and from the red caves of Nagali. If used the right way, the plants could heal many in the kingdoms."

"I don't want any of that here," Tehl barked.

"That's your prerogative as crown prince. But I would like to leave you with this thought: would you let your people suffer because of your own prejudice?"

He blinked. When she put it like that, it made him feel like the villain. "We've done just fine until now."

Lilja cast a glance at his father and he followed her gaze. The king stared at the floor with his shoulders slumped.

"Have you?" Her question was soft.

Anger burned in his chest at her cruel question. "That was a low blow."

"Everyone has lost someone, Tehl, especially those of us who have lived long lives."

He met her gaze and saw understanding and loss there.

"Why let others suffer when you have the power to bring about change for the good? Change will happen, with or without you. Don't you want to shape it into something great for your people?"

His gaze dropped to the floor as he mulled over what she said. Change for Aermia and for him had happened even if he didn't want it to—his mum's death, his father's mental breakdown, picking up the pieces of the kingdom, and marrying Sage. Many unexpected things had befallen his family and himself, but it was because of their choices that things were still going well. He lifted his head and nodded.

"I will think on it."

"That's all I ask." She clapped her hands together and pushed off the table. "How do you think your advisors will react to the news of the Scythians' advancements?"

"Disbelief, anger, bloody panic, and a steeling of themselves for what is to come," Sam drawled.

"Very astute for someone so young," Lilja said. "No wonder Sage likes you. You're very similar."

"You hear that, Tehl? You married the female version of your brother," Sam joked.

Tehl began to retort when Lilja cut him off. "You think you're cloaked in shadows, Samuel Ramses. But just as Sage sees who you are, so do I. Just remember that playing so many roles can blur who we are, even to ourselves. If you wear too many masks, you may forget what you *really* look like."

"Spoken like someone who knows something of it," Sam replied, his tone serious.

Lilja strode toward Sam and clasped his hand in both of hers. "I've lived a long time in the dark, hiding who I am to protect the ones I love. I know something of it. You and I are more alike than you realize. Call on me for anything."

Sam blinked and shifted a hair closer to Lilja. Tehl rolled his eyes, already knowing what was coming. His brother smiled seductively down at the woman.

"Call on you for anything?" he purred.

"Hey now," Hayjen objected.

Lilja leaned closer to Sam. In a move meant to seduce, she ran her hand up his arm and to his cheek. "You're out of your league," she whispered, and then patted him on the cheek twice, hard enough to sting. She spun on her heel, wearing a grin that spoke of vindication, and sauntered back to her husband.

Tehl sniggered at how his brother cupped his cheek and stared after Lilja with both admiration and fear.

"Now that that's over, how do you propose we move ahead with our plans, my lady?" his father asked.

The smile on Lilja's face was positively devious. "We run circles around the Scythians."

"How will we do that?" Gav jumped in.

"With the promise of women, of course."

CHAPTER SEVEN

Sage

Sweat dripped between her breasts as she struggled to place one foot in front of the other. Each breath was wet, like she was breathing water—the air seemed saturated, heavy.

She glanced to Jasmine. Her friend's face pinched with every step. A curse burst out of the brunette's mouth as she stumbled, her knees buckling. Sage reached out and caught her roughly, stumbling and almost going down herself. She strained and locked her knees, barely keeping them both upright.

"You're slowing us down. Pick up your speed or I'll drag you."

Sage clenched her teeth and turned to glare at Rhys.

"He's not worth it," Jas wheezed in her ear. "Just help me, Sage."

She swallowed back her rage and slid her bare arm around Jasmine's back. "Can you still walk?"

"Yeah. It's just my damn ribs. They hurt in the back, too."

"You need more exercise," she said, trying to lighten the mood.

Blue-gray eyes narrowed on her. "You're hobbling as much as I am."

"It's my bloody feet. There's not much skin left." And it was the truth. The soles of her feet were always soft from the rain, so they shredded and cut easily. Each evening, she attempted to clean the wounds and bandage them, but they were always caked with black soil, so it was mostly futile.

She shivered as a drop of water splashed between her shoulder blades and ventured into her half-corset.

"He's watching you again."

Her jaw clenched. She didn't even need to look to know who Jas was referring to. When she'd sat with Jasmine after his forced disrobing, Rhys' eyes had locked on her like she was his prey. At that moment, she'd frozen as he glided across the camp toward her. Jasmine had shaken her out of her stupor, and she had stood to face the monster. His eyes had slowly traced the curves of her body. Sage had forced herself not to back away when he had leaned close to whisper, "Soon..."

It was only one word, but it was enough to keep her on edge for the next two days. She blinked, and the memory disappeared as

Jasmine's face swam into view. "I know."

"You need to be careful."

"I know, Jas," she whispered harshly.

"Even if you have to beg protection from one of the other men, like the leader, do it."

She scanned the circle of men surrounding them, pausing on the large roguish-looking warrior. He lifted his head and glanced her way as if he could hear their conversation. For all she knew, he could. Not looking away from him, Sage whispered, "They're not our friends. They're our enemies."

"Yes, but some men are worse than others."

"Indeed."

Both women fell silent, as it took all their focus to keep painfully trudging on. Sage kept her eyes on the ground to avoid anything sharp that could damage her already severely abused feet even more. She suppressed a shriek when a spider the size of her fist scuttled across the forest floor. Jasmine wasn't so discreet.

"Swamp apples!" she hissed in disgust. "That's nasty."

Sage tuned her friend's grumbling out while scanning the surrounding jungle. Her brows slammed together. Something wasn't quite right. The trees were duller, and the ground had begun to slant downward. The soil between her toes even felt different, scratchier. She dropped her chin, her wet hair flopping limply into her face. With care, she examined the surrounding men. The warriors still walked with a purpose, but something in their stance had changed. She scrutinized it for a moment before deciphering what it was.

Excitement. There was a spring to their step now. Her stomach dropped. What were they excited for?

Her gaze swept the jungle again, searching for the source of their excitement. She blinked. Somehow, she'd missed that somewhere along the line, trees had been thinning. A large, dark hill rose just a stone's throw away. Whatever excited them rested on the other side of that hill.

"What is it?" Jasmine murmured.

"What?" she asked absently, still trying to figure out where the men were taking them.

"Your arm tensed, and you squeezed my ribs."

Immediately she loosened her grip and glanced at her friend, holding her panic at bay. "Whatever is over that knoll is the end for us."

Jas squinted at the dark hill, little lines appearing on her forehead, before she turned back to Sage. "Once we enter where they are taking us, there won't be any escape."

"No," she agreed.

"Then you need to escape now," Jasmine said, only loud enough for her ears.

She jerked. "I'm not leaving you."

The brunette's jaw set. "I can't run. I can barely walk. You can make it, Sage. You have to try. For the both of us."

Everything inside her ached to just run, to escape. Her hand opened and closed against Jasmine's back. "I can't leave you." Guilt threatened to swamp her at the angry expression on her friend's bruised face. "You wouldn't be here if it wasn't for me."

"That's not true," Jas whispered harshly. "I would have tried to help anyone. It just happened to be you. I should have checked the forest better. I wasn't cautious enough. That's on me. Now run. I'll distract them."

Her gaze darted around as she debated the outcome. Could she make it? The answer slapped her in the face as her eyes connected with Rhys. “No,” she said, tearing her eyes away from him and back to Jas. “Even if I could escape the warriors, I would still have to get through a week of jungle without food, water, and a direction in which to run. Not to mention the deadly creatures the warriors had to battle back there. The black felines are still hunting us. I wouldn’t make it. I’d be dead by morning.”

Jasmine visibly wilted. “You’re right, I wasn’t thinking.”

“You weren’t thinking.”

They both stiffened at the deep, accented voice behind them. Sage craned her neck and was met by feathers and coal black hair. The leader.

“You’re wise not to run. You wouldn’t survive in our jungle. Now put all childish dreams of escape and freedom from your mind.”

“Freedom is childish?” she questioned. “I thought your people would appreciate—” Pain slammed into her face, causing her to lose her balance and topple Jasmine. She crashed to the ground, the wind knocked from her. Rolling to her hands and knees, she swayed, trying to see past all the stars swirling across her vision. A metallic tang invaded her mouth. Someone had made her bleed. Again. If it was the last thing she’d do, she’d—

Sage jolted out of her thoughts at Jasmine’s cry. Her gaze cut to Jas, lying flat on her back and clutching her ribs while a boot rested on them. Sage looked up and glared at Rhys. Her vision turned red and all she could see was him and his smug face.

Enough was enough. It was time for him to die.

“Rhys! You’ve had your fun,” the leader admonished.

Sage's hand ran along the forest floor, seeking a weapon. Anything to protect herself and Jasmine. A grim smile tugged at her lips as her fingers closed around a sharp rock. That would do. Slowly, she shuffled closer.

"They need to be punished for plotting an escape," Rhys said.

"They were speaking nonsense."

"I think you've grown soft in your old age. The men see it. You've been soft on these girls. Do you think they'll be handed to you for your obedience?"

She froze at the beat of silence, taking the utmost care not to attract attention.

"The warlord will grant you nothing," said Rhys. "You are nothing."

"Those are large words from a flawed."

The forest seemed to still at the leader's words. Sage watched Rhys through the curtain of her hair, his face turning almost purple. His fists clenched, and his arms began to shake. She closed her eyes, pulled in a deep steadying breath, and prepared herself. A large hand rested on the top of her head, causing her eyes to fly open. Boots she'd become familiar with stood right in front of her. She hadn't even heard Rhys move.

Sage obeyed the tug on her hair as she was forced to meet his cruel, soulless gaze. "This is how you should always be. On your knees."

That was it. She couldn't move because of the hand in her hair, but she still had use of her hands. Clutching her rock, she licked her bloody lips, knowing he'd follow the motion, and slammed the pointy rock into the side of his knee. His eyes widened, and his mouth parted in a bellow right before she received a kick to the gut. She flew backward, her breath rushing out of her. Her shoulders slammed into the ground, and her feet tumbled over her head.

She coughed, trying to get air into her screaming lungs as she brushed her hair from her face. Pain was everywhere. Sage pushed up from the ground and grimaced as a large hand snaked around her waist and pulled her from the forest floor. Rhys struggled with three warriors, trying to get to her. She bared her bloody teeth at him in a smug smile.

He strained harder against the arms restraining him, the veins in his neck bulging. "You're dead! I'll kill you! You're dead," he screamed.

A crazed laugh bubbled up from her belly. "I died in that cell. There's nothing left to kill."

"You shouldn't have done that," the leader muttered next to her ear. "Look at what you've wrought."

Sage's smile faded as she truly *looked* at Rhys. His whole body shuddered, and it was almost as if he had grown in size. Something had shifted in his eyes. She slammed into the hard chest behind her when his bloodshot, feral eyes clashed into her own. The rage-filled man she'd come to know was nothing like the wild beast in front of her now.

His teeth gnashed, spittle flying through the air as he bellowed, "Mark my words, you'll pay."

One of the warriors pushed a flask against his mouth and another pinched his nose. He fought harder, spewing the brew everywhere. Sage watched in horror as liquid and drool dripped down his chin, and he mouthed, "You're mine."

She trembled in the leader's arms for a few minutes as the wild glint in Rhys' eyes died and his usual soulless gaze returned. He growled at the men and jerked his arms from their grasp. Rhys shook himself and sneered in her direction, before limping to his horse and swinging up into the saddle like nothing happened.

"Let's go," he commanded, like he wasn't losing blood each second.

She turned her face and leaned her cheek against the warm chest behind her, shuddering. What *was* he?

"I warned you not to push him."

"Not well enough," she pushed out between chattering teeth. They always did that when she became scared or excited. "What was that?"

"Berserker rage. If those men had not held him back, he would've torn you apart, woman. I keep thinking you've learned your lesson, and yet you keep rebelling. You're lucky today. If you try that with the warlord, he'll kill you. No one will stop him. Your death will be senseless. Be smart. Try to survive."

Sage pulled herself from the leader, took shaky steps away from him, and turned to look at him with a raised brow. "Why?" Why was he looking after her?

He shrugged his wide shoulders. "Women are rare. You're worth more alive."

"Indeed," she muttered, and turned her back to the leader. Jasmine had managed to stand, but still clutched her ribs, her face a map of pain.

"Are more broken?" Sage asked with worry.

"I'm sure. I got kicked by my brother's horse when I was younger. I know what it feels like."

"Beasts," she spat.

"After that display, I don't doubt it." Jasmine's voice wobbled on the end, betraying her fear.

Sage slipped her hand into her friend's, giving strength as much as receiving it. It was a comfort to have someone in which to share the poor circumstances. "We're in this together."

"Together."

***

She thought they were going over the hill.

She was wrong.

She stopped, confused as to why they weren't moving up the hill. Her confusion doubled when the warriors stopped next to an enormous rock and pushed. Her eyes rounded as they revealed a black hole in the side of the hill, a gaping maw which could devour them.

"Where does that lead?" she asked. No one answered. Wherever it was, it was not somewhere she wanted to be.

One by one, they entered the black hole and disappeared. A calloused hand wrapped around her bicep. She winced at the tight hold and leaned away from its owner.

"Don't cause trouble or you'll regret it," Rhys threatened.

Her skin prickled at his proximity, and her heart galloped. He was unhinged; it was boiling right under the surface. Sage dipped her head in a respectful way, she hoped, and wished he would release her throbbing arm.

"Good."

He let go of her abruptly, almost upsetting her balance, but she'd prepared for it. Rhys had a way of being predictable when it came to his abuse. She lifted her eyes to catch the leader's; the small dip of his chin sparked anger inside her. She neither needed nor wanted his approval. She just wanted to stay alive.

The warriors took up formation, surrounding and ushering them toward the opening. Jasmine's hand clenched in Sage's.

"I don't like this. It's a cave!"

"Me neither."

They fell silent as the opening loomed before them. Sage finally let go of any hope she'd harbored for a rescue as they entered the dark.

No one would find them here.

Chapter Eight

Sage

The grating sound of stone against stone etched into her mind.

There was no escaping the inky darkness.

She blinked repeatedly, trying to help her eyes adjust. Someone pushed her from behind and her right shoulder slammed against something cool, wet, and rough. She pressed her hand to the cave wall and ran her fingers over its surface. Porous stone, similar to that which was beneath the Aermian castle. Were they close to the sea here?

Another shove forced her to abandon her exploration and shuffle forward in the pitch black, every step a gamble.

"It's so dark in here, I literally cannot see my hand in front of my face." Jasmine's voice grumped from her left.

Sage's lips twitched. Jas seemed to have an uncanny ability to lighten the mood without trying.

As they trekked through the dark, the air of what she assumed was a passage slowly heated from the press of so many bodies and sweat. She paused for a moment to help Jasmine, only to have a very large, hot, sweaty body press against her back. She skittered away, dragging the brunette with her. Deep masculine laughter rumbled around them and her cheeks heated further, both in embarrassment and anger.

Jas squeaked in outrage. "Who was that?" the brunette demanded.

"What?"

"Someone touched me."

More laughter.

The women huddled closer together as the dark seemed to escalate their fear. The dark was both oppressing and unnerving. It made them too vulnerable.

"Enough."

One word, and the laughter stopped. The press of bodies around them seemed to lessen. Her breath whistled out from between her clenched teeth; she was thankful the leader had command of his men.

After walking for a while, she lost all sense of direction as well as time. The only thing she could discern was that they seemed to be descending, her legs and thighs burning from the slope. Her brows furrowed when she detected faint traces of light, which brightened their surroundings bit by bit. She blinked a few more times as the outlines of the men surrounding her became visible. Something cracked underneath her foot. She paused and squinted at the floor.

Bones.

Jasmine followed her gaze and yelped, pulling them to the side. "Is that...a skeleton?" she asked, her voice shaking.

"It's what happens to those who run away." Rhys' voice slithered over them.

Sage grimly stared at the skeleton. That had been *someone*. It had once been a living, breathing human being, maybe even with a family. Before she could stop herself, she asked, "Why?"

"He was hunted down, hobbled, and then let free," the leader replied.

She finally tore her gaze from the bones. "Free?"

"Free to run until the leren caught him."

"Leren?" Jas asked.

"The man-eater that almost killed you that first day in the forest."

Chills ran up Sage's arms when she thought of the giant black jungle cats that had tracked them through their entire journey. "You let them run free here?"

"No," Rhys whispered in her ear. "We ration their food until another source presents itself."

"You starve them until you want them to hunt someone?" she asked, her tone flat. Just when she thought they couldn't get more barbaric, they got worse.

"They love to hunt prey that runs from them," the leader supplied. "Let's move on."

Sick to her stomach, Sage carefully stepped over the bones with Jas plastered to her side. She shivered at the thought of being hunted in the maze of dark tunnels. Disgust gave way to hysteria, and a giggle slipped out. How fitting. The stone was as black as the Scythians' souls.

Jasmine looked at her askance.

"Nothing," she muttered, and stamped down the hysterical thoughts bubbling up inside her. If she let go now, she'd probably come unhinged.

The group snaked around a corner, and her steps faltered as light poured through a wide doorway. When she saw what lay beyond it, she stopped short. It was a phenomenon unlike anything she'd ever seen. The doorway led to a massive open cavern that hosted what looked to be an entire city, carved from the black stone. Sage squinted, barely able to make out the filthy people scuttling about the curved lanes, carrying all sorts of tools. Lanterns cast a sickly, yellow glow over them and she suppressed a gasp. Were those chain slaves?

"Move on."

The leader jostled her forward, and just like that, she was swept away from the strange underground city. A thousand questions were at the tip of her tongue, but she kept her mouth shut. It wasn't like they would answer her anyway.

The stone hallway twisted left then right, and at the far end were two enormous wooden doors into which symbols had been charred. Four giant men guarded the door, their bare, muscled skin painted with those same symbols. She shivered as their dark eyes zeroed in on her and Jasmine. It wasn't sexual, but they looked at the girls with unveiled curiosity, as if they were some sort of exhibit.

In unison, the guards bowed and pulled open the doors. Her lids slammed shut at the sudden burst of light. One eye at a time, she cracked them and forced herself to move through the doors.

She squinted, the bright light blinding her. Everything was white. The walls, ceiling, and floor were made from white stone polished so brightly she could practically see her reflection. The bare walls sloped into high arched ceilings and the entire place felt cold, empty.

Sage looked behind her just as the doors thudded closed. She blinked. From this side, the door was invisible. The only thing that gave it away was a fine line where the stone didn't quite touch, allowing the doors to glide smoothly.

Her attention was pulled to the floor when she noticed garish scarlet footprints that marred the pristine beauty of the floor behind her. Something about it raised the hair of the back of her neck. She tracked the bloody footprints to her own feet.

"Rhys," a woman greeted.

Her head snapped up. She hadn't heard the woman arrive. She couldn't afford slips like this. Time to focus.

The woman's body was cloaked in furs, with daggers strapped to her thighs. When combined with her lithe, toned body, she was even more a warrior than Sage ever was. She scanned the strong features she'd learned were typical of the Scythians: sharp cheekbones, straight nose, and coal black hair. She paused when she met a shrewd, caramel gaze.

"This is the one?" the woman asked as she moved through the warriors and to Sage, stopping a pace away. Her eyes scanned Sage from head to toe, then back up. She cocked a hip and pursed her lips in a way that betokened disapproval.

Sage tipped her chin up. She'd be damned if she let some random woman intimidate her. Her body was in bad shape, but no one would make her feel ashamed for it; it wasn't even her fault. She eyed the woman as she circled her, and turned just enough to keep her back from the woman.

The Scythian female paused and raised a brow. "You're smart not to turn your back to me. Although..." She scanned her body again. "It seems you were not always smart."

Jasmine shifted by her side, an aggravated gesture. Sage grabbed her friend's wrist and squeezed. They couldn't afford rebellion.

The woman noticed the gesture and grinned. "It seems she has manners."

Sage stiffened.

"She needed training," Rhys replied, his face a mask of smugness.

"Indeed," she drawled in her slight accent.

"Where is he, Maeve?"

"The throne room, where else?"

"Of course."

The woman smiled with fondness at Rhys. Sage blinked, surprised. No one liked him.

"If you release the women into my care, I'll clean them up before you present them to the warlord."

"No, he needs to see them now."

The woman's eyes widened slightly before she schooled her reaction. "Do you think that wise?"

"You think to counsel me?"

Sage shifted closer to Jas when Rhys moved around her to tower over the woman.

"No, my lord," she replied. "But you know how he is."

"I have to agree with Maeve, Rhys," the leader added, stepping into the circle they'd formed in the hall.

Rhys cackled in his deranged way. "You live to disagree with me, Blair." He stepped back and wrapped a hand around her bicep. "*I* brought her here. *I* delivered her. *I* won't have this honor taken from me."

She kept her face blank even though he was pinching her arm.

"You shouldn't hold the Aermian so tightly. Even I can see you're hurting the girl," Maeve admonished.

His cold eyes locked onto her face, and she had to force herself not to run in the only way she could: by retreating into her own head. As appealing as it seemed, however, it was not something she could afford.

"There's beauty in flaws," he whispered near her cheek.

Her stomach heaved. Lord, how she despised him.

His face soured as if he read the thoughts she fought to hide. "We go now," he snarled. "Move!" He released her arm and spun around to stalk away, the warriors seamlessly parting for him.

The men straightened, forming a ring with Blair, the Scythian woman, Jas, and her at the center. Sage stepped forward, only to be tugged back. She met Jasmine's blue-gray eyes.

"I can't move," Jas whispered.

"What?"

"My legs, they've seized."

Sage released her friend's hand and tucked the brunette into her side. "Put your arm around my neck."

Jasmine grunted and did so. "God, that hurts," she hissed.

"It's going to hurt more before it gets better. Brace yourself."

A small cry fell from Jas' lips as Sage held her tightly and began moving.

"You have one extra," a feminine, accented voice spoke from her right.

"She...inserted herself where she didn't belong, and we had no choice but to bring her. We always need more stock."

Stock? What did that mean? She tilted her head down, focusing on carrying Jas and listening at the same time, her ear cocked toward the woman.

"The last few did well."

There was an undercurrent of jealousy in the woman's tone. Interesting. Why would she be jealous of stock? Her foot slipped, and she jerked, jarring her friend.

"Hell, Sage," her friend cursed through clenched teeth.

"Sorry," she mumbled, adjusting her grip. She glanced at the floor and grimaced at the trail they were leaving. If by some miracle they could escape, at least they'd have their own trail of dirty, bloody footprints to return by.

Looking ahead, she caught sight of a set of twenty-foot-tall, engraved, white doors adorned with curling black handles carved from wood. The warriors stationed outside them bowed to Rhys and then immediately looked at her. Was she that different? That odd? To her, *they* were the odd ones, all looking the same.

She was pulled from her questions when Rhys appeared before

her. "You will not speak unless spoken to. You will stare at the floor unless addressed, and you will not embarrass me." He then spun on his heel and disappeared past the ring of warriors.

"He's right," the leader whispered. "Be careful, both of you."

The immense door pushed inward.

Sage took a deep breath and looked to Jasmine. "Are you ready?"

"As ready as I'll ever be when walking to my death," she wheezed.

Sage briefly quirked a smile at her before shuffling along with their procession as it moved through the doors and into the room. Upon entering, her eyes widened and she barely managed to keep her jaw from dropping.

The room was large and domed, its walls at least four stories high, with glass ceiling tiles sprinkled here and there. The white stone floor was broken up by large trees that stood like giants surveying their kingdom. They reached up through the dome and disappeared into a sea of greenery above them.

She was jerked from her inspection when something touched her cheek. Her lips thinned. It was a reaching fern. Nothing else. Just a plant.

She plowed ahead, trying to keep her wits about her, but she still felt like something was off.

"There are no birds," Jas whispered.

The hairs rose on Sage's arms. That's what it was. There wasn't a sound in the throne room except for their own shuffling footsteps. The feeling of being watched had the back of her neck prickling. She scanned the surrounding trees, but found nothing, at least, nothing she could see. That's what worried her the most.

It didn't dissipate as they moved on, but intensified.

The trees opened up and formed a half circle, which butted up against the biggest stone wall she'd ever seen. In the center, a strip of the black porous rock ran from ceiling to floor. She peeked between two warriors to get a better look and caught a glimpse of stairs which led to what she suspected was the dais.

"Nephew, it's been some time since I've seen you in the flesh."

The deep voice rolled over Sage like thunder in a storm, all power. She'd always thought Tehl's voice held power, but his was nothing compared to this.

She stilled when it was Rhys who answered the warlord. "My lord, I'm humbled to be in your presence."

Her insides quivered in fear. This was going to be worse than she thought. The warlord was Rhys' *uncle?* "Oh, God," she breathed.

"He can't help you here," the leader whispered.

She whipped her head around to stare into the solemn eyes of the leader.

"Blair..." the deep voice commanded.

If Sage hadn't been staring so hard, she would have missed it. Just for a moment, hate flashed through Blair's eyes at the sound of the warlord's voice, but it was gone as quick as it came. He broke their stare-off, then pushed through the ring of warriors.

"My lord," he responded, his tone respectful.

"You've done your job well. Thank you for bringing my nephew home safely."

"It was nothing."

"Untrue." A pause. "Did you accomplish your task, nephew?"

"I did," Rhys replied.

"Excellent. And what of your guests? I wasn't expecting you to bring anyone home."

Jasmine sucked in a breath and began to tremble.

Rhys' voice drifted closer. "I've brought you a gift."

"Intriguing."

Sage's heart raced when her enemy pushed through the circle of warriors. He captured her gaze and held his hand out. She stared at it as if it were a venomous snake.

"Come now, Sage, don't be foolish. And mind your manners," Rhys spoke through gritted teeth.

Inwardly, she steeled herself. She didn't have any other choice. Things would go very badly for them if she offended the warlord. Sage turned to the woman, who was currently watching the spectacle, and gestured to Jasmine. "She can't stand on her own. Will you help me?"

Maeve eyed her with annoyance but moved to Jasmine's other side.

Sage squeezed her friend's hand once more, and then placed that same hand in Rhys', her jaw clenching when his thumb rubbed against her wrist. The warriors parted, and she dropped her eyes to her dirty feet as her own personal demon led her like a fine lady toward the dais. Her gaze snagged on his limping gait. Despite the horrible circumstances, she had to hide a grin at his shuffling pace. The bastard deserved that and then some.

Blair's instructions ran through her head. *Don't speak unless spoken to. Keep your head down. Don't make eye contact.* But she wouldn't be led to the warlord like a lamb, cowering and staring at her feet like she was in submission to them. Using her last vestiges of strength, she raised her head and stared ahead.

Gasps surrounded her, and Rhys' hand tightened on hers, but all she saw were warm, black eyes. It shocked her. She'd expected soulless, cruel eyes. The smile lines around the man's eyes spoke of something different. His inky hair hung around his angular face, just brushing his bare, muscular shoulders. He was beautiful. Everything about him called to her, from the straight, proud line of his nose to the stubborn chin and almond-shaped eyes. But it was more than his features; it was how he wore them. Sage kept her face schooled and lifted her chin. Never in her wildest imagination did she expect him to be so stunning, or so young. Her eyes told her he was beautiful when her mind told her he featured in the nightmares of many. It wasn't right that evil could don such an alluring mask.

Her gaze strayed to the lounging felines on either side of him, and she barely contained a gasp. Leren: the man-eaters. Their golden eyes latched onto her as they flicked their tails in her direction. With her head still held high she surveyed the Scythian court; they were every bit as beautiful and cold as she expected. They eyed her with shock and disgust, but also a flicker of fear. Why did they fear her?

"What have you brought me?"

Her eyes snapped back to the warlord, who had sat up from his lazy sprawl, now leaning forward, one elbow resting on his knee.

Hell, he was flawless.

She'd spent time surrounded by handsome men—Tehl, Sam, Gavriel, and Rafe—but this man was regal in a way that left her in awe, rather like a fine painting or well-carved statue.

Rhys tugged her close, pulling her from her gawking, but when he tried to brush a tangled strand out of her face, something inside her snapped. She slapped his hand away and jerked out of his grasp. In an instant, both man-eaters sprang from the dais and to the floor, growling in a way that had fear clawing at her belly. Her instincts told her to run, but she knew that would only sign her death warrant. She reached for her belt and clasped air. Again, she cursed Rhys for taking her weapons. She was now completely defenseless. Slowly, so as to not startle the beasts, she settled into a defensive position, hands held out in front of her.

"Who's this?" the deep voice purred.

She shivered, but didn't pull her gaze from the giant midnight felines.

"This is Sage Blackwell, the rebellion's blade, and...princess of Aermia."

"Princess?"

"Yes," Rhys replied, pride in his tone.

There was a beat of silence, and then, "Sage, I'm so happy you're able to visit my court."

Visit? What a joke. "It wasn't much of an invitation, my lord." It took all her energy to hold still and remain calm. In reality, she couldn't hear anything over the pounding of her pulse and the ringing inside her head.

More curses and murmurs erupted around them. Inwardly, she winced. Probably not the best idea to disrespect the warlord. She felt his gaze hot on her face, but she still didn't look away from the beast that had just licked its lips.

"She's feisty."

"More than you know, my lord."

"Why are you limping?"

She swore she could almost hear Rhys' teeth grinding.

"She fought me and landed a blow," Rhys rushed out.

"Interesting," the warlord drawled. "And her injuries?"

"Earned."

She bit her lip to keep herself from lashing out, but still kept her eyes on the beasts stalking back and forth in front of the immense throne.

"My loves, come back," the warlord cooed.

She studied the felines as their ears flicked back and forth before slinking back to his side, settling like shadowy pools that stained the white dais. Her hands trembled, and she had to clench them to hide it. At least she would not be torn apart by beasts. For now.

The warlord stood from his throne made of stone and thorns. She blinked at his bare, chiseled chest, which also seemed to be carved from stone, and again wondered why he didn't wear clothes. In her mind, a warrior would want as much protection as possible. Sage studied him as he glided down from the dais and toward her. He truly did glide, each movement of his body flowing into the next. She shivered. Only highly trained warriors and assassins moved like that.

Tipping back her head, she maintained eye contact as he approached, halting less than an arm's length away. Stars above, the man was enormous. He had to be well over six feet tall, maybe close to seven.

He completely threw her off balance when he bowed slightly, murmuring, "My lady."

She dipped her chin in acknowledgement. The Scythian warlord straightened, and raised a black brow like he was waiting for something. If he expected her to curtsey, he would be sorely disappointed. She'd crash to the ground if she attempted such a thing.

Rhys stormed to her side and jerked her arm, crushing her skin in his hand. She winced as pain shot through her arm. Black eyes caught hers, and she masked her expression. But he'd seen it.

"Kneel," Rhys demanded.

She locked her knees, not losing eye contact with the warlord. "No."

Before she knew what was happening, her knees cracked against the stone, her palms slapping the unforgiving floor, stinging. Much to her frustration, a tear squeezed out of one eye. It dripped off her face and splashed onto the white floor, mixing with the blood and dirt she'd tracked in. Glaring at the black boots of the warlord, she prepared herself for the beating that was sure to come.

Chapter Nine

The Warlord

He thought it would be another day of dealing with petty bickering, but then his nephew reappeared, and with him, a girl.

The voices inside him quieted the longer he stared at her. The moment she lifted her head and met his gaze, he jolted. Images of the past assaulted him: sad, green eyes, a kiss, brown hair wrapped around his fist, and blood. He blew out a deep breath as the memories faded.

The voices whispered that they wanted her. That she was different. That she was *his*.

The resemblance was striking, and yet, she was unlike the women he'd surrounded himself with. By all accounts, he should've been disgusted by her, offended and repulsed by her green eyes and scars, but he was intrigued. Ensnared. The flawless Scythian women scattered around the room and the dangerous, broken creature before him created an almost laughable contrast.

But as enchanting as her body might be, it was her face that captivated him. It looked sweet, innocent, and honorable. Everything he was not.

She wore a mask of calm, but again her gaze betrayed her. Flames burned behind her eyes; she was dangerous. But what piqued his interest was the small glimmer of fear he detected. It was an interesting combination: fear, hate, and feigned innocence. He had killed for less than the expression she wore, and yet the voices stayed his hand at her insolence. Death clearly didn't scare her, but he did. He both liked and hated that.

Before he really knew what he was doing, he descended the dais, almost desperate to be closer to her. Her obvious hate for his nephew warmed him to her even more. Rhys had always been a pathetic excuse for a Scythian. The moment Rhys struck her, something snapped inside Zane. Only knaves and cowards hit women. It was despicable, and no one touched what was his. Ever. It was an act which was not to be borne. His nephew had signed his own death warrant right then and there.

His gaze never strayed from the woman as he drew closer. Could she be the key to what he sought, or would she be the key to his destruction?

CHAPTER TEN

Sage

A large, calloused hand wearing several rings entered her vision. She stared at it. What kind of joke was this? He couldn't mean to help her up.

"Take it, please," his smooth voice said.

With no other option, Sage slipped her hand into his. He lifted her from the floor, and she swore she heard her bones creak. She met his gaze and dipped her chin as she pulled her hand away. "Thank you."

A nod. He scanned her face slowly, taking all the time in the world. Then, he moved down the rest of her body, stopping here and there to examine a scar, a cut, a bruise. Was he admiring his man's handy work? Looking for ways he could hurt her? She held herself stock-still as he walked around her as if he was inspecting chattel.

"What happened to her clothing?" he murmured, only loud enough for Rhys to hear.

"The other woman needed medical attention. Sage had to use her shirt as punishment for insubordination."

The warlord hummed and paused by her side.

"Is she still pure?" The question lingered in the air.

"Of course, my lord. We wouldn't dare touch what is yours."

She forced herself to hold still when he caressed a scar along her hip, and then her wrist.

"How did she come by the scars?"

"She and I had...a disagreement, if you will," Rhys replied smugly.

Her stomach churned at his lies.

"And the rest? She's been beaten badly."

"All deserved, I can assure you. She brought them on herself. She never stopped fighting."

Another hum. "What do I cherish most in the world?" the warlord asked conversationally.

"Perfection." Rhys' response was automatic.

"What comes second?"

"Our line."

"True," the warlord answered, circling her again. "And who bears our lines?"

"Our women," Rhys drawled.

Sage turned her head to follow the prowling warlord. All his pacing had her on edge. He stopped between Rhys and herself.

"Do we *ever* hurt our women?"

"No," the monster replied, his mud-brown gaze darting from her to the warlord.

He glanced at her arm, and the warlord's lips thinned just a touch. Slowly, he began circling her again. This time, she turned to keep her back from him. She was finished with his inspection.

A small smile tipped up his sensual lips. "I wondered when you would give up your submissive pose. You don't have it in you to bend to someone else's will."

She bared her teeth at him, countering his movements. "You know nothing about me."

"On the contrary, I know everything." The warlord slid behind Rhys and whispered, "You shouldn't have marred her. You know how I feel about that, and yet you disobey me."

One moment, Rhys was staring smugly at her, and the next, he was gurgling on the floor, scarlet liquid slipping from his neck.

Her body flashed hot and cold, and a high ringing filled her ears. A tremor rippled through her body as Rhys gasped and writhed on the floor. Even as death claimed him, he managed to choke out something that would surely haunt her dreams.

"I'll always be on your skin," he coughed, and the light in his eyes dimmed.

She blinked. *No.*

Sage scrambled toward Rhys and dropped to her knees next to

him. Carefully, she held a hand over his parted lips, shaking. Not one breath. "No," she uttered as she frantically grabbed his wrist to feel for a pulse. Nothing. "No, no, no, no, no, no!"

Her eyes darted back to his face, and she gagged at his empty, unseeing eyes. He was gone. Dead in a matter of heartbeats.

No pain. A clean death. No suffering.

An ember of rage caught flame in her gut. How dare he die! "You bastard!" she screamed and slammed her fists on Rhys' unmoving chest. "You don't get to die! Breathe, damn it."

Still, his chest didn't move. He was dead.

He didn't deserve a quick death. He didn't deserve death at all! He deserved to rot and suffer in eternal hell like she did *every day*. A wail came out of her that didn't seem physically possible. "Death was too good for him!"

Sage pulled her hands back and held up her shaking palms. They were red. Covered in blood. She retched, bile burning her throat and flooding her mouth. In a frenzy, she scrubbed her hands over her pants and half-corset, sobbing. She didn't want him on her. Pushing up from her knees, she tried to stand, only for her feet to slip in the gore. Again, she gagged and scrubbed harder, but only succeeded in making it worse. Her body now looked like a garish painting of red, brown, and black.

Even in death, Rhys seemed to win.

Another sob broke loose as she lifted her head. The warlord was observing, completely calm, utterly unaffected by the murder he'd just committed.

"You," she accused. "You killed him!"

A shrug. "He deserved to die for his actions."

"He deserved to *suffer*," she choked out as the warlord's form blurred from her tears.

"My justice is swift. No one breaks my laws without punishment."

"His life was mine!" she yelled. "Mine!" Sage flinched as her voice echoed in the room.

"Was it?" the warlord questioned softly, returning his blade to the sheath at his hip. "Is anything really yours? Every decision you've made has been guided or forced from you. Your life, your body, and even your children will not be yours. He was mine, my subject to deal with."

She had begun shaking during his little speech, tears still pouring from her eyes.

"It was justice." He gestured at Sage. "He had no right to touch you. For that, he had a price to pay. You're too valuable to ruin."

She scoffed and sniffed, looking for Jasmine, while holding her arms out. "Your men have proved otherwise."

The warlord barked, "Blair."

The leader stepped away from the group of silent Scythians. "My lord."

"Is what she says true? Did the men harm her?"

The leader stilled and flashed her a look that asked, *Can you handle our deaths?*

She swallowed, and tried to think through all the madness swirling inside her. She held many lives in her hands. Part of her wanted them all to die, but did they deserve to die because Rhys happened to be part of their party? No.

"Your men did not permanently harm me. They followed orders." The words tasted like ash on her tongue.

"And the other woman?" the warlord asked.

"Anything that befell us was at the order of Rhys." Her nausea rose up again. She'd just defended the enemy. What was wrong with her? She blankly stared at the grisly scene on the floor, no longer seeing anything.

"Indeed." He addressed the leader: "Blair, make sure both women are cleaned, healed, and fed. Also, notify my sister that her son has died."

A large hand touched her arm and something squished underneath. Sage pulled away and stared at the bloody handprint overlapping the silver scars of her forearm. The sight sickened her. She hunched forward and expelled what little there was remaining in her stomach, and watched it splash all over the dirty, bloody floor around her. She wiped the bile from her mouth and stood on wobbly legs, only to come face-to-chest with the warlord. When had he moved? She lifted both crimson-stained hands, and pushed against his chest while stepping back. But she was stopped short and hauled back when his hand wrapped around the back of her neck.

She began struggling, but it felt like she was moving through sap. All her movements were slow and uncoordinated.

"It's easier this way," he whispered.

She darted a look up at him as his finger pressed into her neck. His sensual mouth and black eyes were the last thing she saw before darkness swallowed her.

CHAPTER ELEVEN

Tehl

"She won't say a damn thing!" Sam paced and ran a frustrated hand through his hair. "I've tried everything, and nothing! Nothing works. She's silent as the grave. If I didn't know better, I'd say she might be deaf. All she does when I ask her a question is stare at me expressionlessly, as if she can't understand the words coming out of my mouth." He cursed. "We don't have time for this! Sage is enduring God-knows-what circumstances and—" Sam broke off and swallowed hard. "I worry for her."

Tehl closed his eyes and held the bridge of his nose. "We have to get her to speak."

"What do you expect me to do? Torture her?" Sam snarled.

The anger that had been simmering beneath his skin finally bubbled over. "I don't know!" Tehl exploded. He shot out of his chair and threw a bottle of ink at the wall. "My wife has been missing for over a week in enemy territory. I have no way of knowing if she's even alive." He watched the ink drip down the wall like black blood. "Some part of me hopes she's already dead. Then, she would be spared from Rhys," he admitted. "Do you understand how messed up that is?"

Jeffry, Gav, Sam, and Rafe all stared at him in silence like he'd lost his mind. Maybe he had. Since Sage had been taken, he'd had nightmares every night. She always died in his dreams, mouthing something he couldn't understand with accusing eyes.

"You don't want that," Gav said with sorrow clinging to him. "Mourning a loved one is not something I'd wish on my worst enemy."

A loved one.

Somewhere along the lines, Sage became not just someone foisted on him, but part of his family. She got under Tehl's skin, just about drove him crazy, and ribbed him mercilessly, but that made him like her all the more. He loved her; not like his father loved his mother, but she was a loved one. The realization startled him.

Rafe uncoiled from his spot on the wall and rolled his neck. "Let me have a turn at her."

"Do you think you'll do better?" Sam asked.

The rebellion leader shrugged. "Maybe, maybe not. But I'll try until we get something we can use."

Tehl tipped his chin at Rafe. "I'll go with you."

"Is that wise, son?" Jeffry asked.

He smiled sharply at the Keeper. "No."

The Keeper blinked his eyes dangerously slow. "You're not planning on anything you'll regret, are you?"

"The only thing I would regret is the death of my wife," he said over his shoulder. He then stormed down the winding hallways that made up the labyrinth of cells.

"Do you have a plan?" Rafe asked from beside him.

He sent the rebellion leader an irritated look. "How do you move so quietly? If I didn't know any better, I'd say you were related to Sam."

A small smile played about Rafe's mouth. "I can't help it. It's how I was raised. You didn't answer my question."

"I will study her, and maybe read," Tehl answered.

"Read?"

Tehl pulled a small book out of his pocket and brushed his fingers over the silver filigree. "*The History of the Mort Wall.*"

"You're going to give her a history lesson?" Rafe asked skeptically.

"The last time Sam and I spoke with her, she was a staunch believer of all things Scythia. Sam seems to think she was indoctrinated with their beliefs. If I belittle her kingdom, maybe she'll start speaking. When we captured Blaise, she was the most emotional of the warriors. She had a temper."

"That's brilliant."

Tehl shot Rafe a startled look. "We're agreeing on something again?"

A shrug. "It was bound to happen sometime. We've always had Sage in common."

Guilt churned his stomach. He should've protected her.

"It wasn't your fault," Rafe murmured.

Tehl's jaw tightened, hating that the rebellion leader was reading him. "It was my task to protect her. I promised her family she'd be safe."

"You're not the only one. She's been mine to protect for the last few years, and all I've done is send her into one bad situation after another for the greater good," Rafe scoffed. "What the hell is the greater good? Is there really any good left in the world?"

"Sage and people like her are the good in our world."

"Very astute for someone so young."

Tehl's brows wrinkled. "You're not that much older than I am."

Rafe's lips thinned. "Indeed."

Both men fell silent, lost in their own thoughts. Tehl slowed to a stop at the Scythian woman's cell. Her hair fell in dull strands over her slumped shoulders, her eyelids closed. Even dirty, the woman was extraordinarily beautiful.

The rebellion leader sucked in a sharp breath. Tehl glanced at him and his lips twitched. "Have you never seen a Scythian?"

"I have, but I've never seen one of their women. They're guarded jealously. I can now see why. She's, she's—"

"Flawless," Tehl finished.

Rafe scowled, his scar puckering. "Indeed."

Tehl turned his back on the gawking man and moved to the stone wall across from the cell. He sank down to his haunches, then sat and pushed back against the wall. Tehl ran his fingers over the butter-soft cover of the book, remembering how his mum used to read it to him and his brother growing up. When he was little, it seemed like a bedtime story, but as he grew, he discovered the real value of the book. History meant everything.

He ignored Rafe as the rebellion leader plopped down several feet away and tipped his head back against the stone.

Tehl focused, opened the book, and began reading.

In the beginning, there were five kingdoms with very different peoples: Aermia, Methi, Nagali, Scythia, and Sirenidae. Each people had something very special to offer the world.

The Nagalians had the ability to communicate with the red dragons of the realm by singing. Their bonding led to working in the caves to retrieve rubies.

Methians were a courageous, regal people who lived in the mountains despite their somewhat temperamental neighbors—the griffins.

The Sirenidae lived in the sea, and graced all the peoples with treasures from deep below. They kept fishermen and traders safe on their passages.

The Aermians were a clever, kind people whose borders touched all other kingdoms and became the hub for trade. They welcomed all to their land.

Last were the Scythians, a brilliant, resilient race of people who lived in the harsh jungles, and could create the most amazing healing draughts from their plants. They were healers and warriors by nature.

Tehl read for hours, describing what each kingdom traded, how the people intermarried, how time passed. He read until his throat went dry. Licking his lips, he glanced at the lightly snoring Rafe, and prepared to start reading again.

"Must you drone on and on?" a husky female voice asked.

Casually, he placed the book in his lap and lifted his eyes to the woman in the cell. "Do you have anything else to do?"

She stared stonily at him.

Tehl shrugged. "If you don't mind, I'll continue." He plucked the book from his lap and picked up where he left off.

Unbeknownst to the other kingdoms, Scythia's warlord had grown increasingly obsessed with perfection, and began to covet something that was not his. A woman. One who was promised to another.

Rafe sniggered. "Sound familiar?"

Apparently, the rebellion leader wasn't asleep.

Tehl raised a brow but kept reading. "*Time passed, and the warlord's experiments continued from just healing his people to attempting to alter them so they would never get sick. And he succeeded. His people never became ill. But that wasn't enough; he kept searching for ways to fix his people, to perfect their race.*

When the other kingdoms became aware of his tampering, they immediately sought the warlord of Scythia. He smiled and placated the kings with lies and promises of healing draughts from their lands. But slowly, the Scythian people stopped marrying into any other race, worried that their children wouldn't be healthy. They began to distance themselves, withdrawing back into their jungles, fearing imperfection would infect them.

That was the first sign of danger. The Sirenidae saw the danger and calamity ahead, but no one paid them any mind. So, they pulled back into the ocean and disappeared altogether.

After years, it seemed normal that the Scythians didn't leave their kingdom, and the Sirenidae became a myth. But there was still peace.

As time passed, the warlord became more obsessed with perfecting the world. He hated the bond shared between the people and dragons of Nagali. It was unnatural in his mind that the death of a beast would break a person and change them forever. So, he offered the Nagali king a draught that would heal and alter his people, but the king refused. This angered the Scythian warlord, so much so, he decided to cleanse the Nagali people from the land."

A snort.

Tehl ignored her and kept on.

"Scythians crept into Nagali like thieves in the night. They swarmed the land like locusts and destroyed everything in their path. In a matter of days, an entire race had been murdered, down to the last ruby dragon. Aermia and Methi rallied and moved to meet Scythia in battle. But Scythia never planned to battle them. They had created a sickness that would spread through the people. It was only because of one man that this didn't happen."

"The traitor," Blaise spat.

"Many consider Alexander a hero."

Somehow, she managed to look down her nose at him whilst sitting down. "He betrayed our kingdom. I assure you, he was no hero. Every year, we celebrate his death by dancing on his grave."

Rafe tipped his head forward and looked at Tehl. "They're more demented than I expected."

A mocking laugh poured out of the woman. "The only thing demented here is you. Don't think I can't smell what you are, Methi."

Tehl froze, keeping his face schooled. *Methi?*

The rebellion leader smiled arrogantly at the woman. "With senses like that, you're no better than an animal like me."

Blaise lunged to her feet, only to be jerked back by her cuffs. "I'm nothing like you."

"Don't be so sure. Who do you think your warlord was trying to imitate when he started experimenting on his people? He was jealous of everyone else's abilities."

She spat at him and sat on the floor again, her chest sawing heavily.

"Charming," Rafe remarked.

Tehl watched her as she tried to calm herself down.

She pulled in one final breath and opened her eyes. "Even in this kingdom, staring is considered rude." A pause. "You won't break me."

"I'm not trying to break anything."

"Liar," she hissed.

He crossed his arms and cocked his head. "Truly, nothing broken is useful."

A long blink. "Agreed." Another pause. "Where's the woman? I enjoyed her last visit. She's interesting."

"Come now. Surely, you can use her name?" Rafe needled.

"Sage. I want to see her."

Then the Scythian woman wasn't aware. "So do I," Tehl replied.

Two little wrinkles appeared in her forehead. "What do you mean?"

"You know what I mean, Blaise."

Her attention jumped from Rafe to himself and back again. "Is she dead?"

"No, she's been taken by a man I originally met as Serge," he explained, then took a risk. "A man you're acquainted with. A man named Rhys."

She didn't fidget or look around. She just froze. But her gaze held a glimmer of fear.

"Are you familiar with him?"

Silence.

"Answer me."

Anger, frustration, and panic churned in his gut. All he wanted were a few answers. He didn't want to play the bad guy. He hated it.

He uncoiled from his spot and walked to the bars, never losing eye contact. "Do you know what happens to political prisoners like yourself?" No answer. "Let me tell you. We marry them off." She pulled in a sharp breath through her clenched teeth. Good, she needed to understand the stakes here. "It hasn't been done in many years, but don't think I wouldn't marry you off to the highest bidder. That is your future if you don't speak."

"Do you think I would betray my kingdom because of a threat?" she whispered, disgust clear in her tone.

"No, you're too honorable for that. But I'm not asking you to betray your kingdom."

"Lies, but for the sake of the argument, what do you want from me?"

"Why did he take Sage?"

"I don't know."

"Lies," he repeated her words.

"I don't. If he did, no good will come from it."

"Who ordered her kidnapping?"

She hesitated.

"Tell him, or I swear I'll come in there and rip your tongue from your throat," Rafe growled.

Tehl frowned at Rafe. "Enough."

The rebellion leader snarled but kept quiet. He turned slowly back to the prisoner to lock eyes with her. Her gaze bounced between them, and a half-smile curved her lips. "You're both in love with the princess."

"You're right," he allowed. "She's part of my family."

"The beast and the prince," she murmured. "How scandalous."

"Why has he taken her?"

"If he's taken her, it could be many things. Someone may want her, or…he could have taken her for himself."

"Why?"

"He needs a reason?"

"You're being obtuse." Time for a different tactic. "Blaise, you owe me nothing, but you owe Sage something. She's made sure that your safety and health were a priority. You've been in this prison, but you've been well taken care of. No men have touched you. You haven't been starved or tortured. She has been your champion. I understand Scythians have their own code of honor. Would you really leave your debt unpaid?"

Her fists clenched, and she tipped her head back to stare at the stone ceiling. "You don't need me to tell you why she was taken. It's common sense. She's valuable. She was the most valuable thing in this entire castle." Blaise rolled her neck and peeked at him from under her lashes. "She's not in immediate danger, but she'll wish she was dead."

"Why is that?"

"Scythia is not kind to chattel."

"Chattel?"

She looked him dead in the face. "The women used to birth our young."

Rafe cursed and slammed a hand on the bars. "Why would they even want her? Scythians hate outsiders. She's not one of the flawless."

"There are ways to make sure the young she carries are flawless, even if she isn't. Plus, one can always close their eyes..." A hint of revulsion colored her words.

A wave of disgust washed through Tehl. "That's sick."

She turned away, hiding her face from him. "Flawless or not, no one should be used like that," she admitted.

"I agree," Tehl said, trying to keep his emotions locked down. "Thank you for speaking with us. When Sage returns, I'll send her to you." He pushed away from the bars and strode away.

"Don't expect the same woman," she called after him. "The woman you knew as Sage is dead."

He sped up and wound through the hallways, trying to sort out the conversation in his mind and keep himself from killing the spy striding next to him.

"That woman's toying with us," Rafe growled from his right.

Tehl skidded to a stop and stared at the rebellion leader. "She's not the only one."

"What do you mean by that?"

He snatched his dagger from his waist and slammed his forearm against Rafe's chest, pushing him into the stone wall. "Do you really think I would forget what she said? You're a damn spy."

Amber eyes narrowed on him. "Are you going to trust what that lying wench said?"

"She wasn't lying, but you have been. Why are you here, *Methian*?" he demanded, pressing the blade against the rebellion leader's throat.

"I'm here to help Sage, and make Aermia stronger."

He snorted. "That's utter rubbish. You started the first successful rebellion in Aermia's history. Enough with the lies. What's in it for Methi?"

The large man stared at him and then sighed. "I'm not here to cause trouble."

A sarcastic laugh burst out of Tehl. "What makes you think I would believe anything that comes out of your lying trap? First, you're the Methian prince, then you were the leader of the rebellion, and now you're on my council. How convenient." His own gaze narrowed at a thought slithering through his mind. "Is she aware of who you are?"

Rafe held his gaze. "Yes."

"Damn it," Tehl yelled, and pushed back from the spy. He glared at the stone wall and pointed the dagger at Rafe. "How long?"

"The night before you wed."

"Of course." He laughed. "You were hoping to spirit her away."

"She refused me."

"Only because she has more honor in her little finger than most in their whole body."

A bitter chuckle rumbled out of Rafe. "That's what attracted me to her in the first place. She was so loyal and dedicated to her family. Then I saw her practicing in her meadow. She was glorious."

Something flashed across the rebellion leader's face that made an unfamiliar emotion stir in Tehl's gut. It felt suspiciously like jealousy. "Why does she keep protecting you?" Tehl asked, feeling completely at a loss. "You've done nothing but put her in harm's way, and betray her time and time again. And yet, she forgives you."

The rebellion leader scoffed. "That woman hasn't forgiven me for anything. I have fought tooth and nail for her. I even bribed her with what she wanted most in life, and she still wouldn't leave with me." Rafe glanced to the floor, and ran a hand through his wine-colored hair. "She was mine before she ever met you. *Mine.* If Rhys hadn't betrayed both of us, she never would have been your wife."

Tehl arched a brow. "Rhys wasn't the only one to betray her."

"You're right," the rebellion leader growled. "She was everything I ever wanted, but duty demanded I take care of my responsibilities before my feelings. You understand that."

It was something Tehl understood well. "Duty is important," he acknowledged. "What were these responsibilities that kept you from her?"

Rafe blew out a breath and ignored his question. "She says she forgives me, and yet she holds me at arm's length. I can't help but feel that if I listened to her the first time, none of this would have happened."

"We can't go back. It's useless to dwell on the past, unless it's a lesson to be learned."

"Very wise."

Tehl smiled. "My father used to say that when we were growing up."

Rafe cracked a smile. "He's an interesting old man."

"That he is," Tehl said. "What are you doing in my kingdom?"

The rebellion leader studied him for a long minute. "The Methi have never forgotten the stories of old. They are even part of our education for our young. We've watched Aermia for a long time, and then things started to change in your kingdom."

"The kidnappings," Tehl said.

"Among other things," Rafe answered vaguely. "Then your mother died."

A sense of loss filled Tehl. It had been years, but the loss was still there.

"Your father, in his grief, lost his grip on your kingdom, and things became worse. It was then decided that something had to be done."

"Why? Why meddle in Aermia's affairs?"

"Your kingdom is all that keeps the Scythians from us. If your kingdom falls, Methi is vulnerable. To keep the Scythians at bay, you needed a leader to take charge."

Both Tehl's brows rose. "And that's you?"

"No, it just wasn't your father. We needed someone who would fight for your kingdom and unite it."

"Sage."

Rafe dipped his chin. "One of several possibilities. Everything was going according to plan until you captured Sage. Even then, I thought it would be great for information, but then..."

"Rhys."

"Rhys," the rebellion leader hissed. "That double-crossing son of a whore. He destroyed everything."

"He needs to suffer."

"Indeed."

Both men stared at each other, wearing matching grins, and, for the first time, it seemed like there was no animosity between them.

Tehl took one step closer and held his hand out to Rafe. "This is not the path either one of us planned on traveling, but tragedy, unexpected events, and Sage have shoved us together. For the sake of my wife and the woman that you love, do you suppose we can get on together? For her?"

Rafe eyed him, then clasped forearms with him. "For the woman we love."

"For Sage."

CHAPTER TWELVE

Sage

Sage groaned. Everywhere hurt.

When she finally got up the strength to crack her eyelids, she blinked, and then blinked again. Was there something wrong with her eyes? She saw only darkness, not even a sliver of light. Sage ran her hands along the rough surface upon which she lay. The familiar rough texture of stone met her fingertips. Where was she?

A dungeon?

She tried swallowing and found her throat burned as if she were swallowing fire. After a moment, she was able to croak out, "Jasmine?"

"Here," her friend's voice was a whisper, and it came from somewhere on Sage's right.

"Are y— ?" She broke off, seized by a sudden coughing fit. "Are you alright?"

"Well, I haven't really moved around, but my ribs don't bother me as much, so I guess there's that."

Sage shifted to sit up but stopped short, cool air caressing her skin. She gasped and grabbed at the soft cover around her. What the hell had happened? "What happened to my clothes?" she grumbled out loud.

"They took them and washed you. I watched the whole time. Nothing horrid happened."

She shuddered as the image of Rhys' hungry, soulless eyes flashed through her mind. Shaking her head, she rubbed at her forehead, as if the motion could somehow erase both the memory and the fear it created. "So where are we now?"

"My guess? Some sort of cell."

"How long have we been here?" she asked, turning toward the sound of Jasmine's voice.

"No clue. I've slept on and off, and there's no light. No one's visited us since they left us here. If I go by my throat and belly, I'd say it's been at least a day." A pause. "I'm so glad you're okay. When the warlord grabbed you, you went limp. I fought to get to you, but that Scythian wench held me back. I thought he'd killed you." Her last words were a broken whisper.

"I'm so sorry, Jas. That must have been horrible for you."

Jasmine sniffed. "There was nothing I could do! I've been so damn helpless this entire time!"

Sage sat up and clutched her head as a wave of dizziness washed over her. Once she'd regained her equilibrium, she tugged on the edges of the fabric covering her and tied them into a knot. Even if Jas couldn't see her, there was no way she was going without clothes. Sage scooted in the direction of Jasmine's voice, and paused as something smooth and cool on her ankles halted her. Her breathing quickened as she ran a shaking hand toward the object brushing her skin. Her fingers discovered cool metal encircling her ankle— a manacle.

No...

She was chained... trapped....

"Sage?"

No, no, no, no, no! The words echoed over and over in her mind. This couldn't be happening, not again.

"Sage!"

The harsh tone snapped her from her trance. Pushing her now-dampened hair from her brow, she gave voice to her thoughts. "We've been caged and bound," she whispered, her heart galloping. "We're trapped."

"I'm so sorry."

She started tugging on the iron. "There has to be a way out."

"I already tried."

She pulled harder and pain shot up her fingers.

"Sage..."

She stopped pulling. Suddenly, she felt faint. Why was there no air in the room?

"Sage!"

"What?" she yelled.

"You need to calm down."

"I c-can't breathe, there's no air!" she wheezed. "I can't breathe!"

"Yes, you can. You just need to calm down first." She heard metal slithering across stone just before she felt a hand grasp her arm. "Sage. Inhale through your nose and out through your mouth. I'm going to do it, so you just copy me, okay?"

Clasping Jasmine's hand, she tried to do as her friend instructed, breathing in and out. In and out. She focused solely on accomplishing those two things, and how long they sat in the dark, just breathing, she didn't know. Slowly but surely, her breathing slowed. Sage patted Jasmine's hand when she finally managed to speak without wheezing. "Thank you."

Sage felt her friend shrug beside her.

"My nephew has had episodes since his parents died in a Scythian raid a few months ago. I've since taken charge of their care, so I've had to learn how to calm him down."

She shifted and pulled her sheet tighter around her. "Your nephew?"

"My brother and his wife had twins, a boy and a girl, but I'm raising them now. Or at least, I was..." She trailed off.

"I'm so sorry." She squeezed Jasmine's hand. "You will see them again."

"And you're a damn liar."

"Nothing is impossible."

A snort. "You know how ridiculous that sounds?"

She did, actually. A chuckle slipped out, and then another. Sage laughed and laughed and laughed, until tears streamed down her cheeks and her belly cramped.

"It wasn't that funny."

She wiped her eyes and stared into the darkness. "It's this ridiculous situation. Everything about it is surreal."

"I understand what you mean."

She opened her mouth to continue when she heard what sounded like a shoe scuffing against stone, followed by the scraping of stone as a door was pushed open, and the two girls were left blinking in the newfound light. Sage rubbed at her eyes and then squinted as her eyes tried to adjust. She was barely able to make out the two masculine shapes standing in the doorway. "What do you want?" she demanded.

They ignored her and moved into the room. As her eyes began to adjust, one of the men approached Jasmine and knelt beside her, removing the chain connecting her feet to the floor. The girl attempted to scramble back away from him, but was held immobile by a large hand wrapped around her ankle.

"What are you doing?" Jasmine yelled.

Sage's hand tightened on Jasmine's when the warriors remained silent, trading a look. This didn't bode well.

"Get your hands off me!" Jasmine commanded.

In a coordinated move, the men placed themselves on either side of her and plucked the small woman from the ground, holding onto her arms and feet.

"No!" Jas yelled as she fought.

Sage surged to her feet still holding tight to Jasmine's hand. "Let her go!" Her fist struck out, smashing into the taller of the men. He grunted but didn't release her friend. Sage's sheet fluttered to the ground, leaving her body exposed, but she didn't care about her nudity.

Jasmine let out a pained cry when the shorter one wrapped his arms around her damaged ribs.

"Careful," the taller warrior warned. "Don't hurt her. Can you handle her?"

"Yes."

The taller warrior dropped her flailing feet to the floor and turned to Sage. "Do not make this difficult. We do not want to hurt you."

Sage wrapped her other hand around Jasmine's arm and gave him a defiant look. "Let her go."

"I'm sorry," he said, before he pushed her and tore her grasp from Jas.

"NO!" she screamed as the shorter warrior hauled her friend, kicking and screaming, into his arms. She lunged toward Jas, only to be jerked back by large arms.

"Sage!" Jasmine screamed and reached for her just as the warrior disappeared through the door.

Sage spun on the taller warrior when his arms released her, and sprang at him, only to be tripped by her shackled feet. Her bare knees slammed into the stone, her teeth clacking together at the impact. Tears sprang to her eyes. "Bring her back!"

His lips turned downward. "Forget about her." He picked up her sheet from the floor and tossed it to her. "Cover yourself. Not all are gentlemanly."

She caught it with numb hands, still unable to believe they had stolen Jasmine. "What will happen to her?"

"She will be disposed of."

Disposed of? Her panic doubled. "What are you going to do?" He gave her a sad look and moved out the door. "Tell me, damn it!"

"She's never coming back," he said and closed the door, shutting all light out once again.

"Bring her back!" she screamed, completely blind. Without hesitation, she started wrenching at her shackles. "Come on, you bastards! Bend, break, something!"

No matter how hard she screamed and pulled, they didn't budge. It was perhaps hours that she went on like that, but to no avail. Her breath see-sawed from her chest, and her hands throbbed in time with her heart when, finally, she collapsed against the cool floor, tears streaming down her face. They'd taken her friend. She should have fought harder. Done something.

And now they were both alone.

She cried and cried until there were no more tears, and exhaustion claimed her.

***

Sage woke up, still naked and on a stone floor. She groaned and rolled onto her back, a tear leaking from her eye as she stared up into the darkness above her.

"I'm so sorry, Jas. Sorrier than I could ever tell you," she whispered, her heart so heavy it felt difficult to breathe.

She swiped her eyes with the back of her hand and lay her cheek upon the cool floor. She ached all over at the loss of her friend. It felt like someone had reached into her chest and squeezed her heart. Another tear snuck out. She'd only known Jasmine for little more than a week, but they'd bonded in an extraordinary way, having supported one another through the most gruesome of circumstances. She'd chosen to stand and fight, and Sage admired her for it. Even when she was badly beaten, she stood back up. That endurance and grit had made Sage feel like she could fight harder, too...

But now, her friend was gone, and she was alone. Hadn't they just been laughing together, comforting each other in spite of their circumstance? How could she just be ripped away? Tears welled up in her eyes. It wasn't fair, to either of them.

"Jasmine," she whispered, her tears spilling over. "What did they do to you? How can you be gone? I need you. I need your iron will to keep me going. I, I-" Her throat felt tight, her voice raw. "I'm sorry I couldn't save you and-" She let out a sob. Her breath stuttered as tears streamed down her face, her words barely intelligible. "I'm s-s-sorry that your babies have to grow up without their momma a-a-and now you." She wiped at her nose with the back of her hand. "I'll miss you so much. I'm sorry. I'm so, so sorry." She was choking out breaths now, her cries echoing around her in the darkness. For the second time, she cried her heart out for her friend, her grief overwhelming her.

After her tears had mostly dried, she lay on her back, staring once again into the darkness above, just thinking. She thought of her friend and how it seemed so unfair that no one would know of the enormous sacrifice she'd made just to help a stranger.

"But I do," she said softly, "and I'll never forget it, just like I'll never forget you." She also thought of those two tiny children, the ones no doubt missing their auntie, with no one to care for them. She would do it if she could. She would give those children the love and care they needed and deserved. "And if, by some miracle, I get out of here alive, I'll see to it your babies don't, either." Those children deserved to know about their aunt, and Jasmine deserved to be remembered.

A sense of calm came over her. The pain didn't diminish, but the hopelessness did. She realized she still had a reason to fight and to live. She wasn't just fighting for herself but for those babies who'd already lost so much. When she escaped, Sage could fully mourn, but first, she had to survive.

She was a survivor, not just a victim. Now she had to act like one.

***

Her tongue felt swollen in her mouth, and her lips were cracked. Her arms shook as she forced herself to sit up and lean against the wall. She was wasting away in here. A meager amount of bread and water were delivered each day, but it wasn't enough to sustain her. It was just enough for her to die slowly. That she felt she could handle. It was the darkness that was bound to drive her insane. Her eyes roved the darkness, seeking any sort of light. How long had she been here?

"You've been here for five days, Sage."

She jumped and glanced around, shocked to hear the sound of Tehl's voice.

"Tehl?"

"You're just having a nightmare. Go back to sleep."

Sage blinked slowly. "I was dreaming?"

A grunt. "You have nightmares almost every night. It's a miracle I haven't been stabbed yet."

"It seemed so real," she said.

"Nightmares usually do. Now, go back to sleep. I'll protect you."

"But I…" Something wasn't right.

She ran a hand along the bed and froze when cool air whispered across her chest. Her bare chest. She jerked the sheet over her body and slammed her eyes closed. What was happening? She'd never slept naked in bed with Tehl. Why was she naked?

A masculine laugh rippled through the dark, causing goosebumps to rise on her arms. "You can sleep naked anytime you like, love."

Sage tucked the sheet under her armpits, and pressed her palms to her forehead. She was hallucinating.

She felt a touch on her arm and jerked, opening her eyes only to find she was still surrounded by darkness. "Who's there?" she croaked.

"Just me," Tehl replied.

"You…you can't be!"

"Why not? Think about it logically. How many times have I had to wake up and convince you that you were just dreaming? Thirty? Forty?"

This was starting to freak her out. Where was she?

"You're at home."

"Stop speaking to me! I can't think," she yelled. Sage wrapped her arms around her belly, and rocked back and forth. What had Gav said to do when she had nightmares? "Say what is truth," she whispered. "My name is Sage. I am a blacksmith. I'm the crown prince's consort. Lilja and Mira are my friends. I've never slept naked with Tehl. Rhys kidnapped me." She swallowed. "Rhys is dead. You're not real."

"Very good."

"You're not real."

"I thought we established that."

"My mind is making you up."

"Seems likely."

Sage shook her head. "Why in the world would my mind create you?"

A snort. "Don't ask me to decipher a woman's mind. I almost never know what you're thinking anyway."

"But why?"

"I'm thinking that's a question only you can answer."

"Why couldn't I have imagined my mum, Lilja, Mira, or Gav? Why choose you?"

"I don't understand it, either."

"But you're me," she pointed out. "I'm talking to myself."

"It does seem that way."

She slumped against the wall as her stomach cramped painfully.

"You need to eat soon."

"That's not helpful," she retorted. "I can't control what they give me."

"You'll die soon."

"Not soon," she whispered. "Slowly. At least they've given me enough water," she whispered, curling up into a ball. As hungry as she was, it wasn't enough to keep her awake. Her eyelids were so heavy they closed of their own volition and she shifted her sheet so she was cocooned inside it. "Tehl?"

"Yes?"

Tears burned the backs of her eyes. Just hearing his voice was a comfort, even if his presence was imagined. She slid her hand out of the sheet with a faint tremor. "Will you hold my hand?"

Silence. It was a ridiculous question. She needed the comfort of human contact, but it was ridiculous to ask her hallucination to do so. She started to pull back when she felt Tehl's hand slip into hers and squeeze three times. Tears filled her eyes. Jas did that every night they fell asleep in the jungle. Sage pulled his hand closer and swore she smelled his spicy scent.

"Thank you," she said, grateful.

"You're welcome, love."

Then, she slept.

Chapter Thirteen

Sage

"I'm dying."

"No, you're not," argued Tehl.

Sage twisted her neck to face the direction of Tehl's voice. "I'm not even strong enough to move anymore. It won't be long."

"You have to fight."

She laughed weakly. "I can't fight starvation."

"You're giving up." It was an accusation.

"What do you expect me to do? I can't do anything."

"Don't give up hope."

"How exactly? There is no hope. I'm in enemy territory with no hope for rescue, no hope for escape, and no hope for recovery. The situation is hopeless."

"So, you're going to give up? Just like that? You're going to let Jasmine's sacrifice be in vain? That's selfish and weak."

Her anger flared. "Shut up, Tehl! Why can't I be selfish and weak, just this once? I'm dying, for heaven's sake!" She blew out a frustrated breath. "Just let me go in peace. I can't be strong *all the time*. Why do you expect me to be?"

"Because I'm you."

She blinked. In that moment something occurred to her. She was holding herself to a higher standard than she held everyone else. It was she who never allowed *herself* to be weak. *She* never allowed herself to be taken care of. *She* was harder on herself than anyone else, and *she* made excuses for others when they made mistakes, but for herself, she accepted none. Tears pricked her eyes at the thought.

And then she made another realization. "I don't have to be the martyr."

"No, love, you don't."

"Will my parents be disappointed in me?" she asked.

"No, Sage, your parents are beyond proud of you. They worry, though."

"That's what parents do."

"Indeed, it is."

"What about your father? I worry about him."

"He's not beyond helping. You're proof of that."

Sage thought about Sam and Gav. She never thought she'd want more brothers, but after living with them, she found she didn't want to live without them. They'd become her family. Then there was Tehl. Painfully, she shifted onto her side. "And what about you? Do you need me? Will you be okay?"

"I won't lie and say I don't need you. Even you must be able to see that."

She snickered and then winced when her stomach cramped. "I never know what will come out of your mouth. You make me laugh." A small smile tightened her dry cheeks. "I didn't expect that when I married you. Surprisingly, your awkwardness is somewhat charming."

"Call me 'Prince Charming.'"

"Never," she retorted, and curled up tighter.

"But back to before, I will be okay, you know. I'm a survivor, like you."

She closed her eyes. "I never thought about it that way."

"We're a lot more alike than you realize."

She snorted. "I realize it. I'm just not sure I like it." A yawn. "I need to sleep now… I'll talk to you when I wake up."

"Okay. Sleep sweet, love."

"M'kay."

***

"You need to wake up," Tehl urged.

"I'm too tired."

"Open your damn eyes!"

Her eyelids sprang open at his demand, only to slam shut. Stars dotted her vision, and tears leaked out.

"What have you done to her?" someone snarled. "You almost killed her! What were you thinking? You weren't thinking! Get out of my sight!"

Someone moved into the room and knelt beside her to brush the hair from her face. "Oh, wild one," a deep and smooth voice whispered. "What have they done to you?"

She cracked an eye, only to be blinded by brightness, and immediately squeezed it shut again.

"Close the door!"

She sighed in relief when the darkness returned.

"Sage? I need to move you. Can you open your eyes for me?"

Flopping her head toward the voice, she forced her eyes open. The room was dark, but one sliver of light shone from the door, giving just enough light that she could make out a face in the darkness. "Hello," she whispered.

The face leaned nearer. An extremely handsome face. A perfect face, with eyes as dark as pitch. "Are you here to steal my soul?" she asked.

Her heart stuttered in her chest with the breathtaking smile he gave her. "No. I could never steal something like that, nor would I want to. If I were to keep a soul, it would have to be given to me."

His words didn't make sense, but it was such a pleasure to see something after being in the dark for so long. Not to mention being with someone so stunning. It was almost too much. His dark gaze roamed from her face to the sheet covering her nude body. By the darkening of his face, it was apparent that, as he looked on her, he found no pleasure in it. His face hardened, and she flinched back when he met her eyes.

"I'm sorry." He bowed his head for a moment. "What hurts?"

"Everything."

A nod. He lifted his head and pushed shiny black hair from his face. "I need to move you somewhere I can take care of you. Is that okay?"

Hope fluttered in her chest. "You'll take me out of here? I would love to see the world again before I die."

"You're not going to die," he said with conviction. "I'll make sure of it."

"Okay," she whispered.

He eyed her sheet. "I'm going to lift you and wrap the sheet around you. Can you hold on to it while I lift you?"

She didn't think so, but she wouldn't admit that. "Yes."

A whimper escaped her when he wedged his arm underneath her back.

"I'm sorry," he whispered, and lifted her to her feet.

Pain hit her like a wall, but she managed to keep the sheet barely clenched in her fist, the fabric draping down her front. Cool air chilled the backs of her thighs and back. She swayed into a firm chest as her knees buckled. The warm arm pressed against the bare skin of her back, anchoring her to his chest.

She clenched the sheet tighter in her fist when he tugged on it.

"You need to let go, so I can wrap it around you."

She still didn't let go. It was like her fingers wouldn't unclench.

"I promise I'll not look," he said in a gentle voice. "On the count of three, let go. One, two, three…"

Sage let go, shaking. She hissed as he wrapped the fabric around her sensitive skin, and tucked the ends around her, still holding her against him.

"Brace yourself, I'm going to lift you."

Her nostrils flared as the pain stabbed at her from all over when he swept her off her feet and into his arms. Her arms trembled as she wrapped them around his neck. Everything hurt, and all she wanted to do was go to sleep again.

"Close your eyes. The light will be too much for you."

She took one last glance at the space she had expected to be her coffin, and then peeked up at the man studying her. "Thank you."

"Don't thank me. I'll never be your hero. Now, close your eyes."

His words didn't make any sense to her, but she obeyed as he began moving toward the door. "Open the door."

She hid her face in his shirt when the light draped over them like a long-lost friend. She wished she could open her eyes.

"You'll be able to see soon," he murmured over her head. "But you've been in the dark too long. Your eyes need time to adjust." He shifted her in his arms, but at her sharp breath, he paused. "What?"

She shook her head, his linen shirt caressing her forehead. "It hurts."

"I know. Soon the pain will all be over."

He picked up his pace and the bright light soon faded; even the air cooled.

A creak of leather. "My lord," a masculine voice said then.

"Fetch broth, Maeve, and have Ezra create a draught."

"It will be done."

Silence. Not fading footsteps. Had the other man left?

A door opened and slammed shut. The air heated, and it was like she was breathing steam.

"Everyone out. When Maeve arrives, send her in. Also, close the curtains."

There were more people in the room? She strained to hear any sound, but nothing. Damn Scythians and their sneaking.

"I'm going to set you down. Don't open your eyes."

He placed her on something soft. She sank into it, reveling in the luxury. She heard the rustling of cloth just before large arms plucked her from her new bed. She growled.

"Hush. I'll let you sleep soon enough."

The sounds of lapping water reached her ears, and then they were descending. Warm water soaked her feet, shocking her, and her eyes flew open. It was dark enough that she could just make out a large room with a massive hexagonal pool in its center. And they were in the pool. "Wh-what are you doing?" she squeaked.

"Getting you cleaned up."

"No!"

She blinked up at him. His expression was firm, with a stubborn set to his jaw; apparently, this was happening with or without her consent. His gaze roved her face.

"I'll not ravish you in the pool, if that's what you're worried about. But you need to be cared for."

A blush heated her face. "It's my body."

"True, but it won't be your body if you're dead."

He had a point. "Isn't there a woman who can help?"

"No. I've helped many women birth babes. The female form is nothing new to me. Your modesty has no place here." He descended further, submerging her body in the warm water.

Her jaw clenched when he sat on a submerged pool ledge and pulled her body into his lap, tugging the sheet from her.

He hissed, and Sage squinted down at her bare body. She

couldn't see much, but what little she could make out looked like a collage of colors accented by silvery slashes, but that wasn't the worst of it. It was like her skin was too big for her body. She looked like a monster.

"You're not a monster."

She'd said that out loud? Fatigue hit her hard, and she collapsed against the warlord's bare chest.

"That's it. Just relax," he crooned. "I'll take care of you."

A warm, sudsy cloth started on her hand and carefully moved up her arm. Sage kept her eyes closed, blocked out everything happening to her, and focused only on the warm water and the comfort it gave her. She checked in when he washed her stomach and the tops of her thighs, but his hands never strayed to her important bits.

His hands moved to her head, and she hummed, soothed by the soft touch of his hands through her hair. His hands stilled.

"You like that?"

"Mmmhmm... My mum used to wash my hair and brush it for me. I love it," she said, not knowing why she gave a stranger that information.

"I'll remember that," he rumbled and began washing her hair again.

A few times she hissed as he untangled her matted locks, but for the most part, it was the best thing that had happened to her in a very long time. It was the last good memory she'd have before she died. "Thank you."

"My pleasure," he hummed.

She let herself drift and was almost asleep when a knock jarred her.

"Enter," the warlord called.

"I have everything prepared, my lord," a female voice answered.

Sage pressed against his body, both embarrassed and scared that she still couldn't see the woman speaking. The warlord hugged her closer and ran a hand down her wet hair. "I'll bring her out."

A door clicked softly shut, and the warlord turned toward her. She could feel him regarding her. "Can you wrap your arms around my neck?"

She shook her head, all strength gone.

"No matter," he said and he picked her up, sloshing water around, and ascended from the pool. He placed her feet on the floor and wrapped his arm around her back. A fuzzy towel rubbed against her head and then gingerly wrapped around her body. Once again, she was swept into his arms and moved into another dark room where she was then placed on the softest bed she'd ever felt.

"I can take care of it from here, my lord," the female voice offered.

"No, Maeve."

"Do you think that's wise? You're on edge."

"It's not your concern," the warlord responded and ran a hand over her head again. "I'm going to remove your towel, Sage, but I'll cover you with blankets."

She nodded, not caring as long as she didn't have to move from this spot. The wet towel disappeared, and warm blankets were smoothed over her. She sighed and snuggled in deeper.

"You don't get to sleep yet. You have to eat."

"I'm not hungry."

"You'll eat." His tone brooked no argument. His palm cradled her head, and something was placed at her lips. "Drink."

She opened her mouth, and something warm and savory met her taste buds. She gulped down more and cried out when it was taken away.

"You have to drink slower, or you'll get sick."

Sage nodded. She'd have agreed to anything as long as he brought back the delicious broth. She forced herself to take small sips, but before long, she turned her head away. "No more."

"You hardly ate anything. Just a little more," he coaxed.

"No," she moaned, her stomach cramping painfully.

"Let her be," the female said gently. "It'll take time."

A hand smoothed the damp hair from her face. "Sleep sweet, wild one."

She sighed and did so.

***

She shivered, hearing voices while heat licked inside her veins.

"She needs more," a dangerous voice snarled.

"If I give her more, she'll change," a soft male voice answered. "Do you think she'll follow you meekly when she doesn't even recognize the girl in the mirror? She's just a breeder anyway."

"She's *mine*. I'll do with her what I want."

Why was it so hot?

"But—"

"I didn't bring you here to challenge me. Obey me or suffer the consequences. You know what's on the—"

Stars above, it was bloody hot. She was burning. She

whimpered and rubbed at her skin.

A cool hand touched her brow. "Sage?" a deep voice crooned.

"Burning," she whispered.

"I've got you," the voice whispered.

Something pressed to her cracked lips, and blessedly cool liquid coated her tongue. Instantly, the burning began to dim, and the darkness sidled closer, like an old friend, an old friend Sage welcomed with open arms.

CHAPTER FOURTEEN

Sage

Sage awoke to a pounding in her head. Her limbs felt heavy, and she thought about just going back to sleep when she noticed dull light dancing behind her eyelids. Light? Could she really be seeing light? Or was this another trick of the mind? She bolstered herself and cracked one eye.

It was real.

She lay in a giant room with couches and chairs scattered in cozy nooks. Wanting to see more of the room with its luxurious rug and woven tapestries, she turned her head but immediately regretted it. She brought a shaking hand to her throbbing temple. It was as if there was someone inside her head ringing a gong over and over. Carefully this time, she turned to the right and then froze. A man held her hand, and he was fast asleep in a chair that was far too small for him. It was the warlord. Her eyes ran over his shiny raven hair that had fallen over his face and down his bare chest. Sage blushed and returned her gaze to the hand clutching hers. Maybe if she pulled just right, she could extract her hand. She loosened her grip and tried gently tugging her hand from his.

"What are you doing?"

Startled, she looked up at the man now staring at her. "Moving my hand. It fell asleep." The lie fell easily from her lips. Thank goodness for quick thinking. He ran his thumb over her wrist and let go, still watching her with his onyx gaze. She wet her lips and asked, "Why are you here?"

"Someone needed to care for you."

Her brows slashed down. "Why?" What did the warlord want?

"Because you were sick."

"Because of you," she whispered.

"I never meant for you to be there. To be locked in the dark."

She flinched as the memory of blindness slammed into her.

He leaned closer, his hands laced with his elbows on his knees. "I promise."

She stared at him. Everything told her he was the enemy and a liar, but he couldn't fake the dark circles rimming his eyes. He certainly had been concerned for her. She decided she believed him, but still didn't trust him.

"How long have I been out?"

"Fourteen days."

Panic slammed into her. "I've lost fourteen days? Fourteen? How long have I been here?"

"You've been in my home for six weeks."

Unbidden, tears sprang to her eyes. She'd been locked in the dark for twenty-eight days? She blinked repeatedly and turned her stare to the ceiling as the tears dripped down her face.

"I'm so sorry. I came to you as soon as I became aware of what happened. I didn't order your imprisonment. Someone betrayed me." His tone took on an edge. "They've been dealt with."

A pool of crimson flashed through her memory. "Like you slayed the monster?"

He paused before answering. "Yes."

"They killed my friend," she choked.

"They paid dearly for it."

Fatigue weighed heavily upon her, and she felt her eyes begin to droop, despite her mind whirling with questions.

"Here..." Something was placed at her lips. "Drink this to gain your strength."

She obeyed, not even tasting the broth, just sipping until none was left.

"I'll let you rest."

Sage turned, putting her back to the warlord.

"I'm sorry."

"Sorry doesn't bring Jasmine back," she whispered.

"No, it doesn't." His hand softly brushed her shoulder. "Good night, wild one."

She ignored his touch and stared vacantly at a covered window. Vaguely, she noted a door closing, but she was leagues away in her mind. Six weeks. She'd been gone for *six weeks*. What was happening in Aermia? Were her parents okay? What about the alliance between the rebellion and the Crown? Would it still be honored in her absence? What about Tehl?

"What about me?" he asked, sitting on the bed.

Sage smiled, more tears springing to her eyes. For the first time, she could see him. Black hair, sapphire eyes, and broad shoulders.

"You're here." Her heart stopped when he smiled at her. It was rare for him to full-on smile; when he did, it was a thing of beauty.

"I never left." He looked around the room. "It seems you've moved up in life."

She darted a second glance around the room. "It seems I have."

"The warlord has taken fine care of you."

She dropped her gaze to the coverlet and traced the pattern. "It seems so. He said it was a mistake. That he didn't know."

"Do you believe him?"

"I'm inclined to say no, because of what I've been told about him. But he's different," she admitted. "I can see, but I'm still blind."

"Well, remember we judge on actions, not on hearsay. Examine what you understand to be true. Start from the beginning."

"People have been kidnapped by Scythians. Rhys hurt me." She shuddered and moved on. "He kidnapped me and abused me more. The warlord killed him. I was thrown into prison. Jasmine died," she choked out. "I thought I would die. The warlord rescued me. He has taken care of me."

"Indeed. There might be more beneath the surface than what

appears. Could it be that our council has been blind because of prejudice? Possibly. But have you been led to see something that isn't really there?"

That pierced her. Rafe had lied and lied, and she had gobbled up everything he said. The world wasn't black and white. She understood that now. Her eyes started to slide shut. "I'm tired."

"Sleep, love. I'll watch over you."

***

The next time she woke, a Scythian woman sat next to the bed, reading a book. Cinnamon eyes met hers over the top of a page. The woman snapped the book shut and raised a brow. "It's about time you woke. Your stench is enough to make my eyes water."

"I beg your pardon?" Sage blurted.

"You shouldn't smell like that."

The woman pushed from the chair and yanked back her covers. Sage wrapped her hands around her bare body. How long had she been naked? What had happened to her while she slept all that time?

"Stop looking so scandalized. No one's touched you but the warlord himself."

Her eyes widened. That didn't make her feel any better.

The woman rolled her eyes and helped Sage sit up, then stand. "As if he would take advantage of you looking and smelling like you do. Honestly, you Aermians assume everyone wants you."

Sage blinked and locked her knees when they threatened to buckle. "I meant no offense," she drew out, feeling off balance.

The woman swiftly lifted Sage into her arms, and strode to another room with a rectangular, steaming pool in the middle.

They moved to the edge, and the woman plopped Sage in like she weighed nothing at all. Sage's bottom rested on a stone ledge, and her fingers weakly grasped the side of the pool. She glanced at the beautiful woman who was watching her like a hawk.

"Don't drown. I'm not crawling in there to take care of you like the warlord."

Sage gasped. "He bathed me?"

The woman tsked. "It was nothing untoward, child. You would have died without his care. Do you understand?"

The woman's rebuke had Sage feeling about a foot tall. She nodded her head.

"Now, don't let go of that edge, girl. I need to grab supplies."

What happened? She had bathed naked with that man? Her stomach sank. She was an adulteress. Wait, why did *that* of all things come to her mind? All the slurs which had been thrown her way after she'd escaped from the palace, they now applied.

"You're not at fault."

Sage peeked at Tehl lounging by the pool, looking almost as carefree as his brother.

"I know who you are. I know you would never break our marriage vows."

"But I did..." She blinked at the stone edge, feeling violated. "I bathed with another man."

"Not of your own choice. You were on the verge of dying."

"I'm sorry."

"What was that?" the woman asked as she came bustling back in. Sage glanced to where Tehl had been a moment earlier, only to see the bare stone floor. "Nothing," she muttered. God, had she lost her mind in that cell? Had she died? Was this even real?

"You're thinking out loud you know, and this *is* real. Just wait until I have to untangle those snarls in your mane. Then you'll know it's real. Now hold still."

She submitted to the vigorous scrubbing and ignored the muttering and cursing coming from the woman. And, stars above, she was right. At one point, she may have begged for the woman to simply cut her hair rather than keep yanking on her head so. "We'll get there," was all she said.

When she was finally permitted to leave the pool, she was utterly exhausted. The woman dried her and slipped a linen shirt over her head that was much too large, but Sage didn't care. She was just happy to be wearing a garment. She sat Sage in front of a mirror, and whipped out a pair of scissors from God knows where. She lifted a hand and grabbed the woman's wrist, meeting her cinnamon gaze in the mirror. "I may have been a bit hasty when speaking about cutting it."

"I'm only going to trim off the dead."

Sage eyed her suspiciously but relented. It was hateful, really, to place her in front of a mirror. Her skin was sallow, and the shirt hung off her bony shoulders. She brushed aside the collar and glared at her protruding collarbone. Her gaze travelled to her face. She looked half dead. The black bags underneath her eyes were the most prominent part of her face. When she couldn't stand to look at herself anymore, she watched the graceful woman behind her. It was obvious that she found taking care of Sage distasteful.

"What's your name?" she prodded, hoping to break the silence.

"Maeve."

She jerked.

"Hold still," Maeve chastised, fingering her hair. "It's uncanny how similar you look to my mother," she muttered, absently.

This was the same woman who'd eyed her with disgust when she and Jasmine were first brought in? Blinking, she scrutinized the woman wielding the scissors. Maeve looked so much younger than she had first thought. She frowned. The Scythian woman spoke in a way that portrayed age, but the woman could hardly be a handful of years older than her.

"If you keep frowning like that, your face will be stuck," Maeve said, never looking up from her task.

Her frown deepened. That was something her mother would say. It was odd, to say the least.

True to her word, Maeve only trimmed her hair, and then plaited it simply. Once she was finished, she wrapped an arm around her back. "Back to bed with you, missy."

She helped Sage back to the bed, but 'helped' was probably a generous word. Sage gritted her teeth while she was basically carried back to bed. It was horrible having to rely on a stranger for her basic needs, but she was grateful nonetheless. Sage was the enemy to them, and yet the woman took care to help her. As the woman tucked her in, Sage caught her hand and offered a smile. "Thank you, Maeve. Truly. I won't forget your kindness."

The woman stared at her for a long time, like she was looking deep inside her. "It was my pleasure, my lady." She patted Sage's hand and left the dim room.

Finally alone, Sage allowed herself to fall back asleep.

***

Hands tore at her clothes, and cruel, brown eyes glared down at her. "You're nothing. You'll always be nothing."

She struggled, and the monster pressed harder down onto her.

"No!" she screamed.

"I'll always be on your skin. You'll never get away from me," Rhys whispered into her neck.

She struggled harder, unable to breathe.

"Sage."

"Always on your skin."

"Sage!"

She jerked awake, her entire body shaking. Disoriented, she tried to roll over, only to come into contact with a masculine chest. "No!" She struggled, but her body wasn't fighting like it should. Her movements were sluggish and weak.

"Sage, it's just me. It's just Zane," the warlord murmured in her ear. "Rhys can't hurt you. He's gone forever. He'll never hurt you again."

She collapsed against his chest and cried harder. "He's not gone. He's still haunting me." She trembled, her skin crawling. It was like Rhys' breath was imprinted on her neck.

"They're just nightmares. It's not real." He placed her curled fist over his heart. "Count my heartbeats."

She flexed her fingers, pressed her palm against his chest, and began to count. She reached 562 when her heart stopped racing, her breathing evened out, and she realized exactly where she was and whom she was with. Sage pushed upright, and scooted away from the warlord, pulling the covers around her tighter. What was he doing here? She met his black gaze.

"Thank you, but I would appreciate it if you got out of my bed." She held her breath and inwardly winced. Even she could hear the tremor in her voice. She could not afford to appear weaker than she already was.

He studied her, then climbed out of the bed and stood with his hands in his pockets. She breathed a sigh of relief and ran her eyes over his moonlit-haloed figure.

"You're in my room," she stated.

"Well, technically it's my room, but it's yours until you heal," he replied.

That startled her. "Why?" What was he after?

"Because I can protect you here."

She didn't believe that for one moment. People always have ulterior motives. "Why do you want to protect me? I'm the enemy." She squinted harder, trying to gauge his reaction.

"Are you my enemy? Have I treated you as one?"

"No," she said slowly, "but I can't help feeling there will be a price for your generosity. It's the way of the world. What do you expect of me?"

His laugh danced through the air, raising goosebumps on her arms. She scowled at him while trying to rub them away. What was so funny?

He shook his head. "So suspicious. Here..." He pulled something from his waist and held it out to her, the edge of a blade glinting in the low light.

Sage eyed the dagger, and then the warlord. Was he trying to bait her? What trickery was he weaving?

"It will not bite you. Take it. It's a gift. A warrior should never be without a weapon." He held it out farther.

Sage reached out and hesitated, her hand hovering over the blade. She glanced at the warlord again and decided to just take it, since he was offering it. Pulling the dagger from his grasp, she held it to the light, examining it. It was a simple design, but the hilt fit well in her hand. She balanced it on her palm and smiled. It was balanced well, perfect for throwing. A sense of comfort blanketed her as she palmed the dagger and set it on her lap. Having a means to protect herself meant everything to her. Her gaze flicked back up, and her comfort fled at the intense interest on the warlord's face. She needed to remember that, even with a weapon, she wasn't safe here.

He cocked his head. "What made you this way?"

"What?" His question caught her off guard.

"It's like you expect me to attack you at any moment. What made you so suspicious?"

She thought about lying, but from what she'd seen of him so far, he seemed like someone to see through untruths. So, she led with the ugly truth. "Rhys," she said flatly.

His jaw clenched, then loosened. "Not every man or Scythian is like him."

"True, but not every man is as good as my father," she pointed out.

"I find it interesting that you say your father, not your husband. From what I hear, you have a love match."

Her fingers clenched in the bedding when the warlord glided around the bed before sinking into a chair placed next to the mattress. He moved with an inhuman grace, and with restrained power. She shivered. He was dangerous. She had to stop forgetting what he was.

"Tehl's an honorable man with a good heart," she said softly, inconspicuously pulling the blade from her lap and into her hand. The warlord seemed to miss nothing; he tracked the movement, but said nothing of it.

"Do you trust him?"

"With my life," she replied without hesitation. She did. Tehl had many qualities she didn't care for, but loyalty and honesty were two of his best traits. She trusted him.

"Does he love you?" the warlord asked.

"He does," she said carefully. What an odd question. Where was he going with this? Her sluggish brain couldn't figure it out. Already, fatigue was weighing her down.

"Then why hasn't he come for you?"

That was a punch to the gut. She brushed aside her feelings and focused on logic. "A crown prince has many responsibilities. Running after his kidnapped bride into enemy territory would be foolish. And Tehl is not a fool."

Leather creaked as he leaned closer. "I sent word that you were safe but sick. That your health made it impossible to travel home without an escort. I even sent word that I would bring you to the border."

Home? Her breathing stuttered. He had to be lying. He was playing a game.

"His reply was not what I expected." His voice hardened. "A peace treaty and a threat."

She bowed her head to hide her expression. Tehl threatened the warlord of Scythia? That was a bold thing, but peace? It seemed farfetched. "Is peace such a bad thing?"

"No, but the crown prince's actions suggest otherwise."

"I don't follow," she replied, her brows slashing together.

"Instead of jumping at the chance to retrieve you, he countered with the offer of your skills as a mediator. He said they were unparalleled."

Her heart fell to her stomach. Tehl wanted her to stay here? "What else did the letter say?"

"That as long as you were healthy and whole, he'd bring back his Scythian prisoner in the same condition."

What prisoner? Then it came to her. "Blaise," she whispered.

"What did you just say?"

She cleared her throat. "He used Blaise?"

"Yes." He plucked a mug from the side table and handed it to her. "His wording was quite strong."

"To what end? That doesn't sound like the crown prince at all."

"Men will do whatever is necessary to accomplish their will."

She took a sip and watched him over the rim. "And you?"

He smiled. "I'm no different. But here is my concern. It may not sound like the crown prince, because he's being manipulated."

"By who?" she mused.

"I have my suspicions."

"Humor me," Sage replied.

"I believe it's the Methian running things."

Her fingers tightened on her mug. How did he know Rafe was Methian?

"Excuse me?"

"You heard me, Sage. Don't play coy. You're not unintelligent. You know of the one about whom I speak. He's been manipulating everyone from the beginning." The warlord leaned forward to make his point, energy seeming to teem around him. "Ask yourself this: why would he stir Aermia into a rebellion? How would that really help Aermia at all?"

"We needed a new leader."

"But stirring up a rebellion? Surely, there are better ways to bring about change than a bloody rebellion? Why would he want Aermia weak?"

"I haven't the slightest idea," she deflected.

"Come, now, you're a brilliant woman. Aermia is the central kingdom. It holds all the power."

"True, maybe." She raised a brow. Time to bait him as he'd been doing to her. "What keeps you from going after it, if it's *that* valuable?"

"I've never desired to leave my jungle. We're self-sufficient. I don't need your kingdom, so it has no appeal."

A small laugh escaped her. "The power kingdom has no appeal? I'm sorry, my lord, but I don't believe you."

"It's just Zane."

She ignored his correction, and steeled herself for what she would say next. "Your kingdom has been known for being power-hungry and covetous of others. What you're saying is the opposite from everything I know to be true."

He lifted a hand and tugged at his hair. "Do you like to be held accountable for your family's actions? Or people you don't even know? That's what it's like. I have been held accountable for the sins of a deranged madman with a god complex who died hundreds of years ago. We can't leave this place without being scorned."

The anguish in his voice did something to her. She knew what it was like to be judged by rumors.

"Do you want peace?" she echoed again. The warlord didn't seem evil. If he truly wanted peace, maybe she was exactly where she needed to be.

"I want absolution," he murmured. "I want the voices of the past to quiet."

"I can't give you that, but—" Goosebumps broke out on her arms at the way he stilled at her words, like a predator readying for the hunt. *Be brave, Sage. Brave*. She swallowed and continued: "I can give you a chance to make a difference."

"Be careful," Tehl whispered in her ear. "You're playing a game you don't know the rules to."

She blinked and ignored him, watching the man who held her future in his hands, and quite possibly, the future of her kingdom.

"Do you really think you can erase hundreds of years of bad blood and animosity?"

She chose her words carefully. "No. As much as I would like to say that prejudice will be a thing of the past, it's not possible. Since the beginning of time, man has found a way to label each other, and then judge those labels. There have always been divisions, and there always will be."

"So, what are you saying?"

She stared straight into his handsome face. "I'm saying that I can't change the past, but we can change the future. Together," she added.

His head cocked. "Together?"

"Together."

She flinched when, in a single fluid motion, he stood and leaned toward her, the ends of his hair tickling her cheeks.

"I accept your proposal, my lady."

Her eyes were huge when he kissed each of her cheeks. He smiled at her reaction, his white teeth flashing.

"In Scythia, we seal a deal with a kiss."

She pursed her lips.

"Once you do this, there's no going back," Tehl warned in her ear.

Sage leaned closer, not losing eye contact, and kissed one cheek, then the other.

"It is done," he whispered, his breath washing over her face.

"It's done," she repeated.

For better or worse, she'd just made a deal with the warlord of Scythia.

CHAPTER FIFTEEN

Sage

"You're going to sleep the day away, Sage. Get up."

She yawned and ignored Tehl's voice, snuggling into the bed. When was the last time she'd slept in?

"Remember whose bed you're sleeping in. How are you so sure he won't come and join you?"

A tingle ran up her spine and she stiffened. She wasn't so sure, but the warlord had yet to try anything. "I don't believe the warlord will harm me," she muttered. "He wants peace, I can tell. Now go away."

A voice as smooth as whiskey washed over her. "Now, that's just rude."

Sage jerked up, slipping her dagger from beneath her pillow, gritting her teeth as her whole body screamed with the unexpected move. She blinked repeatedly, her eyes still not focusing right, and frowned at the warlord sitting beside her bed.

"What are you doing here?" Her tone was a little harsh, but this was the second time in a handful of hours he'd shown up in her room, silent as a wraith.

Zane blinked at the dagger and sniggered. "I think that was the weakest threat I've ever received."

A grimace pulled her lips down as she glared at her shaking hand.

"Put your dagger down, wild one." He stifled his smile when she turned her glare on him. "Sorry," he said, not sounding sorry at all.

"I'm sure," she muttered.

"Who were you speaking to?" he asked, changing the subject.

"No one," she responded automatically. How much had he heard of her conversation with Tehl?

"It didn't sound like no one."

"It was a dream." That was partially true. She hadn't been dreaming, but Tehl certainly was not real.

The warlord cocked a brow. "You're lying."

She kept her face impassive. "No, I'm not. My husband can tell you I talk in my sleep."

He shifted his hulking figure in the small chair and steepled his fingers. "Sometimes, when someone suffers a traumatic event in their lives, they experience certain things that are not healthy. These can be nightmares, flashbacks, being on edge, paranoia, and hallucinations. These things happen when your mind can't handle what you experienced. Sometimes, your mind will block those memories to protect itself. I've seen it with my men." A pause. "Blair reported to me what your journey was like."

She pulled her gaze away from his knowing eyes and stared instead at the wall over his shoulder. She'd do anything to lock away her memories of Rhys.

"I've also seen your scars. All of them."

Her spine straightened. "Excuse me? What do you mean, 'all of them'?"

He ignored her question. "I have someone I want you to speak with."

She rubbed at her head. It was like he was speaking another language. "What do you want from me? Speak plainly."

"I want a healer to assess you."

"Why? What are you looking for?" she asked.

"Nothing. He is going to speak with you. That's all."

"That's it? He won't touch me?"

The warlord stood. "He won't touch you. In fact, he's waiting right outside. May I send him in?"

She blinked. The warlord had asked. He hadn't demanded or done what he wanted. He'd asked.

"I guess that's okay."

He smiled at her and nodded to the cup next to the bed. "Drink your broth."

She reached out and took a sip from the mug.

Satisfied, he strode to the door and whispered something to someone out of sight before an extremely tall man entered. It was almost an impossible task for Sage to keep her mouth from hanging open. His white hair shone like a beacon in the dim light. She sucked in a sharp breath as his magenta eyes met hers.

A Sirenidae.

"This is Ezra," the warlord said. "He will visit you every day from now on." He cast a glance at her and walked backward toward the door. "I'll visit you later in the day, and Maeve will be by to help you bathe."

Sage nodded, noting the warlord's departure, but refusing to take her eyes from the man now staring at her. He moved to a divan at the end of the bed and sat down, just observing. Her gaze darted to the door and back to the him. She wet her lips, not sure what she should say.

"It's a pleasure to meet you."

His eyes tilted up at the corners when he smiled, making him even more handsome, if that were possible. She patted at her hair, self-conscious of her state of dress.

"It's a pleasure to meet you, too, Sage. But that's not what you were going to say, was it?" He arched a brow.

"You have unique eyes," she said slowly, gauging his reaction.

His head tipped to the side as he studied her. "You know what I am. Intriguing. So, you've been in the company of a Sirenidae before. Well, a story for another day, I'm sure."

She blinked. She didn't expect him to be so candid about it. "How did you come to be here?"

He waved a hand at her. "My story is short and boring, but I would very much like to learn about you."

Immediately, she was on guard. What information was he after? "My name is Sage Blackwell, and I'm the daughter of a swordsmith."

"A humble beginning."

"A perfect beginning," she corrected.

"Indeed. There's nothing better than being raised in the country with a family who loves you."

The affection in his tone bespoke of a similar life.

"You speak from experience."

Ezra smiled softly. "You're now a princess. Why did you leave your happy home?"

"Because it was the right thing to do." Her generic answer.

"That's a large burden for you to bear."

"It had to be done."

"But surely someone would have stepped up to protect the kingdom?"

She shrugged. "Maybe, but how could I take that chance with so many lives on the line?"

"You protected them."

Glancing down in her mug, she swirled the dark broth. "It's my duty to, if I'm able."

"Who protects you?"

"What?" She frowned at the Sirenidae.

"You heard me. Who protects you? Who has shielded you, when you could not shield yourself?"

Her eyes dipped toward Tehl, now sitting in the chair next to her, his face serious.

"My family."

Ezra nodded. "True, but that's not who you see." He jerked his chin toward the chair. "Who are you seeing?"

She startled, and her lips thinned. "No one."

He held her gaze, his face stern. "Do you know what happens when we push our minds too far?"

She stayed silent. He would tell her whether she wanted to hear it or not.

"They break, and there's no coming back." He paused, his face a mask of seriousness. "If you indulge your hallucinations, your mind will fracture. Can you honestly tell me you could rule a kingdom and protect your people with a fractured mind?"

Marq flashed through her mind. "No," she replied honestly.

"Then you need to let your hallucinations go. Don't encourage them, and don't speak to them." He stood from the couch and bowed to her. "I wish you a speedy recovery." His long legs quickly ate up the distance to the door and he disappeared, the door clicking shut quietly behind him. He was gone as quick as he came.

"He's right, you know," she murmured, not looking in Tehl's direction. It was unhealthy to indulge her hallucinations.

"I know, but you can't wish me away just like that," Tehl said, his tone solemn. "I'm part of you."

"It doesn't matter. I have to," she whispered to the empty room.

CHAPTER SIXTEEN

Sage

Tehl didn't disappear. He was stubborn, that one. He still spoke to her, but now she ignored him.

The Sirenidae had made a good point that first day they'd met. She wanted a healthy mind, and a future. If she kept going the direction she was, she'd end up like Marq, broken and half crazy, hurting the people around her.

Each day came easier, and slowly she settled into a routine. Ezra would visit her in the morning for a brief time. Sometimes they would talk, other times they would sit in comfortable silence. Each day, she grew a little stronger. The warlord always made sure to help her walk, and let a little more light in each day, so her eyes would continue to adjust. It was frustrating to be cooped up in the room, though. She wanted to explore, to get to know the people here.

Maeve's visits, though, slowed to a trickle and eventually stopped. When she asked about the woman, the warlord joked, "Am I not enough?" and that was that.

Days went by, each of them like a dream. She didn't really have a perception of time or even reality anymore. So, one day she shared this with Ezra.

"Do you ever feel like your life is one big dream?"

He set his cup down and watched her in his gentle way. "How so?"

"Like you're not sure what's real. Like the world is moving around you, but you can't see it. You just have a vague feeling that things are changing."

"You feel disconnected."

"Exactly. I'm stuck here in this bed with no way of knowing what is going on. I can barely walk. I'm so frustrated I could pull my hair out. I long to see the sun." She sighed. "I miss my home. Do you understand that? Everything I do seems empty. The only joys I have are when you and Zane visit."

Ezra jerked. "Zane?"

She blushed. "He gave me leave to use his name."

"I see. He's a good friend to you."

Was he her friend? Sage smiled. "He is."

"The warlord has sacrificed much for you. I hope you realize what an honor it is to be held in such esteem."

"You mean because I'm not Scythian?"

"Yes. There's a reason only myself and the warlord visit you. There have been many attempts on your life. We've managed to thwart all of them, but it's been a bloodbath since you arrived." He smiled and shrugged a shoulder at her horror. "The things we do for peace, right? And the ones we care about," he tacked on.

"It's worth it."

"Indeed. Now..." He slapped his hands against his thighs. "Would you like to take a turn about your room?"

Her body was riddled with fatigue, but she wouldn't turn away a chance to move. She hated being stuck in the bed. "Yes, please."

She'd lost some of her self-consciousness over the last few weeks. It wasn't ideal to rely on someone else, but Ezra and Zane had been extremely gracious about assisting her.

She peeked up at the Sirenidae as he helped her from the bed. "We've been speaking for some time now, and I still don't know much about you. How did you come to be here?" she asked.

He stiffened for a moment before continuing their shuffle around the room. "My family was taken from me, and the warlord offered me a chance to help others, so I took it."

"I'm so sorry about your family." Losing her own family, even if temporarily, was extremely painful.

His gaze intensified as he looked down at her.

Was there something on her face? She lifted a brow in question.

He smiled at her and tightened his grip on her waist. "Sage, you're a special girl. I'm sorry for the tragedy in your life."

She nodded, accepting his sympathy, and they both fell into silence, finishing their walk. Ezra helped her into bed and left her with a small bow, his shoulders stiff. When he closed the door, she wanted to slap herself, and, to her horror, cry. Obviously, bringing up his family had been a mistake, and she hoped desperately that it wouldn't ruin their new friendship. She was short on friends these days.

***

The warm water lapped at her skin, relaxing her. Sage had come to love the hexagonal bathing pool. It was a luxury to be able to swim and bathe at the same time. A smile turned her lips up. Maybe she could convince Tehl to install one.

"Sage, wake up."

Speak of the devil. She kept her eyes closed and ignored him while attempting to float in the pool.

"Woman, listen to me. You're not alone."

She smoothed her arms along the water. *He's not real, Sage. Ignore him.*

"You're going to die."

Her eyes snapped open, her gaze seeking Tehl. Sage sputtered, flailing in the water, and wrapped her arms around her breasts.

Ezra knelt beside the pool, his face looking infinitely sad as he leaned toward her.

"Wh-what are you doing here?" she screeched, blinking water out of her eyes. "Get out!"

He dipped his finger into the water and drew a pattern. "You're too good for our world, Sage. You shouldn't be here."

She took a tiny step away from him. Something in his voice was off. It sounded as if someone had died. "Thank you. If you give me a moment, I'll get dressed and come out to you."

His lips tipped up, but he didn't look up from his water drawings. "Do you remember when we spoke of peace?"

Chills erupted along her arms. Something wasn't right. Why was he bringing that up now? She glided back another step, eying the stairs that led out of the pool. She darted a look to the open door. No guards. Could she make it out of the pool to the outer door? Unlikely.

"Yes," she said, slowly twisting toward the Sirenidae. She jerked when her gaze clashed with his.

"I want to give you peace," he whispered, and something akin to determination altered his expression. "I'm going to help you end your suffering."

She balked and opened her mouth to scream, but he lunged. Water closed around her face as he shoved her under. What the bloody hell? Her feet touched the bottom, and she propelled herself to the surface.

Gasping for air, she pushed toward the stairs, panic building in her breast. All she needed to do was make it to the stairs. Her foot landed on one stair, then two, and then three. Hope blossomed. Maybe she would make it.

A shriek flew out of her as a hand grabbed her ankle. Her palms slammed against the stone, and her chin cracked against the step's edge, clicking her teeth together. Dark spots dotted her vision, and the room swirled. She dug her fingers into the stone as she was pulled back, and kicked at his hand.

"Let. GO!"

He jerked harder, and her nails broke, her hands slipping. She sucked in another breath and screamed, the sound piercing the air, and echoing around the empty room.

She scrambled forward when the hand released her ankle, but she didn't make it far. Ezra's arm wrapped around her torso, and his hand slapped across her mouth, cutting off her screams. He towed her back into the pool kicking and screaming.

"Don't do this," she pleaded from behind his hand.

"I'm sorry..." His voice broke. "I have to save you from him. I won't let you be used. You deserve peace after everything you've suffered. I'm going to grant you at least that."

Her eyes widened. He was really going to do it. Ezra was going to drown her.

She pulled in a deep breath through her nose when he kissed the top of her head and pulled her under. All sound disappeared except for Ezra's soft humming. She struggled against him, bit at his hand, raked her broken nails down his arms. But he didn't budge. Panic filled her as her lungs burned, begging for air. She flung her head back and crashed it into his face in a blind panic. She needed air. Now. But even that didn't help. It earned her a hand around her throat.

Unable to hold her breath any longer, she sucked in a breath and choked. Her body spasmed at the invasion in her lungs. It burned. Stories said drowning was peaceful, but those were lies. Her body seized, trying to get rid of the fluid. She tried to claw her way to air, the surface of the pool just above her, taunting her. She gazed at her hair floating around the pool, and closed her eyes. This was how she would die.

Suddenly, something slammed into her, breaking the vise around her torso and throat. She was free. She tried to swim, to move, to do anything, but her body wouldn't obey. How unfair. Freedom was just an arm's reach away, and yet she would still drown.

Something smashed into her chest and pain radiated into her ribs. Why did she have to feel pain? Why couldn't she go in peace? It hammered into her chest, and she choked out water, coughing. She tried to breathe, but all she did was spew water. Sage gasped, gagged, and coughed. God, it was painful. She cracked open her eyes to find Scythian warriors dragging Ezra away. Her ears were ringing, so she couldn't hear what he was screaming, but she caught the last words on his lips before she puked up more water: "Don't drink it!"

She shook her head and panted, staring in shock at Ezra.

His wild magenta gaze latched onto hers. "He'll be the end of you. You're just a pawn. Don't trust—"

Zane lunged from behind her, and, in a move too quick to follow, slammed his fist into Ezra's face, rendering him unconscious. Her muscles locked up at his speed. She stared, wide-eyed, at the warlord's wet, heaving back. *Inhuman.*

She squeezed her eyes shut as another bout of coughing racked her body. A hand soothed down her back as she expelled the rest of the water and collapsed on the floor. Her body trembled, her cheek pressed to the tile. Ezra had tried to kill her. She'd almost died. She shuddered at the thought, and vaguely noticed someone draping a towel around her. She forced her eyes to open. Zane leaned over her, rage and worry battling for dominance of his features. His hand cupped her cheek, his thumb running along her cheekbone.

"Wild one, are you okay?"

Her gaze wavered as tears filled her eyes. "No. No, I'm not. He tried to kill me. Why?" she cried. "Why, Zane? Ezra was my friend. I don't understand."

"I don't know," he murmured, brushing the tears from her face. "I don't know."

She hiccupped and cried harder, snot mingling with her tears. "I-I-I just don't understand."

"People do things beyond reason all the time."

Zane slipped his arms around her wet body and carried her to the bed. He tucked her in, then snuggled behind her, one arm draping over her waist. That small act of comfort broke her. She sobbed and clutched his hand while the shock and betrayal ran torrents of tears down her face. "He was my friend..."

"I know, love. I know."

She cried until there was nothing left, exhaustion immediately claiming her.

***

Sage blinked her eyes open, and for one blessed moment, she felt peace, until memories of the prior day slammed into her. She sat up and swung her legs to the side of the bed, and placed her head in her hands. Maybe if she squeezed her head hard enough, she could erase the memories. She pulled in a shuddering breath and lifted her head, staring sightlessly at the wall across from her. What had possessed Ezra to attack her? She thought they were friends. Had she been blind to his true feelings the entire time? She shook her head and blew out the breath she was holding. Sometimes, people were impossible to understand.

Her stomach pinched, reminding her that she hadn't eaten or

used the bathroom. Sage pushed her tangled hair from her face and stood on wobbly legs. She frowned. When would her strength return? She hated being weak. She rolled her shoulders back and carefully made her way to the vanity, plucking the long linen shirt from the top and continuing into the bathing room.

Her skin prickled uncomfortably when she entered the room. Sage kept her focus on the doorway to the chamber pot. She quickly relieved herself and tugged off the old shirt, each move stiff and painful. She winced when she lifted her arms above her head to slip on the new one that Zane had left. She blinked, her pain forgotten for the moment. When did she start thinking of him as *Zane* and not the warlord? Her brows slanted downward as she stared at the swirling stone tiles beneath her bare feet. She couldn't pinpoint when it changed, just that it had. Her heartbeat quickened at the thought. What else had changed that she hadn't noticed.

She shook her head and smoothed her hands down the shirt in an attempt to calm herself. Change was a part of life, and it wasn't something to be afraid of. Her fists clenched in her shirt when her eyes snagged on a particularly wicked bruise. God, that was ugly. Her lips thinned as she began to notice all the other cuts and bruises on her legs. She didn't even remember how they'd happened.

Without her permission, her gaze darted to the placid pool. Her breath seized, and her heart pounded in her chest. Her friend tried to kill her. Drown her. Her stomach rebelled, and she dropped painfully onto her bruised shins, heaving over the pot.

She trembled as the heaving subsided, then wiped her mouth with her shirt sleeve. Sage panted as the room tilted around her and warped. Her fingers bit into the chamber pot edge as she fought to control the panic that threatened to swallow her whole. She had to get out of there. On clumsy legs, she clambered to her feet and lurched forward, skirting around the pool as quickly as she could and racing for the door.

She burst into her room, and the fist around her lungs loosened. She couldn't be in there; it made her feel like the walls were closing in on her. Her breath sawed in and out of her chest, and she jumped when she caught the reflection of a girl with wild green eyes. The girl was wild, and on the edge of breaking.

Sage closed her eyes and gulped air. She needed to follow Jasmine's advice and slow her breathing. Each breath was a challenge, but with every breath, her heartbeat slowed a touch. She opened her eyes and stared at the mirror. The girl looking back at her was her, and yet, it wasn't. Cautiously, she approached the mirror and lifted a hand to her cheek. The girl mimicked her. She jerked back, startled. How could she reconcile this strange, frightened creature with herself?

She stepped closer to the mirror and touched the cool surface. It *was* her. She couldn't believe how much she'd changed. Her eyes were a deep green, her skin practically glowing and smooth; even her nose seemed straighter than it had been. Her brow furrowed. That wasn't possible. She ran a finger over her nose and gasped when she couldn't find the little bump from where she'd broken it at nine years old. What was happening to her?

She shrugged her left shoulder out of the linen shirt, and shifted to the side to inspect the giant bruise across the back of her shoulder. God, it was ugly. Purple and green, it just looked angry. The door creaked, but she didn't look away from the mirror. She already knew who it was. Zane's reflection moved across the mirror and paused behind her. She watched him watch her, but it wasn't awkward. His presence brought her a sense of comfort. Despite the horrors of the day before, she wasn't alone.

Zane leaned closer, his eyes staying on hers as he ran a hand down her arm before clasping her hand. "How are you feeling?"

She gave him a forced and lopsided smile. "Like my friend just tried to kill me." She gestured to her shoulder. "And like these stupid cuts and bruises are a reminder of that."

His dark eyes studied her before he leaned over to place a soft kiss on her bare shoulder. "You're strong. Each of these is proof of that. The scars and bruises are beautiful." His heated breath slithered across her skin.

She shivered and stepped forward, unease churning in her belly. "But I'm not flawless," she joked.

His hand tightened on hers, and he bridged the space between them, hugging her from behind. His arms were wrapped around her, and his chin rested on her shoulder. "You may not be a Scythian beauty, but as I've aged, I've come to realize that knowing what's inside a person is just as important as what you see. I've seen beauty which disguises rottenness and depravity, but yours isn't that kind. To me, your beauty is flawless."

Her throat tightened at his words, and the back of her eyes burned. "That's one of the nicest things anyone has ever said to me. Thank you."

"No need to thank me for the truth."

She smiled, and her attention shifted her face. "I've changed."

"You have been through much."

"No..." She gestured to her face. "I mean, yes, but that's not what

I was talking about. I mean, I broke my nose when I was nine, and I've always had a bump on the bridge of my nose...but it's gone now. Why?"

His eyes scanned her face. "You were given some of our special herbs to heal the damage to your body. This is just a byproduct of that herb. Are you angry?"

"I'm not sure." And she wasn't. It did feel like a violation; it was just strange to look at her own face and see someone slightly different than she was used to. "I don't look like myself."

"Yes, you do. The same luminous green eyes framed with dark lashes, the same heart-shaped face, and the same honey brown hair. You're still you."

When she continued to squint at her reflection, he squeezed her, pulling her attention back to him. "If you hadn't received that herbed broth, you would've died."

"I don't doubt that."

They stood there together, simply staring into the mirror. For how long, she didn't know. It was only when her legs began to tremble with the effort that Zane pulled her away and tucked her back into bed. She stared into his stunning face and reached a hand out to touch his wrist.

"Thank you for saving my life. I feel like I'm continually in your debt."

"There's no debt." He hesitated. "But I will need you to attend the execution."

Bile crept up her throat. "Execution?"

His face hardened. "Ezra attempted to kill you, and he almost succeeded. You are royalty, and you are my friend. He's earned his death."

"But execution? It seems so..."

"Barbaric?" he supplied, his body tense.

She bit her lip and answered carefully. "I don't believe murder is the answer."

"Really? And Rhys?"

She flinched.

"Was his death okay with your moral code?"

"That was different."

"Was it?"

Her lips thinned, and she looked away.

"Things here are not the same as in Aermia, but that does not make our customs wrong. If you're not careful, you'll let your prejudice color your perception of the world. Don't judge people by your own standards without considering theirs, or you will give them leave to do the same with you."

She swallowed but didn't relent. In her mind, this wasn't a matter of prejudice; it was right and wrong.

"Think about what I have said, Sage. Even if you don't agree with it, your presence is needed there. You don't have to watch, but you need to be there, so he can stand trial. I'll not let him go free. This is my right as his ruler. You may be willing to forgive everyone, but you must remember some people don't deserve forgiveness. They deserve judgment." He placed a soft kiss on her cheek. "I'll check on you later. Don't forget to drink your broth. You need your strength. Sweet dreams, wild one."

He began to stand, and Sage looked up into his face and squeezed his hand once. "Thank you, again."

The hard expression on his face softened a touch. "Anything for you."

CHAPTER SEVENTEEN

Sage

She glared at the curtains covering the window, a single sliver of light having escaped through the crack between them, cutting a swath of light across her room. Every part of her longed to throw back the curtains and see what lay beyond, but her hand hovered above the velvet cloth as she wondered, was it worth the risk to her sight? Her eyes had not fully healed yet, and she knew it was dangerous to expose them to too much light until they were. It had been *so* long though, so long since she'd seen anything outside of these walls. Her rooms had become a prison.

Her hand shook, and she clenched it into a fist. Leaning forward, she let her forehead press into the curtain.

No, she thought, *I can't risk it.* She might enjoy the view, but it'd be short-lived and the action could irrevocably affect her future. The dark fabric tickled her face, and the smell of vanilla teased her nose. It smelled like its owner: Zane.

With an angry huff, she pushed from the window and shuffled toward a divan piled high with pillows, her thoughts on the warlord. Zane had been quiet since Ezra's attack on her. He cared for her and was extremely tender, but once his duty was finished, he left rather quickly.

Sage winced as she sat on the couch and got comfortable, tucking her feet up under her. Did he blame her for what happened? Tipping her head back, she stared at the ornate ceiling. She wouldn't blame him if he did. Ezra had been his friend for many years, and now, because of her, he had to execute one of his closest companions.

The door creaked, and she flopped her head to the side. Speaking of the devil, Zane stepped quietly in, pausing when he caught her staring. "I thought you would be asleep."

That comment cut her. Was he sneaking in while he thought she was asleep, so he wouldn't have to deal with her?

"I'm sorry," she whispered.

His dark gaze moved to her face. "For what?"

"For killing your friend."

His hand clenched on the doorknob, and the door groaned.

Again, she was reminded that he wasn't like her. More powerful. Stronger. The idea should've frightened her, but it didn't.

He glanced at the door and stepped away, prowling toward her. He grabbed an enormous chair and placed it in front of her as if it weighed nothing. He sat down and studied her face.

"Why do you think you killed that traitor?"

She frowned and looked to the side, avoiding his searching gaze.

"Look at me, Sage."

She stubbornly kept her face turned, giving herself time to rein in her emotions. She was one comment away from crying. A finger touched under her chin.

"Please talk to me."

"It's my fault you have to execute Ezra. If I wasn't here, this wouldn't have happened." She looked back at him. "I'm sorry. I didn't mean to cause trouble."

"You have nothing to apologize for. He was the one to break our trust. He was the one to attack you. You didn't force him to do anything. He made his choices."

"Then why?" she paused. "Why?"

Zane cocked his head. "Why what?"

"Why are you avoiding me?" She blushed at her blurted question and stared at her clenched hands. She sounded like an affection-starved idiot.

His hand reached out and stroked her fingers. "You think I'm avoiding you?"

"It's just that, you've been gone, and you're not speaking..." Her brows furrowed. "You sneak in and out. I assumed it was something I did."

He heaved out a sigh. "It's not you, Sage. I wanted to give you time to process what you've been through. I assumed you would want to be alone, that you wouldn't feel comfortable with me around. You've suffered much from men. That sort of trauma doesn't disappear in days, sometimes not years. I figured you would need time."

Her gaze flew to his. "I don't blame you for any of this, Zane. You're my only friend here. It's been...lonely without anyone to speak to."

His smile was blinding, with just a hint of triumph, and just as attractive as everything else about him. She blinked. Who knew teeth could be so attractive? It was distracting.

"I'll make sure to bother you more often." His smile slipped a bit. "On a more serious note, though, we do need to discuss the execution."

The air flew from her lungs. She pulled her hands from his and smoothed the dressing gown across her thighs. "What about it?"

"Are you prepared?"

She'd had time to think about it over the last few days, and had come to a conclusion. "I'm not going." Sage met Zane's gaze as steadily as she could. "I'm sorry."

"You're going."

She blinked at his stern tone. "Excuse me?"

"I told you four days ago that I need you there."

"You told me to *think* about it," she pointed out. "And I did."

He pursed his lips. "That was more of...'think about it and get used to the idea,' because as I said, you have to be there."

"I don't want to go."

"And I understand that, but there's no other option."

"Murder is wrong," she said.

Something angry flashed through his eyes. "You're right. Murder is wrong. So is *attempted* murder. Did you forget that Ezra tried to kill you? That he tried to take you away?"

Pain, and her lungs burning, and watery silence assaulted her mind. Ezra's betrayal wasn't something she'd soon forget. She traced one of her jagged fingernails with the pad of her finger. "I haven't forgotten."

"Then why are you being so difficult?" Exasperation colored his tone.

"Because something is not right!" She stood on shaking legs and ignored the hand he held out to steady her. "Ezra never acted like that. Not once. Something was wrong with him that day. He was speaking nonsense, and he was so sad." The look on his face still wrenched her heart. She paced the floor, leaning her hand against the wall for balance. "We shouldn't be executing him, but examining him."

"There's nothing wrong with him."

"How?" She spun and walked back to Zane. "How do you know?" she asked, staring at his upturned face.

"Because he was interrogated, and I know crazy." He sighed and pulled her down to sit on the divan. "It was another plot to kill you."

"*No.*" She wilted in her seat.

He squeezed her hand. "Yes. You're different and unwelcome to some of my people. You're a threat. One they will do anything to eliminate. I'm so sorry."

She went numb. "This was his plan all along? Ezra planned to kill me the entire time?"

"Our intelligence says yes, this was the plan all along." Zane stood up and then sat next to her. He pulled her into his arms and held her. "I'm sorry, but he was never your friend. He was a spy and a murderer."

Sage stared vacantly at the fur rug beneath their chair. "Murder does not condone murder, though." The arms holding her tightened. She peeked up at Zane from under her lashes, and her breath caught in her throat. It was as if Rhys was looking down at her with his disturbing, soulless eyes. She blinked, and it was Zane staring at her, lines between his brows.

"Are you alright?"

She shuddered and pulled from his embrace. Zane was nothing like Rhys. She couldn't keep comparing every man she met to him. "I'm fine."

She wasn't. Not even close.

"I'll send a dress for you tomorrow and have the women help you with your bathing. Then, I'll fetch you for the execution." He pressed a kiss to her temple and tipped her chin up. "It will be okay, love. I promise."

***

It was not okay in the least. Actually, it was awful.

When the women came in to help her bathe, she nearly punched one in the face when they tried to force her into the bathing room. She had been avoiding the bathing room since her attack, and there was no way she was going in there. She had kept the door closed all week with the hope that it would stop the memories from bothering her. It didn't.

After some heated debate, Maeve barged in and ordered a

bathing tub to be brought into her room instead. Quickly thereafter, the women got her scrubbed and into her dress. It was a black silk dress that sat off the shoulders and dipped into a low back. A black fur and a leather belt hugged her waist with a sheath for her dagger, and the skirt followed the swell of her hips, which had finally begun to fill out again.

Sage sat on the stool in front of the mirror, staring at herself. The Scythian women hadn't even applied any cosmetics, yet she still barely recognized the woman before her. She pulled her gaze from her own face and looked over her shoulder at Maeve.

"What should we do with my hair?"

What was one supposed to do for an execution? Her stomach cramped.

Maeve frowned and dipped her head. "The warlord has something special planned. I'll take my leave." A shallow bow and she was gone.

She returned her gaze to the strange woman before her. How had she changed so much? Surely, the broth couldn't have changed her this much?

"Lovely," Zane's deep voice purred.

She slowly turned to him. "It seems like too much for..." She swallowed. "An execution."

He sauntered toward her. Part of his hair was braided back from his face, highlighting his sharp cheekbones and strong jaw, and he had an earring made from obsidian and ruby in one ear. She scanned the black shirt, leather pants, and boots he'd donned, noting the numerous daggers strapped in various places on his person. She had to admit, she was impressed. He looked good. Better than good—he looked perfect.

He smiled at her perusal and placed the parcel he carried on her bed. Stepping behind her, he laid his hands lightly on her shoulders. "Not too much for a consort."

She twisted back around to stare at the mirror. "This feels wrong, like I'm celebrating his death."

"No, it would be a dishonor if we wore rags."

She gestured at her hair and joked, "Well, my hair is enough of a dishonor."

Zane pulled a shiny lock from her shoulder and rubbed it between his fingers. "Nothing this beautiful could ever be a dishonor." He caught her gaze and kissed the lock of hair.

Heat suffused her cheeks. He was always affectionate, but this was something more, something she couldn't give.

She broke the moment and looked away, trying to ignore the way his stare seemed to burn into the top of her head. Sage startled when his fingers wound through her hair. "What are you doing?" she asked, watching him in the mirror.

One side of his mouth quirked up. "Fixing your hair?"

"You?" She arched a brow.

"I had sisters."

"I didn't know." She didn't know much about his family. He kept that to himself, mostly.

"They died a long time ago."

"I'm sorry."

She sensed the conversation was over, so she closed her eyes as his hands worked through her hair. There was nothing better than having someone play with her hair. She stayed quiet and prepared herself for what lay ahead.

Death, that's what lay ahead.

"Open your eyes."

She peeked at the mirror and was pleasantly surprised by what he'd created. Her hair was braided back from each temple, forming ropes, and twined behind her head like a crown. She turned her neck and smiled at how the rest of her hair tumbled down her back. It was simple but beautiful. "Thank you."

His grin reached his almond-shaped eyes when he held a finger up. "That's not all." He turned and opened the parcel and pulled out a crown.

Her eyes widened. Its base was black metal, shaped into roses and thorns. Rubies and obsidians sparkled, catching the light. He settled the heavy crown on her head, and placed his hands on her shoulders.

"Do you like it?"

"It's beautiful, and deadly," she remarked in awe. "But it's too much."

"It's not enough, wild one. I had it made just for you. It shows your two sides."

She swallowed back her emotions and twisted around to peer up into his inky gaze. "It's stunning."

"It's not the crown, it's the wearer."

Warmth infused her at his compliment, but it quickly cooled. She wasn't going to a ball, she was attending an execution. How she looked was inconsequential. Sage dipped her chin. "I'll wear it proudly."

He offered her an arm and she took it, her dress rustling gently as she moved. At Zane's sharp breath, she looked at him with raised brows.

He blatantly eyed her figure, his eyes roving first up and then back down. "Beauty, where you lead, I shall follow."

She tried to figure out what to say to that. "Thank you for the dress and crown," she said lamely. Her breath stuttered when his burning gaze met hers.

His eyelashes lowered, shuttering his eyes. "My pleasure."

Zane swept her from the room and she blinked hard, her eyes watering at the brightness of the hallway. Warriors snapped to attention and bowed deeply as they passed by. Sage tried not to shrink away from their lingering stares.

"They're just curious," Zane said, under his breath. "You're unusual."

She snorted, finding that somewhat amusing, and she felt some of the tension drain from her body. She continued with Zane down what seemed like an endless stone hallway until they finally veered into a luxurious room. She froze when she caught sight of the creatures which came to greet them. Two black felines slunk from their pillows and rubbed against the warlord and herself.

"Breathe," Zane soothed. "They'll not hurt you."

She released her breath, never taking her eyes from the golden-eyed beasts brushing against her. Her hand clenched in her skirt as one pushed its nose up to her fist.

"She only wants a good scratch."

Her fist clenched tighter. Zane moved behind her and smoothed a hand along her arm and down to her fist, prying her hand from her skirt. He entwined their fingers and placed both their hands on the feline's head. A loud rumbling erupted from the beast, making Sage jump.

"She's just happy. She's purring."

Sage pressed her back into his chest and marveled at how soft the feline's coat was. "What are their names?"

"Nege and Nali."

"Beautiful."

Zane pulled his hand from hers, and moved to stand before her. He jerked his chin at the door behind him. "Through that door is my throne." He let that sink in. "Once we leave this room, I'm no longer Zane to you, but 'my lord.' Do you understand?"

"Yes."

He scanned her face. "This is just a formality. Nothing can make me look weak in front of my people. We can't be familiar."

"I understand." It was an execution. It was to be solemn.

"I will prompt you through everything you need to do."

Panic clawed at her throat. "What will I need to do?"

"Nothing much. You'll basically sit next to me the entire time."

"You'll warn me when it's time?"

He stepped closer and ran his fingers along her face. "You won't have to watch. Are you prepared to see him again?"

She swallowed. "Yes."

"You'll be a spectacle to my people. Prepare yourself for the gawking."

She nodded. "I'm ready."

He scrutinized her, and she watched as he slipped into the role of leader. He was a warlord once again. It disturbed her. He looked the same, and yet everything about him was colder. She took his offered elbow, and clenched her dress in her right hand as both felines flanked them. The immense door caused her to shiver.

Beyond it lay a people who hated her and a traitor.

Beyond it lay death.

Chapter Eighteen

Sage

The door opened, and she barely managed to keep a tranquil expression in place. The door led to the warlord's dais, but that wasn't the most disconcerting thing. It was the thousands of eyes upon them. She'd never felt so naked in her entire life.

He led her around his throne to a small, but equally ornate, wooden chair. He guided her to sit, and gasps reverberated through the crowd. Did she do something uncouth? Sage glanced at Zane for assurance. With his back to the crowd, he allowed a ghost of a smile to cross his face, but it quickly disappeared. Her momentary panic faded until he moved over to stand in front of his own throne. Then it came surging back.

Suddenly, she was staring at the vast crowd. Every eye was on her, and not in a friendly way. She forced a sense of calmness she didn't feel. She was Sage Blackwell and she had been through much in her lifetime. She could do this.

The warlord stood in front of his throne with Nege and Nali sitting regally on either side of him, looking for all the world like a warrior god who'd come to prey on humanity. "Let it commence."

A door opened, and a group of warriors dragged out Ezra. The crowd booed and threw food. Sage barely kept her mask in place at the sight of him. His pale white skin was covered with dried blood and bruises, his face so swollen he could only crack one of his magenta eyes. It was as though he felt her stare, for his eye found hers and stayed upon her. She was shocked to see neither anger nor sorrow, but pity in his face. Did he pity her? Why?

Her breath hissed out of her, and she opened her mouth to object to Ezra's treatment when she felt Zane's large hand settle over hers. Ezra, too, took note of the action, and his gaze slid to the warlord, his expression so filled with hate that it felt like a punch to her gut. Why did he hate his friend? He was the one who committed a crime.

Something was wrong. What was she missing? She shifted uncomfortably beside the warlord when he pressed closer, and Nali pushed against her skirts, rubbing against her knee. She glanced to the feline and back to Ezra, her heart pounding. None of this felt right.

"How do you plead for the crimes of which you have been accused, Ezra of the Sirenidae?"

Ezra stared straight at the warlord. "Guilty."

She swallowed hard.

"Do you have any last words?"

"No one lives forever. Your time will come." He turned to Sage. "But until then, don't be blind, be smart."

Her brows slanted together. It was a warning, but what was he talking about? And why? "Ezra…" she began.

"Enough," the warlord cut her off. "It's time."

Her throat tightened when Ezra's sad eyes met hers, and he mouthed a single word: *Sorry.*

"Proceed." Zane motioned with a bored gesture to a warrior with a large sword.

The man stepped forward and forced Ezra to his knees.

"This isn't right," Sage whispered.

"She should be the one to end his life," a man piped up from the crowd. "It is our law!"

Others cried out their agreement.

Sage stiffened. *What?*

The warlord stilled, and the room seemed to cool. "You wish to challenge me?"

A behemoth of a man stepped to the front of the crowd and dropped to his knees. "I've no desire to challenge you. The woman is not from here and does not know our laws. If she is to understand what it is to be Scythian, it does not make sense to coddle her, my lord."

"And that is for you to decide?"

The warlord's tone made her want to hide underneath her seat, and, wisely, the man stayed silent and shook his head.

Zane's boot entered her vision, and he lifted her chin with gentle fingers. "I'm inclined to agree with him. It is our custom."

"You would like me to do what, my lord?" she asked calmly.

"In our land, the victim exacts justice for the crime." He released her chin and gestured for her to stand.

Sage stood on wooden legs and placed one hand on Nali's head. Zane held a hand out toward the warrior, who strode to them and knelt, holding the sword up. The warlord plucked it from the warrior's hands and held it out to Sage.

"My lady..."

She stared at it like one would a poisonous snake. Did he expect her to pick up the sword and cut Ezra down? He knew her better than that. But when she looked into his black gaze, it held no friendship, no emotion, and it eerily reminded her of the look she often saw in Rhys' eyes. But it had to be her imagination; they weren't at all alike...were they? She shuddered at the idea, but her thoughts were interrupted when Zane prompted her, "Take it, my lady."

With trembling fingers, she carefully pulled the large sword from his hands, but much to her surprise, it took everything she had to keep the sword steady in her hands. She gritted her teeth. How had she lost so much strength in such a little time? A babe was no doubt stronger than she!

Zane swept his arm out, pulling her attention back to him. "After you."

Her legs weak, she barely managed not to stumble as she

approached Ezra, halting before him with the large sword swaying slightly, as her arms strained. The Sirenidae was a shadow of what he used to be. As he looked up, his eyes seemed to plead with her, but she hadn't a clue what for.

Zane raised his voice above the din of the crowd. "As our laws command, it will be done."

Sage's jaw clenched. She couldn't do this. It was wrong.

"I can't do this."

"You have to," the warlord whispered in her ear, his warm breath tickling her neck.

Her stomach rolled. "You misunderstand me. When I say I can't, I mean I won't."

"You must, Sage. You have no other choice. This is the first step to securing peace, to prevent *more* death. This is why the crown prince wants you here, for us to work together. To do that, my people need to accept you and see that you understand them. We need them to see that we are not so different as they think."

But they *were* different, she and Zane. She'd never executed a man, nor forced someone to watch their friend die. It was unthinkable to her, yet here Zane was, calmly demanding she do so. Was one man's life worth the countless deaths of others if she refused? Was her taking of Ezra's life worth a chance at peace?

She stared at Ezra kneeling before her. Tears burned at the back of her eyes, but she wouldn't let them fall. Now was not the time for tears. She hefted the sword and held it to Ezra's neck, wavering slightly. None of this was right. She didn't know why Ezra had done what he'd done, but she was sure he was not so terrible he deserved the death to which he'd been sentenced. Yet could she really let this chance to end hundreds of years of hate and prejudice pass by, merely because of her personal feelings?

"Do it quickly. Right at the base of the throat. He won't experience any pain that way," the warlord coaxed her. "The worst is almost over."

A tear fell from her eye and rolled down her cheek. The worst is almost over? What a ridiculous statement. She'd be tormented with the memory and guilt of this long after this single moment, and she would deserve that torment. This was wrong. Was there a way to escape this choice without inciting a riot—or worse, a war?

"It's okay, Sage," Ezra whispered. He leaned closer to the blade, the sword kissing his neck, his eyes understanding, his voice forgiving. "It's okay."

It was his forgiveness which undid her.

She simply would not do something which violated her moral code, and it was wrong of him to try to force her. She would do her utmost to secure peace, but not at the price the warlord was asking. The cost was too great. Peace gained by murder was no peace and she would not give up another part of herself to appease someone else.

Throwing her shoulders back, she stood taller and smiled at Ezra. "I'll not do it," she said loud enough only for Zane and Ezra to hear.

Her brows furrowed as her words wrought a range of emotions skittering across Ezra's face, which she found difficult to interpret, but very quickly, they disappeared. His eyes met hers and she was surprised to see a determined look in them. She had just begun to pull away the sword when the Sirenidae did something that would haunt her until she died; he smiled sadly and brought himself down onto her blade.

A cry stuck in her throat. She was paralyzed as he fell to the ground, crimson staining the white floor. Numbly, she let go the sword, allowing it to fall from her fingers and clatter to the stone floor.

"No," she breathed. She tried to drop to her knees to help him somehow, but a large hand kept her from doing so. "No!"

"Calm yourself before you ruin everything," Zane commanded, steel in his voice.

The Sirenidae writhed for a moment, then stilled. He was there one moment and gone the next. A dull roar filled her ears, and her knees threatened to buckle.

"Look away."

For the life of her, she wanted to, but she couldn't. The world took on a dream-like quality, and everything blurred around the edges.

He'd killed himself. Her chest heaved. Ezra had taken his own life.

"*Why?*" she whispered. Why would he do such a thing? She lifted her hands and stared at her shaking palms. What had she done?

Vaguely, she was aware of Zane leading her from Ezra's body and toward the dais. She craned her neck and watched as the warriors collected the Sirenidae's limp form. It wasn't right. He should have still been there.

"You've done well, love. You've secured peace."

She slowly spun to the warlord, his praise turning her heart cold. "If it was done, it was by no action of mine," she replied woodenly.

"But the people believe it was, and that's all that matters." He smiled.

Sage looked past him to the Scythian crowd and realized that the thundering in her ears was actually cheering. Bile burned the back of her throat. How could they be *applauding* death? It was disgusting. Somehow, she ended up on her chair next to the warlord's throne. She blinked at how Zane's olive hand held her creamy one. Both different, but both stained by death. Chills erupted over her arms, but she didn't bother to rub at them. The sea of celebrating people warped into swirling colors, Ezra's beautiful magenta eye blank at the forefront of her mind.

A tug on her hand turned her attention to the man at her side. Zane gave her a searching look. "I'm sorry."

A seed of bitterness took root at the empty words. Sorry? Well, so was she. He stood and guided her from her seat and down a few steps to a table piled high with all types of food. She simply stared. The aromas, normally enticing, upset her stomach even more.

"We're to eat?" she asked, incredulous.

The warlord glanced at her. "It is our custom," he said sharply.

They expected her to eat after...

She pulled a breath through her nose and pressed her lips into a firm line, hoping it would prevent her from vomiting all over the table. Zane placed her in a seat and took the one beside her. What she assumed was the warlord's inner circle surrounded them and took their places at the table. People in power always surrounded themselves with other powerful people.

The warlord gave some sort of speech, but Sage tuned it out, thwarting each of his subsequent attempts to pull her into his conversation. She couldn't focus her own scattered thoughts, let alone carry on a conversation, most especially during this barbaric and morbid celebration.

Relief filled her when the feasting finally seemed to consume most everyone's attention. The questions and blatant stares decreased as they focused on the bounty of food. She scanned the table and paused when she met a familiar gaze. Blair. He looked much the same as when she'd last seen him except that tiny wrinkles appeared between his brows when his dark eyes met hers.

She stared back, blankly, before noticing the woman in the seat next to him. The shock of red, curly hair pulled Sage out of her dream-like state. Hazel eyes peeked out from a freckled face as the woman arched a brow at her. Sage blinked, but continued staring. The woman wasn't Scythian. Her round cheeks and soft pink lips lent her an air of youth, but the fine lines bracketing her eyes betrayed her age. The woman pushed back from the table and placed a hand on her belly. Sage glanced down to the redhead's belly. A very pregnant belly. Sage's stomach soured even further. A pregnant woman came to an execution. Did the redhead have a choice? Or had she been conned into attending as well?

The woman's other brow accompanied the first as she placed her fork down. Some of Sage's disgust must have been apparent. She wiped all expression off her face and ignored the woman's questioning gaze.

Sage's forehead wrinkled as something occurred to her. The only women present besides herself seemed to all be in some stage of pregnancy. Odd. She shifted in her chair and picked at the food the warlord had placed on her plate. Was that too some sort of strange custom? Community birth planning? A snort escaped her.

"My lady?"

Sage tried to keep her thoughts from showing on her face when she glanced at the speaker, a beautiful Scythian woman with a headful of raven braids. "Yes?"

"When are you due?"

"Due?" She searched the Scythian's face. What did she mean?

"When is the child due?"

Child? The idea was so out of place, it struck her as hysterical. She laughed aloud and shook her head. "I'm not with child." At her words everyone at the table stilled and quieted, their eyes moving from her to a spot behind her. Did she say something wrong?

An arm slid across her shoulders, Zane's cedar scent tickled her nose. "It's much too early to be speaking of children. You've barely met her." The censure in his voice was clear.

The Scythian woman blanched and stared down at her plate. "Forgive me."

"There's nothing to forgive," Sage said with as much feeling as she could manage. The Scythian woman gave her a weak smile and picked at her food, while her warrior husband was stiff, his eyes glaring at his wife. Again, odd. Why would he be angry about a simple question?

She thought dinner would be the end of it, that she'd be able to flee to her room and grieve, but boy was she wrong. Drinking and desserts followed, and as each hour passed, it became more unbearable. All she wanted to do was escape, to mourn the loss of her friend. Maybe scream and throw things a bit. The surrounding depravity sickened her. These people were celebrating like this had been the grandest of events and not an execution. It was as if his death phased them not at all. She swallowed thickly and sipped water from her cup, trying to ignore the gruesome commentary on Ezra's death that was currently taking place at her table.

A heavy furry head landed in her lap, and she did her best not to jump. Sage looked down to find large golden eyes peeking up at her. She set down her cup and slipped a hand underneath the table, praying the beast wouldn't bite it off as she scratched Nali's soft ears. The big cat let out a rumbling purr, but none of the revelers reacted.

They were most likely too deep into their cups. Disgusting.

"She likes you," Zane murmured into her ear.

Sage ignored his proximity and continued to pet the beast, tucking her thoughts away. "She's beautiful."

"She is," he breathed the words against her skin.

His nose skimmed her jawline and then something wet touched the lobe of her ear. Sage jerked away and gaped at the warlord. "What are you doing?" she demanded, her hand sinking into Nali's fur.

His smile was lazy. "Tasting what's mine."

She stiffened and then leaned closer to stare into his eyes. Zane misunderstood the action, and leaned in even closer, triumph lurking in his eyes. Sage placed a hand on his chest. "Are you drunk?" she asked, infusing her voice with as much disdain as possible.

"Not at all," he scoffed, plucking her other hand from the arm of her chair and nipping at one of her fingers.

She yanked back her hand and closed it into a fist. She glared at her fist for a moment, seriously considering punching him. He caught the gesture and something akin to anticipation crossed his face. Her nose wrinkled. He was drunk.

"I'm leaving."

His hand snaked out and clutched her skirts. "You're needed here."

Leaning forward, she whispered in his ear, conscious of the advanced hearing of the others. "I am not needed. This display of celebration over a man's death is disgusting. I've done what you've asked me."

"He wasn't a man. He was Sirenidae."

He said it so matter-of-factly that she almost missed it. The prejudice. The hate for Ezra's race. She pulled back and searched his face, his eyes confirming what she suspected.

"You actually believe that? That Ezra wasn't a man because he was Sirenidae?"

A shrug and a haughty look was all the answer she received. She waited for some sort of emotion to bubble up inside her at his response, but there was nothing. Apparently, everything inside her was numb. Sage tugged at her skirts in his hand and then touched his fist when he didn't release them.

"I'm done. Let go."

He just stared at her.

"Allow me to leave, or I'll make a scene," she hissed, and she meant every word. She'd create a scene so fantastic that it would go down in Scythian history.

His black eyes traveled to her face, then he nodded. "Goodnight." His fist released the crumpled silk of her skirt, dismissing her like a servant.

If he thought to humiliate her, she didn't care in the slightest.

She'd endured much worse and she was much too numb to care anyway. All eyes moved to her when she scooted her chair back and stood. "Goodnight..." She dipped her chin and spun on her heel, her black silk dress flaring with her every stride.

The thrones loomed before her, seeming to grow with every step she climbed up the white stone dais. She skirted around the thrones and moved to the door behind them. Her hand paused on the handle as she took one more look at where Ezra had died. It was pristine, the shiny white stone glaring at her, showing no evidence of what had happened earlier. It was wrong. Like they had wiped away the crime. Like it didn't exist. The air in the room seemed to evaporate the longer she stood staring.

Hurrying through the door, Sage almost closed it on her feline shadow. Nali slunk through the door behind her and traipsed out into the hall. Using her memory, Sage navigated the hallways, not surprised when warriors materialized and followed her. Sage glanced down a side hallway and skidded to a stop, not believing her eyes.

"Jas?" She blinked, and the hallway was empty. Her heart pounding hard in her chest she stared at the empty space. She could have sworn she'd seen her friend standing in the hallway. Oh no. Would she start hallucinating Jasmine, too?

She shook herself and spared the silent guards a glance before continuing on. The sadness and anger she'd been waiting for crashed into her, and she gasped at the force of it. She picked up her speed and shoved the emotions down for the moment. There was no way she would cry in front of the warriors. They turned a corner and her door came into view. She hustled through, slammed it in the warriors' faces, and placed her back against it.

Her chest heaved, and angry tears spilled onto her cheeks. Everything was so muddled. The Scythians' display was barbaric and revolting, and yet she'd been forced to participate. What kind of person did that make her?

She pushed through her door and Nali jumped onto her bed, circling a few times before snuggling down, but Sage could not lay down. The emotions coursing through her had her feeling on edge and she began pacing the room. She ran a hand through her own hair and winced when one of the crown's metal thorns pricked her finger. She'd forgotten it was there. She glanced to the mirror and examined her reflection. She was shocked to realize she looked like a queen, but not an Aermian queen—the enemy's queen. She stormed up to the vanity and placed her hands on it, staring into her reflection.

"Who are you?" she asked herself. "What are you doing?"

"You're surviving," Tehl answered from her side.

Sage stared at him. His visits had become less frequent ever since she'd stopped speaking with him over the last couple weeks. "Am I really?" She returned her attention to the face in the mirror. Was she doing what she had to in order to survive, or merely following along because it was easier than fighting?

"You're being hard on yourself and it's partly because you lost someone today. Your legs are shaking so hard, I'm not even sure how you're still standing."

Now that he mentioned it, she realized her legs were shaking and she was on the verge of collapsing. She let out a scream of frustration. "Why am I so weak? I should be healing, or healed!"

"I don't know."

The crown glinted in the low light; it seemed to taunt her the longer she looked at it atop her head. In a fit unlike her, Sage yanked the obsidian crown from her head, along with a few hairs, and lobbed it across the room.

"Do you feel better?" Tehl asked drolly. "Anger won't help, you know. It'll make you vulnerable and prone to mistakes."

He was right.

A deranged chuckle burst from her. "Tehl, you're not even here and you're right. It's uncanny and it's unfair." She dropped her chin to her chest and glared at her clothes. It sickened her to have anything Scythian touching her skin.

"The dress is beautiful," he said. "Keep in mind, though, men generally only have dresses made for women they feel belong to them."

She bit her lip. It was time to stop talking to her hallucinations. It was dumb to keep lapsing. "I can't speak to you, Tehl." She glanced at him. "I appreciate that you helped me survive, but you're not real, and it's unhealthy to speak to you."

His face was serious, watching her. "I know, Sage. But I'll be here when you need me."

She turned from him and stepped toward the bathing room. Her feet stumbled, and her hands clenched as memories assaulted her of her drowning. Her eyes turned to slits. She'd let fear rule her too much as it was. It was time to fight. Her fear ended now.

Chapter Nineteen

Sage

She was proud of herself. At least one positive thing had happened in this nightmarish day. She had changed and washed the cosmetics from her face in that cursed room; she'd never taken her eyes from the pool, and her heart was still pounding from it, but still, she'd done it.

Sage knotted her dressing robe over her body, still feeling

naked. The lack of underclothes was something she just couldn't get used to. It made her vulnerable and she hated it. Her eyes wandered over to where the crown lay on the floor. It was beautiful and skillfully made, but she could hardly bear to look at it, as it brought gruesome memories to the forefront of her mind. Its beauty would be forever tainted by the stain of death.

Quickly, she plucked it from the rug and returned it to its box. She then placed it by the door with the black dress neatly folded atop it. They were beautiful, to be sure, but she could not bear to keep them.

She moved to the end of the bed and leaned a hip against it, eyeing the enormous ball of fur occupying that space. "Where am I to sleep?" she asked Nali. "You take up the whole bed." She wanted nothing more than to crawl under the covers and sleep.

Nali cracked an eye before slowly stretching out onto her back, her belly up. Sage's hand flew to her mouth as she gasped. Nali's belly was crisscrossed with silver scars. "Oh my, you poor thing. What *happened* to you?" Who had done this to her?

Carefully, Sage placed her hand in front of Nali, waiting to see how the beast would respond. The feline's ears flicked to the side and she sniffed Sage's fingers and bumped them with her nose. Sage smiled and scratched under Nali's chin, feeling a sense of kinship with the powerful creature.

"You and I are the same, it seems; both of us scarred. What a pair we make. I have to admit, I didn't think we'd be friends. I was sure you were going to eat me." Sage laughed to herself, and Nali let out a little chuff when Sage slowed her scratching. Her door swung open and she dropped her hand to her lap, any sense of peace evaporating through the doorway. Sage felt like a cat with her hackles raised; there were so many things she wanted to say to Zane, the fury and confusion from earlier welling back up inside her. But who would she receive, Zane or the warlord? She gasped when he came straight to her and pulled her off the bed and to him, his arms encircling her waist. She stood frozen as he buried his face into her neck and hair.

"I'm *so* sorry, Sage. This was never meant to happen. What a hellish day."

Sage remained stiff in his arms. "You're right, today was a day from hell."

He pulled back and clasped both of her cheeks, his gaze darting over her face. "You're angry?" It was a question.

She shook off his hands and shoved at his chest, though she couldn't even move him an inch. "You lied to me," she accused. It wasn't as eloquent as what she'd been rehearsing in her head, but it was a start.

He sighed heavily. "I did not lie to you."

"You *said* I wouldn't have to watch! That all I would have to do was sit by your side and it would be over." She stepped away from him and pointed a finger in his direction. "How could you subject me to that? You knew how I felt about the execution already, and yet, at the behest of your people, you forced me not only to watch, but *participate!*"

"What did you expect me to do? Cave to you in front of my kingdom? That would've made me appear both weak and inept as a ruler. Doing so would have been dangerous, not just for you but for me as well!"

"Are you serious?" she yelled. "Standing up for what is right is not weak!"

"How was it wrong? It was all according to law."

"But it's barbaric!"

His face turned to stone. "And what of Aermia's hangings?"

"We don't personally have to hang them ourselves."

"Well, maybe you should," he retorted, "Perhaps you'd consider it more carefully, then."

She tugged on her braids, realizing he had a point. She'd never been comfortable with that particular aspect of her government, but that was not the whole of it. "It wasn't only the manner of execution – it was your reaction. You practically held a festival!"

"Be reasonable here. There's one less murderer in the world. Shouldn't that be cause for at least *some* rejoicing?"

Sage gaped at him. "He wasn't a murderer, and you know it. He was sick. He attacked *me* and yet, I saw it plain as day. His attack made no sense. But, that aside, even if he was just a murderous person, his life was still precious." She narrowed her eyes at him. "Death should never be celebrated."

Zane held his hands out placatingly. "I know you're having a hard time accepting what happened and that's natural. You've been through some tragic experiences in the last couple weeks, Sage. But you have to realize: abuse, murder, ravishment; none of them make sense. So, stop trying to make sense of his actions." He gave her a pitying look, "Sometimes, you just have to accept that someone is bad and move on. I've done it, and so can you. If you don't, it will eat you alive inside."

That spiked her anger. "Don't you dare! How dare you just chalk this up to some 'poor, broken Sage' situation. I'm not blind. I know what I saw, and he wasn't a murderer. Something was wrong that day! And you–" she jabbed a finger in his direction, "don't you talk down to me about 'letting go'! Of course, I understand letting go. You know how much I've already done so!"

He tossed his hands in the air. "I don't pity you. I'm trying to explain something to you, but you're so focused on your anger that you won't listen. I'm trying to help you understand that some people are just evil."

"First of all, like I already said, that doesn't justify your people's rejoicing over that fact! You don't get it, Zane! What happened today was horrible. It was wrong for so many reasons."

"No. It's you who's missing the point. You're skewing the situation." He ran a hand through his hair and blew out a frustrated breath, "I don't understand why you can't just be reasonable here."

"Zane, I am being reasonable. You can't say that just because I don't agree with your opinion I'm unreasonable. That's tyrannical and unfair!"

He began pacing the room, his hands clenching and unclenching as he gestured wildly to punctuate his sentences. "But *your* opinion is wrong, so yes! You do have to agree with mine! What is *wrong* with you right now?!"

Sage didn't even know what to say to that. What exactly did he expect her to do? She opened her mouth to say just that when he stopped abruptly, his attention snagged by the neatly packaged crown and dress sitting by the door. Slowly, he strolled to it and bent down, opening the box and pulling out the crown.

"Why are these by the door?"

If she could have thrown the gifts in his face, she would have. "I will not accept such generous gifts, *my lord,*" she bit out, knowing he hated when she used his title. "It's too much."

He narrowed his eyes at her. "I told you to call me Zane, and you *can* accept them. They were made specially for you." He pulled the crown from the box and frowned, first at it and then at her.

She pulled her lips into a tight smile "And as much as I appreciate the thought, I will not accept it. I cannot. It–"

"It what?!" His hand tightened on the crown. "Isn't to your liking? After everything, you would scorn my gifts, my generosity?"

"That's not what this is about, I–"

"What then?! You spite me out of anger? Have I not done my best to care for you? To meet all your needs? Why isn't it enough?"

He suddenly seemed more agitated than the situation merited and he was starting to make her nervous. "Zane," she said soothingly, "That's not what I meant. It *is* enough. And that's why I won't accept these. You've taken care of me, protected me, and even given me your room. I can't possibly take anything more from you."

He seemed not to hear her words. "I should've known better. None of this was enough. It's *never* enough," he whispered heatedly. He turned to face her, still holding the crown. "Wild one, what game are you playing with me?"

Something about the query and his posture raised the hair on the back of her neck. A strange glint had entered his eye; whatever was going through his head made her heart pound. He seemed different, dangerous. He cocked his head and, almost offhandedly, remarked, "You obviously have a keen mind, yet you still give in to the weakness of your kind. Why do you refuse logic and why do you refuse me? I admit I find it both infuriating and fascinating."

She frowned at him. Now, that just didn't make sense. Her gaze bobbed to the crown. What was going on? And why did her refusal of the dress and crown upset him so much?

Sage stepped behind the bedpost and held onto it to keep her hands from shaking. Her movement backward seemed to propel him forward. Step by slow step, he prowled toward her, unnaturally fluid. She'd told him how nervous and unsettled she felt when he did that, so after that first week, she'd rarely seen him move with his Scythian grace. Why was he doing it now? Was it just to unnerve her, because she'd irritated him?

She looked into his face and her stomach dropped when she met his eyes. They were lit with anger and lust, but it was the lust which scared her the most. He'd never looked at her like that before. A little voice in her head told her to run; she wasn't sure if it was Tehl or herself, but she felt for a certainty that Zane was very dangerous right then. She'd have to tread carefully.

"Everything's okay," she said in a smooth, calm voice, hoping to soothe whatever was going on with him. "You can put the dress in my wardrobe if that makes you happy. I didn't mean to be offensive."

But there was no change in his posture. He still eyed her like a predator. Her instincts were screaming at her to run, and run now. Ever so carefully, she gathered her robe in one hand and moved a step back, then another, and another until she'd moved around the end of the bed's other post.

The warlord ran his hand along the opposite bedpost. He studied the wooden frame like it held all the answers in the world and then seemed to speak to it. "Each time I expect you to break, you become stronger. It's beautiful. I..." he turned to face her, "I actually find myself wondering how far I can bend you."

"Excuse me?" His words made her shudder. Something was very wrong here. Even the cadence of his voice had changed, and his speech was almost lilting. It was as though a different person inhabited his body. She placed a hand on Nali in an attempt to steel her nerves. "Are you drunk?" she asked again.

"No, my dear wild one. I'm in agony."

"What do you mean?" Maybe if she kept him speaking, she'd have time to get closer to the door.

"Because I want—no, need—something I shouldn't. When I contemplate the idea, it infuriates me, even makes my gut churn." His eyes narrowed and his lips compressed. "The two of you are far too alike."

Her fingers tightened in Nali's fur, earning her a chuff of indignation, but Sage paid it no mind. She snuck a glance at the door. She knew there was the possibility she was blowing the situation out of proportion and overreacting, but her gut told her something wasn't right. He wasn't in control of himself. A memory flashed through her mind of Rhys in his berserker rage. It was possible the warlord was almost at his edge. He wasn't between her and the door yet, though. He was faster than she, so she might only have one chance. She needed to tread with care.

She took a step toward him and channeled the real concern she felt for her own safety into false concern for him. "What can I do to help? You've helped me so much already." The words she spoke were true. Despite their horrid day, he'd been nothing but attentive and kind up until this point. But if he *was* going to lose it, she would not be a casualty. It was time to get out until he calmed down or got over whatever seemed to be taking him over.

"You can do nothing, Sage," he replied, and then sighed.

She took another step toward him and almost faltered when she saw his eyes track her progress with hawk-like focus. She steeled herself, though, and moved steadily forward.

"Nothing?" She was only a few steps from him and about fifteen steps from the door. She could make it, but she needed to surprise him.

"No. You can't change your imperfections or your heritage."

She stilled. Imperfections? Heritage? The words echoed in her mind, familiar. She'd heard almost those exact words from Rhys when he'd been tormenting her. The memory flashed through her mind: *Inferior heritage, disgusting imperfections...* The air froze in her lungs as something unsettling occurred to her. *Stars above, no...* Had Rhys' insanity been a product of Zane's influence? Could Zane be the originator of those barbaric ideas? But how could that be true? Truth or not, she had to escape *now*.

She lunged for the door, her quivering muscles screaming. Her heart galloped in her chest as she wrenched open the door, but there wasn't enough room to slip into the hallway before he hooked an arm around her. Sage let loose a scream and caught the calm expression of one guard before Zane pulled her back against him and landed a hand on the door, slamming it closed.

Then his breath was in her ear. "You can't run from me. It's only fair, really, as I haven't been able to run from your memory for years."

Memory? She screamed again and lifted her legs to the door, pushing against it with all her might. Just as she hoped, it upset their balance enough that they crashed to the floor. Sage pulled herself to her feet and lunged for the door again. Zane stepped in front of her and held his arms out, a smirk on his face.

She skidded and turned toward the draperies. Maybe she could make it out the window. She zeroed in on a lamp. That would break the glass.

But she wasn't fast enough. Again, the warlord's arms encircled her. "Why are you trying to run, wild one? There's nowhere to go."

"Let me go!"

"Never." He punctuated the word with a bite, latching onto the skin between her neck and shoulder.

She cried out, pain pulsing from the spot he'd bitten. "Please stop, Zane. You're not yourself."

"I am, actually. I finally am." He tightened his grip on her body and dragged her backward, away from the window.

Sage jerked her head to the side, her eyes widened in fear. "No! You're drunk. You don't know what you're doing." He didn't slow down. She clawed at his arms and fought harder. She had not survived the jungle and Rhys only to be ravished today. She'd die first. "Zane, stop! Just think about this first!"

"I'm afraid that's all I've been doing. All day, every day. My control can only last so long."

She screamed again when he pushed her face down onto the bed. She tried to scramble away, but his hand closed around her ankle and jerked her back. She pulled the dagger he'd given her from its sheath and then gasped as he dropped his weight down onto her, pinning her arms and legs, his hand closing around the dagger.

"No," she cried desperately, straining with all her might to hold on to her only weapon.

He dug his finger into the web of her fingers, and like magic, her hand released the blade without her consent. She twisted her face to the side and arched her neck, so she could breathe and keep herself from suffocating in the pillows. "Please don't do this. I'm Sage Blackwell, your friend. Don't do this," she pleaded. "I'm your friend. Work through your berserker rage. This isn't what you want."

"That's where you're wrong. You've never seen what I've wanted and you still haven't a clue." Suddenly, she felt cool metal bite into her neck as he held something to her throat. She jerked, and a sharp edge of metal pierced the fragile skin where her pulse hammered.

"Hold still or you'll hurt yourself," he commanded.

"Go to hell."

"I own it, and I'll make you queen of it. You'll suffer as much as I have."

As he said these words, she felt him squeeze the metal around her neck until it encircled her like a collar. She wheezed at the pressure, choking on her pain and panic. The warlord yanked her back off the bed as she coughed and tried to catch a breath.

"Help!" she huffed, but it was barely audible.

He spun her to face the mirror, one hand banding around her waist and arms, immobilizing her; the other lifted her chin to display what was constricting her breathing. She gasped and tried to look away, but his bruising grip held her still.

It was the crown. Roses and thorns. Obsidians and rubies. Death and Blood. It wrapped around her neck like a beautifully-crafted animal collar.

"Lovely," he purred, watching her reaction in the mirror. "For so long, I've wanted my crown on your skin, it's been unbearable."

One finger slipped from under her chin to caress her lips. "Do you like it?"

Sage tried to bite his wandering finger. "Don't touch me!"

He smiled, looking pleased. "It's too bad you don't share my appreciation, Sage."

How was she to get away now? Letting her legs buckle beneath her, she dropped her entire body weight. If he had been any other man, it would've worked. But she should have known better; he wasn't just any man. She hung in his grasp while he simply smiled at her like she was an indulgent child.

"I guess if you insist on misbehaving, you'll need to be restrained."

"No!" She struggled harder. If he tied her, there was no escape. She ignored the thorns biting into her neck as she fought him. She cried out and threw her head back into his face, stomping on his instep. It did nothing. He simply picked her up and carried her to the wall where he yanked down a tapestry. Her horror doubled as she discovered chains behind it, secured to stone. She screamed bloody murder. *"Help!"*

In a move both smooth and painful, he secured her hands above her head, then stepped back, rubbing his chin as though admiring his work. Her breath see-sawed in and out of her chest, and her legs quivered with exhaustion. She strained against the manacles, and the familiar feeling sent a wildness through her as she flashed back to the dungeon and Rhys.

"I'm not him," the warlord said quietly.

How did he know what she was thinking?

"You're everything like him." How had she been so blind? But why trick her into trusting him? He had her weak and sick when he discovered her in the cell. Or was that a lie, too? Her mind spun, but she couldn't untangle anything with the panic riding her. "Why?" she shouted.

The warlord rushed toward her and pushed her into the wall, both of his arms caging her in. "Because you're too alluring for your own good!" His eyes darted between hers. "I should be disgusted by your imperfections, by your green eyes." He ran a hand along her exposed collarbone. "By your creamy, scarred skin—but I'm not."

Rage flashed across his face; he slammed his hands against the wall, making plaster from the ceiling rain down around them. She cringed back from him. Just how strong was he?

He stepped back and jerked his shirt into place. "I should just take you and get this over with."

Revulsion overwhelmed her, and she pressed herself hard into the wall. "No."

"No?" he scoffed and took a step closer. "Nothing but 'yes' should come out of your mouth. You'd be lucky if I took you." His gaze dropped to her body and stayed there. "You'd love it, revel in it."

She gagged. "That's exactly what it would be: *taking*," she replied, trying to gain his attention from where it was currently fixated. "I would never consent."

"I doubt that," he whispered. Carefully, he reached out a finger and ran it over her chest.

She hunched her shoulders forward in an attempt to make her breasts smaller.

"There's no need to hide. I've seen it all before, Sage. Every inch of your skin has been bared to me." He moved closer, pressing his body along hers, his lips brushing her temple. "I promise it will be so good, but I'll wait. It will be all the more sweet when you cave in to me."

She panted harder, his excitement making bile flood her mouth. "I'll make it terrible. That is *my* promise."

He ignored her comment. "And lucky for me, I can introduce to you all the pleasures of intimacy. In this way, you're different. She was never innocent."

She froze. Who was he talking about? Another woman he'd been with? "You will introduce me to nothing."

Zane chuckled, his voice rough as his hands roamed down her body and wedged between the wall and her butt. "I can tell when you lie, wild one. Something tells me that the crown prince did not touch your flesh." His hands traced from the back of her around to the front, and his fingers slipped inside her robe to caress her bare thigh.

Her breath hitched as he continued his journey upward. She snapped her teeth at the warlord, a smug smile on his lips, his pupils dilated. "Get your hands off me!"

"I've never appreciated our garments, or lack thereof," he murmured, his eyes never leaving hers, as though enjoying her reaction. "I suspect Aermia is different in this way. You have too much modesty. It's useless."

Her panic increased as his hand inched higher. She bucked against him. "Stop!" When that didn't work, she used her last resort. She spat into his face.

The smirk on his face dissolved; he pulled his hand from inside her robe and placed it over the juncture of her thighs.

"Don't test me."

Sage's breathing was shallow. She was very aware that only a flimsy piece of barely-tied linen protected her.

Zane pressed his forehead to hers and kept eye contact. "I can feel the heat of you," he growled and then licked his lips.

"You're vulgar," she spat, turning her head to the side.

"And barbaric. So you've told me," he purred.

He removed his hand and pressed against her, his hips snug with her, and she shuddered, disgusted. She didn't know which was worse, his hands or his body.

He placed a small kiss behind her ear like a lover, not a ravisher. "Sage," he groaned. "What am I going to do with you? I should have just had you bred, but when I saw you in my throne room covered in dirt, grime, and blood, glaring at me with your emerald gaze, I knew you were special. You were the one."

Sage had tuned him out and was staring at the curtains covering the window. Her escape had been so close all along, and yet she had never even dreamed of running. Stupid. Her stupidity never ceased to amaze her.

"You're not stupid, Sage. Far from it, actually. I'd never say this to your face, but it's one of the things I like about you," Tehl whispered.

Relief filled her at the sound of his voice. She wasn't alone. Fingers touched her chin gently and forced her gaze back to Zane's face.

"You have no more energy to fight him off. The time for fighting is over, love. It's time to hide, okay? It's alright to let go. You need not be aware for this. I'll protect you."

The warlord watched her as he pressed his lips to hers. Sage didn't fight, didn't respond. He pulled back and cocked his head, frowning. "Kiss me once like you mean it, and I shall leave you unmolested."

It took her a moment to process what he was saying. She barely had any energy left. "Forever, or just tonight?"

"Forever."

She narrowed her eyes. "I don't believe you."

"You know me, Sage. Have I ever taken anything that wasn't offered?"

The question confused her. Had he ever taken anything? No. But he wasn't in his right mind. Or was he? Was he crazy, or did the berserker rage work differently with him? She mentally slapped herself. Why was she trying to find an excuse for him?

He must have seen her thinking about it and pounced. "I want you willing. I will not force anything from you. It's barbaric and disgusting. Any man can force a woman, but seduction? That takes skill. Come to me willingly and life will continue as it has." He smiled beautifully as he spoke and she hated it. It was so unfair that the rot in his soul wasn't evident on his face. "It's just one kiss. Be reasonable."

It was more than that. It meant her surrender. It would be *her* choice.

"Sage, he's telling the truth," Tehl whispered again. "Protect yourself at all costs. Just imagine me when kissing him."

She squared off with the warlord. "One kiss."

Anticipation flashed across his face. "One."

She expected him to maul her right away, but instead, he paused, his eyes softening as he simply looked at her. He then crooked a finger beneath her chin and raised her face toward his, his thumb tracing the curve of her lower lip.

"Flawless," he whispered and touched his mouth to hers. He drew his hand down her neck to the hollow of her throat just below where he'd forced the metal collar. His breath caressed her skin and her entire body tensed. This was so wrong. She didn't know if she could do this.

"Just breathe. It'll be okay, love," Tehl murmured.

One muscle at a time, she tried to force her body to relax. His arms wound around her so tightly she could hardly breathe. His hands spanned her back before leisurely exploring her curves, their trailing path leaving her skin crawling. He held her securely against him and tangled one hand in her loose tresses, cupping the back of her head as he first brushed his lips across the bow of her top lip, then her full bottom lip, his touch feather-light. When he began softly nibbling at it, she started shaking. This was too much. *I'm sorry, Tehl.* Everywhere he touched felt dirty, and guilt pooled in her belly.

He pulled back, his fingertips touching her chin and tracing her jaw, catching the wet trails of tears she didn't know she'd shed. "It's all right, love. Open for me."

More tears burned in her eyes, but she closed them to keep them from falling. This was her choice, no matter how sick and twisted it was. He cupped the side of her face gently, and kissed her like he could consume her. One tear squeezed out when he moaned quietly. She sucked a deep breath when his hand slid down, fingers brushing across the tender skin under her jaw, then trailing over her abused neck.

Stars above, she couldn't do this. It was too much. She turned her head to the side to break the kiss. His mouth traveled across her jaw and along the side of her neck, following the path of his hand. His fingers caught the edge of her robe and pushed the fabric off her shoulder. The cold air made her shiver, and her eyes slammed open as he nipped at her collarbone.

Tehl stood behind the warlord, staring at her over Zane's shoulder. He gave her a tender look. Sorrow rose, howling inside her, choking her. All that time she spent fighting Tehl, making him the villain, blaming him, and yet he wasn't the monster of her story, he was the hero. He'd always been the hero, albeit an awkward one.

Zane lifted his head, his hooded gaze scorching her. "That was as exquisite as I imagined it to be."

Sage stared at him, knowing he'd taken something from her she'd never get back. His hand slid down into her robe to cup her bare belly.

His fingers caressed the skin, and his smile was all male satisfaction. "Just imagine what you'll look like when you're swollen with my child."

All of her muscles locked down. "Excuse me?"

He graced her with one of his heart-stopping smiles. "You'll make a wonderful consort, and our children will make the most powerful warriors. Just imagine Aermia and Scythia ruling together."

"You're out of your damned mind," she blurted. "I'm married."

"No, I promise you, you are not." His smile was sin and the devil rolled into one. "Wild one, do you remember when I saved you from that hole? Healers were necessary, and so was an examination."

"What?" she asked through numb lips. He couldn't mean...

He cupped her cheek, a tender look on his face. "I had to be sure.

I couldn't make you mine if you'd been used. Imagine my excitement when my healers informed me you were pure. Your marriage is void if not consummated. You, my love, will be my queen. And make no mistake, I won't make the same mistake as the Aermian prince."

"I will never marry you. I'll die first." She meant it.

He chuckled like she was amusing him. "There are a great many things that you, my love, will do for those you love."

"You're just like Rhys," she whispered. "He said something similar to me once."

The warlord scoffed. "He's nothing like me, but a cheap imitation. I'm the original."

"How could I be so blind?" she muttered.

"It's not your fault. You're young and naïve still. Time hasn't jaded you or turned you into a suspicious shrew. It's a good thing."

"You disgust me."

"Disgust can turn to love."

He was delusional. "You can take many things from me, but my love will not be one of them."

The warlord studied her. "I have plenty of time, but I think you need a visit from the dead to inspire you to action."

Dread filled her. "The dead?" she croaked.

"Yes, I think Jasmine needs to visit."

CHAPTER TWENTY

Tehl

Sweat dripped down Tehl's forehead and into his eyes. He swiped a quick hand across his brow, his eyes never leaving his opponent. It took only one moment of distraction to lose your life.

His arms screamed in protest as he met his attacker head-to-head, their swords flashing in the morning light as they crashed into each other. Tehl clenched his jaw and pushed against their crossed swords, hoping to upset the other's balance.

"You'll have to do better than that," his brother heckled.

Tehl spun out from their lock and retreated, his teeth bared in a ferocious smile. He kept his steps light as he maneuvered around Sam and met each thrust and cut of his sword. Every move was calculated on his part for, slowly but surely, he was wearing his opponent out.

"You have enough yet?" Tehl taunted him.

Blue eyes, so like his own, narrowed on him. "Big words for the man who passed out after yesterday's bout."

He glared at his brother, but didn't take the bait. He knew better than to let anger take reign over his actions. Giving into anger made you sloppy; it made you lose. Instead, he coolly assessed his brother's form as they sparred. The spymaster had been favoring his right side for the last five minutes.

Having ascertained what he needed to, Tehl lunged. As he moved in a sequence of attacks, Sam dropped to the ground and slid under Tehl's arm, only to pop up behind him and place his sword on the back of Tehl's neck.

"You lose."

"Swamp apples," he muttered. The crown prince's chest sawed in and out as he fought to catch his breath. He slid his sword into his scabbard and yanked his sweat-soaked shirt over his head. A whistle had him turning his neck and arching a brow at his brother. "What?"

"By the time Sage gets home, she won't even recognize you with all those muscles and bruises."

Tehl scowled and shrugged on the clean shirt an Elite had handed him. He didn't bother with the buttons and crossed his arms over his chest, self-consciousness striking him.

His brother barked out a laugh. "Only you would be embarrassed by that comment." Sam took on a thoughtful expression. "Maybe I should have my wife kidnapped...then I could be motivated enough to look like you."

His levity disappeared. It was like his brother had thrown cold water on him; as if he needed a reminder of his worries. "And you say I never watch *my* mouth."

Sam's smile faded. "What would you have me do? If you can't laugh about it, why live?"

"Well, it's not funny," he growled back.

"You're right, it's not, but it's how I handle things. You know that."

Tehl shook his head. "Well, this time it's not right."

Sam scrubbed a hand down his face. "What then? Ought I to deal with this situation like you? Work constantly, hardly eat, and spar while you're supposed to be sleeping? How's that working for you, huh? You know you're at the end of your rope, so you tell me which of our coping methods is healthier."

Tehl dropped his head to stare at the sand beneath his feet. His brother had a point, but it didn't make this any easier. He was occupied enough with his duties as ruler during the day that he simply forgot to eat, but at night... Well, at night he found he just *couldn't* sleep. His dreams frequently featured Sage these days and in them, he was always searching for her, but she always died right before he reached her. He rubbed his chest. Her scent had even begun to fade from their room. He swallowed hard and met his brother's sympathetic gaze.

"It troubles me... more than I'd like to admit." That wasn't something he'd planned on sharing, but it was true.

Sam crossed the circle and clasped his arm. "I know. The black bags beneath your eyes attest to that. When was the last time you had a decent night's sleep?"

His response was automatic: "The night before she disappeared."

His brother sucked in a breath. "As long as that?"

Anger sparked inside him and he shook off Sam's hand. "How can I sleep, knowing she is suffering or she might be...?" He couldn't finish the thought.

"She's not dead. We have to believe in that."

"It's been over two months." He paused, his face sober. "Honestly? There's a part of me that almost hopes she is," he confessed, though the admission caused a familiar pang of guilt. He watched his brother's expression, awaiting judgment for his words, but none came. He blew out a relieved breath. It seemed his brother understood that in some situations death was a mercy and a kindness.

"She's strong. She'll make it through this," Sam assured. When his brother didn't seem relieved, he added, "She will... She has to."

"Even if she does, in what condition will we find her, Sam? Will she still be Sage, or will she be a shell? Or perhaps worse?"

"We can't know and it's better to leave the *what if*s alone. You can't worry over something that might never happen."

"I know." And logically, he did. But since Sage had snuck into his life, things weren't as clear and logical as they used to be. His attention shifted to Garreth, who was striding in their direction at a clipped pace, his limp barely noticeable.

"News, my lord. We've finally received news!"

He exchanged a shocked look with his brother, before they both ran toward the man.

"What news?"

"We've received a letter from Scythia. It's awaiting you in the war room."

"Make sure Lilja and Hayjen are notified," Tehl commanded, already heading that way.

"They're here already."

Tehl simply nodded and sprinted into the palace. The hallways and doors blurred as his mind focused on one thing: getting to the war room and reading the contents of that letter. He burst through the doors and scanned his council as he took his chair. "Where is it?"

"Here, my lord." Gav held out a sealed letter.

Tehl stared at it for several heartbeats, slightly afraid of the information it contained. He took a breath and commanded, "Please read it, Gavriel."

His cousin nodded and cracked the seal with his dagger. Gav first scanned the document and then began reading:

"'To the lord of the Aermian kingdom, the warlord of Scythia sends his greetings.

It was somewhat of a shock when we discovered one of your messengers bearing a missive. It's been a long time since Scythia's been in contact with the outside world, so please excuse my manners if they offend.'"

Gav pulled in a breath and continued: "'Many years have passed since the atrocity my ancestors committed against Nagali, yet my people continue to suffer for crimes which they did not commit. It has been hundreds of years. I understand that a crime of that magnitude can never be wiped away, nor should it. But I offer to make atonement in the way of restoration. I want to restore what was lost in Nagali. With time, we can honor those who have fallen.'"

Jeren scoffed. "How could one atone for that? Bring all those dead back to life? Even with the use of science, I'm sure that isn't possible."

Tehl ignored his outburst and nodded to Gav. "Please continue."

"'Most of my people have never been outside Scythia, nor encountered someone of a different race. The beliefs of our ancestors have slowly faded over the years, leaving us an isolated people with a bloody, shameful history. But I believe my people deserve to experience life beyond our kingdom, so I will accept your olive branch. It is our desire to reach an understanding that will bring both our kingdoms into lasting peace and prosperity.

"'However, I'm a cautious man, and I can't help but feel suspicious of the fact that this treaty coincides with the arrival of a certain female in my kingdom. She has assured me, though, of your good intentions, and I must say it is only by her counsel that I accept your offer, albeit somewhat blindly. She has also advised me that, as neither side will feel safe in each other's territory, I should find an alternative. Therefore, I propose we do so in the middle, or, in this case, where it all began. In Nagali. There's a palace near both our borders where we can begin negotiations. It's prudent to let you know that Sage Blackwell is very well looked after. Our interactions have become a special part of my day and I admit, I cherish our intimacy. In fact, one would be remiss in not seeking her stimulating company whenever possible. I have, of course, offered to bring her to the Mort Wall for your retrieval but, dedicated as she is to peace, she has thus far insisted on staying.'"

"Lies," Lilja hissed, her eyes flashing. "My Sage would never stay there! Especially not without consulting her family!"

Gav nodded and began again. "'Also, I hope you've shown the same consideration to my woman, Blaise. It's important to me she continues unharmed and well cared for.'" Gavriel's hand tightened on the letter. "'I'm sure you can relate to my concern, as, it would be likewise unpardonable if Sage were to fall ill or be hurt during her stay in our nation.'"

"That's a blatant threat," Zachael snarled.

"'But have not a care, I'll do my utmost to keep her safe, warm, and loved during her time here. My messengers will be on their side of the Mort Wall and are instructed to wait until they receive your response. I send my best wishes and hopes that you continue on in health and prosperity. Your humble servant, Zane Ziy, Lord of Scythia.'"

There was a beat of silence before his council erupted.

"You can't trust a word of that document!" Lelbiel stated.

"He wants us to meet him in Nagali? Where the man-eaters roam unchecked? Surely, it's a trap!" William shouted.

"It would be a terrible place to wage war," Zachael retorted.

"And he presumes to threaten us! *Us*!" Jeren yelled.

"Silence!" Tehl's father commanded over the din.

Tehl looked to his father, who'd been silent until that moment. "What say you, my king?"

His father's face was stern. "The warlord mentioned some valid concerns. We don't know what's been happening over there, thus we cannot say for a certainty that he was the one to sanction the attacks and kidnappings which have been taking place."

"I respectfully beg to differ, my king," Lilja said softly.

His father looked over to the Sirenidae. "Can you be sure that the same man is leading?"

Her lips thinned. "No, I cannot. I lost my contact within Scythia fifteen years ago, but I believe they are the same. I can't give you proof, only my experience and my observations."

The king dipped his chin. "Thank you. We need to be cautious, but we must also have our minds open." He turned to William. "Is Nagali such a bad middle ground? From his letter, I know of the place he speaks. It's just beyond Scythia and Aermia's borders, at the base to the Kugami Mountains."

Old William's face scrunched up as he thought. "I need to study the area to be sure."

"I have extensive maps of that area," Lelbiel added. "They might need some updating, but it's nothing the scouts couldn't take care of."

"Good," the king remarked. "Son, your thoughts?"

Tehl stared at his father, the air around him seeming to turn to water. *Safe. Warm. Loved.* Drowning, he was drowning. "Did no one miss the statement of 'safe, warm, and loved'? Or his use of the word 'intimacy' when he spoke of their interactions and his enjoyment of her 'stimulating company'?" Silence descended as his voice echoed around the room. "What is he doing to my wife?"

"We can't know for s—" Sam began.

Tehl stabbed a finger in his direction. "Don't you placate me. You're the spymaster and the trickster of words. Was that not blatant verbiage for sex?"

Sam snapped his mouth shut and his eyes shuttered. "It was."

"Do you have any doubt of her having been abused at his hands?"

"No, I don't," Lilja whispered, answering for Sam. "Even if she looks whole and beautiful when we see her, we won't know what she's suffering inside."

The very idea brought on a flood of unknown emotion. He'd

always been awkward when it came to feeling so, because he didn't know how to react; he packed his feelings away in a box. But today, the box would not close. Rage, anguish, and frustration all poured out of him. He slammed his hands against the table and let out a roar. He ignored the shocked looks on his councilors' faces as he shoved back from the table, his chair clattering to the ground behind him. "Why do we need to accommodate this monster?"

"Because it means Sage's life."

Tehl swung his gaze to Rafe. "What?"

"If we do not accomplish this and put on the most amazing show for the Scythian warlord, she will die." The rebellion leader paused, staring him in the eye. "Or worse, he'll keep her."

Tehl inhaled deeply, getting his anger under control. His emotions had been getting more and more out of hand the longer he went without news of Sage. He sparred and it helped; the energy he expelled calmed him for a time, but it wasn't quite enough. He righted his chair and took a seat. One by one, he scanned the council, pausing on Zachael. "Our army?"

"Close, but I'm afraid we still need more time."

He nodded and tucked that away. "Then I guess that leaves us one option." His voice took on a dangerous edge. "We accept the good warlord's invitation and prepare to give him hell."

CHAPTER TWENTY-ONE

Sage

She shifted painfully from one aching foot to the other. Stars above, everything hurt. At one point in the night, her legs had collapsed. The metal manacles had bitten into her wrists, and it'd taken everything she had not to break down. She didn't, though, and she wouldn't. She wouldn't give him that satisfaction. After several torturous hours, she'd finally found the strength to stand again.

She tilted her head back against the stone to stare at the dark ceiling, thinking of the previous night. For hours, she'd berated herself and examined each of her conversations with the warlord. After his display last night... Sage shuddered. When she'd looked into his deranged eyes, she'd felt her soul grow cold. She'd been scared in her life before, but something about last night had been worse than anything she'd ever experienced. What kind of monster's lair had she wandered into? Even now, she didn't know, and there was a part of her that still hoped Zane would walk in nursing a hangover. She hoped he wasn't truly evil.

She banged her head against the wall at the last thought. That part of her was foolish but insistent, and she didn't quite understand it. It was like she wanted him to be... What *did* she want him to be? Her friend? A good person? In the light of day, Sage could see it for what it was. It was a longing. She longed for safety, for home, for her family, for her friends, and for Tehl, but in lieu of those things, it seemed her mind sought those things in Zane. Something was wrong with her.

The door slammed open and cracked against the stone wall. She swallowed hard when the warlord sauntered in and smiled boyishly. He moved toward her, her customary breakfast in his hands.

"Good morning, wild one. I hope you slept well."

Inwardly, she quelled. Everything was normal about him—well, the normal she'd come to know up until very recently. Gone was the hard, imbalanced, and calculating man from last night. However, neither did he rush to her side with apologies, nor help her down from the wall. That in and of itself told her something. Was this some sort of game to him? Or was he truly not well in the mind?

He placed her food on the nightstand and then pinched a piece of bread from the loaf, holding it out to her. "Are you hungry, Sage?"

She eyed the proffered food skeptically. "Is it poisoned?"

His deep chuckle washed over her, and she dared to peek at him. What she saw made her gasp. He was smiling at her with love and adoration. What in the world? Was he normal again?

He popped the piece of bread into his mouth, never losing eye contact, and brushed the back of his fingers along her cheek. After he'd swallowed, he asked, "Will you eat now?"

"Will you unchain me?" she ventured.

"Not right now. As much as it pains me to have something so wild and exotic chained like a slave, it's really in your best interest. You'll have to stay this way for your protection." He actually had the audacity to look hurt by it, as if he was not in control of the situation.

"In what world is this protection?"

Rather than respond, the warlord pinched off another piece of bread and placed it at her lips. Sage took the morsel from his fingers and chewed slowly, confused by the brilliant smile he gave her. Had the kingdom been turned on its head? Everything felt off-kilter.

He held the broth to his lips and sipped, then offered it to her. She placed her lips on the cup and slurped, watching him over the rim. What was his game?

A hand brushed her collarbone and then her chest. Sage sputtered and jerked back, knocking the broth from his hand. It crashed to the floor and stillness filled the room, as if awaiting violence.

Sage coughed and glared at the warlord through watering eyes. His reaction, though, wasn't what she'd anticipated. Instead of responding angrily, he let loose a heavy sigh, gathering the broken pieces of clay into his hand.

"One day, Sage, you won't fear me as you do now. You'll accept my kindness without question, and my touch without shuddering. This, I vow."

Not in this life. But she kept her thoughts to herself, staring at the broth that had soaked her robe, rendering the thin fabric translucent. Color heated her cheeks when she realized the fabric was translucent. The warlord stood and stilled as he, too, seemed to notice. Her breath froze in her lungs when he moved closer.

"Goddess," he whispered. "Lead, and I will follow." He looked into her face and touched one finger to her blush. "Do not be ashamed of such beauty. It's a gift many covet, and yours is natural. That's rare. It's a treasure."

"One that is mine," she whispered.

He leaned closer, his words whispering over her skin. "One that is *mine*. This time it will be my choice."

She went rigid at his statement. "You're mistaken...or just deranged." She inwardly winced. She needed to tread carefully. If she needled him too much, there could be a repeat of the night before.

He took a step back and studied her, amusement touching his face. "I like this side of you, Sage. The warrior queen I met in my throne room all those weeks ago is starting to peek out again."

"My lord?" A warrior stepped into the doorway with a bow.

"Yes?" Zane answered, glancing over his shoulder.

"We have what you requested."

"Ah, yes!" The warlord turned back to her and clapped his

hands. "I've arranged a gift for you. Bring her in."

A warrior swung into the room, toting someone Sage had never dreamt she could see again. "Jas?" she whispered, tears springing to her eyes.

Jasmine stared at her and lunged forward. "Sage!"

The male holding her jerked her back. "Do not speak in the warlord's presence unless asked. And bow to your betters." He tossed Jasmine to the ground. She landed on her hands and knees. That had to be painful, but her friend didn't utter a sound of complaint as she knelt before the warlord.

Zane stepped up to Jasmine, and a sound of protest escaped Sage's lips. He glanced back at her with a raised brow. Some of her distress must have shown on her face, because he gave her a warm, reassuring smile which did nothing to reassure her. It rather did the opposite. He turned back to Jasmine and leaned down, tipping up her chin. Sage ran her eyes over her friend's face. There weren't any bruises or cuts, just what seemed to be evidence of lack of sleep.

"Aermia has a way of creating enchanting creatures, despite their imperfections, don't they, Phoenix?"

The warrior nodded and watched Jasmine with a look that spoke a bit too much possessiveness. "Indeed. If nothing else, their spirits are to be admired."

"I agree," Zane murmured, turning Jasmine's face from one side to the other. "Her blue eyes are off-putting, but her facial structure and build are amenable. She'll do nicely."

Nicely for what? Sage stifled her question for fear of his reaction while handling her friend.

"Stand, woman," the warlord commanded.

Jas stood and kept her gaze pinned to the floor. He spun her around and led her by the hand until she stood an arm's length away from Sage. Jas' eyes met hers and tears dripped down her face.

"I'll give you a minute. Enjoy your gift, wild one." The warlord let Jas go and moved to speak with the warrior.

Jasmine rushed to her and wrapped her arms around her. "Oh, God. I never thought I'd see you again."

A sob escaped her. "You died," she choked out. "I was told you died. I lost you, Jas. I've mourned you this whole time!"

Jasmine pulled back and clasped Sage's face. "But I'm fine. I'm here, you see? I'm here! Are you okay?"

"I'm fine."

"I saw you at the execution."

Sage's stomach dropped. "You did?"

"You look different."

A chill ran down Sage's spine. "Is it bad?"

The skin around Jasmine's eyes tightened. "Not bad, but," she hesitated, "you're starting to seem… flawless."

The idea sickened her. "It wasn't by choice," she whispered.

"I don't doubt you. The power to choose is a rare commodity here."

Sage caught movement over Jasmine's shoulder as the warlord made his way back toward them. Panic filled her. "I love you, sis."

"Love you, too, sis," Jas croaked.

The warlord closed a hand around Jasmine's arm and pulled her from Sage. "That's enough." In a quick move, he drew a dagger from his side and placed it at her friend's throat. His gaze captured Sage's. "Do you love her?"

"You know the answer."

"I fear you will be unruly without something to hold you in

check."

Sage's gaze wavered to Jas and back to the warlord. "Have I been unruly?"

"No, but I can sense rebellion building within you. I've dealt with rebellion before, so I know what it looks like." He frowned and blinked as if willing a memory away. "I need your compliance in all things."

"I promise," she answered quickly.

His smile became bitter. "I know you, and I've told you not to lie to me." He slashed the skin of Jasmine's shoulder, making her cry out and try to pull away from him.

"No!" Sage jerked forward with a cry, only to have her chains pull her back. "Leave her alone! She's done nothing wrong."

"You're right, Sage, she hasn't. But you have. Look at the price of your lies." He pressed his finger into Jasmine's wound and her friend's face turned white. His face was a mask of anger when he returned his gaze to her face. "Look what you made me do, Sage! I hate this! Now, answer me."

"I didn't lie!" she shouted, continuing to tug on her manacles.

"More lies!" He moved the dagger back to Jasmine's throat. "Swear to me you'll be obedient, or I'll slit her throat where she stands. Choose carefully. Her life is in your hands."

"I'll obey. I'll obey. Just let her go!"

He observed her. "I believe you, this time. Phoenix! Grab your woman and send for a healer."

The warrior glided forward and took her pale friend from the warlord. Jasmine stared at her and didn't even bother to struggle.

"Don't take her away! Please!"

But the warrior paid her no mind and slipped out the door with Jasmine in tow. Sage tore her gaze from the door after it closed to glare at the warlord.

"Damn it!" He wiped the blood off his hand, his agitation apparent as he jerked his fingers across the fabric. "I hate this."

She wanted to hit something. "Why?" she whispered, knowing he could hear her.

Zane cocked his head. "I can see your anger, Sage, and that's only natural. But, remember what you promised. How you act in the future will affect Jasmine. Your transgressions will result in punishments for her, and I'd hate for you to witness that."

"You're sick."

He gave her a tender look. "You think that now, but I think, in time, you'll understand." He reached for the bread and held it out to her. "You need to eat."

She wanted to refuse, to spit at him and shout obscenities, but she didn't. Like a good little captive, she bit into the bread and ate every bite.

The warlord lifted a lock of her hair and rubbed it between his fingers. "Adjustment periods are always difficult, but don't worry. It'll get easier." He pursed his lips and stared at her wrists. "You're bleeding," he said flatly.

Sage blinked and looked up at her hands. Sure enough, blood was dripping down her arms. She hadn't even noticed it.

"You must not harm yourself, or I'll have to take drastic measures. Do you remember your first cell?"

Terror overwhelmed her. Darkness.

He nodded. "I see that you do. I'll be back later to clean your wounds, but I'd like you to think about what your actions have wrought today. I hope you choose to do better next time. I don't want our lives to be like this. I desire peace. This fighting gets old."

Peace? What a joke. The promise of peace is what he'd lured

her in with the first time. He might utter pretty words and make fine promises, but that was all they were. "I meant what I said," she said softly. "Did you, Zane?" Something glinted in his eyes. Pleasure. She thought back to what she'd said. Zane. She'd used his name. Sage filed that away. That information could prove useful later.

"I always mean what I say. Have I broken my word?"

"No."

"Show a little faith, wild one."

"Do you think you deserve my faith and trust?"

"Have I ever hurt you?" he countered.

She glanced up to her bloody wrists and back to him, saying nothing.

"You did that to yourself. Think about it, Sage. Have I ever really hurt you? Have I left scars on your body, or ever taken a hand to you?"

"No," she drew out. "But you've wounded me just the same."

He cocked his head as he regarded her. "You are the crown jewel of my accomplishments. I have a feeling we will change everything."

"Change everything how?" Unease rolled in her gut.

"By ripping apart the world, piece by piece. Then, once we're done, we'll reshape it into something better."

CHAPTER TWENTY-TWO

Jasmine

Her shoulder burned, and the men hovering around her weren't helping the situation.

"What did you do to anger the warlord?"

"We told you to keep your mouth shut! Why can't you do what you're told?"

"She's reckless, Phoenix. She'll get us all killed."

"Enough," Phoenix growled, lifting her arm to clean the wound.

Jasmine winced and stared past the men crowding her. The image of Sage chained to the wall in a translucent robe was frozen in her mind. What had the warlord done to her? She looked like herself...but not. She winced when Phoenix probed her arm.

"Careful," she growled. "That hurts."

The gigantic warrior glanced at her and then back to his task. "It was necessary."

"What happened?" Mekhl demanded.

"You know I can't reveal that," Phoenix rumbled as he began to bind her arm.

"He used me," she replied flatly.

"For what?" Orion asked, crossing his arms.

"To control—"

"As a demonstration." Phoenix cut her off with a glare, then turned it on the others. "Don't risk all our lives and positions for something as petty as curiosity. Others have disappeared for less." He pinned her with his cinnamon gaze. "And you should know better. It's time to keep silent."

She bit her cheek and looked away. It rankled her that when he demanded her silence, she gave it. She had to admit, she felt guilty for it, she felt like a coward. But she knew she was also being smarter. She'd fought at the beginning. Oh, how she'd fought. But all it led to was punishment. The beginning was the worst. Nightmares still plagued her of the examination forced upon her, and the subsequent drugging that ensued afterward. She'd awoken here, with Phoenix, Mekhl, and Orion staring at her. A tug on her arm pulled her from the memories.

"All done," Phoenix murmured, and then began to clean up his healing supplies.

"Thank you," she said and stood with a stretch. "I think I'd like to go on a walk now."

"No."

She blinked at Phoenix's hard tone. "No?"

He stood to his full imposing height and stared down at her without any emotion. "You've been confined to our home."

"Confined?"

"You're too important to let wander."

His statement didn't comfort her; it did just the opposite. Up until this point, she'd played her part, and in return, they'd allowed her a certain amount of freedom. For instance, she could go for walks, as long as she was escorted. It was the only time she was free of fear, guilt, and self-loathing.

"This is because of our little trip today?"

"Yes. Don't think of sneaking out. The warlord stationed his personal guards outside our door."

Her stomach dropped.

"Is he interested in her?" Orion asked, a hint of worry in his tone.

"No, he's busy with his Aermian consort." Phoenix shook his head. "But Jasmine's a means to an end."

Anxiety churned in her gut. What an apt phrasing: a means to an end. She was an exhibition, a slave and a broodmare already, but now she was to be a means by which a maniac would control Sage. She cast a glance to the men speaking quietly. She hated that they wouldn't hurt her. At the beginning, she'd expected them to beat or torture her, but instead they'd included her in their lives: they spoke with her, took her for walks. But it wasn't because they cared for her personally, not at all. Rather, she was their property, and, as their property, their responsibility; rather like a well-cared-for animal.

She swallowed hard and stared blankly at the wall. The worst part was the night, not because of what she remembered, but because of what she *couldn't* remember. Her breath came heavier as she thought about each night. Apart from the first night, every night since she'd been taken from Sage was a giant blank. No matter how hard she pushed, the veil of darkness wouldn't lift. She could only guess what happened in those blank spots.

The first night still plagued her during daylight hours. She'd been frightened and curled up in a corner. The two walls to her back had brought her a little comfort, while three huge warriors had stood and studied her like she was some sort of animal in a menagerie. They hadn't moved forward to touch her, nor had they spoken. They'd just watched. She'd stared back, terrified to take her eyes off them for even a second, lest one of them attack her.

It had shocked her when, after a few hours of their staring contest, her eyes began to droop. Sleep hadn't come easy when she didn't know what would come next, but her exhausted body won out and demanded sleep, if only for a second.

Apparently, that second turned out to be the whole night, for when Jasmine had blinked her heavy eyelids open, she was no longer in her corner. She iced over when she realized she was in a bed, and not alone. She'd jerked to the side and tried to scramble away. A heavy hand had landed on her thigh, halting her escape. She'd stared at the hand and the warrior sprawled out next to her. He had regarded her in a quiet way and then, slowly, pulled his hand from her leg before wordlessly getting up. He then simply strode away.

She had shivered and leapt from the bed, taking the sheet with her. Her body had not appreciated the maneuver. She hissed, the pain from her ribs robbing her of breath. How did she end up in that bed? She hadn't been able to sleep a full night in days, for every little sound woke her, yet she'd slept through being moved?

When she'd taken another step from the bed, she'd felt an ache in her lower body and the world came to a screeching halt. Her hands trembled, and her lip quivered. That could mean only one thing. Her innocence, had they stolen it? She'd pulled in a deep breath, and bravely pulled the sheet back to examine her body: her old clothing was gone, replaced with a simple nightgown that reached the knee. She had swallowed at the notion that someone had cleaned and changed her, and she never even felt it. What else had happened? Her hand had lifted the hem of her nightgown and paused.

"You can do this, Jas. Don't be a coward."

She'd sneaked a glance to make sure none of the warriors were watching her, and then yanked up her nightgown. Nothing. No blood, no bruising. She had then jerked the nightgown down, shivering, and moved back into the corner, the familiar comfort of the walls to her back. Nothing seemed amiss, yet her body told her something was different.

Jasmine blinked at the hand on her arm and pulled herself back to the present. She looked up into Mekhl's face with a raised brow.

"How are you feeling?"

"Tired," she replied automatically. It was like she couldn't get enough sleep, but that was to be expected with all the healing her body had had to do the last couple months. *Months.* Her heart squeezed. She had been away from the twins for so long. How much had they changed? Did they still miss her? Were they being taken care of?

Orion's soft voice washed over her: "Where do you go when your gaze glazes over?"

"Home," she whispered without thinking.

"This is your home," Phoenix stated, taking a step closer.

"No." She shook her head with a sad smile. "This is my prison."

Phoenix scoffed. "Your prison? Do we have you chained to the wall like the warlord has his woman?"

"She's not his woman."

Orion slapped a hand over her mouth and stared at their door with hard eyes. "You cannot speak like that, Jas. You need to control your speech."

She pried his hand off her face, one finger at a time. "It's never stopped me before."

"You've seen what it's like in the obsidian pit," Mekhl said. "If you cannot control yourself, we will be banished or executed."

Death didn't scare her, but the obsidian pit did. She'd barely managed to catch a glimpse of it before the warriors had taken Sage and herself before the warlord. Curiosity had led her to take her walks there. It wasn't as beautiful close up. Slaves lived in abominable conditions, starved, filthy, beaten and bloody. The depravity and sin in which the Scythians conducted themselves was sickening. Any woman was considered fair game there by the barbaric warriors. She'd had a few close calls herself. If it hadn't been for one of the men, she'd have been raped, or worse. Regardless of how bad it was down there, she kept visiting. It was like she needed to see the terrible conditions to keep herself from doing something stupid—like attempting an escape. Plus, it was one of the few ways she could do something to help. Only Orion knew that she smuggled food down there to feed some of the people.

She turned to Phoenix with her arms crossed and stood tall as he regarded her. "I would choose death before that."

"Brave, but you may not have a choice. You're now part of the warlord's circle. If he comes for you, there's nothing we can do."

A chill skittered down her spine. The way the warlord had examined her with his cold, calculating eyes had pulled the warmth from her body. He was every bit the monster she'd imagined him. But it was when he spoke she saw that he was also insane. Her heart ached for her friend. Had Sage been with him the entire time? What had she experienced at the hands of such a man? Goosebumps broke out on her arms. Her friend looked so different. So foreign. She'd touched Sage's face, needing assurance that her friend was still there. Sage's beauty had become something almost unreal. She resembled the warlord in that way, and it frightened Jasmine.

Rubbing a hand over her arm, she eyed the men, each observing her. It was times like these that she felt guilt. She could be suffering so much more, and yet she wasn't. Even though she hated being a captive, she appreciated the men she'd been sold to. They could've been like that bastard Rhys who'd just enjoyed inflicting pain, but they tended her wounds, spoke to her, fed and clothed her. Really, they didn't ask anything from her except obedience when in the public eye. Yes, it could be much worse.

Times like those were the most trying. She hated acting the slave in front of other warriors, it was demeaning. But it was then she remembered the twins. This wasn't about her anymore. They needed her, so it was her responsibility to do everything she could to survive and eventually get back to them.

"You could always let me go." At their silence, she tried another tactic. "Do any of you have children?"

"No, but by the stars, we hope to in the near future," Mekhl said, his voice holding reverence.

"Before your people took me, I was a mother."

The three men stilled.

"I have twins in Aermia, ones that I desperately miss and adore. I want to go home. They need me."

Phoenix strode forward and lifted her chin. "Lying about children is despicable. They're rare in Scythia and precious. How dare you use them as a way to sway us!"

"It's true. Their names are Jade and Ethan and they're three years old."

His lips thinned. "We know you lie. The healer certified your purity after your examination."

She jerked her chin out of his hand and glared at him. "They are mine, but they're not from my womb. Your people attacked my village, killing my brother and his wife, leaving the twins alone in the world except for me. They became *mine* from that point on."

Phoenix dipped his chin. "Apologies."

She didn't want to acknowledge it, but rarely did they apologize for anything. "Accepted."

"So, you have children?" Mekhl asked.

"I do, and I miss them so much. I worry about them constantly."

"Why are you just telling us of them now?" Orion demanded.

She looked from one man to the next. "Because you need to

know what your kingdom's crimes have wrought, and what sort of place and people you expect me to embrace as home."

"You will never go back there," Phoenix said, softly. "Even if it was possible to grant you escape, you wouldn't survive the trek through the jungle. You barely survived the first time. The best thing you can do is put those children out of your mind. I'm sure your village is taking fine care of them." Something warmed in his eyes. "I'm sorry for what you suffered, but we can't change what's happened. If children are something you want, I'll give them to you. There would be no greater joy in the world than for me to have my own young."

Jasmine choked on her retort as he finished. Phoenix was offering her something that he thought she wanted. He was trying to help, even though it did the opposite. "Could you forget children you'd left alone and helpless?"

Phoenix glanced to the side, his jaw ticking.

"With the way you speak of children, I know the answer is no. Please don't expect me to forget them. They're everything to me. And, as for your offer, I appreciate it, but the answer is no. I don't want to bring more children into this world. It's too dangerous."

"If that's what you wish," Mekhl murmured.

All Jasmine's energy seemed to abandon her, leaving her with a headache and a desire for a nap. "I need to lie down," she muttered and left the group behind her.

She climbed onto the bed and stared at the wall. She had too many problems to solve. Maybe life would look a little simpler after a nap.

CHAPTER TWENTY-THREE

Sage

She'd spend the rest of her life chained to the bloody wall.

She hung against the chains, not caring about her wrists. They were scarred already. What was a little more?

The warlord had left her strung up for five days. *Five days.* By day three, she'd pleaded with him to let her down, her arms numb and her legs feeble. The memory of his response still nauseated her.

He'd kissed her on the temple and cupped her face gently, gazing at her with affection. "This hurts me as much as it hurts you," he had said. "It kills me to have you tied up like this, but it will be better for us in the end. Soon, you'll long for my company." His nose nuzzled at her ear. "To crave my affection." His hand drifted from her cheek to her pulse beating wildly at the base of her throat. "To beg for my touch." Another soft kiss against her temple. "To come to grips with what it means to be *mine*."

To her everlasting shame, she'd told him exactly what he wanted to hear.

But he'd stared right through her with a sad smile. "They don't sound like how I imagined. One day, though, you'll mean those words. Until then, we both must suffer."

And suffer she did.

Each day, she submitted to him wiping her down with a cloth, feeding her from his hand, and conversing with her like they had before. Upon waking today, she was filled with a hopelessness she'd never before experienced. Sage wanted to close her eyes and just sleep forever.

The bathing pool was just in sight, and she had a sudden revelation. She now understood why Ezra had tried to kill her. Somehow, he had seen this coming. In the only way he could, he had tried to save her. Even now, staring at the pool, she wished he had succeeded. That peace Ezra promised? She longed for it and didn't even have the energy to be ashamed of her thoughts.

The door banged open, admitting the savior-turned-tormentor.

His wide, handsome smile should've put her on guard, but at this point, she didn't care what happened.

"I have news I'm sure you'll love."

She hung her head, tuning him out.

A finger slipped under her chin and lifted it up. Black eyes met hers. His smile slowly faded as he studied her. Minutes or hours might have passed as he gazed at her face. "It's done," he whispered in awe.

It took her a moment to realize he was smiling at her—not his normal smile, but the smile that made her heart flip and her chest warm. Despite everything that had happened, when he smiled at her like that, it made everything a little better. Shame filled her. Stars above, she was pathetic.

"It's time for you to come down, wild one."

A slow blink. She couldn't even rouse herself enough to get excited. What if he was just playing with her, only to snatch away her hope?

"Send for Maeve," he commanded.

The warrior who stood just inside his door spun on his heel and disappeared through the door.

"Okay, my lovely. It's time."

Zane moved in close and wrapped an arm around her waist. He lifted her, taking all her weight off her wrists and feet.

Tears sprang to her eyes at the instant relief, and pain swamped her. Her forehead landed on his shoulder as she breathed heavily. A small cry escaped her when he moved her arm from the one manacle and placed it around his neck. Hell, it hurt so bad.

"I know it hurts, but it will get better. I promise."

Her body trembled against his as he removed the chain from the wall and laid her down on the bed. His hands circled her arms and rubbed at them. More tears blurred her vision.

"It hurts."

"Patience. This will help."

Sage bit her lip to keep her cries of pain locked away as he worked feeling back into her arms.

"You sent for me, my lord?"

The familiar feminine voice had Sage searching for its owner. Maeve was as beautiful as she remembered—and just as disapproving. The woman's gaze scoured her and rested on the warlord's back. Something flickered across Maeve's face, and quick as lightning, disappeared. But Sage had seen it. It was an emotion with which she'd become very well acquainted over the years.

Hate.

Sage dropped her eyes to the warlord before the other woman saw the surprise on her face. Maeve had sung the warlord's praises the last time she'd been here, so what had changed these last few weeks?

"I need you to have a bath drawn for Sage."

Maeve started for the bathing room.

"Not in there. Bring one for the room."

Maeve paused and muttered, "It will be done, my lord."

"That's not necessary, my lord," Sage whispered, knowing even then Maeve heard the words. "The pool in the bathing room is adequate."

When he lifted his head and pushed his hair from his face, she forced herself not to cower. A coldness emanated from him, giving his face cruel lines.

"You'll never bathe in that pool again."

"Why?" she whispered.

He reached out a hand and brushed her cheek so softly that his touch could have been a butterfly's wing. "He almost took you from me. I'll never forget, and I don't want reminders. You'll not bathe in there again."

She swallowed and nodded her head in understanding. Some tension in his broad shoulders fell away, and he went back to rubbing her arms. Sage glanced over his head to the woman staring at her with an unreadable expression.

"Maeve?"

"Right away, my lord."

Sage stared at the covered window, listening as a tub was brought in and then the hot water, one pail at a time. The window was so close. If she could walk the fifteen paces, it would be within her grasp. But as close as it was, it was plenty far away. She'd never escape through there. Plus, part of her was afraid of opening that curtain. She had no idea what she'd find on the other side.

A finger traced her brow. She turned to Zane and stared up at him, silently accepting the touch.

"Are you ready for your bath?"

"Yes."

Even though he'd cleaned her as she hung there, she only felt dirtier. Maybe if she scrubbed hard enough, she could scrub away the last five days.

He took her hand and helped her slowly sit up the rest of the way.

"If you'll give us privacy, I'll make sure she's well taken care of," Maeve said.

"I'll stay." The warlord's tone left no room for argument.

Maeve gaped for a second, and then her expression hardened. Even her feet widened like she was getting ready to physically fight an opponent. "It's not proper, my lord. I assure you, I'll take the utmost—"

"No." His icy tone doused the room. "Do not tell me what's proper, sister. I'll not take any chances with her. Now, please do as I command. Help her undress and care for her, but I'll not leave."

Sage swallowed and stared at Maeve over the warlord's shoulder. She was Zane's sister? The woman looked ready to retort, but she inhaled deeply and seemed to forgo any further argument.

"It will be done."

"Thank you, Maeve." He stood and moved toward the pool room. "I'll give you privacy to change," he called over his shoulder.

If she could muster a grain of humor, Sage would've snorted at that. The man hadn't given her privacy in days. He'd been the one to bring her a chamber pot in which to relieve herself, for God's sake. Sage turned to the Scythian woman, scrutinizing her. She didn't care for the haughty look Maeve was giving her. It wasn't her fault she was in this situation.

"Quit scowling at me and help me up, please."

Maeve shook her head and strode to her side. Her nose wrinkled as she got a good look at Sage's robe. "You stink."

She shrugged, not offended in the least. She did stink.

"Can you walk?"

"I cannot," Sage replied without shame.

Maeve mumbled something under her breath and slipped an arm behind Sage's back. "I'm not carrying you."

Sage nodded and painfully shuffled toward the bath.

"Place your hands on the tub's edge, and I'll help you out of your robe."

Sage did as she was told and shivered as the Scythian woman stripped her of the soiled cloth. Maeve sucked in a sharp breath. Sage peeked over her shoulder to catch Maeve looking like she'd bitten into a lemon. Sage ignored her and managed to slip into the tub. A sigh slipped out as warmth caressed her aches. Fingers lifted her hair over the tub's edge.

"This will need a good brushing before I can wash it. It's a mess."

Sage's eyes slowly closed, and she hummed deep in her throat as Maeve began to brush her hair. There was something so soothing about it. In that moment, homesickness slapped her so hard she lost her breath. She wanted her mum, wanted to be hugged and held by someone who loved her.

She opened her eyes and stiffened. The warlord knelt by the bath, watching her with an intensity that made her gut clench. How long had he been watching her? She crossed an arm across her chest and one to the juncture of her thighs. "Wh-what are you doing?"

"Watching my consort bathe, as is my right."

She shrank deep into the tub, wishing to disappear from his heated gaze.

"My lord, you're making my job difficult. No doubt you wanted her to relax during her bath?"

"Indeed," he murmured. He smiled, all seduction, and skated his fingertip across the top of one of her breasts. "So beautiful."

Everything cried out at the violation. There was nothing she wanted more than to slap his hand away, but she didn't. She let him touch her. She had to.

He sighed, and his midnight-black gaze flickered above her head. "I know what you're alluding to. I'll leave you, but just know that if anything happens to her, there will be consequences. I'm leaving the door cracked so the guards can listen." He glanced back at her face. "I'll see you soon, wild one." Zane pushed from the floor and glided on silent feet out the door.

Sage stared at the closed door, wondering if it was a trick. Was he just waiting on the other side for her to get comfortable, so he could lunge back in?

"You can breathe now," Maeve murmured, her accent lilting.

The breath she was holding rushed out in a torrent of air. Her pounding heart didn't slow, though. How often did he sneak up on her without her knowing?

"He's gone now."

"What?" Sage asked.

"The warlord. I can no longer hear him."

It unnerved her that she was surrounded by people so much more powerful than she was. Here in Scythia, she was the prey. A shudder worked down her spine at the thought.

Maeve poured water over Sage's hair and began to wash it. Minute by minute, Sage's unease abated. A calm quiet settled over the room, giving her a small sense of safety and comfort.

"Thank you," she whispered, while staring blankly at the wall ahead. "I know this isn't something you'd wish to do, but I appreciate it nonetheless." After spending days chained, she was sure she couldn't have washed her own hair even if she'd been given the option, and the idea of the warlord doing it made her sick.

The fingers in her hair paused. "You're welcome," Maeve said gruffly. She finished up with Sage's hair and moved gracefully around the tub. Holding a rag, she sank to her knees in one fluid movement. "Your wrist, please," she asked, holding her hand out.

Sage pulled her hand from the scented water and held her abused flesh out for the Scythian. Maeve's lips tightened, but other than that, she said nothing. The Scythian woman took painstaking care of her arms, washing the wounds until they were clean. Sage startled when Maeve's hand clenched against her wrist. Her yip of pain made the Scythian woman loosen her grip, but the glint in her eyes and thin lips spoke of anger. Sage followed her gaze. Ah, her scars.

"They're not as bad as they seem," she murmured.

"How did you come by them?" Maeve whispered, her tone uncharacteristically soft.

"A Scythian thought he'd have fun with me." Her words were slow and lifeless, even to her own ears. "I'm sure you know him." Sage arched a brow. "You were there when the warlord executed him."

Maeve paled, her normally olive skin turning a sickly color. She dropped Sage's wrist into the water and clutched the side of the tub. "No," she breathed, anguish on her face.

Sage's brow furrowed at the intense reaction. "I'm sorry if he was your friend." Her brows furrowed when one tear dripped down Maeve's face. Was he more than a friend? A husband or lover? She searched her mind for something to say to soothe the woman, but she came up with nothing. Rhys was a monster.

"All of them, were they from—" Maeve stuttered.

She pitied the woman, but she wouldn't lie to her. "He personally etched each and every scar into my body himself."

Maeve placed a hand on her own stomach and panted. "I had no idea. I—" She shook her head. "How can a little boy grow into such a man?"

She blinked and tried to make sense of Maeve's words. A little boy? She hadn't noticed it before, but Maeve looked familiar. She studied her a moment.

No, she thought. It couldn't be possible. The Scythian woman looked hardly older than she and yet... when she thought of it, she couldn't remember seeing anyone that looked older than 30 at the execution or the feast. Could it be possible? She *was* the warlord's sister, but the mother of Rhys? That seemed too far-fetched. "Were you his mother?" she whispered.

"I was," Maeve whispered back, staring at her neither with malice nor friendliness.

A thousand questions flashed through Sage's mind, but only one came out. "How?" she breathed. "You're too young."

Maeve gestured to her face. "I'm older than I look."

A product of Scythian tampering? Likely. "Like the Sirenidae?"

A bitter smile twisted the woman's lips. "Something like that."

Stars above, what kind of creatures did the Scythians create? Panic squeezed her chest. Had they been experimenting with her, too?

"What has he been giving me?" she demanded, grabbing Maeve's wrist.

Maeve's gaze shuttered. "I don't know."

"Don't lie to me," Sage said desperately.

"I'm not. You think he shares his plan with me just because the same blood runs through our veins?" The Scythian woman shook her head. "You're still so young and naïve. You've no idea what you're doing."

"I'm surviving," she said simply.

"No one survives him, child. No one."

That she could believe. "And you, how have you survived?" Sage asked. Maeve might be abrasive, but Sage was sure she wasn't insane like her brother.

A mirthless laugh burst out of the woman. "I didn't. I gave up pieces of myself until all that remained was this perfected shell."

Sage stared hard at the woman, who stared back evenly. "If that were true, you'd have killed me already."

"How do you know I won't?"

"You fear him," she said simply. Maeve's expression didn't change much, but the tightening around her eyes betrayed her. "You wouldn't risk his wrath, not for yourself, but for the ones you love." Sage leaned her chin against the tub, never taking her gaze from the Scythian woman. "You have shown me kindness."

Maeve scoffed.

"You can pretend all you want, but I see the good you try to hide under your rough persona. You're kind to me in spite of everything. I'm not Scythian, your brother wants me, and..." She paused and continued in a soft voice, "I'm the cause of your son's death... I'm sorry for it." It wasn't his death she was sorry for, but that it caused this woman pain. No parent should ever have a child die before them, let alone witness it.

The Scythian woman studied her. "Why apologize? You hated him. I saw it the moment you looked at me when we first met. Surely, his death pleases you?"

A part of her, the dark twisted part, was happy he was dead. But that part also sickened her. She should never rejoice in the death of someone, no matter how depraved they were. A life was still a life.

Sage pushed her thoughts away and answered, "Because no matter what he was to me, he was still your son and that means something to you."

Maeve's brows rose in surprise, and then her face settled into its normal stoic expression. "How?"

"How what?"

"How are you so…so good?"

A dark chuckle slipped from Sage. "There's nothing good about me."

Maeve shook her head. "You should hate me, based on association alone."

"I could say the same about you. But that's the type of thinking that got our kingdoms into this situation in the first place."

"He doesn't deserve you."

Sage's eyes widened.

The Scythian woman stiffened and shot to her feet. "Enough of this conversation." She blurred from the room in a burst of speed, then was standing before Sage holding a towel out for her in less than five seconds.

"Get out. He's coming."

Using all her strength, Sage heaved herself up, water sluicing off her body. Maeve held a hand out and helped her from the tub, wrapping the towel around her just as the door burst open.

"I've wonderful news."

Sage turned carefully and clutched the towel tighter to her

body as Zane's gaze heated, slowly running over her barely-clad form. Time for a distraction. "Good news?"

He lifted his hand, holding a letter, and grinned. The boyish smile softened his foreign, otherworldly beauty into something warm and approachable. Shame washed over her at the errant thought.

"Aermia has responded!"

"Responded to what?"

"My letter, of course."

She forced herself to not step back when he pushed into her space and clasped her face between his huge hands.

"Soon, we'll have peace."

His smile was positively infectious, and she had to force her mouth flat to keep it from answering his. What was he really up to? He didn't desire peace, he desired control. So, what was his game?

The warlord seemed to know her thoughts, and his smile turned a little dangerous. "Oh, dear Sage, I long for peace. Peace of mind that no one can steal from me, that my line will continue, and that the Aermian dogs won't interbreed with my people."

She swallowed hard, very aware that he could crush her skull between his hands as easily as cracking an egg. Still, she spoke her mind, "I'm Aermian."

His eyes darkened, and a fevered light entered them as he stared at her. "Much to my chagrin." He pressed closer, his nose touching hers, his breath puffing across her lips. "You are my greatest crime against my people," he whispered. "I hate that I want you. It would be easier to kill you. Believe me, I've mulled over the idea at great length."

Stars above. Her insides were quivering with fear. He had said it so matter-of-factly, like he was speaking of the weather, not that he'd pondered murdering her, all the while holding her like a lover. Something dangerous crossed his face and then cleared the next second, leaving her shaken.

"But I cannot do it." A disappointed sigh escaped him, ruffling the hair at her temple. "Despite your inferior birth and flawed genes, I want you, and I hate you for it. Yet, there's something about your scars and green eyes that calls to me."

There was nothing to say to that. It was the ramblings of a madman. A madman who somehow managed to sway her emotions and who she was still inexplicably drawn to. A dangerous madman.

He kissed her forehead and then stepped back to address Maeve, who stood next to the mirror, still holding the brush. "This is good news for you. It means you will see your daughter sooner than we thought. You shall have her back in your arms by the end of the month."

Maeve looked like he had slapped her. "My lord?"

He waved a hand toward her. "It's been too long since I've seen my niece. Her punishment is over. I'm sure she's learned her lesson. Now, leave us."

Maeve placed the brush on the vanity and quickly left the room, leaving the warlord and Sage alone. He turned to her and reached out to brush a finger along her bare arm, leaving goosebumps in its wake.

"How was your bath?" he asked, strolling slowly toward the vanity.

"It was refreshing," she said.

He picked up the brush and jerked his chin toward the bed. "Put on your new robe and then come and sit. I'll brush your hair."

She glanced at the semi-translucent robe he'd brought in and back to the warlord. "Will you give me privacy?"

"I've been generous enough for today."

Sage swallowed and slowly stepped up to the bed. She peeked over her shoulder to find the warlord leaning against her vanity, legs crossed, watching her. Turning back to the robe, she inhaled deeply and picked it up. He expected her to wear that?

"You still aren't changing. I think someone wants me to dress her myself."

Panic fluttered in her chest at his softly-spoken words. Carefully, despite her shaking hands, she slid her arms in without dropping the towel, and closed the robe before letting the towel fall to the floor. As fast as her shaking fingers could move, she tied it closed and smoothed the fabric.

Turning, she almost stumbled when she caught sight of herself in the mirror. The robe reached the floor and trailed behind her, but that did not mean it was modest. It clung to her curves in a way that was seductive; the fabric was just see-through enough that it gave tantalizing peeks of what was underneath. Sage pulled her hair over her shoulders to cover her chest.

Zane tilted his head as he studied her face. "Come to me, consort."

Rafe would have been proud at how she kept her mask in place, not reacting to the heated way the warlord gazed at her, or his use of 'consort.' She put one foot in front of the other and sank onto the stool.

He pushed off the vanity and moved behind her, all grace and danger, and began to brush her hair. She avoided watching him in the mirror, his perfection almost too much to look at. What sort of sick game was he playing? One moment, he was cutting her friend open, and the next he was brushing her hair. Everything inside her was muddled, leaving nothing but confusion.

Her jaw flexed as he gathered up the hair falling over her chest. She might as well be naked for all the good this robe did. Light fingers brushed her hair over one shoulder, and his lips ran along the skin of her neck in an unhurried way.

A shudder worked through her body.

He peeked up at her, his eyes glittering, his hair tickling her collarbone. "Kiss me."

She shook her head.

"Remember the cost of your rebellion, wild one."

If Tehl were there, he'd tell her to fight the warlord, no matter the cost. But friends protected each other, so that's what she did. She protected Jasmine.

She twisted her neck and met the brush of his lips.

Her stomach churned, and she willed her mind to go blank. *Wrong, wrong, wrong*, her mind screamed. The warlord softly touched her chin and skated his fingers down her neck to rest above her heartbeat. The kiss lasted far too long, and she felt dirty from the inside out. No amount of scrubbing would remove the guilt and taint from her soul.

Finally, he broke away; she gasped out a breath as his lips left hers. He looked stunning, and innocent, which was the farthest thing from the truth. There was nothing innocent about him or the way he was gazing at her.

"This pleases me, wild one."

Another piece of her heart shriveled in her chest. She just bet it did.

His thumb traced her lips. "One day, you'll look at me like you did before. You'll see reason. We just need to be patient until that day comes."

He'd wait a long time.

He pulled her up from the stool and led her toward the bed. He sat and tugged her onto his lap. Her heart jackknifed in her chest and she squirmed, uncomfortable. Hands landed on her hips and squeezed. Sage peeked up at him.

"You need to stop squirming, wild one," he said through gritted teeth, "or I will forget my promise, and eating will be the last thing we will be doing."

Hell. She froze like a deer scenting a predator.

Zane plucked a grape from a platter sitting on her bed and held it to her lips. "Eat, consort. You must keep up your strength, so you can heal."

Her lips parted, allowing him to push the grape into her mouth. She chewed slowly and stared blankly across the room. A healing that she wouldn't need if he hadn't chained her to the wall for five days. Another grape entered her vision, and she glanced up at him, hoping her feelings were well hidden from the monster wrapped in this deceiving package. How could she ever escape him?

Her answer was clear. There was no escape.

CHAPTER TWENTY-FOUR

Tehl

Tehl stepped into his study and examined the draperies, his brows furrowed in confusion. It seemed that his curtains were giggling. He closed the door and cocked his head, listening. Well, it certainly couldn't be an assassin, or even a lady come to seduce him; the giggle was much too childish. The corner of his mouth twitched at the small purple shoes peeking out from the bottom. If he had to venture a guess, he would say there was a certain small girl hiding herself behind the material.

Feeling mischievous, instead of just whipping back the curtains as he might normally do, he began speaking to himself in a loud voice, affecting bewilderment. "My, my, it seems as though my study is full of humor today."

Another soft snigger slipped from the draperies.

"I wonder, could there be someone hiding in this room?" He crossed to his desk and peeked underneath it. "Well that's odd. No one is under my desk. Where else might someone be?"

He stomped dramatically to a tapestry, which hung on the far wall, and yanked it back. "Huh. No one behind my tapestry." Tehl then crept quietly toward the curtains and whipped them back. "I found you!"

The girl let loose a screech loud enough to burst his eardrums and then fell into a fit of giggles.

He smiled to himself. "Isa?"

She pushed a shock of fiery red curls from her face and looked up at him with enormous violet eyes. She grinned and jumped to her feet, wrapping her delicate arms around his leg. "Uncle!" she squealed, "I surprised you!"

Tehl pulled her up and swung her into the air, landing her in his arms for a bear hug. "Isa, darling. It's been so long since I've seen you!" His heart warmed when she wrapped her arms around his neck and squeezed. It didn't even bother him that her unruly curls were tickling his nose. "I've missed you so much! When did you arrive?"

"Today. Papa sent for me and now I get to live with you! In the castle!"

He stared at his three-year-old niece, slightly shocked at how different she looked from the last time he'd seen her. Her limbs had slimmed, her face was sharper, and it occurred to him that he had already missed a lot of Isa's life. He didn't like that idea.

He was pulled from his thoughts when a small finger tried to smooth out his brow.

"Uncle, did I make you sad?"

It was incredible that, even at her age, she was so aware of the feelings of others. He brushed a curl from her face and smiled, cupping her cheek. "Of course not, Isa. You could never make me sad. Is your papa aware of where you are?"

She glanced to the ground and then looked up at him sheepishly. "No."

Tehl rolled his eyes. Of course, the little rascal had escaped notice. She was infinitely more devious than any of them had been growing up. Turning on his heel, he opened the door and addressed the guard stationed outside: "Inform Gavriel that his daughter is with me." The guard nodded and bowed before striding off down the hallway.

"What would you like to do, Isa?" he asked as he closed the door and moved toward his desk.

"Can I paint?"

He kissed the top of her head and sat her on his desk as he took his own seat. "Sadly, I don't have any paints. Can you use a quill?"

"Uh huh."

Tehl eyed his niece in doubt. "Are you sure?"

Her little nose wrinkled. "Nurse's been teaching me. I can do it."

He had to hide a smile at the indignation in her little voice. "I'll make sure to have colors brought to my desk, so the next time you visit, you can paint."

She grinned and snagged the quill out of his hand. "Okay, Uncle."

There was something magical about having her here with him. He'd always loved children. They were so honest in their affections and full of vivacity. Reaching out a hand, he ran it over her curls. When was the last time he'd felt so light, so happy? He couldn't remember. He banished the glum thoughts and began working on his own paperwork. The two continued that way for quite some time. Every once in a while, she'd ask him a question that he would answer, and then she'd go back to her swirls.

"Uncle?"

"Yes?" he answered, continuing his correspondence.

"Where is Auntie?"

He jerked and shot her a questioning look. "Auntie?"

"Aunt Sage. Papa wrote in his letter that I would get to meet Auntie and that she'd teach me how to use a dagger." Her eyes widened comically. "But Nurse said that wasn't proper."

For the life of him, he couldn't figure out how to respond. His mouth opened and closed a few times as he thought about explaining what kept him up most nights. "Your auntie..." he drew out, "isn't here right now."

Isa's pixie face fell. "When will she be back?"

"Soon," he deflected. Hopefully soon, but hope was never on his side.

His door burst open and in stormed Gav. When he spotted the two of them at Tehl's desk, he skidded to a halt and a small smile replaced the scowl he'd been wearing. "I see you've acquired a helper."

"Papa!" Isa grinned and held up a paper with squiggles all over it. "Flowers!"

"Those are beautiful pictures, darling," Gav said.

Tehl squinted at the paper she held up. Nothing in that even closely resembled flowers, but when she held it up for his inspection, he just smiled and nodded as well.

Gav strode to the front of the desk and lifted Isa to the edge. His cousin's face turned serious as he gazed down at his daughter. "Isa, what did I say about staying by Nurse?"

Isa ducked her chin.

"Look at me, Isa." The little girl peeked up at her father. "What did I say?"

"Not to run off?"

"And what did you do?"

"I wanted to see Uncle."

"I understand that, but I asked you to do something, and you disobeyed me."

"But I wanted to—"

"Isa," Gav admonished. "Don't argue with me. I told you we would visit later. You scared your nurse and me. It's not safe for you to wander the halls like you did at home. Because you disobeyed, you're going to bed early tonight."

Isa's shoulders slumped forward. "Sorry, Papa."

"I know." He wrapped his arms around her and hugged her to his chest. "I appreciate you apologizing, and I love you."

"Love you," she sniffed.

"Nurse is going to take you for a snack and then a nap."

"No nap," Isa complained.

"Not a choice." Gav turned toward the door. "Mrs. Clairette!"

An ancient-looking woman opened the door and stepped inside. "My lord?"

"Isa is in need of a snack and her nap."

The older woman nodded and held her hand out. "Isa? Come, child."

Isa hid her face in Gav's shirt. "I don't want to go, Papa." She peeked up at Tehl. "I want to stay with Uncle."

He was about to assure her she was welcome to stay when he caught Gav's expression. "Well, the quicker you go and eat your snack and take a nap, the quicker you can wake up and have dinner with me. Maybe we'll have cake for dessert."

His niece's eyes rounded. "Cake?"

"Yes."

Isa squealed and wiggled down from his desk, all but sprinting to the nurse. She waved to them over her shoulder as she left. "Bye, Papa! Bye, Uncle!"

Gav blew her a kiss while Tehl simply waved, the little girl now following the old woman without a complaint. He closed the door behind them and turned to his cousin, smiling. "You finally brought Isa home! Why didn't you tell me?"

"We were going to surprise you tonight, but," Gav scowled, "apparently Isa couldn't wait. I wish that Mrs. Clairette could keep a better eye on her."

"By the way Mrs. Clairette squinted around this room, it seemed as though she couldn't see," Tehl said. "How old is she now?"

Gav ran a hand through his raven hair. "She's old. And sadly, old enough that I now need to find someone else to take care of Isa."

"But hasn't Mrs. Clairette taken care of Isa since birth?"

"Yes, but Mrs. Clairette can't live at the palace. Her husband is older than she, and her children and grandchildren live around my keep. I can't uproot them all just for my daughter. The journey here has already worn her out. I'm not saying they're unwilling. I'm sure that if old Will was healthy enough to make the journey, they would do it, but honestly? It's just not possible."

"What are you going to do, then?"

"I'm not sure. I hate the idea of trying to find another suitable companion and caretaker for Isa."

"Have you told Isa?"

"No," Gav grimaced. "It will break her heart, I'm sure."

Tehl opened his mouth to answer when the door slammed open. He rolled his eyes at his brother. "Will you ever learn to knock?"

Sam powered to his desk and held out an envelope. "Not when there's news."

He plucked the envelope from his brother's grasp and brushed his thumb over the black wax seal. This was it. Everything hinged on the contents of this letter. He glanced up at his brother and then Gav.

Pulling in a deep breath, he snatched the letter and ripped it open. All the air rushed from his lungs. It was just three sentences.

We are in accord. Your letter pleased me. We will meet in one month and embark on something our kingdoms haven't experienced in hundreds of years: peace.

Tehl's jaw hung open. This was unreal. He turned to the two men at his side. "He agreed. We're set to meet in one month."

Sam moved around the desk and pulled him into a hug. "Just one more month, brother, and then we'll have Sage in our arms.

She'll be safe."

Emotion clogged his throat. They were almost there. Only thirty days until he had his wife and advisor back. "I need to tell her parents," he said absently.

"Do you think that's a good idea? To give them hope?" Sam asked.

Tehl ran a hand through his hair. "I've got no other choice. I can't keep this from them. And even if I don't say anything, I'm certain Lilja will. Honestly, though, I'd rather…"

"You want it to come from you," Gav supplied.

"Yes, and I'm due for a visit anyway." He blew out a breath and handed Sam the letter. "Alert the war council. We'll meet this evening." He rounded the desk and clapped Gav on the shoulder. "Tell Isa I'll be back for dessert."

His cousin nodded and, just as he was exiting the room, his brother called out, "Give the Blackwells my best."

***

Tehl tensed as the door swung open, revealing Sage's father. The man looked fairly healthy, but also very tired.

The older man stepped up to him and wrapped him in a hug. "Welcome, son."

He released Tehl and stepped back. The heat of the forge enveloped him, the warmth draping over him like a warm blanket. A small smile pulled at his lips as the older man sat him down and poured him a drink. Tehl sank onto the bench and took the cup of ale with a muttered, "Thank you." Colm sat and sipped his ale, all the while watching him over the rim.

"What's eating at you?"

"Is it that obvious?"

"Yes, though I've also come to know you a bit over the last couple of months."

Tehl swallowed. "I've had word."

Colm paled and placed a bracing hand against his workbench. "Sage? Is she…is she all right?"

"She's alive."

Tehl shot to his feet as the older man leaned forward, visibly sagging. "Colm!"

The older man grabbed Tehl's hand and yanked him to his knees before pulling him into another hug.

"So, she's really alive?" Colm rasped, his eyes full of tears.

"She is."

Sage's father let loose a heavy sigh and pulled back. He quickly wiped his face and stood, extending a hand to his son-in-law. "We need to tell Gwen."

Tehl clasped his hand and pushed off the floor, looking the other man in the eye. "Is she strong enough to bear it? We may be getting her back, but I'm not sure in what condition we'll find her."

The older man's face hardened. "Condition?"

"She's been in Scythia this whole time. Specifically, with their warlord," he finished softly.

"No," the older man breathed, looking green.

"He's assured us that she's been well taken care of and is in good health, but…"

"It's damn Scythia. You can't trust a word they say!" Colm thundered.

"I know, but what other choice do I have?"

Colm's face fell. "You've none, I know."

"I have to balance my feelings for Sage with the good of the whole kingdom." He slumped onto the bench and hung his head. "I'm tired, so tired. Each day I awake only to find myself stuck in the same nightmare from the day before."

A large hand settled on his shoulder, and his father-in-law's deep voice washed over him: "We don't blame you."

"How could you not? I'm the reason she's gone."

"Do you really think that's true?"

A bark of laughter escaped him. "No, I suppose not. Somehow, she still would have found a way to be in the middle of this mess."

The man chuckled. "She never could stay out of trouble."

Tehl sobered. "I worry."

"We all do."

He nodded. "Where's Gwen?"

"She is sewing by the fireplace."

"Are you sure she can handle this?"

He nodded once. "She's stronger than most."

CHAPTER TWENTY-FIVE

Sage

Time stretched and blurred, only measured by the warlord's visits. It sickened her how easy it was to fall into a routine with him. It was now second nature to accept the food he offered from his hands, his kisses, and his care. The night he released her from her punishment, he moved back into his suite.

She had tried to sleep on the couch, but all it took was a

reminder of his threat for her to trudge back to the bed. Her skin had crawled when he'd slipped into bed, but he had left her untouched. She hadn't thought she'd sleep, but exhaustion had pulled her under. The next morning, she'd awoken in a panic, barely able to breathe. A close inspection, however, revealed that he'd left her unmolested. He'd left her to the silence of his empty room.

The silence was the worst.

Her thoughts ran in a continuous loop in his absence. Day by day, she was losing what was left of her mind. She reflected on her mistakes, her misjudgments, her unnatural attraction to the warlord, dying, and back to the warlord. He consumed so many of her thoughts.

After being starved of human interaction for so long, she looked forward to when he'd visit, to the gentle touches bestowed upon her. One day, she realized that she wasn't scared when he came to bed, and that his side had slowly encroached onto hers, until he slept curled around her. It disgusted her that sadness blanketed her when he left in the morning. She craved his company, but didn't understand why. It was wrong, depraved, and yet she couldn't help it.

"Wild one?"

Sage blinked and glanced over her shoulder to catch the warlord watching her. "Yes?"

"Come here."

She pulled her fingers from Nali's fur, earning her a chuff of discontent, and moved to stand in front of him. He leaned forward and brushed a kiss across her lips with a smile.

"I have news for you."

"News?"

"It's time for a trip."

"A trip? You mean, I get to leave this room?" Even she could hear the desperation and excitement in her voice. She was pathetic.

"Yes, we leave now."

"Now? So soon?" Her heart raced. What brought this about?

"It's safer to travel."

"Where are we going?" she asked. Maybe he'd tell her.

"To another one of my castles."

She hid her frown at his evasion. How would she ever escape if she didn't know where she was?

"I need to pack." She scanned the room. It held nothing of hers. The only thing she truly cared for was the black feline staring at her through a slitted eye. Turning back to the warlord, she shrugged. "I have nothing to pack."

He cupped her face with a grin. "I've already arranged clothing to be packed for you. Something befitting a queen." She stiffened as he caressed the crown collar around her throat tenderly before settling his palm on the side of her neck. "I don't understand how you do it, but you bewitch me. Something about you ruins all of my best-laid plans."

"Ouch." Sage pulled away from him and rubbed her neck. "A thorn poked me," she explained. The collar stopped bothering her after the first couple weeks, but every so often it would hurt something terrible. Her brow furrowed as the room spun. "I don't feel so good." Zane's arms wrapped around her as her stomach plummeted, and she stumbled.

"Are you alright?"

"I'm exhausted." Her temple pounded, and she lifted a hand to her head, blinking. Just barely was she able to focus on his face. Concern was evident in his expression, but his eyes spoke the truth. Calculation. Her heart sank. This was planned.

"Did you drug me?" she asked weakly.

Zane swept her feet out from underneath her and carried her to the bed. "I had to. You wouldn't be reasonable about traveling. I can't risk you trying to escape and getting yourself hurt. This is for your own protection."

"Zane," she whispered, struggling to sit up. "But I promised."

"I know. That's why Jasmine is coming as well."

She shook her head to keep awake. "You're bringing my friend?"

"I couldn't rely on you being logical with what's ahead of us. I don't plan on hurting her. I'm bringing her to protect you, really."

"How does bringing her protect me?" she mumbled, the words becoming hard to form.

"It protects you from doing something stupid." He pressed a kiss to her lips. "I will explain it all when we arrive."

"Liar," she whispered, her eyelids too heavy to keep open. He didn't explain his plans to anyone. He was too suspicious. Too cautious. Too controlling.

"Goodnight, wild one."

He'd lied. Again. Hurt her. Again. Tricked her. Again. When would the deception end?

Never.

Chapter Twenty-Six

Sage

When Sage came to, everything was blurry.

She blinked several times before the world came back into focus. When it did, she found herself in a massive tent with tiny lanterns hanging from its ceiling. There were furs covering the floor, and the lanterns cast a soft glow over the space, casting deep shadows in the corners. Where was she and why couldn't she move her limbs? What had Zane given her?

She felt movement on her right and, when she turned her head to inspect it, found herself nose-to-nose with Nali. The black feline swiped her rough, long tongue from Sage's chin to her temple. She scowled at the beast.

"Nali! No kisses!"

If Nali could have rolled her eyes, Sage was sure she would have. She was about to scold her further when the murmuring of voices caught her attention. She lifted her neck, attempting to see farther. One tent flap was tied back, giving her a view into a connecting room.

In it, the warlord stood, hands braced against a table, surrounded by warriors. Even after everything he'd done, something about him called to her. Was it his unearthly looks? His charisma? Whatever it was, it disturbed her, deeply.

Almost as if he heard her thoughts, his dark gaze cut to hers, entrapping her. A shudder rolled through her. Everything about him was all sorts of wrong. A stunning smile curled his sensuous lips at her blatant stare, and she jerked her eyes away, staring instead at the canvas wall. Her eyes traced the flickering shadows in an attempt to calm her beating heart.

The murmurs died down, and she had to force herself not to glance in his direction again. She could feel his attention on her, but maybe if she paid him no mind, he'd leave her alone.

"Consort," his smooth, deep voice called.

She was never that lucky. Sage continued to stare at the wall, her fingers tightening in Nali's fur.

"Look at me, wild one."

Sage stared harder at the shadows.

She heard him sigh before he moved to kneel before her, cutting off her view of the wall. She focused on staring at the laces of his shirt.

"I know you're angry with me."

Angry didn't even begin to describe how she felt.

Another sigh. "You needed protection, and this was the only way I could protect you."

"By drugging me?" she whispered, still not looking up.

"You know the dangers of jungles. I needed to transport you safely. The risk is too high, and you're too important."

Her gaze flew to his face. He was serious. His expression showed tender emotion and something deeper than passing affection. She hid her dawning horror at this revelation and forced herself to remain still as he cupped her cheek. "Don't hide from me. I hate it."

"I'm right here," she whispered.

"Don't lie to both of us. You're a thousand leagues away, Sage. I know the symptoms. I invented them."

She swallowed and focused back on his laces. "I can't move my arms," she said, changing the subject.

"It will be a while until you can."

He pushed back from the bedroll and began unlacing his shirt.

"What are you doing?" she asked in a high voice.

"Undressing. It's time for bed."

Panic fluttered in her breast, and her breathing turned shallow. She was completely at his mercy. She couldn't fight back even if she wanted to. He stilled and cocked his head.

"Hell..." He dropped his hands with a scowl. "I'm not going to accost you. Have I not told you that? I will never take from you!"

She didn't believe him for one second, and her expression must have shown it, because he let out an irritated huff as he jerked off his boots before stomping to the bedroll, pulling back the fur covering her, and sliding in. Her heart pounded as he rested on one elbow and leaned over her, earning a growl from Nali.

He glared at the beast, then looked back to her. "I've not *ever* taken from you, have I?" he demanded.

"No," she whispered, conscious of the fact he had complete control. Now was not the time to challenge him.

He scanned her face and brushed a stray hair from her cheek. "I regret what happened that night. I've never been that close to losing myself. It sickens me when I think of it."

Sage didn't regret it, not one bit. It had shown her who he truly was, and she now understood that the other person she'd come to know was merely a persona, one invented for her benefit.

"I hate that it was necessary," he whispered. "Do you think I liked seeing you chained to my wall?" He shook his head, his hair brushing her face. "I hated every moment of your punishment. It hurt me as much as it hurt you."

Sage doubted that, but still she remained silent. She was getting good at that these days.

"One day, you'll understand. I wait for that day," he whispered and pressed his lips to her cheek. He pulled back, a tender smile on his face. "Until then, I can content myself with only holding you."

Zane wiggled his arm underneath her head, twisted her to face Nali, and pulled her into his arms.

She squeezed shut her eyes as he curled his large body around her, holding her like she was precious, even though she already carried scars from his cruelty. She inhaled sharply when his other arm snaked across her waist and rested against her stomach. Her moment of alarm passed quickly, though, as the warmth of his body cocooned her and fatigue settled over her.

"Are you hungry?" His breath moved the loose hair around her ear.

The idea of food did not appeal. "No."

Warm lips brushed the skin below her ear. "All right, love."

Goosebumps broke out along her arms at the whispered endearment. His hand moved from her stomach and passed along her arm, soothing her goosebumps even as he caused more to erupt. Her skin prickled, hyperaware of him as he intertwined his fingers with hers, the metal of his ring kissing her. He turned her hand and brushed his fingers along her wrist.

"Sleep, wild one."

She hissed as something pricked her wrist. "Again?" she asked, not even shocked that he'd drugged her.

"For your protection. When you wake, we'll be at the palace."

"You mean the prison," she slurred as Nali faded into a black blob.

"*My* prison," he whispered, and darkness once again claimed her.

***

Awareness came to her in the form of warmth. Sunlight filtered through her eyelids and warmed her face. Her fingers twitched, and then brushed over the material under her. A bed. It was a real bed, so they weren't still traveling. Sage took stock of her body, flexing her fingers and toes. Her muscles were stiff, but at least she could move them this time.

With care, she rolled to the side and scooted just out of the light. Cracking her eyes, she took stock of her new prison. Two huge doors were opened toward her, revealing a sprawling red stone balcony that boasted a view unlike any she'd ever seen. She stumbled to her feet, lurching toward the balcony. Pain stabbed at her temples and her stomach heaved, but none of that mattered. She gasped, and tears poured down her face when the cool breeze wound around her. She was outside, *finally*. So many emotions coursed through her. She blinked several times, trying to remember the last time she'd seen the sun.

Smiling, she leaned on the intricately-carved railing to get a better view and then gasped. The balcony hung in the air, a two-hundred-foot drop below her. Pine trees stood like giants on the mountainside below, and red sand peeked out between them.

They had to be in Nagali.

She craned her neck. Above her, similar balconies adorned what seemed to be a castle, and the structure itself had been built into the mountainside. It amazed her how seamlessly the castle blended into the rock. Her gaze traced the exotically-upturned roofs, and the way each story of the castle was smaller than the last, reminding her of a tall, castle-sized cake.

Prying her eyes from the architectural marvel, she turned back to the view. It was stunning and foreign. Part of her mourned for the land. How no one now enjoyed its beauty. Part of her was in awe that she'd get to experience something that she'd only read about in books.

Her eyes still watered at the bright light, but she didn't care. She was outside. She didn't realize how much of her longed for the outdoors, craved it. Dark green forest and red sand gave way to more familiar trees and golden fields. Her heart squeezed in her chest, and another tear slipped down her face for another reason entirely.

Aermia. Home was so close, and yet so far away. It was a cruel joke.

She shot a glance at the open doorway. She could spare herself the pain and go back inside, not force herself to gaze upon what she'd lost, but she didn't. She craved the view. While she felt pain and loss, she also enjoyed the beauty and the freedom of being out there, and it was more than she'd had in a long time. So, she sank to her knees and took it in, sitting until her butt went numb and the sun had moved across the sky.

The air was colder now, and a shiver worked through her, though she still didn't move. The sunset was the most beautiful thing she'd ever seen, the sky painted with rich reds, oranges, and purples.

"It's beautiful, isn't it?"

Sage barely kept herself from jumping at the sound of his voice. Slowly, she turned to the warlord. He stood, arms and legs crossed, one shoulder leaning against the stone wall. The wind ruffled his inky hair, giving him a softer, tousled look. But it was a lie, just like everything else about him. Her traitorous heart flipped when he gave her a lopsided smile and pushed off the wall, holding his hand out for her. She slipped her small hand into his large one and allowed him to pull her to her feet.

Zane spun her to face the sunset and wrapped his arms around her, his chin resting on her head. "You like your view?"

She swallowed and nodded.

"Did you sit out here all afternoon?"

"Yes. It's beautiful."

"I hoped you would." He paused and hugged her tighter. "There's something wild and exotic about this land that makes it easy to lose yourself in it." Zane lifted a hand and pointed to the far-off river. "Our company will arrive soon."

Sage squinted and then gaped when she spotted what he was pointing at. It was an army. "Who is it?" she asked, her heart pounding in her chest.

He pulled his hand back and rested it on her beating heart. "The Aermian council."

Her pulse kicked up another notch. "Why?"

"The time has come for treaty negotiations."

"A treaty?" She all but choked.

"Rather boring business, but something we must discuss nonetheless. Come."

She took one last glance at the fading sunset and followed him in. Sage took in the rooms as he went about closing and barring the doors.

The walls were a soft cream fresco, accented with a few colorful mosaics. One particular scene was of a red dragon drawn on the wall across from the bed. She walked up to it and ran her hand along the dragon's scales, fascinated. Had they used jewels to create this picture?

"I should've known you'd be enticed by the dragons."

Sage jerked her hand from the mosaic like she had been caught doing something naughty. Spinning on her heel, she eyed the warlord. "It's beautiful."

He shook his head ruefully and began rolling his sleeves up.

"Out of all the pictures that caught your eye, it was the abominations that drew your attention."

"The stones caught my eye," she said, knowing it was only half the truth.

"They're rubies," the warlord said. "The palace is filled with them."

The room fell silent, the only sound the crackling of the fire.

The warlord let out a sigh and moved to one of two large chairs placed beside the fire. He turned them to face each other and then sat down. He glanced at her and held out a hand. "Please sit."

His serious tone turned her blood to ice. Cautiously, she moved to the seat across from him, doing as he requested. She clasped her trembling hands together and held her breath, waiting for him to speak. The intensity of his gaze made her want to squirm, but instead, she straightened and lifted her chin. If things were going to be bad, she wasn't going to cower in her chair.

"Tomorrow, the Aermian delegation arrives."

She stayed silent.

"And along with them, the crown prince."

Tehl was coming with them? How stupid. Sage kept her face carefully blank as the warlord scrutinized her reaction to his words.

"You will need to be on your best behavior when they arrive."

"I'll see them?" she asked.

His smile held a dangerous edge. "Yes, from my side."

His words settled in. She was going to stand at his side, like a traitor, like the consort he was always calling her. Bile burned the back of her throat, but she held herself in check. "Is there anything else I should know?"

The warlord leaned forward and pulled one of her clenched hands from her lap, lacing his fingers through hers. She stared at their hands and prepared herself for what would come.

"Know that attempted escape will result in quick and violent retribution." His hand squeezed hers. "Look at me."

She lifted her eyes at the command and felt as if the world had dropped away. Heat simmered in his gaze, but his expression was all calculation.

His lips curled up on one side. "If you make a mockery out of me, I will destroy your friend, then the Aermian delegation, and then everything you hold dear."

He said this casually, as if he were merely speaking of the weather. It chilled her to the bone. He meant every word. She could see it in his eyes.

Sage swallowed past the lump in her throat and spoke in a low tone, like she was trying to soothe a dangerous beast. "And what do I tell my husband?"

He jerked her out of her chair and onto her knees in front of him. Her knees stung as he traced her face with one fingertip.

"He's not your husband, wild one." His hand skimmed up to the thorn collar and settled around her throat. He squeezed once gently, just enough for her to know he had complete control and held her life in that moment. "Do you know what this collar represents?"

She forced out a soft, "No," and was pleased with how her voice didn't shake.

"In Scythia, it is not just a method by which women adorn themselves, it is a statement of ownership. Of marriage." His nose rubbed against her temple. "Where do you think your cuff custom originates from? Scythia," he breathed. "You may have been married to the enemy, but it was never consummated. But my claim…" His lips curled against her hair. "It's been validated by a doctor."

Sage gasped and jerked back, staring into his dark eyes. "That's a lie!"

A lazy grin spread across his face. "Is it? How could you prove otherwise? You've been unconscious for five days. And if any of the delegation ask about your room arrangements, they'll be made aware of the fact that you've been sleeping in my bed for months."

Horror filled her. He was right. To anyone on the outside, it would seem like everything he was saying was true. And then, something dawned on her. The execution. It had been for show, for his people to bear witness that she was standing at his side. If anyone from the Aermian council looked at the evidence, it would seem very much like she was a traitor. A bitter laugh escaped her, causing surprise to flash across the warlord's face.

"That was disgustingly ingenious. You are a monster after all."

He smiled. "A monster to some, a hero to others. Who's to say what I am to you?"

"My death," she breathed.

"And your life," he whispered.

CHAPTER TWENTY-SEVEN

Tehl

The day had come.

He patted down his horse, murmuring soft words to the beast. "We have a long way to go, Wraith, and this time, we'll have a companion." He flicked a glance at the mare behind them. "But I need you to act honorably, okay? We don't have time for your attitude. Sage's mount will be spending a lot of time with us, so just get used to it." Wraith nickered and nudged his pocket. Tehl pulled out the apple piece he'd placed inside it and held it out. "Be good."

Tehl spun and faced the mare creeping up on him. She was tall, around sixteen hands, with a bold face and an off-center stripe on her face. He plucked the other quarter of an apple and held it out to her with a smile at how her ears perked. "You and I are newly acquainted, but I promise you'll like me once you get to know me." The mare stepped forward and lipped the apple, crunching down happily. He stroked a hand down her neck and patted her chest. "There's a good girl. You'll like your new mistress. She's a little like you. Beautiful, smart, and spirited."

"We're ready," Sam said, striding toward him. Right behind him were Rafe and the Scythian woman, scowling at his side.

"Is she secured?" he asked his brother.

"As much as possible. Lilja and Rafe will ride next to her. I doubt she'll give us much trouble. We're taking her home."

Blaise shifted her glare from the rebellion leader to Tehl. Something about her troubled him. It was obvious she hated them, but it also seemed like she was afraid. But why? What was she afraid of? Going home?

"Are you ready?" Sam said, interrupting his thoughts.

Tehl shook his head and patted the mare once more, and then moved to Wraith. "Let's ride."

He was about to hop into the saddle when a familiar voice stopped him from doing so. He glanced over his shoulder to catch Gwen pushing through soldiers and warhorses. He released the saddle and turned toward her as she barreled into him. Surprise, then affection, blindsided him as the petite woman wrapped her arms around him in a fierce hug.

"Bring her back to us," she muttered into his vest.

Tehl squeezed once and then released her. "I'll do my best."

Gwen scanned his face and then cupped his cheek. "Take care of yourself. You're part of the family now, too."

Emotion clogged his throat. "Thank you."

She graced him with one last smile and wrapped Sam in the same fierce embrace. The Blackwells were an unexpected gift that Sage had brought with her into their marriage. Determination filled him as he swung up and into the saddle. He'd bring Sage home. If for nothing else, for the sake of her family.

***

Tehl squatted by the Potam River and stared at its dark surface, reflecting on the last few days. They'd been long and exhausting as they rode hard toward the Kugami Mountains. The small army that followed his retinue slowed them down considerably, which kept Tehl in a foul mood. He scowled at the water. If it had been just him and a smaller party, they would have arrived in a few days, not eight. He glanced at the silent, dark mountains which grew larger every day, and prayed they'd arrive soon. Time was of the essence.

A sharp puff of air left his lips as he splashed the icy water over his face and across the back of his neck. If it weren't so cold, he'd be tempted to bathe, but he could see his breath. It wouldn't be long until fall waned and gave way to winter.

He cast a glance over his shoulder at the camp of men. Scattered fires were burning like fireflies in the night, illuminating the outlines of the faithful protectors of his kingdom. He shouldn't be so negative about their presence. They were heroes in their own right and were necessary for this plan to work.

He turned back to the water's edge, his reflection shining in the moonlight. He peered at himself. It was a rough, hardened stranger who gazed back at him. Black bags had permanently made camp beneath his eyes. During the day, he put what could be happening to Sage out of his mind, focusing on what he could control, but at night, there was nothing to occupy his mind. His lips pulled downward, and he stood, kicking at his watery reflection. He needed to stop moping and focus on what was most important.

Spinning on his heel, he strode toward his tent and tossed back the flap. His advisors stood around a table, strategizing with maps of the Nagalian palace and Kugami Mountains.

Rafe acknowledged him with a lift of his chin and continued speaking: "The Nagali favored open floor plans, so a frontal attack from the Scythians is unlikely."

Tehl stopped next to the Methian and scanned the map as Rafe pointed to lines representing an underground system.

"This is where the danger lies. Even with William's maps, we're not familiar enough with the tunnels to actually use them, and that's risky."

"Then why bring them up?" Jeren asked.

"Because the warlord chose this place for a reason. We may not know the tunnel systems, but I've no doubt that the warlord and his men do. We need to keep in mind that with their enhancements, they are faster than anyone you've ever fought, and their sight, hearing, and sense of smell are superior in all ways. We need to tread carefully."

"How will we beat such an opponent?" Lelbiel asked. "By all accounts, we are inferior."

"Only in physical ways," Lilja said, her white brows furrowed in concentration. "That doesn't mean we can't outsmart them. Their warriors do what they're told and don't deviate from their commands. We can use that to our advantage. Surprise will be our greatest weapon."

"But surely, the warlord has planned for such attacks?" Madden said.

"No doubt. One so corrupt does not keep power without calculation and skill, but he is at a disadvantage as well." Zachael smiled with a hint of malice. "He may be familiar with Aermia, but not us. It's a weapon we can wield."

"And Rhys?" Tehl asked. "He was in our midst for quite some time." He cast a glance to Rafe. "How much information does he possess?"

Rafe's arms crossed and his eyes narrowed. "Enough to be dangerous, as you well know."

Tehl gnashed his teeth. He expected nothing different, but even talking of the traitor made him want to kill something. "Sam..." He turned to his brother. "If the warlord does not let her go, what of Sage?"

Sam scanned the group. "We'll get her out..."

"That's it?" Zachael asked.

His brother stared down the weapons master. "The more people aware of the plan, the more likely it will fail. It's safer if only a few of us have pieces of the information. That way, if one of us is captured, our whole plan won't fall to pieces."

The weapons master dipped his head. "Understood."

"Should I be worried?" Tehl asked.

"You should always be worried when it comes to the spymaster," Gav grumbled while scrutinizing one of the maps.

Old William growled and pushed away from the table. "I hate that we're going into this blind." He gestured to the table. "We can't plan anything until we know where we'll be staying. At least he can't surround us with his army," his advisor grumbled. "The Nagali chose well when they built their palace into the Kugami Mountains."

"My question is, why this place?" Sam asked out loud. "Sure, it's a fortress, but Scythia hates all things Nagali. So why not somewhere else? Yes, the mountains hobble us, but they hobble him as well. What's so special about this place? I feel like we're missing something."

"He's proud of his accomplishments, and he enjoys mind games," Lilja offered. "He could have chosen it for the purpose of showing us what Scythia is capable of, to remind us of what they've conquered, or maybe just to keep us guessing. We can't know. The best we can do is stay alert and plan for anything and everything."

"Indeed. We've discussed all we can for the evening," Tehl said with a hint of finality. "I'll see all of you tomorrow morning."

His council bowed and left his tent one by one, until only Lilja, Hayjen, Gav, and his brother remained.

"May I speak to you privately, my lord?" Lilja asked.

Tehl nodded, fatigue riding him hard. Hayjen clasped him on the shoulder, kissed his wife's cheek, and then led Sam and Gav out of the tent. Tehl and Lilja stared at each other, both silent and unmoving. Her unnatural stillness unnerved him.

"Out with it, Lilja. You're never one to beat around the bush." He pulled a pouch from his waist and took a swig of the spirits, ignoring her stare. When Lilja still didn't answer, he pulled a chair over and sat in it, gesturing to the one across from him. Holding out the pouch, he offered, "A drink?"

The Sirenidae glided to his side and pulled the pouch from his hand, taking a swig. He wasn't surprised that she didn't cough at the liquid that burned like fire. Nothing surprised him anymore.

She sank into the chair across from him and leveled a look he couldn't decipher. "You're tired."

He chuckled at that. "That's nothing new."

"Are you prepared for Sage's return?"

"Yes. I didn't fathom how much of an impact she had on my life," he answered honestly. Lilja smiled at him, and something loosened inside of him. He never had to put on a pretense with her. He could be blunt and honest, maybe even to the point of being rude, but she never judged him. "I miss her."

Lilja's magenta eyes misted. "I do, too." She blinked a couple times and took another swig of spirits before handing it back to him. "When I asked my question, I meant something different, Tehl. That place..." She pulled in a sharp breath and looked at the rug. "It strips you down until you don't know who you are anymore."

"Sage is strong." She was. He truly believed she could survive whatever came her way.

"She is, and I still worry for her." Lilja pinned him with her gaze. "I worry for you."

"Me?"

"Yes."

"Why?"

"Because when you finally see her, it will break you."

"I'm not that easily broken."

"Indeed." She leaned forward, her face very serious. "How will you handle it if she's pregnant?"

Her words slapped him in the face. "Pregnant?" he croaked.

It was possible, but it wasn't something he even wanted to contemplate. Lilja reached out and touched his clenched fist.

"Will you be able to accept another man's child?"

"Children are blessings." He meant it. Children were precious. Tehl glanced up when Lilja squeezed his hand.

"That is admirable, but really look inside of yourself. This won't be just any child, but that of your enemy. Can you accept your enemy's offspring as your own?"

He opened and then closed his mouth. A 'yes' was on the tip of his tongue; his throat worked, but no sound came out. Could he really raise a child that wasn't his? Yes. But his enemy's?

Lilja squeezed his hand once more and sat back. "This is not an easy task, but it is one that falls on your shoulders. She will need you; your support, your strength, your acceptance, and your love. Are you prepared to give those things to her?"

"Yes." That was easy.

"And the child?"

Tehl exhaled and nodded. "It doesn't matter how a child was created. Scythian or no, the child is an innocent, one that I will welcome into my home and raise as my own, no matter how difficult it may be."

A smile lit up Lilja's face. "Then you're a good man."

He shook his head and ran a hand over his face. "If I was a better one, we wouldn't be in this situation."

"Do you really believe that?" the Sirenidae asked.

Guilt weighed him down. "With my whole heart."

"Maybe Sage isn't the only one who needs support, strength, acceptance, and love."

"Do you think that is possible for us?" he asked, holding his breath as he waited for Lilja to reply.

"Do you think her parents, or Hayjen and I, would've allowed your marriage to take place if we believed you'd be unhappy forever?" She smiled at him like she held a secret. "We all care for Aermia, but if you think for one moment that we would have allowed our girl to attach herself to an unworthy man for the kingdom, you're daft."

Her statement struck him as funny. He chuckled, which turned into a full laugh. Lilja looked at him like he'd lost his mind, and maybe he had, but her expression just made him laugh harder. His stomach cramped, and tears blurred his eyes. With much effort, he managed to get control of himself and wipe the tears from his eyes.

Lilja grinned at him. "Laughing is good for the soul, isn't it?"

"My mum used to say that."

"What was so funny?"

"Your statement. After spending time with the Blackwells, I should've realized this was part their decision, too. It seems I have many more people to be thankful to."

Sam pushed into the tent, interrupting them. His gaze darted between the two of them. "Gav," he shouted. "I told you it wasn't Tehl laughing. Lilja made him cry."

Tehl scowled at his brother and rubbed his eyes hard. A hand on his shoulder pulled his attention up.

Lilja's eyes were sparkling with mirth. "I've brothers, too," she mock-whispered just loud enough for his brother to hear. "They never grow any less bothersome."

"My lady! I'm wounded."

The Sirenidae rolled her eyes and strode toward his brother. "I'm sure nothing could wound you on account of your battle prowess."

Sam's eyes narrowed playfully. "I get the feeling you're playing with me, Lilja. What a cruel thing."

She sniggered and swept around him. "You haven't seen my cruel side yet." She paused before the tent flap and swiveled to look at Tehl and his brother. "We'll reach the castle tomorrow. Sleep well. I'm sure it will be the last time any of us do so until we leave that accursed place." She glanced through the flap. "I better relieve Rafe before he kills the Scythian wench. They squabble like crows."

With that, she disappeared outside, leaving the brothers to stare after her.

"She's a magnificent woman," Sam commented.

"Lilja's certainly unique," Tehl answered and shifted into a more comfortable position, waiting for his brother to sit and have his say. "How much did you hear?"

"Not much. Only your deranged cackle." Sam plopped into Lilja's vacated chair, swiped the spirit pouch, and stared at it. "It's been a long time since I've heard you laugh like that."

"It's been a long time," he admitted. His mind then turned to the possibility of a pregnant Sage.

"Your serious face is back," Sam noted. "Will you share your burdens with me?"

Tehl leaned forward, his elbows on his knees, his hands clasped. "What if..." His voice cracked. He cleared his throat and tried again. "What if she is carrying a child?"

Sam stilled and then took a swig of the spirits before answering, "Then you do what you do best."

"And what is that?" Tehl really didn't know. Everything was falling apart around him. Nothing seemed to go the way he planned.

"You care for her and the child."

"Care?" he scoffed. "Gav is better suited for it than I am."

"Not true. You're stunted when it comes to understanding others' emotions, I'll grant you that. But you care for those close to you. You've been caring for all of us for a long time. Just keep on doing what you're doing."

Tehl shot to his feet and began pacing the tent, his brother watching him.

"Speak, brother, I'm listening."

"I can care for the child, but what of Sage?"

"What of her?"

He stopped pacing and pinned his brother with a look. "How do I heal rape? I don't know how to deal with that. When I think of it..." He broke off as rage filled him. He glared at the chair, wanting to throw it. "I want to kill him. I want to tear things apart."

His brother's face clouded over. "If he has, he will pay."

"That's my point!" Tehl exploded. "How can I care for her with all this hate and rage inside of me?" His hands curled into fists at his side. "How can I get her back if I'm this out of control?"

"You're not out of control, brother." Sam stood and clasped him on the shoulder. "You've borne this better than anyone."

His jaw clenched, and he looked to the side, his fears spilling out of his lips. "What if we can't get her back?"

"We will," Sam said resolutely.

"And what if we do and the Sage we love died in Scythia?"

Sam grabbed him into a rough hug. "Then we'll welcome her home and get to know this new version of her."

Tehl nodded and thumped his brother's back a few times before pulling away. "Thank you."

His brother clasped his forearm. "I'm with you. You're not alone." Sam scanned his face. "Get some sleep if you can. Tomorrow is the big day." He slapped Tehl on the shoulder and then moved to his bedroll.

A new sense of strength filled Tehl. They would get Sage back.

He glanced at his own bedroll. It was doubtful he'd get any sleep, but he needed to try. Tomorrow, they would change history.

Chapter Twenty-Eight

Tehl

It was more beautiful than he expected. Golden grass gave way to rich, green pine forests; the earth shifted from a deep brown to an intense red. He scanned the castle looming in front of them, anxious. Somewhere inside was Sage. She was so close.

"Breathe, my lord."

Tehl glanced at Zachael. "I am."

The weapons master scoffed. "Not evenly. Remember your training."

He nodded and pulled deep breaths in and out as they ascended the mountainside toward the castle. It was eerie how pristine the Nagali palace still was. Not a single tower or wing looked run down or in any need of repair. It was exactly how it looked in history books.

His men circled nearer on their horses as they moved ever closer to the palace. He couldn't see the Scythians, but he knew they watched. Everyone was on edge as they crested the mountain path, finally arriving at the palace gate.

Silence met them.

Tehl scanned the area, hyper aware of his surroundings. It was like the mountains also held their breath, waiting. His gaze snapped to the metal gate when it groaned and swung inward, a group of dangerous-looking Scythian warriors just inside it.

The largest one stepped forward. It was the same warrior they'd encountered all those months ago outside of Sanee. The one who'd shot down his own men. Tehl schooled his face, one hand tightening on his reins, causing Wraith to toss his head. He loosened his grip and straightened in the saddle, his other hand on the pommel of his sword.

"My lords and ladies," the warrior's deep voice boomed, echoing off the surrounding stone. "Welcome to Palace Kamugi."

Tehl dipped his chin but shot a look at Lilja, who had let out an uncharacteristic gasp. He blinked at her odd behavior. She never let anyone know they'd surprised her. He turned back to the warrior who was staring at the Sirenidae. Was this the warrior Lilja had been given to? He pushed the thoughts away and focused on the warrior.

"It's our pleasure to join you in negotiations. Where is your warlord?" Tehl asked.

The warrior bowed and then stepped to the side. "Unfortunately, he's been detained and could not greet you himself, but accommodations and refreshments have been arranged, so you can refresh yourselves and rest until dinner is served, where my lord will later join you." He gestured to the other stoic warriors. "My men will care for your mounts."

So, that was how it was going to be. "Indeed, send my thanks to your lord," Tehl said, his voice ringing clear. He swung off his horse, his men following his lead. The warlord refused to greet them? What sort of game was he playing? He lifted the reins over Wraith's head and pulled him forward, keeping his gaze sharp.

Sam sauntered up to Tehl's side and smirked at the warrior. "It's a pleasure to see you again," he said to the large warrior. "I didn't get your name the first time we met."

The warrior stiffened, the feathers in his long-braided hair fluttering in the air. "It's Blair."

"Our thanks, Warrior Blair," Lilja purred in a voice that had Tehl glancing in her direction.

At that moment, everything about her screamed unearthly. Her hips swayed as she sashayed up to the warrior, drawing all the eyes of the Scythian men. Even in disguise, she was the most sensual creature he'd ever come in contact with.

Tehl snuck a glance at the warrior and didn't miss the flash of interest in Blair's dark gaze as the Sirenidae glided to a stop in front of him, her hip cocked and hand held out. The commander carefully took Lilja's fingers in his gigantic hand and kissed the back of hers prettily, his gaze locked on the woman.

"My pleasure, my lady," he rumbled against her skin, then straightened and held an arm out.

Lilja flipped her hair and handed her reins to a warrior standing to her left. "I believe it shall be," she murmured, taking his arm.

How did her husband feel about the warrior lusting after his wife? Tehl glanced at Hayjen, who stood behind, watching his wife with a blank mask. Whatever he was feeling, it was deeply hidden.

Tehl's gaze moved to Blaise, standing proudly in the middle of the Aermian delegation.

"Are you not going to welcome me home, Blair?" her question hung in the air.

The Scythian warrior bowed shallowly and straightened. "It is a happiness to see your face again, Blaise. Your mother has missed you dearly."

"And my uncle?"

Blair froze for a second. "I'm sure he'll rejoice in your return as well."

Her cheeks sucked in, and she glanced to the side. "Where is my mother?"

"In her suite, I assume."

Blaise nodded and strode from the group and into the palace.

He shot a look at his brother. The first piece was in play. Sam slid his gaze away.

Tehl handed his reins to a Scythian warrior and kept his face pleasant as the warrior glared at him. The air was taut with unease, hostility, and suspicion. Their peace accord was already going well.

The palace courtyard was like nothing he'd ever seen, and he had to force himself not to gawk. The castle was immense and intricate, it's winged roofs decorated with dragons that sat like little guardians on the tips. Looping gold filigree curled around peaked windows, and bright-colored flowers burst from every little crack. The colors were overwhelming.

"Shall we?" Blair asked, staring at him, with Lilja's arm tucked into his.

"Lead the way."

The warrior spun on his heel, and he and the Sirenidae led the procession upstairs and into the palace.

The inside was even more beautiful than the outside. The high, cream, arching walls created a long tunnel, scattered with tall windows that illuminated the ancient art on the walls—ruby dragons sleeping amongst children, Nagalians riding on dragons, people singing and working alongside their beasts. Each mosaic was more beautiful and fantastic than the last and just as heart-wrenching.

"What a tragedy," Gav muttered under his breath.

Sadness blanketed him as well. An entire people gone. He pulled his eyes from the depictions of the past, disgusted. Scythia had destroyed everything. Tehl stared at the warrior's back, trying to get himself under control. It wouldn't do to hurl accusations around at peace negotiations. His lips curled at the thought. Negotiations. There wouldn't be any negotiations if he had anything to say about it.

Time. They needed more of it to discover what the Scythians plotted, as well as to move their own soldiers into play, but it seemed to be the one thing they lacked.

They trekked up level after level of the castle, each unique. He ignored the murmurs of their party. He was sure the historians and scribes were soaking up the rare chance to see the art of the extinct culture.

Finally, Blair stopped and moved them to a hallway that looped back on itself, creating a circle of doors. Tehl eyed the "servants" stationed outside his door and muffled a snort. If the men standing outside the doors were servants, he'd eat his horse. They were warriors, through and through. So, the question that begged to be asked was, were they there as jailers, protectors, or spies? Definitely two of the three.

Blair nodded to two warriors who stood at attention outside two large doors and flung the doors open, gesturing to him with a bow. "Your rooms, my lord."

Tehl cast a glance at his party, who were all being shown into their own rooms, before moving into the suite. It was beautiful, designed in a way he'd never seen. Rich colors decorated the curtains bracketing the large balcony window, lush rugs carpeted the red stone floor, and exotic art complemented the walls.

"Is it to your liking?" the warrior asked.

"It is." He paused and noticed Sam meandering off into another room. "My delegation?"

"They will all be housed in this same corridor."

"And the warlord?" Tehl asked, the question hanging in the air.

"He hopes you and your delegation will join him for dinner this evening."

"We accept his invitation with thanks," Tehl murmured in an attempt to be respectful. He clamped his lips shut from asking about his wife. If the warrior had any information about Sage, he doubted the Scythian would share it with him.

With one last bow, the commander strode out of the room and closed both doors behind him, leaving Sam, Gav, Rafe, Lilja, Hayjen, Zachael, and Tehl in the room.

"That went as well as I expected," Gav said while walking around the perimeter of the room.

"Indeed," Rafe added, inspecting the balcony. "This place, it smells like death."

A shiver worked up Tehl's spine. There was something eerie about the abandoned palace. No, not abandoned, just empty. He shook it off and shot a glance at his brother, who was peeking underneath the bed. "What did you think of it?"

"Tactically, it's a brilliant place to stage a massacre."

Everyone's attention snapped to Sam.

His brother stood and tapped his temple. "Think about it. It's the perfect place to corral people. Looping walkways, narrow stairways, and every passageway looks identical. It would be easy to get lost if you're not familiar with the place." He shrugged and shoved at the bed, only budging the colossal piece of furniture but a few inches. "Some help, please."

Hayjen and Tehl both stepped forward and heaved the bed over. His brother smiled and flipped back the rug, revealing a hatch in the floor.

"But if you know where the tunnels are, well…" Sam's blue eyes glinted dangerously. "We won't be so difficult to corral."

Zachael dropped into a squat, his black-and-silver hair falling into his face as he ran his hand along the door. He lifted his fingers, his eyes narrowing. "No dust. What does that tell you, Sam?"

"It's been in use. Recently."

The weapon master's lips thinned. "We should be prepared for company." He flicked a look to Tehl. "Also, consider everything said in this room to be public knowledge. Even if they don't attack, there's no way to know who's listening."

Tehl stared at the hatch. "We need to station someone down there."

"I'll do it."

He clashed eyes with Rafe. The rebellion leader let a ruthless grin take over his face, puckering his scar so that it looked even more fierce. "Don't you want to be at the delegation?"

"Yes, but I can guard during the night."

"And when will you sleep?" Gav asked without snark. "You will need rest, or we will all be in danger."

"They won't get past me," Rafe responded with confidence. "During the day, I'll station several men down there."

Tehl noticed Lilja staring blankly out the window. Hayjen stood silently behind her, his hands rubbing her arms. They both were uncharacteristically quiet.

"Lilja," he called softly.

The Sirenidae glanced at him with a sort of sorrow in her eyes.

"Thank you," he murmured. "I know this is painful for you and I wish you didn't have to bear it, but I'm thankful you're here, for Sage." He stepped closer, lifted her icy hand, and kissed the back of it. "I'm in your debt."

He began to pull away when she wrapped her arms around him in a fierce hug. "I'd do anything for Sage, but know I do this for you, too, Tehl."

Tehl squeezed her once and smiled at Hayjen, who stepped forward and hugged him with a lot of back-slapping. He was warmed by the gesture. He'd always had his family for his friends, but since Sage came into his life, his friends seemed to expand day by day, and he couldn't be more grateful.

"What's next?" Rafe asked.

"Now, we wait."

CHAPTER TWENTY-NINE

Tehl

He hated waiting.

Tehl paced the room as the sun set, blazing pinks and oranges splashed across the sky. "Are we supposed to go down unescorted?" he growled, tugging on his blue velvet vest, eyeing the sinking sun.

"Calm down, brother, or you'll tire yourself out. The night is still young."

He pulled in a shuddering breath. "I need some air." He strode across the room and joined Rafe on the balcony. The rebellion leader's head was tipped back, eyes closed, his wine-colored hair lifting in the breeze.

"Have you worn out your boots yet?"

Tehl wrapped his hands around the banister and rolled his shoulders back. "Not yet, but I'm on my way."

An amber eye peeked at him. "You need to calm down."

He scowled at Rafe, his jaw clenching. "I'm trying. It's like I'm trying to burst out of my skin," he confessed. "I want it to stop."

"It's being so close that is difficult," Rafe commiserated.

"What a sad pair we are," Tehl said dryly, scanning the other balconies in view. None were close, but in a pinch, he could possibly maneuver down if the need arose. Was Sage trapped in one of those rooms? He tore his eyes from the windows below. "Does the worry ever end?"

A bark of laughter escaped the rebellion leader, only to be carried away in the wind. "It only gets worse the longer you love someone."

Tehl mulled over that, scowling. He worried over his father, his brother, his cousin, but nothing compared to the agonizing pain and worry he carried over Sage. Was that what love involved? He caught Rafe observing him from the corner of his eye. "What?"

"You are the only one I could ever deem worthy of her. You've sacrificed much for her." The rebellion leader leveled him with a look. "Things your family doesn't even know."

Tehl straightened, knowing exactly what he referred to. "How?"

"The how doesn't matter right now, only that my respect for you has grown." Rafe held out his forearm. "I promise, from this moment forward, I will leave your mate alone."

"My mate?" he repeated, to make sure he'd heard correctly.

"Your mate," Rafe reiterated without so much as a blink.

Tehl took the offered forearm. "Thank you." And he meant it. He knew how much the rebellion leader loved Sage, even if he had a poor way of showing it.

Rafe smiled, but it was bitter. "Just take care of her, or there will be consequences."

He smiled back. "Naturally."

A knock at the door had everyone straightening.

"Let's go get our girl," Lilja whispered.

Zachael pulled open the door, admitting a different warrior. The man bowed and gestured to the side. "Dinner is served. If you will please follow me..."

Tehl strode forward with Rafe and Zachael at either side. In the hallway, the rest of his delegation stood in their finery and bowed at his entrance. He nodded, but kept up with their escort as they were led through a series of twist and turns, finally arriving at a gigantic black door painted with golden dragons. The Scythian pushed the door inward and it split in half, revealing it was in fact two doors instead of one.

Tehl glanced at his brother and nodded as if to say, *Here we go*. He threw back his shoulders and stepped into the room just as the servant's voice rang out:

"Crown Prince Tehl Ramses and the Aermian delegation."

The dining room was immense. To say it was opulent was an understatement. Rubies the size of his fist hung from black metal chandeliers that highlighted the elaborate paintings on the ceiling. But that wasn't the most interesting part. What was more intriguing were the exotic people staring at his group, complete silent. A chill ran down his spine when he noted just how similar they all looked to one another. A man stood at the head of a table and held a hand out to the woman next to him.

Tehl's breath seized in his lungs as he got a clear look at the woman. "Sage," he mouthed.

His wife sat serenely next to the warlord, her face a pleasant but placid mask. His heart jumped, beating so hard he swore everyone could hear it. She was alive. Whole.

A pinch on his arm pulled his attention from Sage to Sam. His brother's lips lifted in a smirk, but his eyes held a warning.

"Steady," Lilja whispered. "Calm."

Tehl barely registered her words, but he gave a curt nod in acknowledgment and centered himself. Tonight wasn't for reunions, no matter how much he wished it. Tonight was for battle. A battle that involved words. A moment of dread gripped him at the thought. He was terrible when it came to speaking pretty words, but Sage's life depended on it. He pushed the thought away and focused on his wife.

She rose gracefully and placed her hand in the warlord's. They moved around the table gracefully, step by step, and Sage never looked more like a queen than in that moment. Tehl froze as two gigantic man-eaters sauntered after the couple. *Stars above.* His mind told him to run from the predators prowling their way.

"That's the biggest cat I've ever seen," Sam breathed. "How in the blazes did he acquire those?"

"With skill, I'm sure," Lilja whispered.

Tehl tore his gaze from the felines and back to Sage. Her expression was pleasant, pleased even, but he knew what that really meant. She was scared. He squinted, but otherwise kept his expression schooled. Her court mask wasn't the only thing that looked different. Sage looked like an altered version of herself, more polished than the wild woman he'd taken as his wife. She looked... flawless. That thought caused unease to churn in his gut. Was it simply his being away from her so long that meant perhaps his memory was inaccurate, or could it mean something more?

With great pain, he pulled his gaze from her and met the pitch-black eyes of the man escorting her. It felt like he'd been slapped in the face. He'd always considered himself a good judge of beauty, male and female alike. But the man—if you could call him that—was beyond anything he'd ever seen. Tehl had never felt more disheveled and self-conscious. The warlord smiled at him, and the hair rose on the back of his neck. Tehl knew a predator when he saw one.

In that moment, Tehl put aside any faint but fanciful notions of peace. The man escorting his wife did not want peace. But what did he want? He'd find out soon enough. Tehl straightened and pulled himself together as the warlord and Sage halted just out of reach.

The warlord's deep voice washed over him, both powerful and smooth with a hint of accent: "Welcome, Crown Prince Ramses."

Tehl dipped his chin. "I thank you for the invitation to join you. I also look forward to our new endeavor for peace."

"I likewise look forward to our future." The warlord's dark gaze swept over the group and paused on someone behind Tehl before coming back to him. "I can't wait to meet your delegation." He turned and smiled at Sage. "I trust you know my companion."

His thoughts stilled at the look the warlord gave Sage. There was too much heat in his smile to just be polite. Far too much.

The warlord lifted Sage's hand, and she glided forward, her green gaze meeting Tehl's. His world tilted on its axis and righted at the sight of her whole. She was here, safe. He kept his feelings shuttered and took her offered hand, placing a chaste kiss on the back of it instead of pulling her into his arms for a hug like he wanted to. "My lady..."

"My lord," she murmured, her voice music to his ears.

It was ridiculous. Since she'd disappeared, he'd almost forgotten how beautiful her voice was. He breathed in and smiled that she still smelled like herself. She looked different, but still was Sage. "Thank you for taking such good care of my wife. I cannot tell you how much she's been missed," he murmured against her skin.

Sage smiled and gently tried to pull her fingers from his grasp. He tightened his grip for several seconds before he allowed her to step back. The light in her eyes dimmed and her mask slipped into place. The hope he held inside died at her reaction. She appeared whole on the outside, but he knew the inside would tell a different story. He forced his hand to keep from clenching and smiled pleasantly at the warlord studying him.

"It was my pleasure." The warlord lifted Sage's hand and turned it over, kissing the inside of her wrist.

Tehl didn't react to the sexual gesture and kept his façade in place, but inside, he was seething.

"She's been an absolute treasure to have in my home. Now, let's eat," the warlord said. He wrapped Sage's arm in his and spun on his heel.

A flash of rage burned through Tehl at the manner in which the Scythian ruler held his wife. He blinked, surprised at the strong emotion. He couldn't risk showing his hand and endangering everyone, so he shoved his feelings aside. With forced casualness, he followed them to the table littered with Scythians.

Two chairs sat at the end of the table. The warlord sat Sage at one and stood in front of the other. "Please, sit, and let dinner begin."

Tehl placed himself on the other side of his wife and sat at the same time as the warlord. His brother glided to his other side and sat with a flourish all his own. For once, Tehl was thankful for his brother's antics as they pulled much of the attention off of Tehl and onto Sam. He glanced across the table and nodded to Gav, who sat beside the behemoth of a warrior who had escorted them to their rooms earlier. Blair, the commander. Tehl acknowledged him and then eyed the servants placing tray after tray of food on the table. Traditional Aermian, and what he assumed to be Scythian delicacies, littered the table, the spicy, savory, and sweet aromas wafting temptingly through the air.

He nearly jumped when a rumbling sound erupted next to him. Tehl glanced down to the floor and caught the golden gaze of a feline. The hair rose on his arms. If he so much as moved his hand he could touch the beast's fur.

"That's enough," Sage whispered softly and placed a hand on the feline's head.

Tehl blinked, and swore he saw the feline smile smugly before pressing against Sage's leg. He eyed the leren for only a moment more before forcing himself to turn back to the table. He inhaled the spices teasing the air and placed a few foodstuffs onto his plate, then turned to the warlord with a practiced smile, not surprised to find the Scythian ruler was studying him. "The fare looks delicious. I thank you for the hospitality shown to my men and myself, Warlord Zane. Our rooms are exquisite, and the view, breathtaking."

A twinkle entered the warlord's eye as he plopped a piece of fruit into his mouth, flashing white teeth. "It was my pleasure, Your Highness. And I might thank you for returning my niece home safely. Not everyone is so honorable."

Tehl nodded. "It was my pleasure. Blaise was no trouble at all."

The warlord released a booming laugh. "I wouldn't go that far. She's a handful and enjoys causing mischief wherever she goes. Isn't that so, niece?"

Tehl glanced down the table to Blaise.

She set her spoon down prettily, dipped her head. "As you say, my lord."

"Cheeky," the warlord mumbled, eyeing his niece. He raised one eyebrow before dismissing her and returning his attention to his plate.

Tehl turned and peeked at Sage next to him, who was picking at her plate. "Are you not hungry, my lady?" he asked, wondering if there was something wrong with it. Was it poisoned?

Her bowed head lifted just a touch; her gaze flitted to his for a fraction of a heartbeat and then back to the food on her plate.

"I'm afraid my stomach is unsettled, my lord."

"Wild one, why didn't you tell me?" The warlord sat forward, a flicker of concern on his face.

Wild one? Anger heated his gut. The warlord had a pet name for his wife? That didn't bode well.

"It's nothing," Sage murmured.

The warlord scanned his plate and plucked up a little yellow fruit and held it out to her. "Here, this will help."

Tehl expected her to take the fruit from the warlord, but the air in his lungs froze when she scooted closer and ate the fruit from his hand. From the corner of his eye, he caught Gav gawking for only a moment before he recovered. The warlord smiled, brushed her lip with his thumb, and caught a drop of juice. Tehl watched as the Scythian leader sucked it into his own mouth. The move was blatantly sexual, and completely inappropriate. His hands clenched into fists under the table.

The warlord's obsidian gaze wandered from Sage to Tehl, a small smirk on his smug face, like he knew what the crown prince was thinking. Sage's small hand slid over Tehl's and squeezed once before retreating. He kept his expression schooled into something polite. Sage continued to eat like nothing had happened, so he followed her cue.

He sipped his savory pumpkin soup while scanning the table. It was ridiculous. The entire group, Aermians and Scythians alike, was silent, each pretending they weren't all sneaking glances at the other. The dislike and mistrust were evident with each glare or false smile. He met Gav's purple gaze before dropping his eyes back to his soup. No one wanted to be here, including himself.

"Is the soup to your liking?" a deep voice rumbled.

He glanced at the warlord. "It's delicious."

"Not a man of many words, are you?"

Tehl leaned back into his chair and cocked his head. "I've found that people like to dance around a problem with too many fine words and end up accomplishing nothing. I hate wasting time. Why not say what you mean the first time?"

"Why not, indeed?" The warlord swirled his wine in his goblet and dipped his chin. "I, too, believe in being straightforward and honest. So, I'll say this..." His dark gaze intensified. "I desire peace. My people deserve more than being punished for the sins of their ancestors, but prejudices long ingrained are hard to remove. This won't be easy, but I believe it possible."

Tehl regarded him thoughtfully. His words didn't seem false, but that made him wary. The best lies were ones rooted in truth. He turned to Sage, who was listening intently, but had remained silent. "And what of you, Sage? What do you think? You've lived with both our peoples."

She twisted and stared him dead in the eye. "Peace is always possible. It just depends on how much one desires it."

"A wise observation, my lady," Zachael murmured, pulling her attention. "May I also say you're looking well."

"Thank you," she said with a small smile.

"Your presence in the ring has been missed."

"The ring?" the warlord asked.

"It's where we train," Sage explained.

Zachael smiled, faint wrinkles creasing around his mouth. "She's a tough opponent. Our men nursed battle wounds and wounded pride daily."

"What a fierce little consort," the warlord said.

Sage stiffened.

Tehl frowned. Nothing the warlord said was offensive that he could note, so why was she upset?

His heart beat a little faster as Sage pushed back from her chair and stood. Tehl was on his feet, along with all the other men out of respect. She curtseyed to the table and caught his eye just for a second before she turned to the warlord.

"I find myself fatigued. I must beg your forgiveness for my early departure."

The warlord plucked her hand from the table and kissed the back of it, lingering far too long. "As you wish, wild one."

Sage pulled her hand from his grasp and glided away from the table without a backward glance.

His fingers clenched around his fork.

What had the warlord done to his wife?

CHAPTER THIRTY

Sage

She huffed out a breath as she exited the dining room, Nali quick on her heels. Four warriors materialized from the dark, surrounding her and leading her back to her prison. The tension in her body increased as they wound their way through the abandoned palace. Tehl kissing the back of her hand flashed through her mind. He looked every bit as handsome as she remembered, and his eyes just as kind. Heat built behind her eyes. Little did he know what a traitor she was...what an adulteress.

The pressure built in her chest, and Sage grasped at every last thread of strength she had. She wouldn't cry in front of these men. They'd report it to Zane, and that was the last thing she needed. All she had to do was make it back to the room. There, she could release her feelings.

The warriors led her around a corner, and the double doors to her room became visible. It was both a relief and pain to see them. Sage ignored the warrior who opened the door and moved into the dim room. The door slammed behind her, and the sound seemed to echo, although it was probably just in her broken mind. Her shoulders hunched forward, and soundless sobs burst out. She stumbled toward a chair and gripped the back of it.

It killed her to ignore her friends and family. Tears dripped down her face, remembering the smile Zachael gave her. The weapons master was like family to her, and while the situation couldn't be worse, she was grateful to see him.

Her hands tightened when she thought of how Lilja had stared. The woman attracted attention everywhere she went, but tonight she'd dressed somberly, her hair covered, and her eye color changed. Fear had gripped Sage when she'd spotted her Sirenidae friend. If the warlord figured out what she was, there was no telling what he'd do.

The pain in her chest increased as she reflected on Tehl's expression when the warlord had made her eat from his hand. Shame and humiliation scorched her cheeks and her hands shook. The entire dinner had been a farce, a test to see if she could be trusted to play her role when the talks began on the morrow. It was sick and demented, just like him. Rage flowed freely through her veins, and a giant crash had her blinking. She stared at her outstretched hand to the vase that had shattered into a million tiny pieces at her feet. When had she picked that up?

The bedroom door slammed open, and Sage spun to face the warriors bearing down on her. Nali released a hair-raising growl and loped to her side, making the warriors halt. They eyed the mess and the man-eater. One brave warrior edged closer and placed a gentle hand on her arm, pulling her away from the broken vase.

"I dropped it," she said.

He stared at her for a moment, disbelief on his face. He obviously didn't believe her lie for one second. She hissed an angry breath when he brushed his hand along her legs, and then her arms.

"I'm not hurt," she said.

"I'm following my commands, my lady." He finished his search, satisfied, and jerked his chin toward the other men. As quickly as they entered, they exited, leaving her behind with only her regret, the black feline, and a broken vase for company.

A shiver worked through her body as a cool breeze blew into the room. She snagged the blanket off the bed and threw it over her shoulders before moving out to the balcony. The black beast pressed into her side, and Sage laid a hand on her head, gazing at the night sky. Bright stars twinkled like gems on velvet. A shuddering breath escaped her when she caught sight of fires burning in the distance.

The Guard. Aermian soldiers.

So close, but so far away. It was cruel, really, to see her escape and not be able to attain it. It could have been seconds, minutes, or hours that she stood gazing out into the dark.

A warm chest pressed to her back; muscular arms wrapped around her, fingers digging into the blanket and her hips.

"Are you going to stand out here all night?" the warlord's deep voice whispered in her ear.

It was unfair how musical his voice was. It could corrupt the most prudish maiden. He was the devil, plain and simple.

He took her hand and tsked. "Your hands are as cold as ice. Come warm them by the fire."

She allowed him to pull her from her sanctuary—one last glance at the encampment. Even though escape was improbable, the Aermians' presence still comforted her, inspiring hope.

The warlord drew her to the fire, where Nali had curled up for the night. Sage sat on a low bench in front of the heat, still cocooned in her blanket. The flames hopped from one side to another in a happy dance of orange, yellow, and red. Her skin prickled, and she pulled the blanket tighter, trying to ignore the huge man studying her.

"You did well tonight."

Sage jerked and craned her neck to meet his eyes. "I did nothing tonight."

"Precisely. You played your part remarkably. You should've seen the expressions of the Aermian delegation when you ate from my hand." An amused chuckle rumbled out of him. "Thank you."

"I didn't do it for you," she muttered. She tensed and dropped her gaze to the swirling rug beneath her feet, wishing she could take back what she had said. Her words were careless. Careless words killed people.

The warlord sank to his haunches and lifted her chin. Bravely, she met his gaze, not flinching at the way he scrutinized her face. One finger traced her eyebrow, then down her temple and cheek.

"I suppose not, consort," he rumbled, leaning forward to press his lips against hers in a kiss so gentle it made her feel like weeping. "Some days, I feel like I could forget the past," he said, his words whispering across her skin.

What past? It threw her when he let her glimpse his softer side every so often. It was just enough to make her second-guess herself and look for something good.

He held his hand out. "Let's go to bed, love. Tomorrow marks the beginning of our future."

Trepidation filled her as she once again followed him to the bed. When she got to its edge, she stared at it like it might bite. Each night went this way. She feared what might happen in that bed, but soon the fear gave way to exhaustion, and she'd find herself wrapped up in Zane's arms come morning. With a huff, she flung the cover off her back and tossed it onto the bed. Sage crawled into the bed and turned onto her side to watch the warlord strip off his boots and shirt. It made her feel like a lecher, but she'd rather stare at him while he undressed than turn her back to him. No use in making herself more vulnerable than she already was.

He caught her eye as he shrugged his shirt off, the moonlight highlighting his muscles, which rippled with his every move. Despite everything that had occurred, he was still the most beautiful thing she'd ever seen. He crawled into bed and scooted closer, never losing eye contact, and placed his hand in the curve of her waist.

She glanced down at his arm and shivered, pulling the cover tighter, unsettled that the heat from his hand burned through the fabric and seemed to imprint itself on her skin like it belonged there.

"Wild one?"

Sage peeked up at him from underneath her lashes. "Yes?"

"You touched him tonight."

Licking her lips, she attempted to calm herself. His tone might have been casual, but it was anything but. It was the calm before the storm.

"It wasn't anything."

"The way he looked at you wasn't just *anything*, consort."

"Do you want peace?"

Her question must have startled him, because his intense expression melted into confusion.

"Have I not made that clear?"

"I was securing peace."

His gaze shuttered. "Is that what you think you were doing?"

"I know him," she said, avoiding using Tehl's name. "Your display upset him. I didn't want the peace accord to be destroyed before it had a chance to succeed." Sage meant every word. Her people didn't understand the kind of creatures they were dealing with. 'Deadly' was the word that came to mind.

His expression was unreadable as he lay there staring at her, searching for something. He must have found it, because he smiled at her and brushed her hair from her cheek.

"I believe you, Sage."

A breath she didn't know she was holding leaked out of her.

He hitched his arm around her, pulled her against his chest, and rolled onto his back. She stiffly held herself against his side, her ear over his heart. Sage hated him in that moment, because he was so human. His heart thumped in his chest just like hers, steady and calm, the calm she craved when everything was so messed up and confused.

"Sleep, wild one."

Almost against her will, her body softened and her eyelids grew heavy. But she wouldn't fall asleep until he answered the question that had been plaguing her since he pointed out the Aermian camp in the distance. "Zane?"

"Yes, love?"

"Will you harm my people?"

Silence.

She lifted her head and met his dark gaze. He lifted his hand and cupped her cheek.

"As long as they don't harm me or mine, I'll leave them unharmed. I want to make the kingdoms a better place."

By what means? she wanted to ask, but instead she whispered, "Do you promise?"

"You have my word, consort, and you know I keep my word." His heated eyes bore into hers, making it clear what he was speaking of. He hadn't taken her yet. He'd kept his promises, all of them, even the one she didn't want to remember.

"Thank you." She placed a hand on his heart and leaned closer to brush a kiss along his cheek. The small intake of his breath clued her into something she hadn't expected. She affected him, but it was more than lust, more than his insane need to control her.

A small part of him might care for her.

Sage pulled back and curled up by his side. The thought startled her and gave her a little seed of hope. Somewhere, deep down inside him, he had good qualities. No one could be completely bad. But she wasn't his salvation, a way to fix his wrongs in the past. Without him knowing it, he'd just given her the key she'd need. It was a dangerous risk to take, appealing to his heart, but if it succeeded, it might mean her freedom.

His hand curled around hers, and his lips pressed to the top of her head.

Freedom. She dreamed of freedom.

***

The morning came too fast, and before she knew it, she was standing before a mirror dressed like a queen. She grimaced at her reflection. With its rich red silk and black fur, her dress screamed Scythian royalty. Her gaze slid to the warlord buttoning his black vest over a black silk shirt. It shouldn't have surprised her; black seemed to be his signature color.

As if feeling her gaze, his almond-shaped eyes peered up at her from impossibly thick eyelashes. "Yes, wild one?"

She shook her head and turned back to her own outfit, her eyes snagging on the collar around her neck. Anger buzzed in her veins. It wasn't right that something so beautiful could represent something so disgusting.

"Something wrong?"

Sage wiped the look from her face as the warlord sidled up behind her and placed his hands on her shoulders. She wanted to test her theory, but baiting him before the peace talks wasn't beneficial for anyone. "No." She shook her head. "Just tired."

He squeezed her shoulder and squinted at her head. A smile pulled one side of his mouth up. "Well, your hair is wide awake," he commented wryly as he brushed down a stray hair.

The moment was surreal. It was times like these that confused Sage. They were so mundane, so human. It scared her how easy it would be to stop fighting, to let go, to let the warlord devour her. He'd been her friend at one time. He could be that again if she let go.

He placed a quick kiss on her thorn collar. "This looks so beautiful against your skin."

Her heart fell. And that's why she would never comply. When he let his human side out, it was brief and beautiful, like a shooting star, but the darkness that raged after it was brutal.

He straightened and held an arm out. "Are you ready to change history?"

Sage nodded and ignored her sour stomach. What sort of changes was he planning?

***

Tables and chairs had been placed in a loose square, while unshuttered windows allowed the mountain breeze to pass through a ballroom. It didn't escape her notice that she didn't quite sit in the middle of the group as the position of mediator dictated. Her chair was slightly to the left, closer to the Scythian side.

The Aermian delegates, the Scythian delegates, and leads were given seats, their places marked with nameplates of onyx inlaid with silver. Pitchers of water, juice, and ale were at all the tables.

Scythian scribes she'd never seen before sat on lush pillows against the wall, ready to take notes, while the Aermian scribes sat at a table behind the crown prince.

She scanned the Scythian side, only knowing three of the nine delegates: the warlord, Maeve, and Blair.

Her heart squeezed as she twisted to the right and stared at all the familiar faces. Zachael, Gav, Tehl, Sam, Hayjen, Lilja, William, and Jeren. Even the stodgy Jeren was a welcome sight. But it was the man with golden eyes and wine-colored hair that pulled her attention. Rafe sat watching her, his face blank, but in his eyes, she detected a familiar look.

Sage smiled inwardly. The warlord was a master tactician, but he'd never met Rafe. If there was a way to escape, he'd figure it out. She scanned the group once more and moved back to the man she'd skipped. His dark blue gaze nearly knocked the wind from her lungs. He was more beautiful than the phantom her imagination had conjured.

"Good morning, wife," Tehl murmured softly.

She swallowed hard, ignoring how the warlord stilled at the crown prince's soft-spoken words. "Good morning, my lord. I trust you slept well?" she said, her tone polite, nothing more.

"I did. The accommodations were excellent, thank you."

She nodded and tore herself from his intense gaze only to be ensnared by the warlord's. He looked cool and collected, but Sage saw something different. She saw rage brewing beneath the surface, one she didn't know if she could survive a second time. He looked to Tehl and then shot her a look; she blinked. Had that been hurt in his eyes? What was he thinking? She tore her gaze from the warlord and pushed aside her thoughts. She had a duty to do.

With care, she rose from her chair. "I welcome all to the peace delegation that will change the very fabric of our kingdoms," she recited from memory. "Today, we'll embark on something historic that has not been attempted in one hundred years. Today, we strive for peace."

Silence settled over the solemn group of men and women as her words died in the echoing space. She curtseyed to the table. "It's my honor to mediate this peace accord. It is my hope that we can reach an understanding that will benefit both our lands and peoples." She held a hand out toward the warlord and the crown prince. "Please step forward to begin our discussion."

Tehl moved to her right side, and the warlord prowled to her left. "Please repeat after me: I pledge to seek the advantage for both our peoples as lord and ruler of my kingdom." Both men repeated after her, and she held a hand out to each man. A measure of calmness settled over Sage when Tehl placed his hand in hers, combating the fear that the warlord's grip instigated in her. She placed the men's hands together. "Let it be done."

Tehl and the warlord shook hands in the Aermian custom and then kissed each other's cheeks in the Scythian custom before moving back to their seats.

Sage swept an arm out and sank into her chair, her wobbly legs grateful for the support. "Begin," she announced.

Relief washed over her. Her part was done for now. Now, she listened and watched.

***

Her worry was for naught.

The morning had started off awkward for everyone seemed reluctant to speak, but after an hour of stilted speeches, Sam had managed to crack a joke that broke even the most stoic Scythians' demeanors.

Each Aermian delegate had a speech prepared that was eloquent and overly polite, and each of Zane's delegates followed by making a speech of their own. The first day was wasted on pretty words that were anything but sincere, but at least they'd gotten the ball rolling.

She rubbed between her brows. A throbbing pain in her head made itself known just as the Scythian at the end of the table, Phoenix, finished his speech. The delegates had spent all day speaking, yet nothing seemed accomplished.

"Are you all right, consort?" the warlord asked. Tehl and Lilja's gazes turned to Sage.

"My head hurts," she said, offering a weak smile. All the stress of the day had led to rising pain that stabbed her eyes.

"We're finishing up here," the warlord murmured. "Why don't you retire to your room until dinner?"

She glanced at the window, noting the sinking sun. "I will." Sage stood, curtseyed, and slipped from the room. She stumbled a step and placed a hand against the rough red stone wall. The hallway lurched, causing her stomach to do the same, and the grapes she'd nibbled on for lunch threatened to make a reappearance.

"My lady? Are you all right?"

Sage glanced to the warrior who was watching her with trepidation. "No, I need to rest."

He nodded, and she forced herself upright and lurched after him. She managed to stumble into the room and crash onto the bed, the pain so overwhelming that stars dotted her vision. Nali grumped, but otherwise didn't move when Sage cuddled up to the big animal.

"Do you need anything, my lady?"

"The curtains," she mumbled, burrowing into the coverlet and pressing her face into Nali's fur.

A rustle of cloth reached her ears, and then blessed darkness closed over her. "Thank you," she whispered.

Silence, and then, "You're welcome."

The door clicked closed.

She grimaced and prayed that sleep would claim her quickly.

***

Cool skin touched her forehead, and she followed it, seeking comfort. Her hand shot out and wrapped around the wrist, moving it back to her forehead.

"Wild one, I need you to let go, so I can give you something for your head."

"No," she moaned. "No draughts." A whimper escaped her as another wave of pain slammed into her.

A curse reached her ears. "You're so frail! Every time I turn around, there's something wrong with you! Let me help. I can heal you."

A large hand slipped behind her neck and something cool was placed at her lips. Sage pushed through her pain and opened her eyes to stare at the warlord's angry face.

"What is it?"

"Something for your pain."

"Are you telling me the truth?"

His face darkened even more. "I'm not poisoning you."

"That's not what I asked," she croaked.

"It's only for the pain."

She searched his face, not sure if he was lying.

"Drink it, or I will make you. Stop choosing to suffer when I can fix you."

And there it was, the threat to take away her right to choose. But even if she did choose, it wasn't really a choice. Another wave of pain crashed into her. Attending the talks in this state wasn't possible, and she needed to be there. It was an easy choice. By way of answer, she opened her mouth and drank the draught.

He laid her down and brushed her hair from her face. "Not terrible, was it?" He placed a kiss on her cheek and rubbed his fingers along her scalp. "Why do you have to be so stubborn? You make no sense sometimes. Women are such fickle creatures."

She breathed a contented sigh as his fingers released some of the pain assaulting her.

"I can't miss dinner, but I'll make excuses for you." He stroked her cheek and then disappeared without a sound, leaving Sage to snuggle back into bed.

CHAPTER THIRTY-ONE

Sage

Sage woke up, tingling with awareness. She curled her hand around the dagger underneath her pillow. It was comical that the warlord let her keep it as she'd tried to use it on him once, yet he'd disarmed her so quickly that the dagger was more of a symbol of her helplessness than anything else. She was, however, thankful to have it this night—because there was someone in her room.

Listening intently, she kept her eyes closed and her breathing even. She forced herself to stay calm and to not move a muscle. A Scythian assassin would be stronger and faster, and she was virtually blind in the dark. She needed to keep still and lure the assassin toward her. It was a risk, but at least if the intruder was close, she could attack first and catch them by surprise; then maybe she'd have a chance.

Blessedly, the pain in her head was gone, so she could really focus. One breath, two breaths, three breaths, and there it was. The scent of mint. She snapped her arms out, clutching a shirt, and jerked with all her strength, throwing the assassin over her head. With speed she didn't know she still possessed, Sage rolled onto her knees and threw a knee over the intruder. She grabbed a handful of his hair and yanked back, holding her dagger's tip to the assassin's throat.

"Give me one reason why I shouldn't kill you right now?"

"Because I'm your brother, and I love you."

She stilled and let the dagger fall from her hand. "Sam?"

"And I'm much too handsome to die so young."

Sage scrambled backward, across the bed, her eyes darting across the darkness, seeing nothing. "You can't be here," she whispered urgently. If the warlord found him here, he'd kill Jasmine without thought and perhaps slaughter the entire Aermian delegation. She jumped from the bed and skirted around the furniture by memory to get to the window, pulling it back so just a touch of moonlight entered the room.

Sam sat on her bed, watching her.

"I've missed you."

Those were the last words she expected to hear. She both

cherished and loathed them. He stood and held his arms out. Sage was ready to step into them but, thinking better of it, halted after only a pace.

His brows furrowed, and he snuck a glance toward the door. "You're right. We don't have time for a reunion right now." He stalked on silent feet to a trapdoor beneath the rug in front of the fire. "Let's go."

She swallowed hard and clenched her fists. Every part of her wanted to go with him, to just leave this place and the horrid memories, but she couldn't leave Jasmine. And even if that was not an issue, the warlord was too cautious. If Sam was here, it had to be by design.

"No," she whispered.

Sam froze and flew back to her side. "What do you mean 'no'?"

"No," she said, watching emotions ripple across his face. Sam rarely let his emotions show. Sam clasped her cheeks in his palms and his eyes darted between hers. He dropped his hands and wrapped his arms around her in a fierce hug. "I don't know what he's done, or what you've had to do to survive, but none of that matters. All that matters is going home to your family and friends who love you. Don't you want that?"

More than he knew, but he hadn't had to live like she did. "I won't go with you."

His embrace loosened and slowly, he released her and stepped back; this time, his spymaster's mask was in place. He reached a hand out and fingered her gauzy robe. "What is he holding over you?"

She slapped his hand away, stared him in the eye, and lied. "Nothing that concerns you, my lord. Now, please leave."

"I'm not leaving until you explain yourself." He gestured to her state of dress.

She slid a glance to the closed doors and back to Sam, shame coloring her cheeks. "I owe you nothing."

Sam cursed, his jaw clenching. "You owe the kingdom everything, and the warlord nothing."

"I owe him much. He saved my life and has taken care of me." The words tasted like ash on her tongue, partly because part of her believed that.

"He's using you."

"No more than the rebellion or the Crown did. Now, leave." Before the warlord stormed inside.

His face was a stone mask. "We can't protect you from him if you don't leave with me, *right now.*"

A sad smile touched her lips. "No one can protect themselves from him." Her words lingered in the air as Sam stared at her in silence. After a moment, he turned on his heel and snuck back to the trapdoor.

He glanced over his shoulder, the moonlight turning his hair silver. "You're playing a dangerous game. One that could destroy you." He smiled carelessly, pulling the trapdoor down. "Be seeing you soon, sis."

Her heart dropped to her feet as he disappeared down the dark hole, the trapdoor closing soundlessly. She fell to her knees, the pain so acute she couldn't breathe.

She'd let her chance to escape slip away. Sage allowed herself a moment to mourn and then pulled herself to her feet. Wallowing served no purpose, and she needed to calm herself before the warlord arrived. She needed to have a clear head when he arrived.

Muddled thoughts led to poor choices in words, and bad decisions.

Sage stoked the fireplace and slid the rug over the trapdoor Sam escaped through. Not that it would make a difference. Zane was almost impossible to hide things from. She wilted into a chair and picked at her robe, pondering if she should change or not. The warlord would smell Sam on her like a bloody animal. There was no hiding his visit. She might as well just wait.

Two hours passed before the warlord sauntered into the room, closing the door behind him. Sage ignored his entrance, staring into the flames as he moved to stand across from her.

"How are you feeling, Sage?"

"Better," she said, still not looking in his direction.

The crackle of the fire filled the silence that descended between them. Not companionable or comfortable silence, but the kind that is brewing with tension and unsaid words.

"I'm proud of you, consort. You've done well."

She glanced at him, her face schooled. "Why are you proud?"

He glided toward her, all Scythian grace, and cupped her upturned face. "You didn't betray me."

Her suspicions were confirmed. "You knew he'd break in."

"I did."

She scanned his unearthly face and reached up to pull his hand from her face. "Why?"

"I needed to know where your loyalties lay." A breathtaking smile burst across his face. "I needed to know who you belonged to."

"I belong to myself."

"No," he breathed, leaning closer. She could smell the wine on his breath. "I *own* you."

She shot to her feet and rounded the chair, putting it between them. "You made me lie to my family."

The warlord chuckled. "Your family? That boy isn't your family."

"Do you even know the meaning of family?" she spat.

His face soured. "Family means nothing."

"I understand that after what you did to Rhys." Sage snapped her mouth shut, not able to take the words back.

"There are consequences for betrayal. Family is no exclusion."

"What made you like this?" she whispered.

"A sick old man and a twisted woman."

He sprang and grabbed her around the throat. Her hands pried at his as he lifted her and pushed her against a low dresser, the wooden top biting into the back of her thighs. He forced himself into the cradle of her thighs and met her gaze.

"You're a reminder of what's wrong in the world."

Sage gasped when the warlord squeezed the collar, the thorns digging into her skin. He released his grip slightly, so she could pull in a breath.

His gaze scanned her face, softening slightly. "And yet, you're all that's good."

"I don't understand," she whispered.

The warlord's chuckle chilled her. "You wouldn't. No one could understand the deranged old man's obsession with perfection or his covetousness of things that didn't belong to him."

"Who was he?" Sage ventured, trying to keep him talking.

His dark eyes emptied of all emotion. "My father."

She swallowed hard at the way he stared right through her.

"Everything was flawed in his mind, except for a Nagalian

beauty he managed to steal and take as his wife. She was his prize, his goddess. She became pregnant. He anticipated the birth of his son—surely, he'd be as flawless as his mother! But the son was born resembling himself, and looked nothing like his goddess. So, the experimenting began." His empty black gaze focused on her. "Now, his mother had always hated the boy. He was a symbol of all that she had lost, all that was taken. But as the boy aged, he changed and grew into a striking figure, one who had no equal, except for his mother. And she took notice."

Her stomach sank. She hoped he wasn't saying what she thought he was saying.

The warlord smirked. "She couldn't help herself. It was only reasonable she'd be attracted to him. He wasn't really her son anymore, or so she told herself and the boy."

She thought she might throw up.

"He didn't know it was unnatural until his sister told him. Shame battered him every time she touched him, and he reacted, but his mother consoled him with logic. They were family. Naturally, they would love each other."

"Oh, Zane," she breathed, nausea threatening to overwhelm her. "I'm so sorry."

He jerked, his hand tightening around her neck briefly. "For what?"

"For your pain."

Anger darkened his face. "I don't need your pity."

"It's not pity. It's sympathy."

He leaned closer, his eyes darting between her eyes. "I can see that."

"What happened to your family?" She needed to know.

"They died, all but his beloved sister who protected him when no one else would."

"Maeve?"

"So smart," he murmured and trailed a hand down her bleeding neck. "Remember this, wild one, science doesn't lie or manipulate. It is truth." His hand skimmed down to her belly and caressed it. "But it does have consequences. Even I couldn't anticipate how it would affect our women and their birth rate."

Oh God. The room swirled around her in a kaleidoscope of color. All the pregnant women at the execution flashed through her mind. *When are you due?* Bile burned her throat.

"You look so much like her," he whispered, still staring at her flat belly. "This time, it will be different."

His mother. Sage swallowed, trying not to gag. "I'm sorry," she choked out.

"It was long before your birth."

"How long?" she ventured to ask, terrified of the answer.

"Since the purge."

The room spun. It couldn't be. It wasn't possible, but as Sage stared at the warlord, his dark, knowing gaze searched her face. The beautiful monster in front of her was far more dangerous than she ever realized. How was it possible for a man to live that long?

"Why?" she croaked. "Why would you do such a thing? All those people."

"They wouldn't let me cleanse them." His gaze traveled to her neck. "You're bleeding," he said, as if he'd just noticed the damage he'd caused.

She wanted to scream when he plucked her from the dresser and carried her to the bed. Her skin crawled at his touch. Sage panted hard as she tried to sort through her emotions. She'd been sleeping with the most notorious war criminal her land had ever seen. She'd let him touch her skin. Every part of her felt defiled.

The warlord uncorked a vial, poured it into a cup, and held it out to her. She stared at the cup and weighed her options. Did she drink it to appease the creature of death and darkness before her? Or did she fight an ancient monster who had once been human? Her gaze lifted to the warlord's, and what she saw there killed her. Not only could she see the monster, but she could also see the abused little boy.

"No."

His hand clenched on the cup, cracking it.

Sage shoved all the emotions down and reached out, touching the warlord's trembling hand. "I'm not something to be fixed, Zane." He stilled at her use of his name. She lifted her other hand to her throat. "You did this. It's not fair for you to erase it like it never happened."

"Life's never been fair, consort."

"True, you and I both know that." As much as she loathed to admit it, they had something in common. They were survivors. She pushed his hand down and dug deep for her bravery. Slowly, she rolled up onto her knees, so they were at the same eye-level, and cupped both his cheeks. "I'm sorry for what you've suffered," she whispered. "Truly, I am, but that doesn't condone what you've done." He began pulling away from her, but she tightened her hold and lied. "But I will help you change."

"Change is impossible for me."

She agreed. But she said, "Change is never impossible. And I will help you."

He pulled her hands from his face and rubbed his thumb along her cheekbone. "Wild one, you may look like her, but you are nothing like her. She was sick and selfish. You are honorable and kind." He pressed a kiss to her temple. "I'll call for Maeve and have her see to your wounds."

Sage nodded, trying not to puke. As soon as he closed the door, she ran for the railing and released all the contents of her belly. Tears streamed down her face. How could everything go so wrong? A knock had her swiping at her tears and turning to the door.

Maeve opened the door and paused when she caught sight of her. She carefully closed the door and strode to the balcony, carrying a basket. Her cinnamon gaze swept across Sage's face and neck, and her lips pulled down. "Come with me, child."

Sage followed Maeve back into the room, all her emotions raw.

Maeve pulled her to a chair and knelt before her.

She swallowed hard and turned to stare at the fire as the Scythian woman cleaned her wounds.

"Where else does it hurt?"

She pointed to her hips. "He grabbed me."

Maeve brushed aside the robe and hissed.

Sage glanced down at the angry purple bruises already forming.

"What did you do?" Maeve muttered.

"What did I do?" she hissed. "This is clearly your brother's doing."

"Well, you must have set him off."

"Because I look like your mother?"

Maeve jerked. "What?"

"You heard me," Sage whispered. "How can you want your daughter to return to this? How?"

"I can protect her here."

"Can you?" She stared straight into Maeve's eyes. "Can you protect Blaise from him?"

Silence.

"He's more dangerous to her than anything else she could possibly encounter."

"What do you expect me to do? Leave her as a prisoner in Aermia?"

"No." Sage clasped the woman's hands. "I will protect her. I could keep her away from here, keep her safe."

Maeve scoffed. "You can't even protect yourself."

"If you help Jasmine, Blaise, and I escape, I can."

Time seemed to stand still as the Scythian woman stared at her, thinking. After a moment, she glanced at the door and then back to Sage. "You want me to betray him, then?"

"I've seen the emotions you keep hidden from him. Don't lie to yourself or to me. He may be your blood, but we both know he's more a monster than a man, a murderer."

Maeve pulled in a breath and squeezed Sage's hand, something shifting in her eyes. Sage didn't know how she hadn't before noted the ancient wisdom in the woman's eyes. "Can you promise me you will do everything in your power to keep my daughter from here? And to keep her safe with you, wherever you go?"

"I will," Sage vowed.

"Then I will retrieve your friend and Blaise…and I will help you escape. I can't promise you will live, but you won't die by his hand, and you'll be free."

Hope fluttered in her chest for the first time in a long time. Sage leaned forward and kissed both of Maeve's cheeks.

The Scythian woman stood and smiled down at Sage. "Thank you."

She grabbed Maeve's hand before she left. "Will you be okay?"

Maeve's smile turned dark. "Zane's not the only one who's been around a long time. Don't worry about me, child. All will be well. Prepare yourself, for the journey will be both difficult and dangerous."

She stood and strode to the balcony, filled with nervous energy as she anticipated what was to come. Gazing at the fires of the army burning in the distance, she took a calming breath. *Soon.*

Soon, she'd escape this hell.

Soon, she'd be home.

And soon, she'd be hunted by an ancient master hunter.

Soon couldn't come fast enough.

CHAPTER THIRTY-TWO

Tehl

Tehl swirled the pungent amber liquid in his cup, mulling over the day's events. It had gone smoother than expected. Part of him wondered if the warlord really did want peace, though. The talks seemed legitimate, but then again, it could have been well-orchestrated play-acting to cover the warlord's true agenda.

He threw back the contents of his drink, his eyes watering as the spirits burned the back of his throat and warmed his belly. Dinner had been another horrid affair, both groups merely staring at each other, occasional whispers echoing in the giant room. More upsetting than their people's inability to communicate was the empty seat beside him.

In the past, it had been difficult to control his emotions, but manageable. But when Sage didn't show up for dinner, he had to employ every trick he knew to keep his feelings locked away. Panic was the first one to grab hold of him, then helplessness. Luckily, Gavriel had asked after Sage, leaving Tehl time to compose himself and pulling the warlord's attention elsewhere.

He frowned into his empty glass. Even when the Scythian leader wasn't watching him directly, the warlord seemed very aware of everything Tehl did. What almost tipped him over the edge wasn't the fact that Sage didn't come to dinner, but the way the enemy referred to his wife. It was intimate, and Tehl hated it, hated how he didn't know if it was the truth or simply a means by which to manipulate him. His hand tightened on the cup. It was probably both.

Tehl glanced over his shoulder as Sam entered his room, shutting the door only to fall heavily against it, his shoulders slumped.

"Sam?" Lilja called, rising from her perch on the divan.

"Music," Sam whispered. "I need music."

Tehl turned and placed his cup on the table near the fire. "Why? What for?"

His brother lifted his head, devastation clear on his face. "I need it."

Short. No explanation.

"Hayjen?"

The tall man met his wife's gaze, disappeared into the adjoining room, and reappeared with a fiddle. He lifted his bow and began to play a haunting tune that rose the hair on Tehl's arms.

Lilja eyed Sam. "Now speak."

Sam dragged a hand over his face and pushed from the door. His stride was clipped as he approached the silent group of people lounging around the room. "We have a serious problem."

That got Tehl's attention; Sam must have needed music to prevent their conversation from being overheard. "What is it?" he asked in a low voice.

His brother opened his mouth and then closed it, shooting a glare at the door behind him. Sam strode to a desk situated in the corner and poured whiskey into a cup. He tossed it back and then pulled in a deep breath before speaking. "She refused."

It was only two words, but they knocked the wind from Tehl's lungs.

Hayjen missed a note, but quickly continued playing.

"Why?" Zachael breathed, devastation clear on his face.

"I don't know. I—" Sam shook his head. "Why would she do this?"

"Did she give you any hints?"

"Nothing." Sam cursed and kicked at a log. "Absolutely nothing."

"She's been with the warlord for months," Lilja murmured, almost hesitant. "She could be under his influence somehow."

"That's nonsense," William retorted. "She seems not the kind of person to be unduly influenced."

"That's the problem, though," Rafe rumbled. "It's not always something one can control."

"How did she act with you?" Lilja asked.

Sam tugged at his hair. "She attacked me." A goofy smile flittered across his face and disappeared. "To be fair, I did sneak up on her when she was in bed. But when she recognized me, she embraced me. I saw Sage, or a glimmer of her, before she locked her old self away and then disappeared." Sam's fingers curled into a fist, his arms shaking. "She...she told me that she owed the warlord everything, and that he was using her as much as..." His brother hesitated. "As much as the rebellion and Crown."

He froze. She thought he was using her? She compared him to the Scythian warlord? Tehl clenched his hands, trying to ward off the pain those words caused him. Something wasn't right. Sage could be reasoned with despite her emotions. Those words weren't reasonable at all. They were nonsense.

Hayjen played straight into another song, his fingers flying over the strings.

"That's not what Sage believes," Lilja reasoned. "I know, because we've talked about it. Those words aren't her own; they have to be someone else's." She shot a glance at her husband. "Hayjen and I have rescued girls who have been inflicted with this type of torture. They're manipulated into believing things that make no sense at all. It seems crazy to us, but seems absolutely real to them."

Jeren stepped closer, his head bowed. "So, you're telling me that our consort has been deceived by our enemy?"

Lilja nodded gravely.

Tehl's advisor, Jeren, glanced around the room and held up his hands. "You all know that I have not hid my dislike for Sage, but in the time she was with us, she changed things for the better. It's with a heavy heart that I say this, but someone needs to." He pulled in a deep breath, looking very old. "Sage is a wealth of information for both the Crown and rebellion. If the warlord has accomplished what you suspect, Captain Femi, then it is logical for us to examine those consequences."

"No," Gav growled.

Tehl met Jeren's gaze. "You think she's working with him. That she's a traitor?" Tehl didn't attack the man for the accusation. It was logical. If the warlord wanted information, Sage was his key.

Jeren glared around the room. "The crown prince believes me," he uttered softly.

All eyes swung to Tehl. "It makes sense. Think of it. She's the perfect piece for him to use in his game."

"So, you're naming her a traitor?" Zachael asked calmly.

"No," Tehl glanced at Lilja. "I am just saying that he's hurt and manipulated my wife. We don't have any idea what information she may have unwittingly given him."

"What a brilliant idea," Sam hissed. "Even if she was able to reason through all his lies, her actions would be proof of treason. The warlord has created an intricate trap." Sam's brows slashed downward. "We're still missing something. Sage was afraid."

Sage never let anyone see her fear. That in itself was disturbing.

"What kind of fear?" Rafe questioned.

Sam squinted at the ornate ceiling. "Fear for me." He dropped his chin down, blankly staring at the group. "She wasn't afraid for herself. Sage was protecting me."

"That sounds like my wife," Tehl muttered. His brows furrowed when something tugged at the back of his mind. He blinked. The girl from the village. "Sam. The girl." Sage would never leave the girl behind.

"What girl?"

"The girl from the village."

"Of course," Sam exploded. He glanced at the door and continued in a lower tone. "Sage would never leave anyone behind."

"Do you think she's protecting the girl and so not being manipulated?" Jeren asked.

"I'm sure he's manipulated her, but if Jasmine is alive, Sage wouldn't leave her behind. What better leverage for the warlord to have? Sage would probably risk her own life, but the life of a friend?"

"What do you suggest we do?" Rafe asked, watching Lilja.

The Sirenidae scanned the group as Hayjen's song came to a crescendo. "We play our parts. We must be content to watch and wait for her signal."

"And you believe there will be one? A signal, I mean?" Jeren asked.

"I would stake my life on it."

"Then, we wait," Tehl said.

"We wait," Lilja echoed.

CHAPTER THIRTY-THREE

Sam

And they waited.

Five days passed in a flurry of pretty speeches, veiled threats, and reluctant compromises. Each day, he prayed that Sage would give them a signal: a look, a cue... anything really. But she didn't. She sat at the end of the table, a ghost of her former self.

Sam glanced at his brother from his seat at the dining table.

Tehl sat in his chair, sipping wine from a goblet, looking regal, as if the world were there only for his amusement. But Sam knew what lay beneath the surface of that façade. It was evident in his brother's gaze resting on Sage, the tightness of the skin around his mouth whenever the warlord needled him, and how tightly he clenched his goblet. His brother was worried, angry, and dangerously close to losing his temper.

Sam sighed, lazily scanning the table. A pair of cinnamon eyes snagged his attention. They were perusing him with interest, so he cocked his head and smirked at her. The one called Maeve didn't simper, flush in embarrassment, or look away. She simply held his gaze and raised a goblet of wine to him. That wasn't something he experienced every day. For once, he felt like the prey, not the predator.

She broke their stare-off and whispered something in her daughter's ear. Sam glanced between mother and daughter, discreetly observing them. Things rarely shocked him anymore, but seeing two women who looked like twins, but were mother and daughter was an eerie experience.

Maeve glanced at him from beneath her dark lashes, a sensual smile curling her lips.

"I'll take my leave," the warlord said as he stood. He held his hand out to Sage. "Consort, would you like an escort to your room?"

Sam schooled his expression as Sage placed her hand in the other man's and swept out of the room with the Scythian.

Her room? Liar. The warlord didn't let her out of his sight.

His gaze shifted to Tehl. His brother stared in the direction of the couple before tossing back the last of his wine emotionlessly. It seemed like his brother fractured a little further as each day passed. They didn't have much time before Tehl broke and did something that got them all killed.

He turned back to Maeve as she daintily dabbed at her mouth and stood. She turned on her heel and sauntered out of the room. At the last second, she peered over her shoulder and met his gaze, winked, and disappeared from view.

Intriguing. She was flirting with him, but why? He swirled his wine and sniffed the fruity liquid while scanning the table. Both delegations were still watching each other apprehensively, though some of the tension had departed the room with the warlord. Sam caught the eye of Blaise and smiled widely, knowing his dimple was on display. It was a smile that always worked for him.

Her lips thinned as she bared her teeth.

Well, almost every time. Apparently, she still hadn't forgiven him for his interrogations.

Sam pushed back from the table and bowed to Blaise in a courtly fashion, earning looks from many at the table. He strode from the room, keenly aware of the attention he drew. He kept smiling as he exited the room, keeping his stride lazy while examining the hallway with a sharp gaze. One never knew who was lurking about.

He sauntered past a curtained window when something grabbed the back of his vest and yanked him back. Sam pulled a dagger from his waist and spun, using the momentum. He blinked in shock as his dagger was plucked from his hand, and he was yanked into the dark and slammed against a stone wall. He tried to surge forward, but the body pressed against him held him in place.

"Calm down. I'm not going to kill you."

A soft, flowery scent curled around him in the dark space. A woman.

"I find I must warn you that I like being taken captive, my lady," he purred as his mind scrambled for an explanation. He blinked, his eyes adjusting to the dark space. *A secret hallway. How unoriginal. Where did this one lead?*

"I don't doubt that, Prince."

His eyes narrowed at the voice as he focused on the woman holding him, just able to make out the shape of her face. Maeve. "I'm flattered, but I must say that you have me at a—"

"Enough," she whispered. "Time is short. Do you wish to take your princess home safely?"

Sam stilled, sensing a trap, and answered carefully. "We all wish for our loved ones to be safe."

A small growl from below his chin. "We don't have time for pretty words. Sage is in danger. If she doesn't escape, he'll kill her."

His body tensed. "Why tell me this?"

"Because I'm going to help her escape our warlord and put his tyranny to an end."

He forced a chuckle out while he ran through the possible reasons she'd really approached him. "That sounds an awful lot like treason, my lady. The Aermian delegation is here for peace. We'd never jeopardize our endeavors."

Maeve scoffed and released her arm from his throat. "Please, we all know why you're here, but you'll not succeed."

Sam almost reached for a blade, but thought better of it. The woman had been able to restrain him in seconds. Plus, he didn't know if her superior eyesight included some form of enhanced night-vision. He straightened his vest. "This has been exciting, but I must be returning to my room. It's been a long day that I'm sure we'll repeat tomorrow."

"She said you'd be difficult. I don't expect you to trust me, but I do expect you to trust someone you've sworn yourself to."

He stilled. "What do you mean?"

"She said to tell you that when you helped to arm her, you promised to support her even against your own blood; you became her brother in truth."

His mind flashed back to Sage sobbing while trying to attach her dagger sheaths before her wedding, and how she shook so hard she couldn't clasp them. He'd never shared that with anyone. He was also sure Sage and Gav wouldn't have, either. This was Sage's sign. "What do you need from me?"

A sigh of relief. "You need to pick a fight tomorrow."

"That sounds dangerous."

"Not a physical fight, but you need to raise an issue that the warlord will never accept, and that Aermia will never budge on."

"And that is?"

"His experiments."

A chill ran through him. "He's still experimenting?"

"That's neither here nor there, but he'd never agree to give up his perceived rights. It'll be an insult he won't be able to ignore."

"He'll have to change his game," Sam murmured. "That's dangerous."

"It'll be enough to ensure the delegations escape from this place, and also allow me time to get the girls out of this hell."

"Girls?" he asked.

"Be prepared to rescue three girls. Span your men along the Scythian border. They won't be able to cross near the Nagali border. There will be too many warriors roaming the area."

"It'll be done." Sam's mind raced, thinking on all the things he needed to put into motion in order for this to succeed. It would be difficult, but not impossible. "And you promise to get her out safely?"

"I promise nothing but freedom."

"And what does that mean?"

"If I cannot free her, she'll die a clean death. I won't allow her to suffer another moment more."

His lips thinned. He hated it, but he didn't understand what Sage had suffered, so perhaps that was the best she could offer. If his sister-in-law was willing to die rather than suffer any further by the warlord's hand, it must be unimaginable. "And what do you get out of this situation?" No one did anything for free.

"I judged you to be an honorable man, so I'm trusting you with a piece of information precious to me. One of the women who will be escaping with Sage is my daughter. You know her by the name of Blaise."

He blinked. The Scythian woman they'd returned. It was a possibility she was a spy. But even if that was the case, he'd welcome her with open arms if it meant having Sage safe at home.

"She's the only light in my world." Maeve's face snapped to the side. "Our time for speaking has ended. I hope her trust in you is warranted." She popped up on her toes and kissed both his cheeks. "Take care of the girls and keep them safe." Her hand curled around his arm, and she pushed him out of the dark and into the window alcove.

Sam spun and caught a glimpse of her face before the door closed silently, only showing a wall of stone where the door once was. He breathed heavily, panic tugging at his gut. It was a gamble trusting her, but ignoring her words was a bigger gamble.

He sucked in a huge breath. No matter what, the peace talks

could only end one way. In war. The delegation would honestly risk little to go along with her plan. It was Sage who risked everything.

They had nothing to lose, and everything to gain.

***

He entered the room and caught Hayjen's eye. "I would love some music."

Lilja grabbed the fiddle and handed it to her husband, her gaze never leaving Sam. Rafe, Gav, Zachael, and Tehl all focused on him as Hayjen began to play.

"We have our sign," he whispered.

Tehl shot to his feet. "What?"

Sam shook his head. "I can't tell you the specifics, but I have a plan set in motion. I'll need everyone's cooperation. You each have a role to play."

"What can you tell us?" Rafe asked.

"I'll speak with each of you personally, and Lilja?"

Her serious eyes met his. "Yes?"

"I'll need your help."

She nodded.

Tehl strode over to him, his face displaying heavy fatigue, worry having created shadows underneath his eyes.

"What do I need to do?" Tehl asked.

"Ruin the peace talks."

A dangerous smile crept across his brother's face, making him resemble a mercenary more than a prince. "With pleasure."

Sam released a breath. "So, we begin."

Chapter Thirty-Four

Sage

It was another day of speeches and promises she knew would never come to fruition. It was a pretty little play. She'd been discreetly yawning behind her hand when Jeren snarled something at Blair.

"We will *never* accept your tampering in Aermia. Your monstrosities end here," the Aermian counselor hissed.

She still felt the shock of his words in the pit of her stomach. How had they gone from trade to this? The room seemed to drop in temperature as the warlord leaned forward in his chair, the lines of his body rigid.

"I suggest you leash your delegate before he says something he'll regret," the warlord growled.

The crown prince eyed the warlord and straightened. "I apologize for his utter lack of tact, but not for his intent. I understand that your people's crimes are in the past and should stay there. But my people's fear and hate for the way you use science has not. If we are to obtain peace, then we need assurances that all your tampering has ceased as well."

The warlord cocked his head. "Haven't I already done so?"

"So you say."

"Are you implying I lied?" the warlord asked casually.

The hair on the back of her neck stood. She knew that tone intimately. It spoke of danger and pain.

"No, I am not," Tehl said. "But we're concerned not about your past deeds, but rather your draughts used for healing. They go beyond what is natural."

The warlord's brows arched. "You don't want me to heal my people?"

"In order to forge our peace alliance, we require all altering to cease. We want no part of your tampering in Aermia."

"You presume to command me?"

"No." Tehl shook his head. "But from leader to leader, you understand what it means to protect your people." His gaze hardened. "And I will protect my people. I will not allow Scythian draughts in Aermia."

"Even if we could heal the disease that plagues your people?" the warlord asked tightly.

"Even so. We will not risk the danger and corruption. This is non-negotiable."

The air seemed to leave the room as the warlord stood. He flung his arm out in her direction.

"Does Sage look corrupted? She's alive because of those draughts. I'd venture to say she's even healthier now than when she was under your roof."

Sage inwardly winced at the warlord's dig and held her breath when Tehl stood. He turned and pinned her with his sapphire gaze. She blushed as he leisurely scanned her before turning to the warlord.

"You're right. She looks healthy, but she also doesn't look like my wife." He flicked a disgusted look in her direction. "She dresses and speaks like a Scythian, not an Aermian." His teeth clenched together. "And apparently, she sleeps in a Scythian bed, too," he growled.

The floor seemed to fall out from below her, and the room swayed. She begged him with her gaze to look at her, to let her explain, but all her words caught in her throat. Their lives hinged on her silence. She swallowed down her explanations and focused on the two men staring each other down. One smug, the other disgusted.

The crown prince lifted his chin and stared the warlord in the eye. "Will you comply for peace?" The question hung in the air.

The warlord stared at her with an unholy glee in his eyes just before turning to the crown prince and replying, "I will not."

"Then we are at an impasse," Tehl said.

"No, we are at the end," the warlord said.

Both men watched each other for a tense second before the crown prince dipped his chin. "So be it. Let the record show that Aermia and Scythia did not come to a peace agreement. The laws of our forefathers will still be upheld." He glanced at Sage. "You have no place among my household. Traitors usually receive death, but since you are my wife, I will grant you mercy. You shall be exiled."

Her heart cracked into a million pieces, but her mask was as flawless as ever when Tehl turned and strode from the room. Heat built at the back of her eyes as the delegation left, refusing to even look in her direction.

***

She blinked constantly, the stars wavering around her.

Six hours.

It had been six hours since the last of the peace talks began.

It had been three hours since the Aermian delegation had named her a traitor.

It had been one hour since they closed negotiations and abandoned her.

She stared into the dark, the wind whipping her clothing around her and chilling her tears. A muffled sob slipped out when she remembered Tehl naming her an adulteress, nothing but condemnation and disgust on his face.

Sage lifted her robe and scrubbed the tears from her face, all the while trying to catch a glimpse of the fires burning in the distance. Before, they shone brightly, beacons of hope, but now they wavered like mirages, false promises. Even now, thinking over the day, she couldn't believe that Tehl thought her a traitor. He was smarter than that. Despite the evidence, he knew her, knew she would never betray him.

But you have already, haven't you?

Sage swallowed down the pain and focused on what she knew to be true. Her name was Sage Blackwell. She was married to the crown prince who was brave, honorable, and intelligent. She had four brothers, and that included two sworn brothers. Sam, the cunning spymaster, and Gav, the warrior with a heart of gold. Neither one of those men would hurt her.

Sage welcomed the cold air as it helped to clear her thoughts. Sam had tried to rescue her six days ago. He knew where to find her. Her brows furrowed, and she pulled her robe closer to her body. He already knew she was in the warlord's chamber. Not only that, but she'd sent Sam a message. So, why did Tehl name her an adulteress and traitor today? It didn't make any sense.

"Wild one, are you going to stand out there all night? I can't possibly keep you healthy if you keep putting yourself at risk."

Rubbing at her arms, she spun to face him, then meandered into the room ever so slowly. The warlord lounged in a chair by the fire, eyeing her with an emotion she couldn't decipher.

"Have you been crying over those fools?" he asked softly.

She forced her hands to stay by her side instead of scrubbing at her face like she longed to. "I'm a woman. We're emotional creatures," she said with a half-smile.

He set his goblet down and stalked in her direction before clasping her face in his hands. She tilted her head back to meet his black gaze.

"If I didn't have any morals, I would have cut them all down where they stood for what they did to you," he whispered. "I have half a mind to hunt them down."

Fear shot through her at his words. "But you won't?"

He scanned her face. "No, I won't, but not only for you. When Aermia bows before me, it will be because they were weak and they failed."

His words incited a shiver. She pulled her robe tighter and gently pulled from his grasp. "It's been a long day, and I'm tired."

"Of course, consort."

She shuffled to the bed and turned her back to him, afraid he could see all of her thoughts and feelings swirling in her mind. He released a sigh and strode around the bed to tug the draperies across the window. Her skin prickled when his belt jingled and his clothes rustled. Her eyes slammed closed as his weight sunk into the bed, and a heavy arm curled around her.

"Sleep, wild one. Tomorrow will have its own worries."

"Wise," she whispered, very aware of how his hand slipped into her robe and pressed against her bare stomach. "It must be because of how old you are."

The warlord stilled and then chuckled, shaking her body. "Sage, you never stop surprising me. Never change."

"Change is inevitable."

His laughter died off, and a light kiss caressed the back of her neck. "True. You and I will change the world."

She stayed silent and forced her body to relax. He was right, each day had its own worries. She had to focus on one thing at a time. Now wasn't the time to decipher Tehl's actions; now was the time to escape.

***

Sage jerked away, her heart pounding. She blinked furiously and sat up, the warlord's arm slipping into her lap. She scanned the room, but nothing looked out of the ordinary. She frowned and glanced at the warlord. He was asleep.

It must have been a dream.

She released a heavy sigh and stared at his handsome face. Awake, he was devastatingly handsome, but asleep, his face was a mask of serenity and peace, angelic. She traced one of his eyebrows and brushed his dark hair from his cheek. In that moment, she could almost forget his atrocities. The thought sickened her. Did a pretty face sway her that much?

"Sage."

She jerked and rolled out of the bed, glaring at the source of the voice.

"Maeve." Sage glanced at the warlord and back to the Scythian woman. "Is it time?"

Maeve slipped all the way through the curtains and shook her head. "It's time. No questions."

Her eyes rounded as she glanced at the warlord.

"Now, Sage. He won't wake for some time. The drug will keep him down."

She swallowed hard and climbed onto the bed. The part of herself that she hated most mourned leaving him. She pressed a kiss to his temple and placed her forehead against his. "I know there's a shred of good inside you, I've seen it, but I cannot stay here with you, hoping I can coax it out. You're too broken, and you'll break me. I'm sorry."

Sage crept from the bed and shivered as she moved through the curtains and into the cold night air. Maeve smiled sadly and glanced toward the room. "Wait here. I need to secure him."

The Scythian woman slipped away, silent as the night. Meanwhile, she wrapped her arms around herself and waited for Maeve to return. It seemed like an eternity before the woman emerged, just as silently as she left.

They both moved to the balcony and Maeve lifted a rope. "I need you to secure this under your armpits"

Sage nodded and took the rope from her, securing it around her body with numb fingers. Maeve tugged on it and then tied it around her waist.

"I'm going to lower you down first and then follow. Blaise has secured our weight. Make sure to hold on, or the rope will bite in painfully. This is the most tedious part of our plan."

Sage nodded and placed her hands on the railing. She'd never been afraid of heights, but putting her trust in another to keep from falling hundreds of feet was no simple thing.

"Breathe in and out. You can do this, Sage. You're strong," the Scythian woman whispered.

She could do this. She had to do this.

Carefully, she slipped one leg over the railing, and then the other, spinning so she was facing the railing, her bare toes clenching the stone ledge.

"Slide down to your knee and edge your body off."

Gritting her teeth, she did as she was told. Her legs dangled below, and her fingers bit into the railing.

"Let go of the railing and grasp the rope."

Sage counted to three and released the railing. For a breathless moment, it felt like she was falling. Then the rope bit into her underarms. She snatched the rope and pulled upward. The pain receded, but her arms began to shake as she swung below the balcony. She glanced up to catch Maeve slipping over the edge, lowering them. Sage's stomach lurched as she dropped a foot and then another.

It shouldn't have surprised her that Maeve held their weight so easily, but it was still amazing to see the petite woman using just her arms to lower them. It was faster than she liked, but even that felt too slow. Every second they were in the air, she felt like the warlord would lean over the railing and haul them back up.

They passed seven levels when Sage caught sight of Blaise. The Scythian woman was holding the other side of the rope. The curious side of Sage's mind was intrigued by the pulley system that they'd rigged, but all of that was forgotten when Blaise locked eyes with her and whispered, "You need to swing toward me. I can't reach you."

Sage nodded and steeled her nerves. She couldn't think about it, she had to just do it, so she began to swing. Her stomach twisted as the rope creaked and groaned, but it held. When Blaise wrapped her arms around Sage's legs, she offered a little prayer of thanks. She then clambered down to the balcony, her legs shaking, and tugged at the rope tied around her.

A flask entered her vision. "I told Mum she was crazy. I've never seen anyone attempt that."

Sage grabbed it and took a large swig. The spirits burned away some of the jitters and the cold. She wiped the back of her mouth and handed it back. "Thank you for not dropping me."

A grunt.

Toes landed on the railing above her head and then Maeve dropped into view, landing without a sound. "Pull the rope,

Daughter." She turned and offered Sage a hand up. "We need to get you changed."

Sage shivered and followed her into a much smaller room. Leather trousers, boots, a linen shirt, and a fur vest were laid out on a trunk.

"I think these will fit you."

"Thank you," she whispered and stripped off her skimpy nightgown and robe. She'd lost most her sense of modesty. All she wanted was to feel *real* clothes against her skin.

"One moment," Maeve murmured. She poured some sort of oil in her hands. "We need to oil your entire body. It will change your scent."

"Okay."

Heat burned her cheeks as Maeve left no inch of skin untouched. Maeve grinned at her reaction for only a moment before sobering. "This is not a time to be shy. This is life or death. You've never faced a foe such as he."

Again, her stomach twisted. She knew.

Once Maeve finished, Sage yanked on the trousers, socks and boots, and then laced her half-corset. She threw on her shirt and quickly buttoned up her vest. Maeve handed her a ring. Sage eyed it. "What's that?"

Maeve flipped back the top of the ring revealing a sharp needle. "This holds a poison that will paralyze a Scythian." She flipped the top of the ring closed and held it out to Sage. "This is a last resort."

She pulled the ring from Maeve's palm and slipped it on the middle finger of her right hand. "What next?" she whispered, feeling a little more like her old self.

"We disguise you. Come here."

She turned and sat on the trunk as Maeve instructed her to do. The Scythian woman quickly did her hair in a Scythian braid.

"If anyone possibly sees you, you'll look Scythian. They won't look twice." Maeve stood and glanced at the silent Blaise. "Are you ready, Daughter?"

"Yes, Mum. I removed any trace of our footprints."

"Thank you." Maeve moved to the wall and pressed on a red mosaic tile piece. A door swung inward soundlessly. "Time to go."

Sage stood, but paused. Both Scythian women glanced at her with raised brows. "Where's Jasmine?"

"Safe," Maeve answered. "She's waiting for us."

"You swear?" Sage scrutinized the woman.

"I do. I would not leave that poor girl to the warlord's wrath."

Sage believed her and so moved into the dark hidden passage. She turned and watched with rising dread as Blaise wiped off everything they touched and threw her clothing into the fire. Blaise scanned the room once more and moved into the hallway, closing the door.

Darkness surrounded them and blinded Sage.

"From this moment onward, you mustn't say a word until I give you permission. Do you understand?" Maeve said, her tone grave.

"Yes, but I can't see."

"Hold on to my belt until your eyes adjust."

Each step, each breath was torturous. They felt too loud. Panic swirled in her belly at being in the dark. It reminded her too much of how she ended up here. She stifled a hysterical laugh. Well, the warlord had done something for her. Her eyes were still used to the dark, so it was easier to see at night than it used to be.

They took endless twists and turns, descending staircase after staircase. Her ears popped, and she shook her head to dislodge the fuzzy feeling it created. Her mouth dropped open as the hallway opened up into a cavern. Sage scanned the area once and followed Maeve around its rocky edge.

"Blaise, I need light."

A few seconds later, a soft glow came from a bitty lantern in Blaise's hand.

Where did that come from?

Maeve took the lantern from Blaise and weaved around the precarious rockface. Now, Sage knew why they needed the light. She almost wished it was dark again; then she wouldn't have seen the jagged rocks below, looking like giant teeth ready to swallow them.

She trod softly behind Maeve and into the next cave where she skidded to a stop, her mouth hanging open. Something enormous slept in the middle of the cave. A red, scaled mountain breathed.

"Wh-what is that?" she stuttered, knowing exactly what it was, but not believing her eyes.

"It's sedated."

"How?" she breathed as she pressed her back to the cave wall glittering with rubies.

"The warlord."

Two little words. But enough to make her hair stand on end. She could scarcely pull her eyes from the myth slumbering on the floor, its massive wings curled against its sides, tail tucked around it. It reminded her of how Nali slept. "But it's a *dragon!*"

Maeve eyed her and picked up her speed. "It is, but we don't have time for explanations. Let's move."

Sage forced dragons from her mind and ran, her boots

thumping on the floor. They ducked into another tunnel and weaved until they reached another room. She stumbled as Jasmine pushed from the wall and ran toward her. They crashed into each other, hugging.

"You're here, you're really here," Sage whispered.

"You got away," Jasmine cried.

Sage pulled back and smiled at her friend. "I can't believe it." She glanced at Maeve who was hugging Blaise fiercely.

She released her daughter and pulled Sage into a huge hug. Maeve pulled back and looked to each girl. "You all are strong in your own way. From here, you rely on each other. You have no one else. If you don't work together, you won't survive. The warlord will hunt you relentlessly, so you must get over the border as quickly as possible. There will be help waiting for you." She glanced to the side. "Nali."

Sage's eyes widened as the black feline slunk out of the dark and brushed against her hip. She ran her hand over the cat's head and glanced at Maeve.

The Scythian woman smiled. "Nali bonded with you, so you're now her mistress. She'll protect you from danger and ward off other predators who might normally try to hunt you. Heed her warnings and watch her reactions closely. I promise you, she will save your lives." She scanned the group of girls again. "Live long, happy lives. Fight, love, and live."

Blaise stepped closer and wrapped her arms around her mum. "Let me stay. I can help."

"No," Maeve murmured. "He'll destroy you. I couldn't take it if he took you from me, too. I love you, Daughter, more than anything."

"Love you, Mum." Blaise pulled back from her mum and wiped her eyes. She glanced at Sage. "Are you ready?"

Sage sank her fingers into Nali's fur and slipped her hand into Jasmine's. "Hell, yes."

For better or worse, she'd be free and, at the very least, she'd die that way.

Chapter Thirty-Five

Tehl

He kept his mask in place as they entered the camp. His guard moved from their tents and bowed low as their party rode by, their gazes scouring the group for the one person missing. The one person he was supposed to bring home. But he did the opposite. He condemned her and left her in that snake pit.

Pressing his heels to Wraith's side, he urged him forward and shot a glance to his brother, who was as collected as ever. He trusted him, but it was all he could do not to wrap his hands around Sam's throat and throttle him until he spilled the plan.

A relieved breath passed his lips when his tent came into view. He slid from his mount, gave the faithful beast a good pat, and nodded to the elite stationed outside his tent. Pushing through the flaps, he maneuvered around the table and chairs scattered about the room and snatched a bottle of spirits from a pack on the floor.

"Drinking?" Sam's voice said. "That's a poor tactic to deal with life."

He spun on his brother and defiantly took a swig.

Sam just arched a brow.

The whiskey burned his throat. Tehl slammed the bottle down and began pacing. His hands trembled by his sides, pulling a laugh out of him.

"What's so funny?"

He held his shaking hand up. "I've always been in control, had things planned. But this?" He waved his hands in the air. "I can't tell up from down. All I feel is anger." Even now, his rage boiled, seeking a target.

"I understand."

Tehl froze, his eyes narrowing on Sam. "How could you?"

"How could I what?"

"How could you possibly understand what it's like to leave your wife to her death?"

Sam wisely stayed silent.

He ran his hands through his windswept hair, guilt and fear rolling in his gut. "We left her there." Sage's pale face flashed through his mind. "I condemned her."

"It was only a show," Sam reasoned.

"But she didn't know that!" he shouted. "You can't pretend you didn't see the despair in her face. Sam..." His voice broke. "She looked at me like I'd signed her death warrant."

Sam strode to his side and pulled him into a rough hug. Tehl stiffened, shock radiating through him. It was like Sam was attempting to hold the pieces of him together. His brother thumped him on the back and released him.

"I understand it was difficult, but you played your part perfectly." Sam eyed him seriously. "Are you ready to hear everything?"

"Yes," he said gravely. "Gather the others."

His brother studied him a bit more and nodded.

Tehl collapsed into a chair and ran a hand down his face. He couldn't fall apart right now. Too many depended on him. Sam had never steered him wrong. He needed to trust in his brother, his people, and himself.

Lilja pushed through the tent, followed by Hayjen, Rafe, William, Gav, and Zachael. The Sirenidae took one glance at the whiskey and grabbed the bottle. Tehl smiled as the willowy woman took a deep pull and passed it along to her husband. She grinned at Tehl while wiping her mouth with the back of her hand. She patted his knee, moved around him, and plopped into a chair to his right.

The group kept silent as they found places to sit while whiskey was passed around. Sam murmured something to the Elites stationed outside the tent and let the flap fall. He walked to the table and placed both hands on it. "Where do you want me to start?"

"How about the beginning?" Rafe said sarcastically.

Lilja scowled at the rebellion leader. "Hush, Rafe. We don't have time for your sass." Rafe's eyes narrowed, but he stayed silent. The Sirenidae turned her attention to Sam. "How did Sage give you her sign?"

"By means of Maeve."

Tehl frowned. "The warlord's sister?"

"Yes," Sam said.

Zachael held his hands up. "Wait, you trusted the warlord's flesh and blood with Sage's life?"

"No, *Sage* entrusted everyone's safety to Maeve."

Tehl kept silent as that soaked in. If it was a trap, surely they would have been cut down before they reached their army. "How did she contact you?"

His brother smirked. "She pulled me into a darkened hallway, quite forcibly I might add... I always like a woman with a little spirit."

William snorted and ran his fingers along his grey mustache. "She'd break you, boy."

Sam shook his head, his expression sobering. "Of that, I have no doubt."

"What was her sign?" Gav asked. "Sage could have shared any information with them. How do you know this woman was legitimate?"

"She spoke of our time right before the wedding. Our promises."

Understanding passed between the two princes. Sam met Tehl's stare.

"Sage would never divulge something like that to anyone."

Tehl only knew of what Sam and Gav had done for her, because he had stood outside the door. His wife was a strong woman who didn't like anyone to see her weak, thus it was unlikely she would have shared something so personal. The Scythian woman must have been telling the truth.

"What did the Scythian woman have to say?"

"She had a plan." Sam tipped his head back to stare at the canvas ceiling. "I did everything in my power to devise a way to bring Sage home with us." He dropped his head. "Every outcome led to death for someone. Maeve's offer afforded us ignorance, escape, and safety, to some degree."

"And what of Sage?" Hayjen rasped.

"Her fate lies in the hands of Maeve."

Tehl's stomach plummeted. He had a hard time allowing himself to trust the woman, but prejudice did no one good. No one was completely evil, just as no race was completely bad. His hands clenched and unclenched. He would have to accept her help and trust her.

"We've followed your directions as you asked. What is the next step?" With Sam, there was always a next step.

"We keep moving."

"Because we'll be watched," Rafe supplied.

His brother nodded. "The warlord is a shrewd man. It would've been stupid not to send scouts and patrols to roam the borders, especially with a third of the Aermian Guard camping outside his border."

"Where do we rendezvous with Sage?" William asked.

Sam winced. "That's the hitch. I don't know."

Tehl blinked at his brother. "That complicates things."

"Indeed."

"When were they to attempt escape?" he asked.

"Tonight." Sam said.

"They won't make it across the border," Gav growled. "It's too dangerous."

"That's why we need to keep moving," Zachael supplied. "If it was me, I would stay near the Scythian border, but move as far down as possible and then cross."

Rafe cursed. "That's only if she can survive the Scythian jungle. Did you see how pale and soft she looked?"

"It's the drugs," Lilja growled. "They give women drugs to keep them docile and weak."

Tehl's jaw clenched. "Bastards."

She reached over and clasped his hand. He didn't know if it was for her benefit or his.

"The journey will be difficult, but she won't be alone, and she has a guide."

"Who?" Gav asked.

"Blaise."

"You mean our former Scythian captive?" Zachael asked.

"Yes."

"Why would she do anything for Sage?" William jumped in.

"Because her mother doesn't want her in Scythia," Tehl whispered to himself. It made complete sense. Maeve was Blaise's mother. All eyes turned to him. "Blaise is the warlord's niece, so it stands to reason Maeve is her mother. Am I correct?"

Sam dipped his chin. "She fears for her daughter, so she aided us to aid her kin."

"That's not possible," William argued. "They're the same age!"

"Things are not what they appear in Scythia," Hayjen murmured.

"Downright unnatural," the old man grumbled, lacing his fingers across his stomach.

"So, she has a guide, and a protector of sorts. How will she make it past all the patrols?" Rafe growled. "Two women won't survive against a dozen warriors."

"Three women," Sam corrected. "Jasmine is with them as well."

"I have that covered," Lilja spoke. "I have someone on the inside who will protect our girls."

"How?" Sam demanded, his eyes like chips of sapphire.

"It was a long time ago."

"That's not a damn answer! I've lost so many spies. And you've had someone on the inside the entire time?"

Lilja lifted her hand placatingly. "I wasn't aware he was alive." She glanced around the room. "What matters is that the girls will have some protection."

Tehl blew out a breath and stood, lacing his hand behind his head. "So, we keep moving. We stay close to the border, and we leave men discreetly behind, watching closely for sign of them."

He hated the idea of someone else finding her.

"It's the only way, brother. We can't be everywhere at once," Sam reasoned.

"If we pace ourselves, we might be able to keep up with them. It's too dangerous to traverse the jungle at night," Rafe said. "So, we travel when they travel, and sleep when they sleep."

Tehl spun in a circle, scanning the group and finally meeting the rebellion leader's amber gaze. "So be it."

"We'll get our girl back," Zachael said with confidence.

How did he end up with such amazing people at his side, guiding, supporting, and helping him? Some of them, he knew, were due to his wife. A debt he wouldn't soon forget. "Thank you," Tehl said. "I will never forget what you've done for the crown, myself, and for Sage."

"Our pleasure, my lord," Hayjen answered.

"We are all with you," Gav added.

"Together," Rafe murmured.

"Together," Tehl echoed.

CHAPTER THIRTY-SIX

Sage

Her adrenaline had long since worn off. Fatigue weighed her down, but she couldn't slow their pace. There wasn't time. She glanced up through the leaves, noting golden streaks of dawn chasing away the dark velvet of night. She worried. How long until the warlord awoke and discovered her gone?

Not long enough, she was sure.

Sage picked up her pace, her weak muscles protesting the use. A branch caught her foot and she stumbled, catching herself against a tree. Deep breath heaved from her lungs, and her nails dug into the smooth trunk beneath her palm. She had to move, but she felt like she couldn't.

Jasmine paused, glancing behind her. "You okay?" She whispered the words, as if the jungle itself was listening and reporting.

"Yes."

Blaise halted, scanned the area, and strode toward them. She pulled a draught from the pouch at her hip and held it out.

"Drink it."

Sage eyed the concoction. "What is it?"

"Something to help keep up your stamina," Blaise darted a look in Jasmine's direction. "Only drink half. You must share."

She didn't want to drink it, but she did want to escape the warlord. Gingerly, she pulled the vial from Blaise.

"Thank you," she said and uncorked the draught.

A pungent odor filled the air. Hastily, she gulped down half. Her eyes watered, and she fought not to gag at the bitter taste. *Disgusting.* Swallowing quickly, she handed it off to the wide-eyed Jas. Her friend eyed it with disdain.

"Drink it," Sage commanded. "We don't have time to dally."

Jasmine threw back the rest of the draught and coughed, her face screwing up. "What's in that stuff? That's worse than my mum's carpe and onions."

Blaise took the empty vial from Jas and tucked it back into her satchel. "A bit of this and that. Can you continue?"

Sage rolled her shoulders and assessed her body. She felt

stronger. "How fast does that react?"

"It's immediate, but it will wear off. We need to move. You move slower than our people and that's a major disadvantage."

"Lead the way," Jas said, waving her hand.

Blaise took the lead and began to jog, followed by Jasmine, and then Sage. The jungle seemed less daunting in the daylight than the night, but Sage knew that was a deception. The daylight predators were more cunning and better disguised.

A flash of black pulled her attention. Nali slunk through the trees just out of sight. Their silent protector reassured her. Last night, the beast hadn't left their sides. Several times, her feline protector warned them of danger or scared away other predators. If it hadn't been for Nali, Sage was sure they wouldn't have been able to travel; they'd have been dead within the first few hours.

There was something both peaceful and intimidating about the silence broken up by their boots thumping against the damp earth. The jungle blurred around her as they ran. Sweat poured down her back and between her breasts as they moved deeper into the jungle. Every once in a while, Blaise would pause and cock her head, no doubt listening to sounds Sage couldn't hear. It was in those times, she was thankful for the Scythian woman's guidance. She knew escaping the warlord would be difficult, if not impossible, but after traveling with both Nali and Blaise, she realized she never would've made it out of the palace on her own.

Blaise wove around a tree and stopped. Sage slowed next to Jas and crept closer. Blaise held her hand up, stopping her. Her heartbeat pounded in her ears and she held her breath. The Scythian woman's shoulders relaxed, and she peeked over her shoulder back at them.

"It's past time we ate. Come on." She waved them through the fronds, disappearing from view.

Sage quietly followed, licking her cracked lips as the babbling of a brook reached her ears. Water. She was so thirsty. She could probably drink a whole lake and still, her mouth would feel dry. Surprise and delight brought a smile to her face when she pushed through the lush green foliage. Fronds, orchids, vines, and trees of all sorts wove together and arched over the brook, creating an arbor over the water. It was one of the most beautiful things she'd ever seen. It was a hidden paradise.

Blaise knelt, cupped her hand, and dipped it into the water, scanning the area even as she drank. Sage moved to her side, impressed with the woman's foresight. She was so thirsty that all she wanted to do was dunk her head in the stream, but despite their paradisiac surroundings, she knew that was dangerous. It was one of the first things her papa taught her when hunting in the forest: you never let your guard down. It only took one mistake to die. The cool water soothed her parched throat, and she heard Jasmine's contented sigh as she wiped water onto her heated face.

Jas pulled her pack from her back and dug through it. She pulled out dried meat, berries, and bread, and then began distributing some of it to Blaise, Sage, and herself. It was a little hard but delicious, and before she knew it, she'd finished her small meal. She groaned as she forced herself up from her crouch and stretched her back. Blaise also stood, twisting side to side to stretch, as Jas packed everything back into her sack.

Sage tipped her back and squinted. The trees completely blocked out the sun, but dim light that surrounded them suggested that darkness wasn't far off. Her brow furrowed. Whatever was in the draught was a miracle. All the water she drank seemed to crash down on her at once. She would be vulnerable when relieving herself.

Sage eyed Blaise. "Will you watch my back? I need to go to the bathroom."

Blaise jerked her head toward the stream. "Go in there. It will carry your scent away." The Scythian woman turned her back to the stream.

Jas gaped. "You're going right here?"

Sage smiled and shrugged a shoulder. "Would you like to go into the jungle by yourself?"

Jas sobered. "Point taken." Her friend spun around to give her privacy.

She quickly finished up and stood guard as each woman followed her example.

Blaise shouldered her pack and glanced at the brook. "We have only a few more hours of light. I would like to hide our scent and tracks, so we'll be traveling through the stream."

She glanced between Jas and Sage.

"The water will disguise your steps, but you still need to move quietly. We don't want to attract any unwanted attention."

Sage nodded and waved to her friend. "Jas, you move in the middle."

The girl snorted. "You're weaker than I am."

"But I'm trained in weaponry."

"If I only had my bow," Jas grumbled as she fingered her dagger. "This won't do much good. If whatever predator, whether beast or Scythian, gets this close, I'm dead."

Sage stepped into the stream, the rocks slippery underneath her boots, and moved forward without a word. There wasn't much to say. Jas was right. If a predator got that close, it was probable they'd die.

Her senses went on high alert as she entered the arbor that arched around the stream. It was a double-edged sword. The foliage afforded them great coverage, but it also hid danger from them. The progression was slow, which rankled her, but she understood the necessity of it, for the warlord had abilities she'd never dreamed on. Just the thought of him hunting her raised the hair on her arms.

She glanced behind her as the feeling of uneasiness intensified. Nothing but the calm stream. She faced forward, her hands clenching two daggers. Something was off. "Blaise," she whispered.

Blaise paused and peered over her shoulder. "What?"

"Something's not right."

The Scythian woman frowned and scanned the area. "I hear nothing."

Jasmine spun and stared at her. "I don't-"

Something scaled slammed through the arbor above them, crashing into Jasmine. Shock prevented Sage's scream as a giant snake pulled Jasmine under the shallow water with its girth. Blaise leapt onto the snake, straddling its slick green flesh. "The head," she shouted.

Sage blurred into action, scrambling through the water. She stabbed her daggers through its skin and the head whipped up, hovering in the air with its beady eyes locked onto her. Jasmine jerked upward, coughing up water, and screamed as it coiled around her. Sage shifted to the side, the serpent mimicking her. What was she supposed to do? If she killed it, its weight would still pin Jasmine. "Blaise," she called.

The Scythian woman stabbed again and the snake twisted and struck at her. Blaise rolled away just in time.

"What attracts it?" Sage shouted.

"Blood!"

"Jasmine?"

"Yes?" Jas croaked, her nails scrabbling at the snake coiled around her.

Sage adjusted her dagger and pressed the point to her forearm. "Get ready." The blade bit into her skin and pain radiated from the wound. She squeezed her hand close and let the blood drip down her arm. It was like the world slowed. The snake stilled, Jasmine screamed, and Blaise froze. The serpent's attention snapped to her and all she could see was its gem green eyes with black vertical slits. She caught Blaise's gaze and nodded once before all hell broke loose. Time sped up as Sage spun and began sprinting along the water's edge, keeping her focus on the ground in front of her. Everything inside her demanded she look back, but she didn't. She kept her gaze ahead. One, two, three steps, fou-

A screech flew out of her as the serpent crashed into the back of her knees, knocking her into the stream. Sage flipped onto her back and scrambled backward as an enormous serpent head hovered above her. She swallowed back her scream and held her bloody arm out to the side. The snake locked onto it and slid forward. Its scales hissed as they scraped along the rocks. Her whole body trembled as it neared. *Stars above, it could probably swallow her head whole.*

She pulled in a deep breath as its heavy weight crashed onto her legs. One, two, three seconds- Blaise leapt onto the snake and slammed her sword through its skull. It thrashed for three heartbeats and then fell to the ground, unmoving. Sage scrambled back, pushing the snake off her.

"Is it dead?"

Blaise climbed off the snake and kicked it in the head. Nothing.

"It's not coming back from that," Blaise muttered.

Sage trembled and skirted around the snake's carcass and ran toward Jasmine. "Jas? Jas, are you okay?"

Jasmine moaned, still pinned beneath the dead snake. Sage tried to push it off, but barely moved the cursed serpent.

"Blaise! I need your help! I can't move it. It's crushing her."

The Scythian woman appeared by her side and hauled the snake off like it weighed nothing.

Jasmine's face was white and she was panting, obviously in pain. Sage's hands hovered over her friend, not knowing what to touch. "What's hurt?"

She cracked her eyes, tears flowing down her face. "My ribs. Broken."

"Swamp apples." Sage grimaced and smoothed Jasmine's hair from her face. "I need to find out how many."

"Do it," Jas said between clenched teeth.

Carefully, Sage began prodding her ribs. A sigh of relief slipped out when she finished the right side. All of them were intact. She'd counted six ribs when Jasmine cursed and cried out. Sage met Blaise's serious, dark gaze.

"Two are broken."

"Damn it," Blaise growled. "That will slow us down."

"Sorry," Jas wheezed. "It wasn't my plan to almost get squeezed to death and eaten today."

A surprised chuckle burst out of Blaise. "Well, next time you should plan better."

Sage blinked as the woman smiled at her friend. That was shocking. She was stunning when she smiled; it completely transformed her face. Blaise raised a brow at her staring.

She shook her head and mumbled a quick, "sorry," while scanning the darkening jungle. "We need to find shelter."

"We also need to dispose of that snake. It's like an arrow pointed to where we've traveled."

An idea struck Sage. "Would Nali eat the snake?"

Blaise grinned. "She would indeed."

She eyed the thirty-foot snake. "Can you haul that?"

"Its weight won't be a problem, but it will get caught on rocks."

Sage winced at the mental picture that inspired. "How much farther until we leave the brook?"

Blaise pointed. "Only about fifty more paces."

"Okay."

Sage stood, her wet clothing clinging to her body, chilling her. "I'll carry Jasmine, you get the snake."

"I can walk," Jas argued.

She squatted and placed her hands under Jasmine's armpits. "Yes, you will, 'cause you're going to have to. Brace yourself, though. This will hurt."

Jasmine growled and spat curses as Sage helped her upright, wrapping an arm around her. Jas shivered, her teeth clacking together.

"Bloody hell," Jas snarled.

"You'll be better in no time. Only fifty paces until we leave the stream. We can do this." Sage moved in careful steps, trying her best not to jar Jasmine while scouring the plants caging them in.

Blaise grunted behind them. "This beast stinks." A pause. "I hate snakes."

"I have to say, I'm with you on that one. I now hate them, as well." Jas muttered.

Five paces till they reached a gap in the arbor, Sage stopped and pressed her finger against her lips. She propped Jasmine against the greenery and pulled her daggers from her sheaths, creeping forward. A hand touched her shoulder, halting her progress.

She met Blaise's gaze. "Let me go ahead."

"We go together."

The Scythian woman studied her and nodded. Both women crept forward and peeked out into the jungle. Birds chatted their goodnight songs, but apart from that, nothing stirred. Sage jerked when a rumble came from above. Her gaze flew to the trees and a familiar pair of golden eyes peered down at her.

"Nali," she breathed. The feline stretched and jumped from the tree to the ground, sauntering toward them.

Blaise stiffened.

Sage glanced at the woman from the corner of her eye. "What is it?"

"Nothing."

"Nothing?"

Blaise scowled and crossed her arms, never taking her eyes from the beast. "I'm still not sure that beast's not going to eat me."

"Nali? She's a lamb."

Blaise chuckled. "You know nothing of her kind. They're vicious man-eaters. I've only ever known of a handful to bond with humans."

"Huh. Interesting." She shrugged. "If you're worried, I'll let you present the snake to her. I'm sure she'll appreciate it."

"I'm sure." Blaise eyed the area. "Darkness is approaching. We need to get up into a tall tree, and rest." Her lips flattened as she stared at Jasmine. "Tomorrow will be worse for her, but we are going to have to push harder."

"I understand," Sage breathed.

Urgency thrummed in her veins. Each moment they dallied was another the warlord gained on them.

Blaise scuffed her boot in the soil. "Are you prepared for the next leg of our journey?"

Translation: are you prepared to die?

"I am," Sage said solemnly, and lowered her voice. "I want you to get Jasmine out first, and then you go with her if it comes to that."

The Scythian woman's dark gaze met hers. "You would sacrifice yourself for me? Your enemy?"

"Hopefully, it won't come to that, but," Sage stepped closer and held her forearm out, "I haven't survived this long by hoping for the best. I'm shrewd. You are our best asset if you decide to help Aermia once we arrive. I'm a symbol, nothing more. You hold real power. Your life is worth more than mine."

Blaise studied her. "And if I don't want any part of the coming war?"

"Then, that's your choice." Sage held Blaise's stare. "But know this, women of power, honor, and courage, women like us, are never on the sidelines. We are drawn into the thick of it. I won't force you into anything, but I predict you will be an intricate part of our kingdoms' future."

Blaise shook her head, a small smile on her face. "My mother was right."

"About what?"

"The warlord cannot have you. If he did, the world would tremble at your feet."

Sage scoffed to hide the chill that ran up her spine. "He will never have me."

"Are you sure of that?"

All the air seemed to be pulled from Sage's lungs. Did he possess part of her? The broken, twisted part of her whispered yes, but the sane portion understood it as manipulation. She rubbed at her chest. She felt like a war waged inside of her. But despite that battle of her emotions, she knew two truths: he was the enemy, and Tehl was her home. She had to keep that in mind.

She pushed back her shoulders and lifted her arm again. "I know what's right. That surpasses all else. I won't allow his tyranny to continue."

Blaise clasped her forearm and then kissed each of her cheeks. "I believe you, Sage Blackwell. You make a fearsome queen. Your prince has no idea who he appointed to share his throne, does he?"

Sage walked over to Jasmine and helped her from the ground. "He doesn't know the half of it."

An infectious chuckle burst out of Blaise. "I'm sure."

CHAPTER THIRTY-SEVEN

Tehl

He stood fifty paces from the crumbling Mort Wall, his quieting camp behind him. A cool breeze ruffled his hair as he examined the tall grass blades. Nothing moved, but the creaking jungle trees on the other side of the wall sent chills up his spine.

He eyed the crumbling stone barrier. The wall was a joke, really. After learning about the Scythians, something as common as stone would never keep them out if they were truly determined. So, why had they been kept apart for so long? Was it because of their radical ideas? How had the warlord kept the people complacent? It was human nature to be curious, to want to explore.

A snort escaped him. By fear, no doubt.

He was man enough to admit that the warlord gave him chills. A leviathan seemed downright docile next to the hulking man. He scanned the swaying grass, his hand resting on his sword. Where was Sage? Was she running right now? Hiding? Fighting?

"If you don't sleep soon, you're likely to collapse," Lilja's silky voice called.

Tehl turned toward the woman perched on a rock just to the right of him. She'd sat there in silence for the last few hours. His designated escort. Part of him took offense that his council assigned him an escort, but the rational part of him knew they were right. Scythians were powerful, and he needed someone equally powerful on his side to protect not just himself, but Sage as well.

"I can't sleep," he admitted. "My decisions repeat in my mind. I can't help but wonder if I had done things differently, would we be in this situation?"

"I understand." Lilja tossed a small rock into the silvery grass. "But we can't go back, no matter how much we wish we could."

"I know."

Logically, he did. But emotion wasn't logical.

"Do you have any regrets?" he found himself asking. He cringed at the personal question he'd just lobbed at her.

"Many things," she said. "I've seen much sorrow in my life, but much good. I can't regret the good things that came from the bad."

"That was one way to—" he cut off his words as Lilja held her hand in the air.

Her magenta gaze cut to his as she slid off the rock and into a crouch. Ever so slowly, she raised her finger to her lips. His muscles tensed, his gaze scouring the area for whatever put the Sirenidae on edge. His eyes narrowed as two large shadows shifted on the other side of the wall. Shadows much too large to be Sage.

Lilja shot him a glance and held her hand up, signaling for him to stay. She slunk into the tall grass and disappeared from view without a sound. Tehl released his breath and pulled his sword from his scabbard with care. The blade slipped free with naught but a soft hiss. Yet somehow that slight noise was loud enough that the shadows creeping through the gap in the wall froze.

One heartbeat, two, and then they rushed him. He shifted his stance and braced himself. The two Scythian warriors rushed him, their movements fluid. He blinked as one disappeared into the grass with a muffled yelp. The other warrior paused, noting his fallen comrade, and that was his undoing. He also disappeared without a sound.

The hair on the back of Tehl's neck rose as silence descended. He strained his ears, but he could hear nothing unusual. His gaze ran over the wall and the grass, searching for danger. His breath stuttered as Lilja stood from the tall grass a mere five feet away, looking like an avenging goddess. Her white hair haloed her exotic face that looked like it was carved from stone. It took a few times for him to find his voice.

"Are you alright?"

"I'm fine," her lyrical voice washed over him. She turned toward the wall. "Why are you here?"

Silence. Who was she speaking to?

"Answer me. Old friend or not, I will cut you down if you mean harm."

Only years of practice, and thanks to many of Sam's pranks, kept him from jumping when a deep voice answered the Sirenidae.

"Lil, you always had a way with words."

A warrior materialized from the grass to their left. He made no move in their direction, though. Instead, he lifted his hands up.

Tehl lifted his sword, but didn't move from his spot. His eyes cut to Lilja who glared at the enemy with such anger, it inspired fear even in him.

"You didn't answer me. What are you doing here?" Lilja repeated.

"Helping."

"Helping," Lilja growled. "You're playing a very dangerous game, Blair."

Tehl stiffened and narrowed his eyes on the man. Why was one of the warlord's closest men on his land? And where was his wife? Lilja's hand landed on his chest. He frowned at the arm holding him back. When had he moved? He glanced at the Sirenidae eyeing him.

"You good?" she asked.

"Yes," he said as he planted his feet, glaring in the Scythian's direction.

Lilja turned her attention back to Blair, waiting for him to speak. The warrior held her stare for what felt like minutes until he cursed and pushed his midnight braids from his face.

"You know I couldn't help you."

Lilja's jaw clenched, but she said nothing.

Tehl glanced between the two. What was going on?

The Scythian dropped his hands and crossed his arms over his bare chest.

"You're not being rational about this. I know you, Lil. Calm down and listen to what I have to say."

Tehl winced. There was something he learned while living with Sage, and that was not to tell a woman to calm down when she was upset.

"Listen to you? Are you serious?" Lilja hissed. She wildly gestured to the grass with her daggers. "You brought warriors to my home."

"And you're also aware that if I didn't want to be discovered, we wouldn't have been. I wanted you to catch them. Why would I want that, Lil?"

"Twenty years," she whispered.

The Scythian hung his head. "Twenty years," he said softly.

"Why?"

"I couldn't risk it."

"Nothing?" Lilja's voice wavered, surprising Tehl. "It wasn't possible to spare one moment and let me know you lived?"

"No, it was not."

"I loved you!" Lilja's voice rose. "Mourned you every day for years. I even went into Scythia in search of you. I almost died! If Hayjen hadn't pulled me out, I would have." She chuckled bitterly, tears dripping down her face. "A part of me died when you didn't come home."

"I have a family, Lil. I couldn't leave them." His tone pleaded for understanding.

Lilja gasped, her face crumpling and her hands curling into fists. "How could you after everything we went through?"

"I did what I had to."

She scoffed, wiping her tears from her face. "I guess my Blair really did die in that jungle. He would never have agreed to something so sick."

The warrior's hands clenched. "I didn't force her. Why would you think that?"

"I don't know you," she said, her face hardening. "I'm thankful Gem isn't here to see what you've become."

"Lilja Femi, don't you dare say that! I've loved you longer and better than anyone else in this world. Don't you dare bring Gem into this." He stabbed a finger at Lilja. "You know what's in my heart. Every day we've been apart, I've fought to right the wrongs of so many years ago. I've sacrificed, so that others might have freedom and the life we weren't afforded. I've suffered, so I can remove that monster from Scythia. You and I are the same, so don't you tell me you don't know me."

His gaze shifted to Tehl.

"You're lucky the warlord hates an easy battle, or you'd be dead by now, and your wife in his clutches forever."

"What do you know of my wife?" Tehl growled.

"That he'll never stop hunting her."

"So, she's alive?" He braced himself for the answer.

"Yes."

Relief surged through his body until Blair spoke again.

"But she'll wish she was dead if he catches her."

"Why are you here?" Tehl asked, suspicion in his tone.

"I'm here to offer help."

"And what do you require in exchange?" No one did anything for free.

"The warlord's death."

"Why now?" Lilja asked.

"Because it's time."

Tehl cocked his head and studied the warrior. The way he said the words meant he was resolute... they also meant a rebellion. "You're organizing a rebellion."

Blair lifted his chin. "For someone so young, you're astute."

"I've dealt with rebellion members. I can spot a rebel when I see one."

"You speak of your wife."

"She's taught me much." Tehl said.

"I'm sure. She's a fierce woman."

"Indeed."

"The warlord doesn't trust you," Lilja murmured.

Tehl glanced at Lilja askance.

"He trusts no one, Lil."

"That's why you didn't seek me out."

"One reason."

"And the others?"

"I have four daughters."

"Four?" Lilja croaked.

Blair smiled, his teeth flashing in the dark. "You'd love them, Lil. They're my life." His smile faded. "But they're coming of age."

Lilja's face turned to horror. "He would take your daughters?"

"They're not mine according to the warlord. He gave me my

woman, and he can take her away at any moment, along with our daughters."

Tehl's gut churned. No one should have that sort of power.

"That's sick," he muttered.

"I agree," Blair growled.

Tehl's mind ran over all the information Blair had revealed, and then to Lilja's comment a few nights ago about her man on the Scythian side. "Is this your spy?"

"Yes."

"And do you trust him?"

Lilja glanced up at Tehl and back to the warrior watching their exchange with interest. "I do."

"Will he protect Sage?"

"I already have," Blair said. "And I will continue to do so."

Damn Scythian hearing. "How so?"

The warrior gestured to the surrounding grass. "We're supposed to be hunting your wife ahead of the warlord. I caught your wife's trail a day ago. It was very faint and hidden well. It was easy to miss, so I led the men astray. I will protect her as best as I can..."

"So long as it doesn't reveal your true intentions," Tehl finished.

Blair nodded. "Like I said, the best I can."

"You better," Lilja growled. "She's what's left of my family."

"Family?" Both men echoed.

Lilja flashed Tehl an apologetic smile. "She's Hayjen's niece."

He blinked and then blinked again. Hayjen looked nothing like Sage. Tehl's forehead wrinkled. But Sage looked like her father. Her brothers, on the other hand, looked like their mother and... Hayjen. He shook his head. He'd deal with that revelation later.

"What do you need from me, Scythian?"

"Peace."

Tehl laughed. "Peace? There's no such thing."

"Deal fairly with the Scythians when this is through. Don't let your prejudice cloud your judgment. The people have suffered far more than you, and the warriors are only following orders."

That was fair.

"I can do that." Tehl threw his shoulders back and strode toward Blair, Lilja hot on his heels. He halted before him and held his hand out. "If you're honorable and do what you say, then I will likewise honor our agreement. You risk much to protect my family, so I will extend the same courtesy. If your family needs safety, send them to the palace. I will make sure they're taken care of."

Blair studied him and clasped his arm. "Thank you."

Blair kissed both of his cheeks and stepped back, gaze sweeping the grass to his fallen warriors.

"I didn't kill them," Lilja muttered. "I knocked them out."

"Thank you, Lil. I'll retrieve them and be on my way. May luck be with you both."

"Not luck—skill," Tehl said.

"Indeed," the Scythian warrior said and turned to leave.

"Blair?" Lilja called.

He paused and opened his arms.

The Sirenidae flew into the Scythian's arms. He pulled her off the ground and buried his face into her neck, mumbling words too low for Tehl to hear. Tehl backed away, feeling like the world had turned on its head, with a million questions running through his mind. He glanced at the couple embracing one last time before turning around. If the Scythian had planned to kill them, he'd have already done it. And from the looks of things, it didn't look like he'd be letting go of Lilja anytime soon.

He eyed Hayjen, who was now leaning against the rock Lilja had vacated. The big man nodded to him briefly before his attention moved back over Tehl's shoulder.

"I take it you're also acquainted with Blair?"

"He's a friend," Hayjen said.

"Just a friend?" Lilja and Blair's conversation seemed like it was a lot more.

"Her best friend."

Hayjen saw the doubt he was obviously not hiding well.

"He brought Lil and I together, and he also helped her escape Scythia. They have a bond that words cannot describe."

"Apparently, we too share a bond – one that no one told me about, Uncle."

Hayjen's gaze sharpened. "She told you?"

Tehl chuckled. "Not on purpose."

"Everything Lil does has a purpose."

He sobered and glanced at Lilja. "Good point." The Sirenidae had a brilliant mind. Tehl turned his attention back to Hayjen. "I guess I should welcome you to the family. I take it you're the younger brother?"

Hayjen shook his head. "No, I'm older by several years. Do you understand why we kept such a thing a secret?"

Tehl frowned. Hayjen didn't look more than ten years older than himself, and yet he claimed to be older than Gwen? He squinted at Hayjen while he calculated the man's age. Logically, the man would be over 50 years. Something wasn't right. "How?"

"Lilja. The sea offers many wondrous things."

He rubbed at his eyes while he mulled that over. "Are you telling me Lilja is in possession of something that can grant immortality?" Saying those words felt comical, like something from a bedtime story.

"Not immortality, but a greatly-lengthened life span."

Something like that would be highly sought-after if word ever got out. Lilja would be hunted, and anyone in association with her. People did dangerous things when they thought something could lengthen their life. "You kept this from Sage to protect her."

Hayjen nodded, his face serious. "Now, you understand why that information has been kept a secret. Many would harm my family, or Lilja and me, just to retrieve it." He pushed off the rock and held out his hand. "We didn't keep this from you for lack of trust."

"I understand." And he did. Tehl reached out and clasped Hayjen's hand. "But I hate secrets. They have a nasty way of backfiring. Is there anything else I need to be aware of?"

Hayjen shook his head. "Not that I know of." He released Tehl's hand and glanced at his wife. "I'll make sure that anything important gets passed along."

"I appreciate it," Tehl murmured and pulled back his hand. He blinked and his eyes burned. The lack of sleep was catching up with him.

"You have the next watch?" he asked tiredly.

"Yep," Hayjen said.

"I'll see you in the morning."

"Goodnight."

Tehl strode away from his newly-discovered relative, still

reeling from the information he'd learned tonight. Lilja had a warrior spy at her beck and call, a rebellion was brewing on the Scythian side, Hayjen was Sage's uncle, and he'd sealed an accord with the warlord's right-hand man. He barked out a laugh and ran a hand down his face. Sage wouldn't believe this. He wished she was here, so he could tell her about the craziness that had become his life.

The smile slipped from his face. If the Scythian didn't keep his end of the deal, then Tehl might not ever get the chance to.

CHAPTER THIRTY- EIGHT

Sage

Sage's arms and legs were screaming in pain, but just a glance at Jasmine's pained face was enough to do her best to shove the pain aside. After all, it could be worse; she could have broken ribs.

As they made their way through the jungle, a spider the size of her fist skittered across their path, but she didn't care. It didn't harm them and soon would be off terrorizing someone else with its hairy appendages. The creature hunting them was truly something to be afraid of.

She stopped in her tracks when Blaise paused, listening to the jungle. In the last two days, she'd been doing that more and more often and Sage couldn't help but feel that a noose was tightening around their necks. Each moment of rest, each minute of sleep was disturbed by the fact that it only meant the warlord was gaining on them. They were losing time. It was a miracle they'd lasted this long.

"Damn it," Blaise cursed softly, casting a glance in their direction.

The blood in Sage's veins iced over at the look on the woman's face. Sheer terror.

"What is it?" Jas whispered, her breathing labored.

On silent feet, Blaise strode back to them. "They've caught up with us." She shook her head in frustration. "We can't avoid them. My only hope is that they aren't a part of the hunt, just a border patrol."

"And if they are?" Sage let the question hang in the air.

"Then we'll have to fight." Blaise eyed Jasmine. "We need to get to the river. The wall is close here." She met Sage's gaze. "We need to cross it today. If we don't, he'll catch us before night falls."

Her legs trembled. "How close is he?"

"I'm not sure. If I was to venture a guess, I'd say he was not farther behind than a few hours. The hunt moves much quicker than we do."

"It's my fault," Jas said, hugging her arms around her waist. "I slowed you down."

"No." Blaise shook her head. "We could not have anticipated the attack, but you've handled the pain better than expected."

"I can survive pain. I can't survive captivity," Jas murmured.

"That, I understand well," Blaise whispered. Her lips pursed as she eyed them. "You both look Scythian from far away, but your eyes will give you away. Keep your gaze down and keep silent. Your accents will give you away as well." Blaise pulled in a deep breath. "We're almost there. We can do this."

"I'm not dying here," Jas said with conviction. "My little ones need me."

"Let's move," Sage said.

Blaise nodded turned around, taking off to the left. "Keep a sharp eye. I may have heightened sense, but it doesn't mean I have eyes on the back of my head," she called over her shoulder.

Sage glanced at Jasmine. Her face was pale, but determined.

"Are you ready?" Sage asked.

Jasmine smiled at her and grabbed her hand. "I've been ready for months."

She squeezed Jas' hand once and stepped aside for her friend to pass. Chills skittered down her spine and her shoulders tightened. Her stomach clenched; she couldn't help having a sense of foreboding. Slowly, she spun, her eyes wide as she examined the surrounding trees. Nothing unusual, and yet...goosebumps dotted her arms. It was like the jungle held its breath. But for what?

She swallowed hard and backed away before spinning on her heel and sprinting to catch up to the others. Blaise shot her a questioning look, but quickened her pace now that she'd joined them. The greenery blurred as they ran through the jungle, leaves and vines grabbing at them like unwanted suitors. Panic ate at the pit of her stomach. Time was slipping through her fingers.

She skidded to a stop as they neared the edge of a clearing. Sage's brow furrowed. Why had they halted? She didn't see anything, but that meant nothing in Scythia.

"Warriors," Blaise breathed.

Sage dropped her chin, her eyes glued to the jungle floor. She pulled in a deep breath. She had to maintain her calm.

"My lady," a deep voice answered. "It's a surprise to see you so far from a village."

Her heart galloped in her chest. Hell. She hadn't even heard them approach.

"We were scouting the area," Blaise replied.

"For what?" A gruff voice asked.

Sage stared at the decomposing leaves beneath her boots and stained her ears to hear the surrounding sounds. Were there only two men?

"A man-eater. We'd all like the right to choose our betrothed."

"A lofty goal indeed," the deep voice commented. "I must say that it's rare to find so many women together. Your companions are quite beautiful."

Jasmine shifted next to her, but otherwise kept quiet.

"Their mothers were of..." Blaise trailed off. "Unusual birth."

"Indeed."

Sage sensed a touch of disdain in the warrior's tone. That was something. Disdain she could work with; it was actually a step up from lust. Footsteps moved closer, and a hand smoothed down her braid. Sweat beaded on her forehead as boots entered her vision. Calm, she had to maintain her calm.

"Are you on patrol?" Blaise asked, her tone neutral.

"Yes, we are," the gruff voice supplied.

A finger ran along her jaw and pressed under her chin. Sage clenched her teeth and looked up at the warrior. His dark eyes studied her face as she stared at him. One finger wandered up to trace the bow of her lip. Sage snapped her teeth at him, not able to handle his exploration any longer. "Get your hands off me."

A slow smile spread across his face handsome face. "So much light, so much fire in your eyes," he murmured. "No wonder the warlord kept you."

Horror moved through her. She whipped her knives out and slashed at the warrior. His hand snapped out, grabbed her dagger by the blade, and tore it out of her hand. Sage dropped to the ground, sweeping her leg out. The warrior avoided her kick deftly. She gritted her teeth. She was slow. As Sage regained her position, the warrior disappeared. She stumbled in surprise and then shouted when an arm wrapped around her throat.

"Weak," he whispered. A hand traced her side. "But alluring."

She. Was. Not. Weak.

Sage dug her nails into his arm and tilted her face forward, biting down. A growl filled her ears as a metallic tang filled her mouth. A hand fisted in her hair and yanked. Pain bit at her, but she didn't let go. He jerked her head back again, tearing her teeth from his arm with a bellow. She cried out when teeth bit into her ear.

"How do you like it?" he hissed. "Just wait until the warlord—"

An earth-shattering roar deafened her a moment before something crashed into her. She slammed into the ground, her face pressing into the damp earth. Sage choked on dirt and leaves and almost cried when the weight crushed her.

She scrambled upright, coughing. She spit dirt out and glanced to the side. She froze, terrified, when she spotted the man-eater tearing into the Scythian. Her hands shook as the beast's golden gaze met hers, its lips pulled back from its crimson stained teeth. Stars above, Nali was fearsome.

A scream pulled her out of her stupor just in time to watch Jasmine sneak up on the Scythian pinning Blaise. Her fiery friend swung her arm and smashed a rock into the warrior's head. He yelled and seized a handful of Jasmine's shirt. Sage's eyes connected with Jasmine's right before the Scythian threw her. A scream caught in her throat as Jas tumbled through the air and crashed into a tree. She didn't get up.

Rage exploded inside her. That was it. She was done with people hurting her friends. Ignoring the beast, she forced herself upright and crept on silent feet toward the warrior beating Blaise into the ground. The beast's snarling was hair-raising, but a blessing. It hid her movements. It hid the warrior's death. He raised his fist one more time, and it was his last. Sage struck. He stiffened and then, like a puppet with its strings cut, he collapsed.

"Blaise," she panted. Her breath sawed in and out of her, and her hands trembled as she tugged on the huge man. He wouldn't budge. Sage scrambled to the side, dropped to her butt, and used her feet to push him off Blaise. Pushing to her knees, she knelt next to Blaise. Her heart flew to her throat at the state of her friend. Every inch of skin Sage saw was damaged. Carefully, she placed two fingers at the base of her neck. A pulse. A sigh of relief escaped her before the panic came rushing back in. How were they supposed to cross the river?

She glanced around the area, skipping over Nali and her meal.

Emotion clogged her throat as Jasmine limped toward her. "Are you okay?"

"I'm alive," Jas croaked. "Is Blaise alive?"

"I am," Blaise rasped.

Sage whipped back around. "What is broken?"

"I don't know. It all hurts, so probably everything."

"Can you move?"

"Not without help."

Sage breathed hard while she thought over their options. There was only one. They had to cross the river. They weren't far from it. She could hear it from here.

"Leave me."

She focused back on Blaise. "No."

"Those were part of the hunt, not the patrol. You have to leave now! There's no time."

"I know," Sage growled and slipped an arm under Blaise. "Jas, I need your help."

Jasmine hobbled around Blaise and slipped an arm under her other side, a moan of pain escaping her thin white lips. Her broken ribs must have hurt horridly.

"What are you doing?" Blaise cried as they forced her upright. Tears poured down the woman's face as they began hauling her across the meadow.

"Saving your life," Jas grunted.

"Nali," Sage called. "Leave your meal. I need you."

She didn't know if the feline would follow, but she hoped she would. Every step they took felt too slow. It was like the warlord was breathing down her neck. They broke through the trees, and she about collapsed in relief when Nali loped past them and to the bank.

"I can't swim," Blaise whispered in a pained moan.

Sage glanced from Nali to Jasmine to Blaise and back to Nali, an idea forming in her mind.

"Nali."

The feline eyed Sage, her ears twitching and laying back, a low growl rumbled in Nali's throat.

Sage's stomach dropped. Something was coming. Her urgency doubled. "Nali, I need you to take Blaise across the river."

"Are you mad?" Blaise hissed as they dragged her into the freezing water.

Sage placed a hand on Nali and scratched behind her ears. "Nali, I need you to be kind to Blaise. Take her across the water. Protect her."

Nali strode deeper into the river and paused.

"Jas, help me lift Blaise onto her back. Hurry!"

They managed to get the Scythian woman onto the beast. Sage wrapped Blaise's arms around Nali's neck and met her gaze. "You hold onto Nali with all you have. Trust her. She'll protect you."

"It was an honor knowing you," Blaise whispered.

"We'll meet again."

Sage slapped Nali on the rump, and the beast strode deeper into the water and began swimming. She cut through the water like she was a fish. "Be safe," Sage whispered.

She grabbed Jasmine's hand and ran along the bank.

"What are you doing? We need to cross!"

"Do you see how wide that part was? We'd drown before we made it halfway. Plus, the water is too cold."

Sage sprinted harder and crashed through some trees near the river. Branches slapped at her face, but she didn't register the sting. Panic and fear were ruling her now. Her breathing was rough and she ached to stop, but she tugged on her friend when she slowed. "We're so close, Jas. Just a little bit further."

Jasmine clutched her side, sweat pouring off her forehead. "Sage, I won't be able to swim across the river. I can't do it. There's something wrong with my other arm."

Tears of frustration filled Sage's eyes. They were so close, they had to make it. She sucked in a deep breath and pulled harder. "We make it together or not at all. I will swim us both across." She wouldn't go back to that hell, but neither would she condemn Jasmine to it.

They weren't going back.

With strength she didn't know she still possessed, she propelled them forward. "Jas, just think, the twins are just across the river. Think how happy they'll be to see you."

Jasmine sobbed and stumbled behind her. "I will hold them and never let go."

They crashed through the trees onto the Scythian side of the bank. Sage gasped for air, staring at the impossible challenge ahead of them. The water was so swift. How would they survive? She swallowed hard and glanced to Jasmine, who was simply staring at the river. It seemed like an ocean before them.

Every hair on her body rose when the forest quieted behind them. Hell. He was near. She met Jasmine's wide eyes. "We have to swim now."

Jasmine nodded, and they both scrambled to the water's edge. "Have you ever swum someone across a distance like this?" she panted.

Sage shook her head and kicked her boots off while wading into the cold water. Jas' trembling arm seized her bicep. She met her friend's eyes, trying to emulate a calm she didn't feel.

"You need to swim pulling me. I'll use my legs as much as I can."

"Okay." She wrapped an arm around Jasmine's chest and pushed back into the current. Sage gasped as the cold water wrapped around her body painfully. The river pulled on her, trying to suck them down. Sage gritted her teeth and fought against the current and the cold, keeping her eyes on the Aermian bank. They were so close.

"Sage!" Jasmine's horror filled voice pulled her attention from her strokes.

Sage glanced back to the Scythian bank, and fear clogged her throat, her strokes faltering. Scythian warriors lined the jungle's edge, silent. Her heart stopped in her chest as she locked eyes with the most devastatingly handsome man she had ever laid eyes on. The warlord strolled to the water's edge with his hand tucked into his trouser pockets, completely casual. Somehow, that frightened her even more.

"Did you think you could escape me, wild one?" he asked, smiling softly.

Her breath seized in her lungs. No, she didn't.

"Swim harder, Sage." Jasmine whispered.

Sage pulled her eyes from the master of her hell and pushed with everything she had. She couldn't let him mess with her mind.

Masculine laughter sounded behind them, deepening her anxiety. She knew that laugh. It was gloating, triumphant. She flicked her eyes back to the bank in time to catch him stepping out of his boots and pulling his sword free from its scabbard.

"You know I love a good game of chase. Keep running. I love the hunt."

She battled the panic threatening to consume her. If she panicked, both she and Jasmine died. Sage cocked her head back and gauged the distance to the other side. They were almost halfway, but her energy was waning. She glanced back to the warlord, who was carefully rolling his pants up, as if that mattered when swimming. If he got into the water and they were still swimming, it would be over for them. She knew how fast he moved. They wouldn't have a chance.

Sage kicked harder and stared at Jasmine's honey brown head. Perhaps one of them did. Jas had children waiting for her to return. What did Sage have? Her family was well looked-after, the treaty was in effect, and the crown didn't need her. She breathed out and made one of the easiest decisions of her life. "Can you swim if I get you to the slow part of the river?"

"I think so."

Sage swallowed and forced her numb legs to kick. "I am going to push you into it and then you have to swim."

"No," Jasmine gasped, her cold breath clouding around them.

"Yes," Sage forced out. "Once he enters the water, we won't make it."

"Then they'll take both of us. I won't leave you."

"You don't have a choice. Think of the twins. They need you. You are their only family."

Jasmine's face was grieved. "I don't want to leave you."

"You must." A calm settled over her. This was the right thing to do. She could repay Jasmine for all the pain she'd endured on her behalf. A splash sounded, pulling Sage's eyes to the Scythian bank.

The warlord waded into the water, his face a mask of concern.

"This water is too cold, my love. You need to get out, or you'll get sick. Come back to me, and all of this will be forgotten."

"No way in hell," she hissed between clenched teeth.

He tapped his ear. "I can still hear you."

"I know."

"So that's how it is to be." He shook his head, his dark hair waving in the breeze. He pushed forward and cut through the water like a leviathan.

"It's time, Jas." Sage flipped them onto their stomachs still swimming with everything she had. "Tell my family I love them, that I forgive Rafe, and tell the princes that I'll miss them." Sage shoved Jas with all her might and never stopped swimming. Jasmine pushed toward the Aermian bank clumsily, but at least she wasn't drowning.

Terror strangled her when a hand wrapped around her ankle, jerking her backwards. She clamped her lips together holding in the scream that would only serve to distract Jasmine. Large burnished arms wrapped around her, hauling her into a solid chest. She stared straight ahead, ignoring the giant body behind her as tears of relief pricked her eyes. Jas had made it to the bank.

"You've led me on a merry hunt, Sage."

Her eyes slammed shut as the warlord's voice curled around her. A nose ran along the column of her neck as they bobbed in the river.

"Cinnamon," he growled, "How is it you haven't bathed in days and yet you still smell like cinnamon?"

She remained silent, her body trembling against him as she ignored him. It was so cold. Everything was numb.

His hand slipped up her chest and to her throat. He pulled her head back and tipped it to the side. "You know how I feel about being ignored. Look at me, Sage."

Part of her wanted to obey him. The thought caused bile to burn her throat.

He spun her around and pulled her flush against his body as he treaded water in the river like it was nothing. The warlord scanned her face. "You've been hurt." She hissed when he brushed a wound on her cheek. "If you hadn't run from me, you wouldn't have been hurt." His hand dropped to her waist and kneaded the flesh. She cringed at his attentions.

"Have you nothing to say?"

"I would do it again."

His face transformed into a proud smile that made her stomach drop. "And that's why I love you, despite the unfortunate line you were born from. You have a fire I want to claim."

"There shall be no claiming."

He brushed a wet strand of hair from her face, tenderly, like her father used to do. "You and I both know that's not true." He dropped his forehead to hers and stared into her eyes. "No matter where you go, I will be imprinted on your soul, and in your dreams. We will always be part of each other."

The sick part was that his words were true. If she survived, he would haunt her nightmares for life. "You're right," Sage murmured. She lifted her exhausted arms and laid them around his dark olive shoulders. With careful movements, she spun the ring on her finger that Maeve had given her and flipped the lid. "But in death, you can't haunt me."

"I'll never let anything hurt you."

"You already have." Sage slammed her hand around the back of his neck holding on tight as his eyes narrowed.

"What have you done?" he growled as he ripped her arm from his neck. The warlord yanked her hand up and examined the ring, his grip going lax even as his eyes burned hotter with rage.

"Nothing that will kill you." She leaned closer and placed a kiss on his cheek. "I freed myself from you."

Sage shoved away from him with the last of her strength, managing to break his grasp because of the toxin. The water tore her from him, clawing at her legs and trying to pull her under. She fought it, knowing that drowning was not a peaceful way to go, but she wasn't strong enough. The last thing she saw was the warlord's panic-filled gaze before the river claimed her.

Water tugged her left and right, up and down. Darkness surrounded her as her lungs began to burn. Her body flailed as she clawed at the water, desperate for air. Her body slammed into something, forcing the rest of the air from her lungs. Her face broke the surface, sputtering and gasping for air. Sage blinked at the bank not ten feet from her. How? She heaved in painful breaths as the freezing water beat at her body. It would be so easy to close her eyes and sleep.

She jerked, her eyes springing wide, when a growl roused her. A dark, furry head bobbed up next to her. Sage let out a sob and sunk her fingers into Nali's wet coat. "Help me," she whispered through numb lips.

She was certain her nails were digging into the feline's skin, but it didn't stop Nali from propelling them toward the bank. Slick stones bumped against her knees and feet as they entered the shallows. Her hip dug into the sand, and she couldn't hold on any longer. Sage collapsed into shallow water, her teeth chattering. Nali quickly moved to her side and bit into the back of her shirt, tugging her from the water. Stone scraped her palms as she did her best to aid Nali, clawing her way up the bank. When her hands sunk into sun-warmed sand, she collapsed with her cheek pressed to the earth, water dripping into her eyes.

She didn't drown. She didn't die.

Sage didn't know how long she laid there, savoring the air filling her lungs, the sand and gravel beneath her hands. Only when her body began to tremble so hard her teeth clacked together, did she gain awareness. Painstakingly, she pushed to her hands and knees and took in the surrounding land.

Forest.

Aermian Forest.

She sat on her calves as a sob tore from her. Tears blurred her eyes and dripped down her face. "I made it," she whispered to herself, relieved beyond words.

For a moment, she had thought the river spat her back upon Scythian land, but to be back again was overwhelming. She never thought she'd truly make it. Great, heaving cries broke free, wracking her body. She hunched forward and sunk her fingers into the sand.

She'd made it home. She was home.

Time blurred as bone-weary fatigue set in. Sage studied her bluish fingers, and something inside her head said she should be worried. But for the life of her, she didn't remember why she should worry.

Nali released a heart-stopping growl that finally pulled Sage from her muddled thoughts. The feline hunkered down in front of her, the feline's jet-black fur puffing up menacingly. Fear penetrated the fog hovering over her mind. There was only one reason Nali would growl like that. He'd found her.

Her heart galloped and her stomach rolled. She kept her blurry gaze on the sand beneath her scratched hands. Why was life so cruel? Hadn't she suffered enough? What more could she give?

"Sage."

Her eyes closed, more tears seeping out of the corners. "Tehl," she whimpered. Even after she'd banished his presence from her mind, still he rescued her when she most needed him. He'd give her a reprieve from the awaiting horrors. "You didn't leave me," she choked out.

"Love, I will never leave you."

Her fingers flexed in the gritty sand. "I can't live this life." She gasped for breaths which seemed unwilling to come. "I can't go back to him. I'm not strong enough."

"You will never have to go back. He will never touch you again."

A sad smile tugged at her lips. If only that was the truth. Tehl knew what she had to do. He was part of her mind after all. She sucked in a shuddering breath. "Thank you for keeping me company. I'll always love you for that."

Her shoulders tensed as Nali snarled louder, protecting her from her dark fate. It was only a matter of minutes before everything she loved would disappear forever.

"Sage, you're shivering. I need you to call off your beast, so I can get you warm."

She frowned at the ground. What was he talking about?

"Call off your beast, please. There's no time to waste."

Another snarl. "Look at me, Sage."

She raised her head at the command and every part of her stilled. Nali stood in front of her, snarling with her lips pulled back, exposing huge canines as she warned the enemy away, but it was not who she expected.

A group of men surrounded her, but one stood apart, his hand held out to the man-eater. His tense form suggested fear, and yet he whispered soothing words. Sage attempted to decipher his words, but she couldn't hear anything over the ringing in her ears. His blue-black hair waved in the breeze as he glanced in her direction and spoke a little louder.

"Sage, love, please calm your beast," he begged. "You need a healer."

She jolted and fell onto her bottom, desperately blinking the tears from her eyes. It couldn't be Tehl. What trickery was this? Had she gone insane?

"You're not insane, but you are ill."

Her lips trembled as her gaze traced his beautiful face. He wasn't real, he couldn't be. Her mind must be broken. That was the only logical explanation that or… "I died." No fear, just numbness. A sense of peace settled over her. She could handle death.

Tehl stepped closer, earning another snarl from Nali. "You're not dead. I need you to trust me and trust yourself. I'm real."

She swiped her arm across her face, her tears smearing across her cool skin. Sage focused on him. "Don't placate me with lies, Tehl. I can't stand any more lies. Just be honest with me."

"I am." He shook his head, his face a mask of frustration.

She smiled as he jerked his hands through his hair. The gesture was so familiar, so human.

He eyed Nali and then Sage, his eyes narrowing. "You stubborn wench. It's me."

"My lord, calm down," a deep voice chastised.

Sage blinked slowly. Her thoughts sluggish. Wench? When was the last time he snapped at her? She couldn't remember. She rubbed her sandy hand across her forehead, the rough grit biting into her skin and grounding her. Could he be real?

"Sage!"

Her heart squeezed as she glanced in the direction of the voice. Jasmine stood bedraggled at the front of the group. She was bruised, dirty, and slightly blue, but there wasn't anything more beautiful in that moment than her friend. "Jas?"

"We made it. We're home."

She pointed a trembling finger at Jasmine. "How do I know you're real?"

Jas rolled her stormy eyes. "Bloody hell. Trust us. Trust your husband."

Sage's eyes slid to Tehl, standing patiently on the other side of Nali. Trust. She'd trusted him the entire time she was in Scythia. Why was she doubting him now when he might be real?

"Fine," she growled. Her friend would only badger her until she complied anyway. She tried to stand, only to have her legs collapse underneath her.

Nali's growl grew louder.

"No, Nali," she whispered, and placed a soothing hand on the feline's side. "It's okay. These are friends." Nali's ears flattened, but she held still, her flesh quivering under Sage's hand. "You're going to have to help me stand, girl."

The beast chuffed and held still as Sage wrapped her arms

along her neck and back. Painfully, she hauled herself to her feet with Nali's aid, wavering slightly. Her fingers sunk into black fur as she studied the man standing fearlessly on the other side of her man-eater. He looked real, but could it be?

He smiled at her and held a hand out. "Take my hand."

She stared at his outstretched hand. What if she was dreaming? Sage reached out and paused, her hand suspended in the air. Could she handle the disappointment?

"Don't be a coward, Sage," Jasmine called.

She clenched her jaw and eyed her trembling hand. When had she ever shied away from a challenge, or the truth? Never. And she wasn't going to start now.

Hesitantly, she slid her hand into his. Tehl's callouses caught along her smooth skin and warmed her frozen hand. She gasped, her gaze darting to his.

He shifted closer, brushing against Nali. He lifted their hands and placed hers against his cheek. Whiskers tickled her palm as he leaned into her touch. "Do I feel real to you?"

Sage stared at her hand cradling his face, another sob escaping her. He felt real, but could she trust it? His blue eyes beseeched her, begged her to trust him. Tehl had always protected her and told her the truth, even when she didn't wish to hear it. "Am I alive?

"Yes. Scarred, but not broken."

That truth hurt and yet it soothed. Awe filled her. "You're real." She stumbled around Nali and fell into Tehl's arms. Her nose stung as she pressed her face to his vest, but she didn't care. She pulled in a deep breath, his familiar scent of leather and pine invading her senses. No trick of the mind could imitate his scent. "I made it," she cried.

Heat suffused her as he crushed her against his chest, one hand pressed against her wet head. "You did," his voice rasped. "You made it." His lips pressed to the top of her head over and over as she clung to him. Her eyelids drooped, and she smiled against his vest.

"You did it, Sage. You're home." His arms tightened around her and he whispered it one last time. "You're home."

She was home. A sigh escaped her as her body went lax.

She was finally home.

To be continued...

In Book Four of The Aermian Feuds: Spy's Mask

Thank you for reading ENEMY'S QUEEN. I hope you enjoyed it! If you liked this book, please review it BECAUSE the review rating determines which series I prioritize. If you want the next book in this series soon, review this book♡ Thank you!

If you'd like to know more about me, my books, or to connect with me online, you can visit my webpage https://www.frostkay.net/, check out my Facebook group Frost Fiends, or follow me on Bookbub to receive news about my new releases.

You've just read a book in my AERMIAN FEUDS series. Other books in this series include REBEL'S BLADE and SIREN'S LURE.

If you love SCI-FI, TWILIGHT ZONE, and ALIENS, check out my MIXOLOGISTS & PIRATES series! (More info on the next page!)

THE AERMIAN FEUDS: BOOK ONE

Rebel's Blade
Frost Kay

War. Secrets. Betrayal.

Tehl Ramses is drowning; crops are being burned, villages pillaged, and citizens are disappearing, leading to a rising rebellion. As crown prince, and acting ruler, Tehl must find a way to crush the rebellion before civil war sweeps through his beloved kingdom.

Tehl will do whatever is necessary to save his people. Yet, his prisoner is not at all what he expects...

Fed up with the neglect and corruption of the crown, swordsmith Sage Blackwell steps forward to spy on the crown. She knows the risks of rebellion - imprisonment or death - and yet, she's still willing to take them to protect her family.

But when plans unravel, Sage finds herself facing the devils themselves, her sworn enemies, the princes of Aermia.

Two Sides. One Goal: Save Aermia

Katniss meets Lord of the rings in this epic adventure fraught with mistaken identities, untold secrets, and dark promises.

Mixologists & Pirates: Book One

Amber Vial
By Frost Kay

Never again.

After unwittingly entering the draft for colonization of an alien planet, Allie believes nothing could get worse.

It could.

A failed escape attempt leaves her chained to an airship chair with nothing but her bag, a vial, a wild redhead, and her anxiety for company. Numbing her fear seemed like a good idea… until it wasn't.

It was just one sip.

www.ingramcontent.com/pod-product-compliance
Lightning Source LLC
Chambersburg PA
CBHW030550310726
48979CB00011B/2097/J

* 9 7 8 1 6 4 2 5 5 5 3 1 8 *